❦

Rosie grabbed the reins out of his hands and twitched Ivanhoe toward the barn.

There was something perversely appealing about the way her small body appeared to grow when she was angry. Fire crackled in her brown eyes and lightning seemed to flash and sizzle around her. Bowie could no more imagine a demure Rosie Mulvehey sitting meekly with her hands quiet in her lap than he could imagine her dressed in silk presiding over a tea table.

"Go up to the house," he ordered with a sigh, taking Ivanhoe's reins. Bowie didn't understand why he liked her more the longer he knew her. Sometimes she was so painfully vulnerable that a child could have crushed her.

Shaking his head, he led Ivanhoe toward his stall and a rubdown. When he thought about Rosie blurting, "But I thought you liked me a little," a painful tightening stretched across his chest.

This strange wounded woman whom he'd no right to marry was beginning to get under his skin.

❦

"THE WIVES OF BOWIE STONE is filled with charmingly different characters. It's a wonderfully told story that will steal your heart. Don't miss it." —Heather Graham, author of *Runaway*

MAGGIE OSBORNE

THE WIVES OF BOWIE STONE

WARNER BOOKS

A Time Warner Company

Enjoy lively book discussions online with CompuServe. To become a member of CompuServe call 1-800-848-8199 and ask for the Time Warner Trade Publishing forum. (Current members GO:TWEP.)

WARNER BOOKS EDITION

Copyright © 1994 by Maggie Osborne
All rights reserved.

Cover design by Diane Luger
Cover illustration by Jim Griffen
Hand lettering by Carl Dellacroce

Warner Books, Inc.
1271 Avenue of the Americas
New York, NY 10020

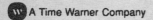 A Time Warner Company

Printed in the United States of America

First Printing: December, 1994

10 9 8 7 6 5 4 3 2 1

This book is dedicated to my husband who has taken it one day at a time for thirteen years. I love you, George. I admire your courage and determination, and I'm proud of you. You are and will always be,
my hero.

Chapter One

Gulliver County, Kansas, 1880

Sheriff Gaine squinted up at the gallows and thumbed back his hat. "Well boys, this is your lucky day."

Four men stood on the trapdoors. Each had his hands tied behind his back and a thick noose looped around his neck. Though it was early in the year and drifts of snow buried the Main Street boardwalk, the noonday sun was hot enough to suck trickles of sweat from the condemned men and from a noisy throng of spectators.

"Seems we got an ordinance here in Gulliver County that states if any of these ladies"—the Sheriff jerked a thumb toward the half-dozen women gathered behind him—"wants to marry one of you sons of bitches, then your worthless life is spared and your sentence considered satisfied."

The eyes of the four condemned men swung to stare at the women who were staring up at them.

1

Sheriff Gaine's upper lip folded into an expression of disgust, implying he occasionally had to administer laws that ran counter to a prudent man's nature.

"If one of these fine Kansas flowers picks you for a husband," he said, scowling up at the gallows, "you'll be taken down from there and marched directly into the courthouse for a hitching ceremony. If you run off afterward, the deal's canceled. Me and my posse will hunt you down, and we'll hang you where we find you. If you ain't picked for a husband—you hang now."

The residents of Gulliver County had heard this speech before. Nevertheless the sheriff continued, allowing the condemned men time to chew over the possibility of reprieve while he explained why this particular loophole existed.

First the war had drawn off the county's males, then cavalry recruiters had passed through and taken most of the remaining men to fight Indians. So few men were left in Gulliver County that Passion's Crossing, the county's largest town, had only one saloon still in operation and only one sorry brothel that offered two whores, both of whom were having trouble making ends meet and were talking about moving on. There weren't enough men left in Passion's Crossing to raise a ruckus on a Saturday night.

More important, there weren't enough men to put in a crop or harvest one, not enough men to raise a barn or repair existing structures. Passion's Crossing had no male labor force.

Sheriff Gaine finished his speech, directed a stream of tobacco juice toward a patch of frozen mud, then addressed the women who would participate in the choosing.

"Who drew first choice?"

"I did," Rosie Mulvehey said, stepping forward. She overheard a few snickers among the spectators and stiffened her shoulders. Let them laugh behind their hands. Nobody in

Passion's Crossing could think it any funnier or any stranger for Rosie Mulvehey to be taking a husband than she did herself.

"Take your time, Rosie. Look 'em over. Ask 'em questions if you want."

Rosie shoved back the brim of the man's hat she wore and wiped a smear of grime and sweat from her forehead. Feeling a tad nervous, she removed a thin, store-bought cigar from her poke, lit it, then exhaled with a small sigh of pleasure, ignoring the respectable women in the crowd who sniffed down their noses and stared at her. She stared back at the respectable women until they jerked their chins up and looked away.

Once upon a time their attitude had hurt and shamed her, but that had been a long time ago, back when she had wanted to be like them. The memory of it embarrassed her and made her angry. She had worn skirts then, and dainty little boots with buttons up the side. She had even curled her hair in clumsy papers special-ordered from Kansas City or Denver. Back then she hadn't smoked and no liquor had ever passed her lips.

A lot of good it had done her. The respectable ladies of Passion's Crossing hadn't accepted her any better then than they did now that she was a hell-raiser. They had averted their eyes from the bruises on her face and body as if they blamed her for her broken arm or ribs, for the cuts and black eyes. They seemed to think she beat the hell out of herself just to offend their delicate sensibilities.

At least now she was legitimately to blame for the icy stares and sniffs of disdain. Every now and again it tickled her fancy to ride into town, get roaring drunk, and shoot up the only remaining saloon. And sometimes, like now, she liked to light up a cigar and blow smoke at the respectable ladies. The hell with them, anyway. Rosie Mulvehey would never be respectable again, so she ran full tilt in the other direction. Now everyone, including herself, understood why she was never going to be a pillar of society.

"Rosie? You changed your mind?"

"I'm just getting a smoke," she said irritably. Hooking a thumb inside her gun belt, she stalked forward to have a better look at the gallows and today's offerings.

They were slim pickings. Not one of the condemned men looked cast-iron and double-bolted. They were a damned dismal-looking lot. One was too old to put in a decent day's work, and Rosie dismissed him at once. The next one had a belly hanging over his belt, more lard than muscle. The third was halfway passable, but he wasn't much more than a boy. He still had peach fuzz on his upper lip.

Feeling her expectations dwindle, Rosie slowed her steps as she approached the last man and squinted up at him. He was tall enough and not too old or too young. He sure wasn't fat. He was skinny as a nail and wore a gray flannel shirt and loose denim pants that looked as if they belonged to a stouter man. His hands were tied behind him, so she couldn't see if he had callouses to prove his worth. What she did see was a wedge of skin at his open collar that was as pale as new butter. He had winter skin, jail skin. This one hadn't seen the sun in a while. And he sure was no beauty.

Not that beauty mattered. Hell, Rosie was no prize herself if it came to that. Still—last night when she had decided to place her name in the draw, she'd been drunk enough to entertain a secret hope that her new husband might be easy on the eyes. Not that she expected to take a shine to him; romance was definitely not part of her plan.

Be that as it might, last night's bender had left her in no condition to judge anyone's capabilities. Rubbing her eyes, Rosie blinked against the harsh winter sunlight, wishing she could see the condemned man better. Part of the difficulty was the huge shiner that had swollen the entire right side of his face, distorting his appearance. The hank of dark matted hair that hung almost to his nose, where it sort of flowed into a ragged mustache that in turn blossomed into a ratty-looking beard, covered much of the rest of his features.

Rosie had never seen a hedgehog, but she imagined it had a face about like this man's: a pointy nose and a hint of eyes poking out of a sheet of hair. It was pretty nigh impossible to make an overall judgment of his looks.

To compound her difficulties in choosing, she was suffering a granddaddy of a hangover that interfered mightily with her concentration. Even if the sun hadn't bounced and shimmered around the hedgehog, she probably wouldn't have been able to focus well enough to obtain a clear view. Moreover, every time she tilted her head back for a hard look, she felt as if she had released a dozen whirling blades inside her brain.

Wincing and wetting her lips, Rosie slid a look down Main toward the square false front of Passion's Crossing's only remaining saloon. She would have given half her bushels of seed grain to nip into Harold's for a quick shot of Brown Blazer.

"Rosie?" The sheriff's voice boomed like a cannon through her hangover. "When I said take your time, I didn't mean we had all day."

"I'm pondering on it," she muttered, annoyed at being hurried along on so important a matter.

When she squinted up at the gallows, she discovered the hedgehog was studying her as intently as she had been studying him. Because of the shiner he could only stare with one eye.

"You any good at farming?" she asked finally in a voice that sounded like two rocks grinding together. It shamed her that she sounded so whiskey-voiced. But then, she'd spent her whole life feeling ashamed of one thing or another.

"I've never farmed."

The hedgehog's voice didn't sound too healthy either; maybe he'd been struck in the throat, which wasn't unlikely. Sheriff Gaine didn't coddle convicts.

The hedgehog's answer astonished her. Rosie couldn't recall ever hearing a condemned man answer a question unfavorably. If it meant the difference between living over the grass or under it, a condemned man would swear he could sprout little pink wings and fly if the woman who was asking sounded as if she wanted him to.

She examined the hedgehog with a glint of interest. "Did you kill the man they say you did?"

"Yes."

His answer damn near blew her boots off. She couldn't believe her ears. And she wasn't the only one. A murmur of angry amazement hummed through the crowd.

"Did you shoot him in the front or in the back?"

The hedgehog's one good eye narrowed, and the lower part of his face moved as if he might be taking offense at the question.

"In the front."

That seemed fair enough. Rosie wasn't bothered that a potential husband had murdered a man; some men needed killing. No one knew that better than she did.

Rosie gripped her gun belt, straightened her shoulders, and tried to look as if she were concentrating. Fuzzy dots speckled her vision and the outline of the hedgehog wavered and blurred. For about the thousandth time she took a silent vow that she would never drink again. At least not until tonight.

"You willing to learn farming?"

The hedgehog had more brass than an army band. He just looked at her out of his one good eye and didn't say a word. Any man with a grain of sense would have babbled promises and assurances. But the hedgehog stood there as if he didn't give a flying damn if he lived or died. He wasn't promising anything.

"Rosie?" The sheriff sounded exasperated.

"I'll take that one," she decided, tipping her hat brim toward the hedgehog. He wasn't much, but he seemed the best of the lot.

With an indifferent shrug Rosie turned and left the gallows to stand in a patch of sun beside the courthouse door and have another smoke while the other women made their choices. She lit up and jutted her chin at the respectable ladies.

At the moment the respectable ladies weren't paying Rosie much mind; they were heaving sighs of disappointment that Passion's Crossing wouldn't have a hanging today. The collective wedding didn't interest anyone except the participants.

Screwing up her eyes, Rosie watched Deputy Sands remove the nooses from around the condemned men's necks and cut their hands free. Apparently all of them had been chosen, although Rosie couldn't see what any woman would want with the old geezer or the lard belly. That they had been picked showed the level of desperation in Gulliver County. Any man was better than no man seemed to be the prevailing wisdom. And who was to say it was wrong? How could a woman alone put in a crop? Or hope to harvest it? How could she keep up a house and outbuildings and miles of fence?

Shaking her head—and instantly regretting it—Rosie ground the cigar stub beneath her boot heel, then fell into step beside the hedgehog as the sheriff led the condemned men and their brides inside the courthouse.

It was colder inside the building than outside in the sun, but at least they were out of the wind. The courtroom had that dingy gray look that seemed to be required of all courtrooms.

Preacher Paulson waited near the judge's bench. He glared at Rosie over the rim of his spectacles. "Take off your hat, Rosie." Showing his disapproval, he ran a frown over her man's work shirt, her gun belt and her soiled buckskin britches. He watched a tangle of dust-dark hair spill out of her hat and fall down her spine before he sighed and set about doing what Gulliver County paid him to do.

"Dearly beloved, we are gathered here together . . ."

Standing next to the hedgehog in the middle of the marrying couples, it occurred to Rosie that she ought to be feeling something. But this was hardly the kind of wedding a young girl dreams about. Back in the days when Rosie had dreamed dreams, the days before Him, she had imagined every detail of her wedding day, except for her intended. That part of the dream had always been fuzzy, but the husband she would take wouldn't be hard to look at and he would like her a lot. So much for stupid dreams.

"Hell fire, you stink," she muttered in disgust, edging away from the hedgehog. She'd been inside the jail a few times herself on drunk and disorderly charges, and she recognized the distinctive stench, except that she'd never smelled the odor this bad or this strong before.

"I apologize, ma'am. If I'd known this was to be my wedding day, I'd have dabbed a bit of whiskey behind my ears," the hedgehog said, not looking at her.

"Stinking of whiskey is a lot better than stinking of jail," Rosie hissed. What was the world coming to when a condemned murderer could make sarcastic comments to his bride, the very woman who had just rescued his worthless hide?

Preacher Paulson leveled a silencing glare in their direction. "Do you, gentlemen, take these ladies for your lawfully wedded wives?"

Everyone except the hedgehog erupted into a chorus of enthusiastic "I do's." The hedgehog appeared to be thinking it over until Rosie dug her elbow into his ribs. He gazed down at her out of his one clear eye and let a goodly pause develop before he muttered, "God forgive me. I do."

It was an insult of the highest order that the hedgehog had to ponder before he decided that marrying her was preferable to biting the noose.

"Do you, ladies, take these gentlemen as your lawfully wedded husbands?"

To pay him back and allow him a minute to recall the noose circling his skinny neck, Rosie didn't answer.

Preacher Paulson raised an eyebrow and peered over the rim of his spectacles. "Rosie?"

Rocking back on her heels, she studied the tin ceiling as if she were entertaining second thoughts. She sucked in her cheeks and shook her head slightly even though it battered her skull to do so. With everybody watching and waiting, she raised a hand and pretended to study her nails in indecision.

"Rosie Mulvehey. Do you or don't you take this man as your lawfully wedded husband?"

She let the silence draw out tight, waiting for the hedgehog to cast her an imploring look or indicate some nervousness over her hesitation. He didn't. Finally, annoyed as hell, she gave what she hoped was an indifferent wave and said, "I guess I have to. I do."

"I now pronounce you man and wife. Gentlemen, you may kiss your brides."

Rosie watched with mild interest as the old geezer, the lard belly, and the boy grabbed on to their brides as if they were ropes thrown to drowning victims.

Finally, placing a hand on one of her revolvers, she faced the hedgehog, jutted out her chin and gave him a slit-eyed look that plainly said she'd rather shoot him than suffer a kiss from him.

Even through all the hair, she could see enough of his expression to tell that her new husband didn't cotton to kissing her either. They stood toe to toe, staring, each daring the other to risk a move.

Rosie had enjoyed her share of staring contests, but this match was oddly disconcerting. First, the hedgehog was taller than she had guessed. To her great disadvantage, the top of her head only reached his nose. Staring up at him was causing hideous repercussions inside her hungover head. The whirling blades shifted to the back of her skull and started shaving away at the top of her spine. Luckily she was accustomed to this kind of pain and could almost ignore it. Grinding her teeth, she bit down and glared into his one open eye.

That eye was also disconcerting. This close, Rosie could see that it was blue, as blue as ever she had seen on a man. Blue as a pansy petal. Blue as a blueberry just before it ripened.

"You try to kiss me, and I'll put a bullet in your private parts." Her eyes were beginning to sting and burn.

"The last thing I want to do is kiss you."

"Good. We're of like mind." They continued to confront each other while the other couples stepped around them and walked arm in arm to the courthouse door. Grudgingly, Rosie acknowledged the hedgehog was no slouch when it came to staring matches. His one good eye was turning as red as she imagined her own eyes were, and starting to tear, but he didn't blink or look away. She didn't either, not even when it began to feel like someone was scrubbing sand between her lids.

She spoke between her teeth. "I'm going to count to three then we'll both turn toward the door."

"Agreed."

She wanted to win badly enough that she welched on the agreement by not looking away on the count of three. The hedgehog welched too. This startled her so much that she disgraced herself with a shout of surprised laughter. But before she let herself laugh, she hit him in the stomach with her fist hard enough that he blinked and made a sound as if the air were running out of him. His blink gave Rosie the win.

Feeling better, she swaggered toward the courthouse door and walked outside. The minute the glare off the snow struck her eyes, she winced and groaned out loud. Pulling her hat brim down to where it almost covered her lashes, she strode toward the buckboard she'd left hitched in front of the general store. The display was sheer bravado. Every step jarred her brain and notched her headache to a higher intensity.

"Is this your horse?" The hedgehog approached Ivanhoe and ran his hands over the horse's flanks, then moved forward to stroke his neck and inspect him more closely. "This is a fine horse. Too fine to be pulling a wagon."

"Ivanhoe is the only horse I have left. The army confiscated most of our stock a couple of summers ago." Frowning, Rosie climbed up and took the reins in her hands. "Get in." She waited until they drove past the gallows the deputies were dismantling before she said more. "I don't have the money to buy a draft horse even if I could find one for sale."

"It's a shame to put a horse like this in traces."

The knowledge came to her in a flash—the way the hedgehog stood, the way he had run his hands over Ivanhoe. She slid a look at his profile, noted the faded army blue of his denims, finally noticed the brass belt plate featuring an eagle enclosed by a silver wreath.

"Cavalry," she said. "The belt buckle says an officer."

He didn't deny it.

"Well?" she asked, turning sharply toward him after they'd traveled half a mile without speaking. "If you're military, how come you're not wearing full uniform? And how come you were tried in a civilian court?"

The hedgehog acted as though he hadn't heard her. He folded his arms across his chest and looked off at the endless fields of snow. Cold wind flapped his hair around the bruises discoloring his forehead. Now Rosie could see that he'd been beaten so badly that pride was the only thing holding him upright. He would require some nursing before he'd be worth a damn to her.

"You might as well tell your story," she said in as reasonable a tone as an irritated person could manage. She snapped the reins. "I guess we're married now. I have a right to know who I'm hitched to."

"You know why I agreed to marry. Why did you?"

His evading her question annoyed her further, but Rosie conceded his curiosity was fair. "I need a cheap roustabout," she said with a shrug. "There aren't any men around to hire, cheap or otherwise. Marrying a convict seemed the best— the only—way to get help on my farm."

The hedgehog wasn't much of a talker. He lapsed into silence again, staring out at the prairie as if there was something out there to see. There wasn't. Just a lone sparrow hawk wheeling above miles and miles of snow-covered grass that stretched as far as the eye could see, interrupted here and there by a bare patch or a sage hillock. There wasn't a tree in sight and wouldn't be until they reached Rosie's farm and the cottonwoods lining Passion's Creek.

"Who was the man you killed?" Rosie asked after another mile. She didn't particularly care, but talking was a more interesting way to pass the time than staring at the prairie. Conversing might even take her thoughts off her hangover. Every jounce and jolt struck needles of pain into her brain.

"Have you heard of the Stone Toes Massacre?"

"The world hasn't entirely bypassed Passion's Crossing." (A bald-faced lie if she had ever heard one.) "We had news of Stone Toes." Frowning, she tried to dredge up whatever she could remember. "It happened someplace outside of Denver, didn't it? A great battle, if I recall." There was something else she had heard, but she couldn't pull the memory through her headache.

"A great battle," the hedgehog repeated. Bitterness roughened his voice. "The Indians didn't fire a shot. Two companies rode into Stone Toes Gulch and slaughtered a village of women and children. There wasn't a warrior within six miles. The men were hunting."

Rosie shifted for a better look at him. "I might have heard something about Stone Toes being a scandal. Then I heard the rumors of scandal were untrue, that it was a heroic battle after all. You were there?"

"Yes."

"Well?"

He pulled a hand through the tangle of hair. "Some men won't accept that the Indian wars are over, the glory days are gone. They're looking for excitement, and they'll create a fight whether it's legitimate or not." His good eye blazed like a blue sun. "The Indians at Stone Toes Gulch had permission to camp on that site."

Interested in spite of herself, Rosie gave Ivanhoe his head and turned her full attention to the hedgehog. Ivanhoe could find his way home with no help from her.

She wished the wind would shift. The hedgehog stank to high heaven, and he was more battered and bruised than she had guessed. He kept swaying on the seat as if he might fall off.

"So. Did you ride down on a village of unarmed women and children?" The question was hard and rude, but she didn't apologize for it.

The hedgehog stiffened on the seat and gripped his knees so tightly that his knuckles turned pale. "I refused a direct order. I led my company back to the post."

Rosie released a long breath. She could guess the rest of his tale, at least the broad strokes of it. The military didn't look kindly on officers who disobeyed direct orders. "You were court-martialed. Cashiered out."

He turned his face into the cold prairie wind.

"What's all this have to do with the man you killed?"

"Do you always ask so many questions?"

"The truth is, mister, I don't give a cuss about you or your story." Color flared in her face. "But you can bet your sorry hide that every soul in Gulliver County is going to know your history before sunset. So I need to know it too. Otherwise, if some flap-tongue makes a remark in my hearing, how am I to know if I should knock his teeth out for the insult or swallow it down and walk on by? I don't care who you are or what you did. All I want to know is whatever is public knowledge so I'll know how much pride I have to swallow. Now that's fair."

She didn't think he was going to answer, and she was working up a good mad about it. A minute before she was ready to explode, the hedgehog finally spoke.

"I was a captain in the Eleventh Cavalry. I refused a direct order from a ranking officer, for which I received a dishonorable discharge." He laid his head back and gazed at the icy sky. "If my commanding officer had not preferred charges, the truth about Stone Toes would never have emerged. Those men could have continued pretending to be heroes. As it was, the *Rocky Mountain News* reported the trial and revealed the truth. Public opinion turned. Men who had been lauded days before were spat at in the streets."

"They should have been spit on. They did wrong."

The hedgehog looked at her for a full minute, but she couldn't tell what he was thinking.

"If you want to exterminate a wolf pack, you don't kill only the male. You also kill the she-wolf and the cubs. That's how the majority of soldiers assessed Stone Toes. Most of my regiment blamed me for the acrimony of those people who object to the slaughter of women and children. A soldier from Company B swore revenge, took leave of absence, and

followed me east." A shrug lifted his shoulders. "Luther Radison shot me in the leg; I shot him in the chest. He died."

"So how come this wasn't self-defense? If you're telling
the truth, how come you were convicted of murder?"

"You know Gulliver County better than I do."

Rosie chewed it over, twisting the reins in her hands. "I
read about this trial. The newspaper said a man who was
cashiered out of the military with a dishonorable discharge
murdered a genuine military hero who had clippings in his
pouch to prove his heroism. That's how the judge must have
seen the situation."

The hedgehog said nothing, but his fingers moved to his
throat.

They rode in silence, ducking their heads against a sharp,
moist-smelling wind. The seat on the buckboard was small
and their thighs pressed together but each ignored the fact.
The warmth was welcome.

A half-mile passed before the hedgehog spoke again.
"There's something I have to tell you."

"So say it." A chill teased Rosie's bones, and she could
count the revolutions of the wheels by the hammer blows in
her head. Her thoughts leapt ahead to the bottle of whiskey
on the parlor shelf.

The hedgehog waited until the farm was in sight before he
revealed what was on his mind. Then he spoke as if the words
were dragged out of him.

"I owe you a debt of gratitude for saving my life."

"I reckon you do."

He faced into the wind, looking at the farmhouse and shabby
outbuildings as they came into view. At least there were trees
here. Groves of wind-bent cottonwoods clung to the banks
of Passion's Creek, a small tributary of the Arkansas. Those
trees could keep a person sane when the vast flatness of the
prairie became overwhelming.

"You said earlier that you need help with your farm."

"If I could plant and harvest by myself, I'd do it rather than take a husband. But I've tried and I can't work enough ground alone to make a profit."

"I'll help you put in the next crop, and I'll help with the harvest. I owe you that much." He shifted on the wooden seat to make sure she was listening. "Then I have to leave."

Rosie stiffened like a dried hide. "Leaving ain't an option, bub."

"Rose—that's your name, isn't it?—I have obligations back east." Something like pain clouded the eye that wasn't swollen shut. "Eventually I'll have to return."

"We're *married*."

"This isn't a real marriage. What we've entered into is a business arrangement more than anything else. You need a hired hand, and I'm willing to be that hired hand in repayment for your saving my life. At least for a while."

"Those obligations back east canceled out the minute Deputy Sands dropped the noose around your weaseling neck! Now the only obligation you've got is to me!" Rosie's hand dropped to her revolver. "Dusting out isn't part of this deal and don't you forget it. If you try to run off before I get a profitable harvest, I'll track you and I'll kill you. I swear it!"

Her teeth ground together and her eyes narrowed to blazing slits. "This farm *must* be successful. Do you understand me? If not this season, then next season. If not next season, then the season after that." She gripped the handle of her Colt so hard that her palm ached. "Once we bring in a profitable harvest, then I don't give a flip what happens to you. If you want to go back east, hell, I'll drive you to the train myself. But if you dust out on me before this farm is profitable, I swear I'll hunt you down and make jerked meat out of you if it takes the rest of my miserable no-good life!"

Suspecting her vehemence had revealed more than she

wanted, Rosie flapped the reins, urging Ivanhoe into a fast trot. Leaning her flushed face into the wind, she studied the approaching farm, seeing it as the hedgehog must.

Her spread didn't look like much. The main house was wood on a sod foundation. Years ago Rosie had lost the battle between paint and the broiling summer sun. She hadn't painted the house, the barn, or any of the outbuildings in three years and the neglect showed in long strips of raw board.

The henhouse and storage sheds were in the same sad shape, and the weight of winter snows had bowed in one or two rooflines. The fencing was a flat-out disgrace. Wind and stray range cattle had knocked down large sections. Without leaves, even the cottonwoods rimming the creek looked stark and dismal.

Rosie scanned her holdings, sighed, and craved a drink.

When she braked the buckboard in front of the house, John Hawkins stepped off the front porch to take the horse's reins. He moved forward, standing tall and as straight as a lodge pole, his ancient eyes sparking with interest at the sight of the hedgehog. Rosie noticed John Hawkins had spruced up for the occasion. He wore a top hat pressed down over his shoulder-length hair, and his coat was brushed. Lodisha must have cleaned his buckskin britches, because they gleamed like butter in the dying sun. A rush of affection eased Rosie's expression. The old Indian was one of the few good things in her life. So was Lodisha, an ex-slave and the best cook in Kansas.

When Rosie came around the back of the buckboard, John Hawkins and the hedgehog were standing a few yards apart, taking each other's measure.

She stepped close enough to John Hawkins to notice he'd slapped some Bay Rum on his weathered cheeks, as if her wedding day were something worth gussying up for.

"This is John Hawkins," she said, looking at the hedgehog. "John Hawkins used to be an Indian. I've known him most of my life." Because John Hawkins set great store on courtesy, she spoke in a formal monotone. Raising a hand, she started to present the hedgehog to John Hawkins. "John Hawkins, this is . . ."

Rosie scowled and stopped speaking.

She'd been married half a day but she didn't know her husband's name.

Chapter Two

"The name's Bowie Stone."

"Captain Bowie Stone," John Hawkins corrected.

"Not any more."

Rosie turned to John Hawkins and her jaw dropped. "How did you know that?"

"If I were still an Indian, I would embrace you as a brother," John Hawkins announced solemnly. "Now I am only a man. I ask the honor to shake your hand."

Feeling uncomfortable, Bowie gripped the old man's hand as they continued to examine each other. He recognized on John Hawkins' face an expression he had observed before. The Indian believed he had outlived his time. In his own culture, he would have chosen a clear cloudless day and a fortuitous site and then he would have laid himself down to die.

Rosie stared hard at John Hawkins. "How do you know Bowie Stone?"

John Hawkins still gripped Stone's hand, examining his eyes through the fall of matted hair. "This is good," was all he said before he released Stone's hand and led Ivanhoe and the buckboard toward the barn.

The wind blowing off the fields of snow sliced through Bowie's shirt and pants. The day's events had so numbed his mind and body that only now did he realize he had no coat or hat. Jamming his hands into his pockets, he rocked back on his heels and swept a glance from the scattering of dilapidated buildings to a sagging fence that tottered across the prairie in a drunken line. When Rosie Mulvehey had said she needed help, he'd had no idea of the enormity of the task she had in mind. Restoring her farm and transforming the hard dry prairie into a lush breadbasket appeared to be an overwhelming and hopeless project.

He couldn't believe that anyone could love this pitiful farm and inhospitable land enough to marry a condemned stranger in an effort to make a success of it.

He also could not get a grasp on who Rosie Mulvehey was. He had noticed her immediately; it was impossible not to. She stood out among the women of Passion's Crossing like a thistle among violets. Stone had seen a few rough numbers like Rosie Mulvehey around the more isolated posts, but he had observed few like her in settled towns.

That Rosie or anything else could interest him at this lowest point in his life amazed him. That he was alive at all was nothing short of a miracle. He hadn't yet sorted out how he felt about it. He had resigned himself to dying, had accepted death as a welcome alternative to a life without honor and without the cavalry. Now, instead of being dead as he had expected, he stood in the yard of a neglected farm that he was expected to restore.

And he had added to his crimes by marrying a bizarre new wife. It was a lot to take in.

"Well ain't you a stinking mess!"

Jerking his head up, Bowie turned toward the speaker standing above him on the porch. A plump black woman wiped her hands on a spotless white apron and eyed him with a hard judgmental gaze.

"This is Lodisha," Rosie explained, grinning. "When Lodisha isn't cooking or cleaning, she's running everyone's life and keeping us in general misery."

Lodisha swept down the steps and marched around him, pinching his arms and waist and clucking her tongue. "Lawd, you is one skinny convict." She shook her head and muttered under her breath. "Don't you be taking them boots and that stink through my parlor, no sir. You take yourself around to the kitchen door and fetch the tub out'n the lean-to. 'Fore we does anything else, we got to git that jail stink off'n you!" Lifting her skirts, she bustled back into the house.

Rosie's grin widened. "Better do as she says. You can't win an argument with Lodisha. She'll wear you down to a nub."

"After you," he said.

Instantly she bristled and her brows crashed together in a frown. "I'll go inside when I'm good and damned ready. You don't give orders and I don't take them, understand?"

Judging from his bride's bloodshot eyes, trembling hands, and the way she kept swallowing, Bowie would have sworn she would have bolted immediately for wherever she kept her bottle. The best ease for a hangover was a soothing nip of the same poison as before. But she stood unmoving in the bare twilit yard, her challenging gaze pushing him around the corner of the house.

Clamping his jaw tight and deciding her hangover wasn't his problem, Bowie followed the sod foundation until he located the kitchen stoop and a lean-to butted up against the house next to the water barrel. Pausing to catch his breath, he listened to the wind and thought he heard Rosie's voice.

Curious, he passed the kitchen door and walked to the far corner of the house. Between the house and a skeletal line of cottonwoods, he spotted her standing beside a rock-bordered grave that had been swept clear of snow.

The fading light softened her appearance and it occurred to Bowie that Rosie Mulvehey might have been an attractive woman if she had worked at it a little. The hair shoved beneath her sweat-stained hat was too limp and dirty for him to form an accurate judgment of its color or texture. But the buckskin britches she wore revealed firm buttocks and shapely legs. He couldn't guess the state of her bosom as she wore an oversized man's work shirt beneath a poncho that had seen better days.

As for her eyes, they were brown and dulled, the whites stitched with red. If her lashes hadn't been stuck together, they might have been long and lush, but he couldn't tell for certain.

Also, she didn't smell any too clean. She reeked of whiskey, tobacco smoke, and old sweat. It didn't really surprise Bowie that Rosie's only hope for a husband was the loophole in Gulliver County's law. But he couldn't help wondering why she appeared deliberately to be doing everything possible to make herself offensive. He couldn't recall ever meeting a woman who actually wanted to be unattractive.

She was talking to the grave in the yard.

"I'm married now," she said to the headstone, kicking at a rock that had tumbled off the border. "Never thought that would happen, did you? Well, neither did I. But it did and now I'm going to make a success of this place. I'm going to bring in the most profitable harvest this farm ever had!"

Bowie experienced an uncomfortable impression that he was intruding on an intensely private moment. Retracing his steps, he opened the lean-to and removed a dented tin bathtub. The tub was heavy and unwieldy and reminded him how battered and bruised he was. Now that the emotional rush of events was behind him, he felt weak as a new pup.

He wrestled the tub to the stoop before the kitchen door flew open behind him and a brown arm dragged him inside.

Twelve years in the military had obliterated any tendency he might have had to excessive modesty. But field habits and the habits of civilization were two different sets of behavior. Bowie's throat burned with embarrassment as Lodisha briskly undressed him, firmly turning him between her hands as if he were a child before she gave him a push toward the tub, which she had filled with steaming water.

"Rags," she pronounced of his clothing before throwing them into the stove's fire box. "Not even good for making patches." She eyed his nakedness up and down. "Get your skinny butt in that tub, Cap'n."

John Hawkins returned from the barn as Bowie eased himself into the tub. On his way to the coffee pot hissing on the back of the stove, John Hawkins paused to give Bowie's naked bruised body a thorough inspection.

Bowie cursed under his breath, feeling a dark flush rise beneath his beard. He had never felt so exposed or vulnerable in his life. The only saving grace was Rosie's absence. If she had come inside she would have witnessed his nakedness as well because, contrary to his expectation, the kitchen and parlor were combined in one large room. The parlor Lodisha didn't want him to trek through was apparently the area of the room nearest the front door. The kitchen was the area nearest the side door. The division between the two existed only in imagination, as far as Bowie could determine.

Only after he was immersed beneath the water and the heat had begun to work its magic on deep bruises and a dozen lacerations, did he begin to identify the invisible line separating kitchen from parlor.

The parlor end of the room was furnished with a ragtag collection of chairs and footstools. A braid rug covered most of the plank floor. There was a table with a lamp, and a bookcase beneath the window.

The footstools were covered with the same faded calico that framed the window. Either Rosie or Lodisha had pasted colorful magazine covers on the walls. Bowie noticed a jug of dried sunflowers beside the lamp.

Before he finished his inspection, a gust of cold wind blew Rosie in the front door. After dropping her poncho and hat on a peg, she proceeded directly to the parlor shelf and poured a hefty splash of whiskey into a tin cup. Closing her eyes, she threw back her head, swallowed the whiskey neat, and sighed with relief.

When Bowie realized she was walking toward him, he sat up and frantically looked around for a towel to cover himself. The water had settled and the steam had diminished. When he glanced down, he saw himself as exposed as a newborn.

"You want a drink?" Rosie asked, standing over him and looking down through the water.

He plunged his hands beneath the surface and covered his genitals from her measuring gaze.

"Oh for God's sake! I'm not interested in your privates," she said. But she watched with a smile as he scrambled around beneath the surface of the water. She made a snorting sound. "Hell, if you've seen one man's privates, you've seen 'em all. If you ask me, none of you have much to boast about. You want a drink or not?"

He managed to control his anger long enough to say yes. Rosie took a cup from Lodisha and poured a generous dollop of whiskey, then extended the cup, grinning when he didn't immediately uncover himself and reach for it.

Bowie swore under his breath. She was enjoying his discomfort, taunting him with it.

This morning he hadn't known any of these people existed. Now he was bathing in front of two women and a man who, after closely inspecting his nakedness, were going about their business as if there were nothing unusual in the circumstance. Lodisha hummed over the pots on the stove, John Hawkins sat at the table sipping his coffee, absorbed in a yellowing newspaper that he held upside down. Rosie Mulvehey stood over the tub, holding the neck of a bottle in one hand and a cup in the other, as deliberately unimpressed as if strange men bathed in her kitchen every night of the week.

Scowling, Bowie pulled a hand out of the water and took the tin cup she offered. Tilting his head, he threw the whiskey down the back of his throat and grimly extended the cup for another splash. Ordinarily he wasn't much of a drinking man, but this had been one hell of a day.

Rosie refilled his cup, then, as brazen as a San Francisco whore, she leaned over the tub and peered through the water, inspecting him from his toes to his throat.

"What the hell do you think you're doing?" Bowie shouted, trying to cover himself. Heat pulsed in his cheeks. Lodisha and John Hawkins looked up and then went back to their tasks.

Rosie straddled a bench, sitting across the table from John Hawkins. She took another nip from the tin cup. "Someone sure worked you over, bub. Near as I can see, you're one big walking ache. Did Sheriff Gaine do that to you? Or was it that bastard, Deputy Sands?"

Bowie stared at her. He was furious that she had violated his sense of self at a moment when he was extremely vulnerable. At the same time his pride was injured by her lack of expression. "What business is it of yours?"

A shrug lifted her shoulders. "I want to know how soon you'll be in shape to work. We have to get those fences mended before plowing time."

"The captain will be ready for light chores by next week," John Hawkins said, glancing up from the tattered newspaper.

"That's about how I read it," Rosie agreed, as if Bowie had no opinion in the matter.

Lodisha bore down on him like a black thundercloud. Before he guessed what she intended, she had lathered his chest, shoulders and back with a cake of lye soap that tore through weeks of jailhouse grime and clawed into his pores. Rosie and John Hawkins watched the process with considerable amusement.

"Up you go, Cap'n. Cain't forget yor legs an' backside." Strong arms jerked him up and Lodisha lathered his buttocks, thighs and calves in full view of John Hawkins and Rosie Mulvehey.

It was humiliating to be scrubbed down like a child before an audience.

"No meat on him at all," was Rosie's only comment. She studied his buttocks and thighs for a long moment; then a flush of color stained her cheeks, and she pushed up from the table. "I'm going outside for a smoke."

Lodisha's hands paused on Bowie's body and he felt her disapproval of Rosie's abrupt departure. Then the kitchen door banged and Lodisha pushed him down into the tub to rinse him and wash his hair and beard. The lye suds hit his swollen eye and Bowie bit down on a shout of pain.

"I can dry myself," he said between his teeth.

Lodisha slapped his hands away and toweled him off. She handed him a shirt and a pair of pants. The shoulders fit, but the waist of the pants was far too large. When he strapped on his belt, folds of material gathered at his hips.

"Better than what you rode in with," Lodisha commented.

"There's someone else around here who could do with a bath," he said sourly.

"Yor right as rain 'bout that, Cap'n," Lodisha said with a

frown. "But me and Rosie got an arrangement. She agrees to a bath after a night in jail and I don' insist no other time."

Bowie watched her stropping a razor strap and tried again. "I can shave myself."

"No you cain't, lest you can do it with yor eyes closed. Ain't no mirrors in this house."

Surprise stopped his protest. Two women and no mirrors? Not even a broken shard? Sighing, he submitted to Lodisha's ministrations.

"Well, well, lookee what we got here," she said happily when she had finished shaving off his beard and mustache and trimming his hair. "What do you think, John Hawkins? A mighty handsome critter was hiding under all that fuzz. Least ways it 'pears so. We'll know for sure when all the swelling goes down."

John Hawkins had watched the shaving, interjecting advice when requested by Lodisha to do so. He nodded agreement.

Bowie removed the shaving towel from around his neck and glanced at the door as Rosie stormed inside. She took one long hard look at him, then whirled angrily on Lodisha.

"Where did you get those clothes?"

"You know where." Lodisha huffed up, but she didn't back away from Rosie's furious expression. "We couldn't put him in them filthy rags he had on." She shrugged. "He got to wear something. Cain't have him running 'round here buck-ass naked."

"John Hawkins—"

"No sir, John Hawkins cain't be 'spected to give up his clothes when we got a trunk full not being used. Now you know I'm right!"

Red-faced and trembling, Rosie ran to the shelves above the stove, reached up to a tin box and pulled it down. Throwing back the lid, she counted out some coins and slapped them on the table in front of John Hawkins.

"Tomorrow you go into town and buy him some clothes." She spun back to Lodisha. "You wash and iron what he's wearing and put everything back in the trunk!"

"We was saving that money for sugar, coffee and extras."

"We'll do without!" Moving in long angry strides, Rosie crossed the kitchen, grabbed the whiskey bottle, then disappeared through a door off the parlor, slamming it behind her.

"What was that all about?" Bowie asked when the silence grew heavy.

John Hawkins and Lodisha exchanged a look, then pressed their lips together and went back to the newspaper and stove.

Rosie didn't emerge from her room for supper.

"Clean up yor plate," Lodisha ordered, ladling chipped bowls full of a second helping of savory venison stew. "This is the last of the venison."

"Rose Mary gave most of the deer to the Hodgson family and the Greenes. It was the right thing to do. There is no man in the Hodgson and Greene houses." Earlier John Hawkins had removed his top hat and placed it on the bench beside him. He wore a calico napkin tucked in the neck of a stiffly starched shirt.

Lodisha talked while the men ate, urging them to take more biscuits or stew, pushing slabs of dried-apple pie across the table at them.

When Bowie finished eating, he smiled at Lodisha's expectant face. "That was the finest meal I've had in weeks, ma'am. Thank you."

"I ain't no ma'am," she said, smiling with pleasure as she picked up the plates. "Jest Lodisha."

John Hawkins stood. "Lodisha does not permit smoking inside the house unless there is a blizzard. We will go outside." After replacing his top hat, he took a heavy coat from the peg beside the kitchen door and indicated Bowie should do likewise.

Outside the night air was sharp and frigid. A glittering black canopy curved above the endless expanse of prairie. Bowie drew the icy air deeply into his lungs and gazed up at a bank of clouds slowly drawing a curtain across the sky. A burst of pleasure tightened his chest. He hadn't expected to see another night sky.

John Hawkins lit two cigars and passed one over. He didn't speak until a satisfactory glow of ash had appeared on the tip of his cigar.

"When I was an Indian, I knew the customs and the laws. I am not always certain of the customs and the laws in my new life. Especially I am not sure of the customs of marriage." He puffed, then exhaled a ghostly plume into the blackness. "If it does not offend any custom or law, I am willing to serve as emissary for the bride's family and I will speak for her."

Nothing better illustrated Bowie's debilitated state than his sensitivity to the cold, he who had bivouacked on bare ground in temperatures well below zero. At the moment he would have preferred to forego smoking and conversation and return to the warmth inside. Male pride and curiosity overcame his discomfort, and he nodded agreement.

"First I speak of the bride's family. Rose Mary's father was a newspaper man, an honest and courageous man. You will find these qualities in his daughter. It must be said that Oliver Mulvehey was also stubborn and rigid in his beliefs. These qualities you will also find in his daughter.

"The mother was like my first wife, a beautiful woman who drew nourishment from men's attention. This is not a quality you will find in Rose Mary. Sadie Mulvehey was weak and foolish. There is no weakness in her daughter and only a trace of foolishness. Sadie Mulvehey married unwisely after

Oliver Mulvehey died. She chose a brutish man who beat her for her foolishness. Sometimes it is necessary to beat a woman, but it is seldom necessary to kill one."

John Hawkins directed a look of speculation toward Bowie before he continued speaking. "Rose Mary is not like other women. This you have seen. You should know also that Rose Mary is generous of heart. She willingly shares provisions with those who turn their faces away from her in town. She keeps to herself and does not gossip. One who earns Rose Mary's loyalty earns it for life. She is intelligent and has a strong back. She does not shy from hard work. Rose Mary is healthy and will bear many strong children."

"Rose Mary Mulvehey is a drunk," Bowie commented, watching the ash on his cigar.

"Rose Mary has faults," John Hawkins agreed. "But she is an honorable woman." He watched the clouds advancing across the sky. "If you had an emissary to speak for you, what would he say of your family?"

"I don't wish to speak of my family," Bowie answered sharply. Eventually he would have to turn his thoughts east, and eventually he would have to confront the enormous problems caused by his marriage to Rosie. But not yet.

"This is not good," John Hawkins said, frowning. When it became evident that Bowie would not explain further, he continued. "I would ask your emissary if Captain Bowie Stone is a patient man. I would ask if Captain Bowie Stone is the man of understanding and compassion that his deeds proclaim him to be."

They smoked in silence for several minutes before Bowie answered. "Don't make a hero out of me because I refused to slaughter women and children. I'm no hero. I've killed dozens of Indians. I fought against the Apache in the Southwest and fought the Sioux in the Dakotas. I was at the battle of the Rosebud in '76. I've devoted twelve years of my life to making the west safe and habitable for farms like this one, and that meant killing hostile Indians. For most of those years I believed what I was doing was right."

"Do you still believe that killing Indians is right?"

Bowie flipped his cigar toward a drift of snow. "I don't know anymore what I believe. The government has cheated, lied, and broken treaties. We've exterminated entire tribes or enclosed them on barren lands and taken away their livelihood, made them dependent for food and life's essentials. It's also true that the tribes have broken treaties, have stolen horses and arms, and have committed atrocities against harmless settlers. There's been wrong on both sides." He glanced at John Hawkins' expressionless face. "One thing is certain. The tide of settlers cannot be stopped. Right or wrong, the tribes will have to accept that."

"This troubles you."

Bowie recalled the Shoshoni scouts who had led the way to the Rosebud River. He had lived with them for weeks, had fought beside them. They were good men, honorable men, and he had respected them as he had respected other Indians whom he had known during his years with the cavalry. But the tribes were outmanned, outgunned, and deemed expendable by a culture they did not understand. Progress doomed the Indian nations to a fate as hopeless as that of their food source, the buffalo, which was now all but extinct. This he also knew.

"Everything I thought I believed in has been swept away. I've done things in the past months that I never believed it was possible for me to do. I disgraced myself and my regiment. I murdered a man. I should never have married Rosie Mulvehey. I no longer know who Bowie Stone is." And he no longer cared.

"I know this feeling," John Hawkins said. After a silence, he added, "If you had an emissary I would ask if one whose life flame burns low can be a good husband to Rose Mary."

"Right now I'm not even good for myself."

"Do not hurt Rose Mary."

Rose Mary Mulvehey was the least vulnerable woman Bowie had met. He seriously doubted that he or anyone else could reach her on a level open to emotional pain. "I've told Rosie that I'll help her put in a crop and harvest it. That seems to be important to her. I owe her and I'll pay my debt. After that, I have other obligations to attend to."

Not yet, he warned himself. Don't think about the senator or Susan or Nate or the destruction of his career. Don't think any further than this moment.

Ebony clouds scudded out of the west, racing to cover the stars. The wind rose and a few pellets of snow eddied out of the blackness, swirling around them. The temperature plummeted.

Bowie wrapped his arms around his chest and shook his head. "How in the name of God can she love this bleak land?"

"Love it?" John Hawkins turned to him in surprise. "Rose Mary does not love this farm, Captain Bowie Stone. She hates it. Her hatred is like a viper in the breast. It poisons her." He caught Bowie's hand, pumped it once, then disappeared in the blackness, walking through the snowflakes toward the barn.

Rosie came awake with a violent start as her bedroom door opened and a wedge of light dropped across her bed. Bleary-eyed and half-dizzy, she struggled upright and managed to find the revolver thrust under her pillow.

"Get out of here!" A man stood in her doorway but she couldn't see his face, just a dark silhouette with the light glowing around him. For a heart-stopping instant her whiskey-soaked mind tumbled backward and she thought it was *him*. Her pulse raced and the revolver shook in her hand. Her throat dried up like an August pond. Then Stone spoke and slowly she released her breath.

"Where am I supposed to sleep?"

"You take one more step and there's going to be a window where your privates used to be!" She brought the revolver tight against the waist of her long johns, holding it as steady as she could in the patch of light so that Stone could see she meant business.

"I'm not trying to invite myself into your bed," he said in a voice of disgust. "I'm merely inquiring where I'm supposed to sleep."

"You can doss in the barn with John Hawkins."

He leaned his forearm against the door jamb, thinking it over. "No," he said finally. She had a feeling he was scanning her puffy face and the empty whiskey bottle on the floor beside her bed. "I'll sleep in the house. I'll take the bedroom next door."

Instantly Rosie's heart crashed against her rib cage. Her eyes widened until they ached. "How'd you know there was a bedroom next to mine?"

"I looked inside."

"You opened the door?" She gazed at him incredulously, her features went slack with confusion and disbelief. She would have sworn that she could be half dead and still hear the hinge squeak on that door. She had believed there was not enough liquor in Kansas to blot out that squeak. Flinging back the quilt and ignoring the devastating eruption in her head caused by the sudden movement, she dashed out of bed and ran toward him with panicked jerky movements. "Get the hell out of my way!"

Rushing past him, she scurried to the other bedroom door and found it a few inches ajar. Swallowing convulsively and fighting a titanic eruption of the shakes, she eased the door full open and let the light from the parlor lamp fall inside.

She leaned across the threshold and scanned the room with frantic eyes.

"Did you touch anything? Disturb anything?"

"I opened the door. That's all."

She sagged against the door jamb and covered her eyes. "Don't ever go in there again! You hear me? Don't go in there." When she opened her eyes, she discovered Stone was studying the way her long johns hung on her body. There was no particular expression on his face; he was just looking. Curious maybe. Maybe surprised. "Stop looking at me."

"I don't believe I ever met a woman who slept in long underwear."

"Well now you have." Careful not to step a toe across the threshold, she leaned forward and closed the door of the second bedroom. The squeak of the hinge clawed down her spine, and a silent scream blew through her mind. She stumbled toward the kitchen, vaguely aware that Stone followed her. "Need a drink of water. God. My mouth tastes like a herd of Texas longhorns tromped through there."

"If you don't like what liquor does to you, why do you drink so much?" Stone watched her bounce from one piece of furniture to another until she reached the kitchen and the bucket and ladle on the broadshelf.

She took the bucket to the table and fell heavily onto the bench. After a couple of stabs at it, she filled the ladle and drank, then poured water over her face, letting it dribble down the front of her long johns.

"I flat can't believe I didn't hear you open that door," she muttered, staring at a point in space. The kitchen was dark and soothing on her eyes except for a glow of banked embers around the fire box. She could hear Lodisha's steady snore rattling the little room off the pantry.

"Who does the second bedroom belong to?" Stone took the bench across the table from her, studying her critically.

Now that he was shaved and barbered, Rosie could see his expression plain enough. He looked disgusted.

"It doesn't belong to anybody."

"There are clothes on the wall pegs, shaving items on top of the bureau."

"Damn it, just forget about that room! It doesn't concern you."

Riled by the questions, Rosie drank another ladle of water after swishing it around her mouth. She saw now that it had been a mistake to come lurching out of bed. The kitchen walls and furnishings had begun a slow spin, picking up speed. She gripped the table edge with both shaking hands.

"Why do you do this to yourself?" Stone asked. She supposed he spoke softly, but his voice roared through her head and she grimaced.

"Leave it be. You ain't got no right to go poking and pushing at me."

"Ain't?" His steady gaze made her squirm on the bench seat. "I looked in the bookcase, Rosie. Goethe, Schiller, Lessing. Shelley, Byron, Sir Walter Scott. You can drop the pretense. You're no ignorant farm girl."

Without warning, her perception of herself split in two. One Rosie Mulvehey sat clinging to the kitchen table, as drunk as a trading-post Indian. The other Rosie Mulvehey hovered somewhere near the ceiling, looking down with revulsion. That Rosie Mulvehey noted Bowie Stone, composed, freshly barbered, and showing disturbing signs that he might turn out to be a daisy of a man. And that Rosie Mulvehey noted the drunken sot sitting across from him in soiled red long johns, her hair matted and dirty, her eyes puffed and almost as swollen as Stone's. That Rosie Mulvehey thought this was a hell of a way to spend her wedding night.

Color flooded Rosie's face, and abruptly she felt like crying. The sudden hot sting of tears mortified her.

"An occasional nip now and then never killed anyone."

"Occasional drinkers don't put away a whole bottle at one sitting. I never knew an occasional drinker who could swallow a bottle and remain upright or have a conversation. That takes someone who's made friends with liquor."

Something exploded white hot against the back of Rosie's skull. When she could see again she was standing in the middle of the kitchen and so was Stone, and she was swaying on her feet and screaming at him.

"I want it to go away! The sound of that goddamned squeak, the wind, the prairie, this farm, and most of all *me*! I wish I could turn the clock back. I wish I could just fly away someplace far and unused and shiny clean!" Raising her hands, she pressed her palms against her ears. "The thoughts come and come and keep coming! I keep remembering. The squeak of that door! And everybody knew, I could tell by the way they all looked at me. But they didn't do anything and I couldn't ask." Her eyes were wild, veering away from the past but seeing it anyway. "Then the creek flooded. And he was dead before I was ready. He cheated me!" A long shudder trembled down her body and her mouth twisted.

"Rosie?" Stone reached for her, but she jumped back and slapped his hands away, wishing she hadn't left her revolver in the bedroom.

"Don't touch me!" she screamed, backing away from him, clasping her arms over her breasts. "I'm dirty! I'm ugly and dirty! Don't touch me!"

"For God's sake. Let me just . . ."

The tears came in a flood, salty and scalding, humiliating her almost as much as the words that tumbled unbidden from her lips.

"I wish it had been me up there on the gallows today! It should have been me."

The room spun faster and faster around her, and bile rushed

into her throat as she flung out her arms and tried to steady herself. It was no use. The room churned around her, the colors whirling and blending into the familiar blackness that would bring relief. She had a moment to focus on Stone's yellow, green, and purple bruises, a moment to register his frown and feel a stab of shame, then she pitched headlong into the blackness.

Bowie caught her before she hit the kitchen planks and swung her up into his arms, surprised at how little she weighed. Her long dirty hair fell over his arm; sour fumes drifted from her open lips. A button popped from the top of her long johns and skittered across the floor, exposing a swell of breast. He stared down at her, trying not to look at her breast, not sure what to do with her.

"Take her back to her room," Lodisha said, stepping out of the shadows. She threw a shawl over her night dress, then flapped forward in a pair of heelless slippers, shaking her head. "Me and John Hawkins hoped she wouldn't drink tonight, her weddin' night. I guess the clothes set her off." A sigh lifted Lodisha's bosom, then she waved Bowie forward through the parlor.

He placed Rosie on her bed, turning her on her side so she wouldn't suffocate if she got sick during the night. The light falling from the parlor lamp softened her features and he suddenly, disconcertingly, had another glimpse of what she might have looked like under different circumstances. Rosie Mulvehey could have been a stunningly handsome woman. Her features were strong and striking, her body well-formed and lissome. He couldn't imagine where she'd gotten the idea that she was ugly. Unkempt certainly, but not ugly.

Curious, Bowie glanced around the small spartan room, noting the lack of female paraphernalia. Her room was as stark and spare as a soldier's. No one would have guessed a young woman occupied this bedroom.

After placing the revolver on the bedside table, Lodisha covered Rosie and smoothed a hand over her forehead, then she flapped toward the door. "Since we's up, we might as well have some of that lukewarm coffee and the rest of the pie."

Stone followed Lodisha's swinging braid into the kitchen and took a seat at the table. "Does she get like this every night?"

"Most nights." Lodisha poured tin cups of coffee and pushed a slice of pie toward him. She tossed her night braid over her shoulder and sat across from him. "Me and John Hawkins is hoping a husband will settle her some. Don't look too hopeful so far." Frowning, she turned her face toward the snowflakes piling against the windowpanes.

"Why does she drink like that?"

"Some folks drink to forget things, but it ain't for me to say."

Bowie finished the pie out of politeness rather than hunger. He turned his coffee cup between his palms. "Was Rose Mary married before?"

"Hoo no, Cap'n. Rosie don't like men nohow. Why you ask such a thing?"

"I was wondering. The grave out in the yard. The bedroom. The men's clothing. I thought maybe they belonged to a previous husband. Who do they belong to?"

Lodisha hesitated, then she patted her bosom and sighed. "I guess I can tell that much. Them things you mentioned—they belong to Frank Blevins, Rosie's stepfather." Her cheerful face collapsed into an expression of scorn and loathing. "He's in the ground and good riddance!"

The answer surprised Bowie. He would have asked more questions, but Lodisha stood and placed the coffee cups and pie plates in a bucket of cold water. She covered a wide yawn, signaling their conversation had ended.

"Where am I supposed to sleep?" Stone asked.

Lodisha's dark eyes widened and then she chuckled. "Lawdy. Ain't nobody thought about that." To Bowie's relief, it didn't seem to occur to her that a husband slept with his wife. Nor did Lodisha mention the unused bedroom, as if that possibility were equally as unthinkable. "Wait here, Cap'n, while I rustle up some blankets and a pillow."

Stone spent the night cramped between two chairs pushed together. He kept remembering the weight of the noose around his neck, thinking that he should have been dead instead of alive and married. His conscience kept him awake, that and the cold seeping under the windows and his bride's drunken snores.

Chapter Three

At first light Rosie tied a wrapper over her long johns and stumbled out into the kitchen, weaving toward the fresh pot of coffee boiling on the stove top. She felt as though she'd been kicked in the head by a mule. After adding a generous splash of whiskey to her cup, she tossed down the coffee, letting the hot liquid scald the fuzz off the back of her tongue.

"Good morning."

The greeting startled her and the last drops of hot coffee sloshed over her wrist. "Don't shout," she ordered Stone, who was sitting at the table, watching her.

"I didn't. You're hung over."

"What of it?" Irritated by his judgmental tone, and irritated to be starting the day with conversation, she poured another cup of coffee, irritated also when she noticed her hand was visibly shaking. "As long as I pull my share of the load, what difference does it make?"

"None to me," Stone said, watching as she eased herself onto the bench and clamped her hands around her coffee mug.

They sat in silence while Rosie frantically tried to remember exactly what had occurred last night. She recalled the shock of discovering the door opened to *his* bedroom, and she vaguely recollected that Stone had followed her into the kitchen. She might have said some embarrassing things.

"Where did you sleep?" she asked.

"We have to talk about that. I don't plan to spend another night sleeping between two chairs." He raised a hand to cut off her insistence that he sleep in the barn. "Not when there's an unused bedroom right here. If that room's so special to you, then you take it and I'll take your room."

Horror darkened her eyes and her shoulders convulsed. "No!" she whispered, shaking her head until her brain banged from side to side against her skull. Since Stone was watching, she didn't grab her head and groan, but, Lord, she wanted to. "No."

"Work it out however you like, Rosie. But I'm not sleeping another night on chairs."

"Lodisha . . .?"

Lodisha turned from the stove and planted her fists on broad hips. "No sirree bob, I ain't givin' up my bed no-how! It ain't me that rode into town and got herself married. So don't go tryin' to sweet-talk me by sayin' 'Lodisha' in that little pitiful voice. I ain't givin' up my bed, and tha's the end a that." Turning around, she banged a pan of biscuits on the stove top, sending shock waves reverberating through Rosie's head.

"I'll ponder on the problem," Rosie muttered. Right now she was in no fit state to deal with a dilemma. She felt like cow flop. Just thinking about the day's chores overwhelmed her.

Her state of mind did not improve when she observed that

Bowie Stone looked fresh and alert, regardless of his claim to an uncomfortable night. And she felt like gagging when she noticed that *his* shirt fit Stone so well in the shoulders. When Stone filled out, he was going to be a big man. Probably virile-looking and handsome. The suspicion made her feel strange and sickly inside.

Already the swelling was diminishing around his eye, and the dark bruising was fading by the minute. A rugged cheekbone had begun to emerge. With his hair trimmed and the beard gone, Rosie could see that Stone had a high, strong forehead and a stubborn jaw. He had an interesting mouth too, she decided, now that she could see it. His lips were wide and firm, his teeth as white as eggshell. Undoubtedly he had cut a dashing figure in his cavalry uniform. He'd probably broken dozens of hearts wherever he'd been posted.

Lifting a hand, Rosie shoved self-consciously at the lank hair falling around her face. A whiff reached her nostrils. Her hair stank of dust and grease and tobacco smoke.

Without speaking, Stone finished the breakfast Lodisha put in front of him, then he stood and stretched his back against his hands. He didn't glance at Rosie as he headed for the kitchen door. "I'm going to have a look around; then I'll see if there's anything I can do to help John Hawkins in the barn."

"Don't you go overdoin' it, Cap'n," Lodisha cautioned. "You give yorself time to heal up, or you won't be no good to nobody, hear?" She followed him to the door and helped him into a heavy coat. "You might wring an old hen and bring her up to the house for supper unless John Hawkins plans to get me that hare that's been coming around. Tell him I see'd that hare again just a'fore first light."

The kitchen door banged behind him, sounding like a small explosion. Rosie permitted herself the luxury of a groan and gripped her coffee cup until the pain passed.

"You should be ashamed of yorself, Rose Mary Mulvehey,"

Lodisha said the minute Stone was gone. "You got yorself a husband now and a fresh start. And what you do?" She slammed a lump of bread dough on the floured end of the kitchen table. "You go off on a bender, tha's what you do. Beats me what you's thinking of, girl. That there looks to be a good man."

"He disobeyed a direct order from a superior officer and got himself dishonorably court-martialed. He shot and killed a man."

"Everybody got a story and the Cap'n got his. Maybe he's lookin' for a fresh start too." She leaned the heels of her palms into the dough, flipped it, and leaned forward again. "Jest look at yorself. If'n you ain't a sorry sight."

Rosie lowered her head. "All my life I've been hearing what a sorry sight I am." She looked into her coffee cup. "But I wasn't troubled last night by some rutting man, now was I?"

Lodisha's expression softened. "Honey girl, you jest forget what yor mama said and what that devil Blevins said. Yor jest as pretty as yor mama was. If you'd work at it some, you'd be even prettier."

"I don't want to be pretty!" A shudder tightened Rosie's shoulders. "The only thing mama got out of being pretty was *him*, and an early grave." She pushed aside her untouched breakfast.

"Sooner or later, you gonna have to do yor duty as a wife, darlin'." Lodisha focused on the lump of bread dough.

"If Stone touches me, I'll kill him."

Lodisha nodded, then came at the problem from another direction. "You need the Cap'n's help if'n you goin' get this old patch of dirt to pay. You don' want him running off now, do you?"

Rosie's head jerked up and her eyes narrowed. "Did he say something about running off?"

"Not yet. But how long you 'spect he's go'n stick around

if'n he has to look at a grimy wife every day and put a drunk to bed every night?"

"Are you saying the only way he's going to honor his promise is if I let him poke me?"

"He's yor husband, honey."

Panic flared in her eyes. "Poking isn't part of the deal! The only way I could save his life and consequently save my farm was to marry him! Being married is just incidental to our arrangement. It doesn't mean anything and he knows that!"

Lodisha divided the dough and shaped it into loaves. "Least you could do is make yorself presentable, tha's all I's sayin'."

"But then he might try to poke me!" A tremor of fear shot through her, and drops of coffee flew across the table.

"You jest think on it, honey girl."

Fighting panic, Rosie hunkered over her cup and brooded.

Bowie stood on the kitchen stoop and breathed deeply of the crystal-clean morning air, drawing the cold into his body. The snow had stopped during the night, leaving a sea of white waves flowing across the ocean of prairie. He didn't believe he could ever learn to love the plains, but this morning he could grasp why some did.

The morning light gave him a better view of Rosie's farm, and the sight was not encouraging. All the outbuildings appeared in imminent danger of falling to the ground. The fences were in worse condition than he had first supposed. There was enough work here to keep a dozen men occupied for two full seasons. If Rosie hated this farm as deeply as John Hawkins claimed, Bowie didn't understand why she didn't walk away and let nature reclaim it. He couldn't see anything worth saving.

When the chill began to penetrate his borrowed coat, he moved forward, walking toward the grave located between the house and the cottonwoods. With the entire prairie to choose from, it seemed strange to place a grave in the side yard in full view of the house windows.

To his surprise there was neither a name nor dates carved on the headstone. The stone was blank, a smooth slab. Yet the rock border was tidy, as if someone regularly tended the site.

Moving on down to the creek, he examined an ice-edged ribbon of dark water. It was only about twelve feet across, littered with stones. A thick collection of animal tracks disturbed the snow lining the banks. Bowie decided this would be a cool, comfortable site in midsummer, shaded by mature cottonwoods and tall willows. So far, it was the only pleasant spot he had discovered.

On his way to the barn, he passed a sagging storage shed, a dilapidated henhouse, a pigsty, and the sunken entrance to a root cellar.

The inside of the barn was warm and filled with the good earthy aroma of hay, horse and the cows crowded up to the feeding trough. John Hawkins was milking one of the shaggy bossies, dressed much as he had been yesterday, except in clothing that showed the effects of hard use.

"Good morning, John Hawkins."

"Good morning, Captain Bowie Stone."

Drawn like a magnet, he went directly to Ivanhoe's stall and offered a handful of grain to the gelding's velvety nose. Ivanhoe whickered and tossed his mane, then nuzzled Bowie's hand.

"This is a good morning for a ride," John Hawkins commented.

The appeal of racing across the snowy prairie, the wind in his face and a fine horse between his thighs, made Bowie swallow hard. God, he missed the cavalry. He missed his life, the bugle in the morning and the good-natured grumbling of his men. He missed the horses and the sharp scent of saddle soap and polish. It pained him to recall the blue and brass of parade review and the pride he had taken in his company's performance. Gone from his life was the joy of order and the crisp tailored comfort of his uniform. His sense of loss was like a hole growing in his gut.

"Maybe in a few days," he said, running his hand down Ivanhoe's sleek neck. He was too debilitated, too weak for the ride he envisioned. Ivanhoe deserved a rider as fine as the horse was himself. After pressing his forehead to Ivanhoe's neck, absorbing the horse's warmth and scent, he left the stall to stand beside John Hawkins, listening to the steady ping of hot milk striking the side of the bucket.

"Does the grave in the yard belong to Rosie's mother?"

"That is Frank Blevins' grave. Mr. Blevins was Rosie's stepfather."

"Tell me about him."

"When a white man dies his character is washed clean. To speak of a dead white man is to speak as he might have been. I have thought about this custom of speaking no ill about dead white men. This is a strange custom, but not without merit, I think. Dead white men are remembered with praise or silence. This is not entirely a bad thing."

"You can't tell me anything about Blevins?"

"He was Sadie Mulvehey's second husband. He was a farmer. This was his farm." John Hawkins leaned back on his milking stool and considered. "According to the custom, that is all I can say."

"Last night you said Frank Blevins beat Sadie Mulvehey."

"I apologize for speaking ill of a dead white man."

"Did he beat Rosie?"

John Hawkins looked at Bowie, but he didn't speak.

"So the answer is yes."

"Now I must decide if my silence spoke louder than my voice would have. I must decide if I have violated the custom.

In some respects it was easier to be an Indian. But, as you agreed, there is no future in being an Indian."

Bowie removed a stool from a nail on the barn wall and placed it beside one of the cows. "It's been a while since I've done this." He rested his cheek against the cow's warm dusty side. "When did you stop being an Indian?"

"I have been nothing but a man for a long time. Sometimes I visit the reservations or I share a pipe with a town Indian. This is good. Indians speak of interesting things that white men ignore. Too bad the Indian life is finished."

The two men completed the milking in silence, then John Hawkins fetched his top hat and a heavy wool poncho from his room near Ivanhoe's stall.

"I am going into town to buy you some clothing. Is there anything else you require?"

"I'd like a mirror so I can shave myself."

Indecision disturbed the wrinkles pleating the old man's face. "Rose Mary does not permit mirrors in the house."

Bowie understood he had placed John Hawkins in an awkward position between Rosie's rules and the desire of her new husband.

"Never mind. I'll buy a mirror the next time I'm in town."

To conceal his relief, John Hawkins turned to the wall to remove a Winchester from a mounted rack. He extended the rifle to Bowie.

"If you feel strong enough to hunt, Lodisha will be wanting a hare for the pot."

Testing the weight and balance of the Winchester, Bowie watched the pale barn light slide along the barrel. The last time he had fired a gun had been to kill Luther Radison.

"Will you ride Ivanhoe into town?" he asked, dropping the rifle to his side.

"I will walk. It is only five miles to Passion's Crossing."

By the time Bowie returned to the house, carrying two hares, he felt more alive than he had in days. For the first time since he had turned his company away from Stone Toes Gulch, he had enjoyed a situation in which he was in charge and at which he had succeeded. Lodisha would have her hares for the supper pot. And Bowie had moved two shots away from remembering his last shot as the one that killed Luther Radison.

As he approached the house, he spotted Rosie and halted in surprise. She was splitting lengths of cottonwood, swinging the axe with an expertise he didn't associate with women. After watching a few minutes, Bowie experienced a reluctant sense of admiration. Not only was Rosie engaged in hard, taxing labor and performing with smooth efficiency; but, considering the hangover she was surely suffering, she was making herself work when every nerve must have screamed in protest. The jolt of the blade biting into the wood would send shock waves rocketing up her arms and ignite an explosion inside her head.

She paused to mop sweat from her forehead and throat, and scowled at him. "You want something?"

"Have you decided where I'm going to sleep tonight?" Having succeeded with the hares, Bowie felt prepared to tackle his most pressing problem.

"You figure it out. I've got too much to do to waste time worrying about you."

"Rosie, about last night—"

A flood of color washed over her face. "Never mind about that."

"I think we should talk."

"There's nothing to talk about, Stone." She glared at him. "Just so you understand . . . this isn't a real marriage. I need a roustabout; you needed rescuing. We got a deal, and that's all there is to it. So don't go getting any ideas."

Lifting the axe, she swung it above her hat, then brought it down with a solid chunk. Bowie watched another minute, then continued to the house.

The instant he stepped inside, the heat enveloped him and sapped his strength. His legs turned wobbly and he felt light-headed. Apparently he hadn't been as ready as he had believed to take on the physical exertion of hunting.

Rising behind her butter churn, Lodisha accepted the hares and ran a sharp eye over his pale face. "If'n I was you, Cap'n, I'd put myself down for a spell. You ain't in the best of shape yet." She chewed her bottom lip, then came to a reluctant decision. "I s'pose you could use my bed for an hour or so."

The question of where he would sleep or whose bed he might borrow suddenly impressed Bowie as wildly ludicrous. There was a perfectly good bed that belonged to no one and was going unused.

"Do you have a basket?" he asked, making up his mind.

" 'Course I do." Looking puzzled, Lodisha entered the pantry and emerged carrying a large woven basket. Bowie took it and walked directly to the door of the second bedroom. When Lodisha realized where he was heading, she gasped and her hands flew to her mouth. "Cap'n," she called, hurrying after him. "Cap'n, you cain't go in there. That bed ain't for use no how. Cap'n—"

He opened the door, frowning at the squeal of the hinge. "Bring me some butter."

"Lawdy, lawdy!" Lodisha wrung her hands in the folds of her apron, watching with wide appalled eyes. As she seemed rooted to the floor, Bowie returned to the kitchen for a cloth and a dab of the new butter.

"Gawdy Gawd," Lodisha breathed, watching him grease the hinge. He kept at the job until the door opened and shut in silence.

The first thing he did inside was throw open the curtain.

Through motes of flying dust, he saw Rosie working in the yard. She jerked up her head at the movement in the window and her jaw dropped. For an instant their eyes locked, then she shouted something, threw down the axe, and ran toward the house.

Bowie drew his arm along the top of the bureau, sweeping Frank Blevins' toilet articles into the basket before he opened the drawers and began to empty the contents on top of the toiletries.

Rosie skidded to a stop in the doorway, panting for breath and scarlet with fury. "You get your butt out of this room right now, mister!" Horror filled her eyes as she absorbed what he was doing.

"You instructed me to solve the sleeping problem and I've solved it. I'm taking this room." He pulled a heavy shirt and a pair of work denims off the wall pegs, folded them and put them inside one of the drawers. The clothing had been worn hard but there was some use left.

"Stop that! Don't touch another thing or I swear, I'll kill you!" She was so furious that her hands shook. She had difficulty removing her revolver from the holster, but she managed it. "I mean it, Stone." Even her voice was shaking. "I'm going to count to three, then you better be out of this room or you're a dead man."

"Frank Blevins is the dead man. He's been dead for three years. It's time you stopped making a shrine out of his room. He's gone, Rosie. Whatever happened between the two of you is finished."

"One." Her breath shot out in short panicked gasps. Her face was crimson and her eyes wild.

Bowie didn't warm to the muddy-colored picture on the wall so he tossed it into the throw-away basket.

"Two . . . get out of there, you sorry son of a bitch!"

He lifted the lid of a moldering trunk and peered inside.

The trunk held a collection of cheap yellow-backed novels, an outdated almanac, what looked like a money pouch, a pair of work boots, and a pile of socks and handkerchiefs.

"Three!"

Bullets exploded around him and smacked into the plastered walls.

The sound of gunfire rang in his ears as Bowie lifted the work boots out of the trunk and held them to the light at the window. There was service left in them so he decided to keep them.

"You! You . . . goddamned, slop-sucking pig! You deserting, murdering son of a whore!" Hysteria thinned Rosie's voice. When he turned toward her, he saw furious tears streaming down her cheeks. "I wish you'd never been born! I wish I'd let you hang! I hate the stinking sight of you!" she shouted.

"There are going to be changes, Rosie," he said quietly. Her violent reaction exceeded anything he had imagined. He wasn't sure what to say to her. "You had to know there would be changes when you decided to bring a husband here." Her frantic expression told him that she was beyond reasoning, but he made the attempt anyway. "Surely you can see that it's idiotic not to use this room."

In answer, she raised her arm, steadied the revolver across her sleeve and fired at him. The bullet cut near enough that he felt it stir his hair before it chunked into the wall behind him. Lodisha screamed and covered her face.

"If you'd kill a man for claiming an unused bed . . . then stop fooling around and get it over with." Calmly, he met her wild, raging gaze. The room was hazy and heavy with the smell of powder and shot. At some level, Bowie felt a detached sense of surprise that he still stood upright. "Go ahead. Do it."

She dashed a furious hand across her eyes and her lips snarled back over her teeth. "I *wanted* this room as a shrine, you stinking cake of cow flop! I wanted it just as he left it so every time I walked past this goddamned door I would remember my promise to get even! I don't *ever* want to forget what he did to Ma and me!"

She shot at him again. This time she nicked him. Bowie felt something like a bee sting nip the bottom of his earlobe. Lodisha sagged against the door jamb and stuffed the hem of her apron in her mouth, her eyes as wide and round as lumps of coal. Bowie touched his bloodied ear and decided Rosie Mulvehey was either the best damned shot in Gulliver County or the worst.

He met the hatred blazing in her eyes. "Whatever happened, it's time to let it go."

Her face twisted, and she waved the revolver in the air. "You have all the answers, don't you?" Her voice spiraled into a scream. "You come in where you don't belong and speak all quiet and calm about making changes as if you were God or something! Well, you don't know what the hell you're talking about. Get out of this room. *Getoutgetoutgetout!*"

"No."

A blizzard of bullets whizzed around him. Chunks of plaster blew off the walls; the window exploded. Bowie heard the curtains crash down, and a piece of ceiling fell heavily behind him. The gun emptied, but Rosie continued to fire as if she couldn't stop, now pointing the clicking revolver directly at his chest.

"Frank Blevins is dead. He's gone. This is my room now for as long as I stay."

She threw back her head and screamed. It was a long howling animal scream that raised the hair on the back of Bowie's neck. There was murder and fury in that scream, and wrenching anguish. He didn't think he would ever forget the sound she made.

At the end, she whirled, making tortured sobbing noises deep in her throat, and she ran out of the house. Three minutes later she shot past the house on Ivanhoe's back, riding flat out like wind made solid. He stood at the shattered window and watched until she was a distant dot against the snowy prairie.

"Jesus Lawd!" Lodisha breathed from the doorway. She stared around the shot-up room.

"If you'll find some rags to plug the window, I'll stir up some patching plaster."

When the flying speck vanished against the horizon, Bowie began the task of repairing his new room. And he wondered just what in the hell he had done.

By the time Rosie reached town, her throat was raw from screaming against the wind, and all her tears were sucked away. What she felt now was a pulsing helpless rage. She seethed inside at Stone's daring to desecrate The Room. And she boiled and writhed to think that her nerve had faltered and that she hadn't killed him as he deserved. At the last critical second she had shied from plugging an unarmed man, even though what he was doing drove a stake into her heart.

Grinding her teeth and cursing, she reloaded her pistols then kicked open the doors of Harold's Saloon and stalked inside.

The walls were hung with red calico and gilt banners. All the dark wood would have given the place a gloomy air if it hadn't been for the chandeliers overhead and a bank of mirrors. Even so, Harold's wasn't half the place it had been a few years past when there were more men in Passion's Crossing.

The place felt deserted, a relic from a distant era. Now dust lay thick on the piano keys; the music man had moved on more than a year ago. Two aging bar girls sat drinking together, looking bored and not caring that their stockings were mended or their once-shiny costumes were limp and dulled with grime. There were only three customers.

Rosie strode directly to the bar, hooked her boot on the rail and took her usual position near the cigar vases and the jars of brandied peaches. This was one of the few spots along the counter where she couldn't see herself in the back-bar mirror.

"Give me a glass and a bottle," she snarled at Harold. She poured two shots and tossed them down in the blink of an eye, hoping they would make her feel halfway human again.

"Well, well. If it ain't the new bride." Lem Sorrenson, the blacksmith, leaned over his shot glass and peered down the bar. "Don't look like you put yourself out any to spruce up for your honeymoon. Or is that a new layer of dirt special for the occasion?" He laughed at his witticism.

"What happened, Rosie?" Shotshi Morris squinted at her. "Your convict husband kick you out of bed?"

Acey James grinned. "Maybe the bastard discovered she ain't no woman at all. I've wondered about that myself."

Rosie tossed back another shot, feeling the hot liquid burn down her throat and hit her stomach like a fireball. She took a cigar from the vase and lit it with a match Lem slid down the counter to her.

"Ain't you going to say nothing, Rosie?" Lem asked, winking at the others. "How's it feel to be a real woman now?"

"You think that there's a real woman?" Shotshi waved at her and laughed. "Reckon ole Lem needs specs."

Rosie smiled at their jokes as she always did, grinned and laughed as she always did. But today it hurt worse than it usually did. She poured another drink, watching the level go down in the bottle, wanting to hurry along the coming oblivion. It was one of the few things in this world that she could count on. Drink enough blazer and eventually the pain disappeared.

"I liked it better when there was music," she murmured. Sometimes she could turn the jokes away from herself.

But not today. The boys were bored, looking for an illusion of excitement, looking for a tale to tell tomorrow. They knew if they goaded her long enough, got her drunk enough, she'd start whooping it up, and tomorrow they'd have another Rosie story to smile over and pass around town. To hurry events along, they chipped in to pay her tab, as she knew they would.

"Hey Rosie," Shotshi said, grinning wide enough to expose a gap where two teeth were supposed to be. "Why don't you just settle the question now, huh? Just lift up your shirt and show us what you got."

"Shut up, Shotshi." Suddenly Rosie felt tired, weary unto death. Aside from feeling the pointlessness of life in general, she had already been worn to a nub by having a stranger in her life. She hated it. Marrying had been a bad, bad mistake. Bowie Stone was right about one thing he'd said, something she'd been too drunk or too hungover to consider: a husband meant changes. She didn't want changes.

She didn't want a man in her house or in her life. She didn't want conversation in the morning or someone making her feel ashamed or unworthy. She did a good enough job of that all by herself. She didn't want anyone disrupting her routine. Most of all, she damn sure didn't want anyone sleeping in *his* bed. Tears of fury and frustration glistened in her eyes, and she turned her face aside so no one would see.

What ate at her the worst was the mounting suspicion that by marrying Bowie Stone she had bitten off more than she could chew. How could she control a man who didn't budge his opinion even when he was being shot at from point-blank range? How the hell was she going to manage a man who didn't care if he lived or died?

A familiar feeling of utter helplessness stole over her, the same despicable helplessness she had felt when *he* was alive. A man she hated was running the show, forcing her to submit to his will, and she didn't see a damn thing she could do to stop it. Worse, she had brought this disaster on herself. She could hardly stand the thought.

Gradually Rosie became aware that the boys had shifted off her as a topic of conversation and were amusing themselves by ridiculing her new husband. Even Harold had moved up close, polishing glasses nearby and listening in.

"... a goddamn Indian-lover. Way I heard, the yellow-bellied coward turned tail and ran right as the fighting started up."

"Too chicken-livered to fire a shot." Lem spit on the saw-dust floor in disgust. "You ask me, they should'a strung him up right there at Stone Toes."

"That ain't how it happened," Rosie said, before she thought about what she was doing.

"Is that right?" They all leaned over their glasses to look at her. "Well s'pose you just tell us what did happen then."

"Stone didn't run away from a fight. He refused to slaughter women and children. There weren't any warriors at Stone Toes, the men were off hunting. So what kind of battle is that? Riding down on women and babies? Besides, the Indians had permission to camp there. They weren't causing anyone any trouble."

Shotshi shrugged. "You think them Indian women ain't going to breed more Indians? You think them babies are going to grow up into Chinamen or something? You know the saying: only good Indian is a dead Indian."

They grinned, goading her. Everything sensible told Rosie to back off. She didn't owe Stone any loyalty. She hated him. She had spent the past fifteen minutes wishing with all her miserable heart that she had killed the bastard when she had had the chance.

"Bowie Stone is not a coward," she stated slowly, hardly able to believe these words were falling out of her mouth.

That she was placed in a position where she had to defend Bowie Stone was appalling and was one more reason to despise his black soul.

"He shot and killed an unarmed man and that's a pure fact. Judge and jury said so. What do you say to that, Rosie Mulvehey?"

"It ain't true is what I say to that. The man Stone killed was tracking him, coming to kill him. Radison was armed and he shot first. If the judge had allowed the full story to be told, the jury would have seen it was self-defense true and simple."

"Is that what Stone told you? Hoo-ee, ain't love blind! Now murder is self-defense." They laughed and poured more whiskey in her glass. "Tha's why the judge sentenced your yellow-bellied husband to hang, right Rosie? 'Cause he committed self-defense."

She understood they weren't going to let up until they prodded her into a performance. Trying to pull up the energy and the inclination for it, she drew out her six-guns and stepped away from the bar, both barrels blazing.

She sent Shotshi dancing across the floor, watching the sawdust kick up around his old work boots as the bullets pocked into the floor. The others laughed, hooted and slapped their thighs.

"Goddamit, Rosie," Shotshi shouted, kicking up his feet. "Watch it, will ya? You're coming mighty close with them shots."

The bar girls looked up from their table and smiled. They clapped their hands and tried to pretend they were having a high ole time.

"I miss the music," Rosie whispered, feeling tired and sad. She kept old Shotshi dancing, but her heart wasn't in it. This time the whiskey didn't make her feel better; she felt like weeping.

Finally, ignoring Harold's pleas, she shot up the painting of the naked Venus hanging above the piano so Harold would get mad enough to call Gaine to come get her and take her off to jail where she could find a little privacy.

It seemed the wind hadn't sucked all her tears dry after all.

Chapter Four

Bowie spent a sleepless night propped against his pillows listening for Rosie's return.

"When she don' come home it means she spent the night in jail, sleepin' off a bender," Lodisha informed him over breakfast. "Means John Hawkins got to go to town and pay her fine and damages 'fore the sheriff'll turn her loose. Eat them biscuits, Cap'n. We got to fatten you up. And don't go leaving spots on yor new shirt and pants, hear?"

While Bowie finished his second cup of hot black coffee, he watched John Hawkins remove one of the tin boxes from the shelf above the stove, open it, and count out a few coins.

"Tha's our bank," Lodisha explained, waving her coffee mug toward the shelf. "First box is for necessities like seed grain. Second box for fines and damages. Third box for books and 'mergencies. Fourth box for luxuries. Ain't nothing in the fourth box. Been a long time since we seen any luxuries 'round this here place."

"I'll go with you," Bowie decided, following John Hawkins to the door.

"You ain't up to walking five miles in and five miles back," Lodisha protested. But she started filling three canteens with hot coffee, and she packed a bandanna with more food than an old Indian and a hungover woman could eat.

Bowie thanked her for breakfast and for the provisions, then donned one of the coats on the peg by the door, pushed on his hat, and stepped into a morning so brilliantly cold and bright that he paused a moment to enjoy the sheer pleasure of being alive to witness it.

After he caught up to John Hawkins, he matched his longer stride to the Indian's steady pace. When they had walked an hour in companionable silence, they stopped beside a gully to drink coffee from the canteens. John Hawkins wasn't winded, wasn't breathing hard. Bowie suspected they paused solely for his benefit.

They didn't speak again until they reached Passion's Crossing and the courthouse jail at the end of Main Street.

Deputy Sands leaned against a porch post, picking his teeth with a penknife. "Couldn't stay away, huh Stone? You missed our hospitality?" He glanced at Bowie's freshly shaven cheeks and clean clothing, considered the fading bruises. "Looks like being hitched agrees with you. Can't say the same for your bride."

"Is she inside?"

"If it was up to me I'd keep her there for being so stupid as to defend a chicken-livered murderer." The deputy's grin abruptly vanished. "You best keep your nose clean, Stone. A lot of folks here-abouts think you oughta be under ground. You step one toe over the line, and me and the boys'll be only too happy to oblige them who'd like to see you get what you deserve."

Stone stopped in the jailhouse doorway. "You said she was defending me?"

The deputy spat next to Bowie's boots. "That crazy no-account was trying to persuade ole Lem and Shotshi how you're a wronged man. Shot up Harold's place and sent old Shotshi on a pill dance in your honor. You might be able to cock-a-doodle a wet-brained drunk like Rosie, but the rest of this town knows better. So you watch yourself, mister."

Bowie stared at him. "You insult my wife again, and you'll live to regret it. And her name is Mrs. Stone, Sands. You refer to her any other way, and I'll take you apart piece by piece."

John Hawkins stepped between them. "I am here to pay Mrs. Stone's fine and damages, Deputy Carl Sands. If it would not inconvenience you, would you be so kind as to bring Ivanhoe around please?"

Sands looked him up and down with mock amazement, then leaned back against the porch post. "I don't take orders from no Indian, John Hawkins. You know better'n that."

"I'll fetch Ivanhoe," Bowie said between his teeth. He left John Hawkins to pay Rosie out and walked around the courthouse to the stable in the rear. By the time he had saddled Ivanhoe and led him around front, Sands was gone, and Rosie and John Hawkins were waiting on the porch steps.

Rosie looked—and smelled—worse than Bowie had seen her look or smell so far. She had pulled the man's hat she wore down to the tops of her ears so no one could see her eyes. Her clothing was filthy and stank of dried vomit. If Bowie had been meeting her for the first time, he wouldn't have guessed she could possibly be a woman. He would have mistaken her for a derelict roustabout whom a sensible man would avoid.

Silently, he handed her Ivanhoe's reins, but John Hawkins intervened.

"I am tired," he said stiffly, not looking at either Bowie or Rosie. "I would prefer to ride home."

Rosie's jaw dropped. "You? Tired?" Instantly she thrust Ivanhoe's reins into John Hawkins' hand. "Take him. John Hawkins—are you sick?"

Bowie hadn't supposed Rosie Mulvehey cared about anything or anyone except her farm and herself. Her genuine anxiety and concern offered an unexpected revelation.

"I am not sick," John Hawkins answered, swinging up on Ivanhoe. Without further explanation, he rode away from them down Main Street.

Bowie couldn't glimpse Rosie's eyes, but he saw her mouth pull down at the corners. "I'll be damned," she said, chewing her lower lip between her teeth. "I've never seen John Hawkins ride in a saddle. He always said he never would. And I've never, not ever, heard him admit to being tired."

"John Hawkins is an old man." But Bowie had observed no evidence that age was a factor in John Hawkins' character. The walk into town had not tired the Indian; he had arrived as fresh as when they left the farm. A suspicion grew in Bowie's mind that John Hawkins had deliberately forced him to spend a few hours in Rosie's company.

It was too late to protest. Bowie thrust his hands into his coat pockets and walked back the way he had come. He made no concession to the wreck of a woman beside him or to the hangover she was certainly suffering. He walked with his usual long stride, leaving her to catch up or lag behind. Given that her head undoubtedly felt like it was coming off, he expected—and hoped—she would fall well behind.

She didn't. She caught up and matched him stride for stride, doing a little kick-step to keep pace when his long legs outdistanced hers. After a mile, Bowie glanced at her, feeling a grudging twinge of respect. Rosie Mulvehey might be a god-awful mess, but she had willpower the likes of which he had seldom seen. She didn't cut herself an ounce of slack. She kept up without a murmur of complaint about the pace he set or about the sunlight glaring off the snow, didn't mention that her head was splitting.

After another half mile at a steady rapid pace, Bowie took pity on her. "Lodisha sent coffee. Do you want some?"

"God, yes."

With a grateful sigh, she sat on a rock and waited for Bowie to remove the canteens hanging around his neck. When he handed her one, she opened the cap and held her face above the escaping steam before she took a long swallow. A strangled sound of pleasure came from deep in her throat, then she upended the canteen and drank again, wiping her chin with the back of her hand.

Bowie gazed at the horizon, wondering why anyone would choose to live in a place where nothing disturbed the monotony of boundless space.

"Defending me wasn't necessary. Don't do it again."

"Even the thought of defending you sticks in my craw. But I have to. You're my husband. That sticks in my craw too, but I don't see what I can do about it. You wouldn't happen to have a bottle of whiskey on you, would you?"

"No." He watched without pity as her shoulders slumped in disappointment. "I mean it, Rosie. Don't cause yourself grief on my behalf. I don't give a damn what people say."

She tilted her head back to look at him from beneath her hat brim. "Did you sleep in the room last night?"

"It's mine now."

"Bastard!" Falling forward, she covered her face with her hands and rocked back and forth. "You no-good piece of horse flop! You're scum! Sludge! I wish you were dead!"

After screwing on the cap of his canteen, Bowie started walking again, not caring if she followed. After a minute he heard her behind him, swearing and shouting names at him, making no effort to catch up. They covered a mile before she moved up beside him.

"Listen, I'm not one for begging, but I'm begging you not to sleep in *that room*. Please, Stone, listen to me. I'm begging you."

Bowie halted and turned with a look of exasperation that she didn't see because he spoke to the top of her crushed hat.

"I'm going to sleep in that room because there is nowhere else for me to sleep. I'm not going to sleep on chairs or on the floor when there's an unused bed a few feet away. Now if you can't accept that, then I'll leave Passion's Crossing right now. Is that what you want?"

They stood toe to toe, two specks on the snowy ruts scarring the prairie. Cold seeped through Bowie's boots. An icy wind plucked at his hat.

She pounded her fists on the sides of her thighs and screamed a long sound of frustration. "You can't leave, you have to stay," she said. "I will always hate your guts for taking his room."

They were both aware what a puny threat her hatred was. Her hatred wasn't enough to send him back to sleeping across two chairs; it wasn't enough to satisfy her need to punish him. They glared at each other.

"Why do you drink so much?"

"Why don't you care whether you live or die?"

Stalemated, they walked on in angry silence, neither willing to explore the other's question.

When they stopped again for coffee and a bite of Lodisha's pie and cheese, the farm lay within sight. Rosie focused on a curl of wood smoke drifting from the chimney.

"I need to know more about you," she said sullenly. The statement was based on necessity, not preference.

"What do you want to know?"

A shrug lifted her dirty poncho. "The get-acquainted type

of bunk. How old are you? Where did you come from? Do you have any family? Like that."

In the distance, Lodisha emerged from the house and walked toward the pigsty, carrying a basin of slops.

"I'm thirty-three. I grew up in Washington, D.C." He didn't want to talk about this. "I had a brother. He died almost four years ago. Is there anything else?"

"Are your parents alive?"

"My mother died years ago."

This time Rosie set out first, leaving him to catch up. "I'm twenty-three. I've spent my whole life in Gulliver County. The only family I have is John Hawkins and Lodisha. The only thing I want is to wring a profitable harvest out of this farm."

"You're only twenty-three?" He couldn't believe it.

Stopping, she turned to face him. "How old did you think I was?"

Bowie stared at her. "I thought you were closer to my age."

"Hell fire! You thought I was thirty? Slop-sucking pig! I don't know how you ever bossed a company! You don't know anything."

Turning on her heel, she stomped toward the house. It was the first flash of vanity Bowie had noticed in her, and he blinked after her in amazement. She didn't care how she looked or smelled, but it offended her that he had believed she was older than she was. Shaking his head, he slowly followed her.

Twenty-three, the same age as Susan. The difference between the two women was so vast that it didn't seem possible they could be the same species. His steps slowed as Susan's features rose in his mind.

Weeks ago she would have received his last letter telling her that he was sentenced to hang. Closing his eyes, he scrubbed a hand down his face. If it hadn't been for Nate, he would have been tempted to let Susan and his father go on believing he was dead. It would be simpler for everyone. But there was Nate, and promises to keep. Eventually, he would have to go back.

Lodisha spotted them coming up the road and hastened to intercept them at the porch. She positioned her bulk in front of the door and crossed her arms over the front of her shawl.

"No sirree bob," she said firmly, leveling a dark stare at Rosie. "You ain't tracking through my parlor stinkin' of jail and worse, no sir, nohow. You know the rules, miss." A black thumb jerked toward the side of the house. "Git the tub."

"I need a drink first," Rosie insisted stubbornly. Her chin jutted. "Let me inside for just a minute."

"No." Lodisha's solid body didn't budge. Her black eyes bored into Rosie. "You ain't taking yor ease until you's setting in yor tub, and tha's final."

Cursing, Rosie tore off her hat and flung it to the ground. "How do you expect me to wrestle the tub out of the lean-to when I'm feeling as weak as a calf?" she shouted. "Give me one little drink to put some iron in my muscles, then I'll fetch the damned tub."

Bowie smiled. "I'll fetch the tub." He winked at Lodisha. "Stick to your guns. Don't give in. Might be interesting to see what's under all that dirt and grime."

"You stay out of this, dammit!"

Lodisha didn't take her eyes off Rosie. "I ain't 'bout to give in, Cap'n. Never have; never will. You go with the Cap'n, honey girl," she said to Rosie. "When the tub's ready, I'll let you inside. But not with them stinkin' clothes on yor hide. Them, you leave outside." A sniff pinched her nostrils.

Cursing and kicking at the snow drifts, Rosie followed Bowie around the house and watched sullenly as he threw back the door of the lean-to and dragged the tin tub out and then up on the stoop.

Lodisha opened the kitchen door. Her expression hadn't softened any. "Off with them clothes."

"I'm *doing* it!"

First Rosie flung down her hat then her poncho. Then she sat on the stoop and thrust her feet toward Bowie.

"What are you smiling at? Make yourself useful and help me off with my boots."

Gripping her boot at the heel and toe, Bowie jerked. When her boot and sock flew off, the smell almost knocked him down. Swearing under his breath and trying not to breathe, he pulled off the other boot and hastily stepped back.

She stood and peeled off her man's shirt and the reeking buckskin britches, throwing them onto the trampled snow around the stoop. When she had pared down to her long johns, she shivered in the cold wind and scowled up at Lodisha.

"Them too," Lodisha said firmly, nodding at her long johns.

"Ah. Well." Bowie cleared his throat and backed away, studying her baggy long johns. "I'll just go out to the barn and check on John Hawkins, make sure Ivanhoe's rubbed down."

He backed up another step. Rosie stood with her spine to him, as rigid as a marble statue.

It wasn't until he had turned and started toward the barn that he realized the pink firing her cheeks wasn't a reflection off her red long johns. She'd been blushing.

Pausing beside the root cellar, he thought about that, taking grim pleasure in the revelation that something on this earth could make Rosie Mulvehey blush. Remembering how she had made a point of humiliating him when he was in his bath, he turned on his heel and returned to the house.

A splash went up from the tub when he entered the kitchen, followed by some frantic thrashing that sprayed water across the plank floor.

"Get the hell out of here," she shouted. "Lodisha, for God's sake throw me a towel!"

Grinning, Bowie walked past her into the parlor and returned with the whiskey bottle. He poured a splash into a cup. "Would you like a drink?"

She was curled up under the water, her knees pressed to her chest. Murder blazed in her eyes, replaced by longing when her gaze dropped to the cup in his hand.

"Give it to me," she demanded. She licked her lips and swallowed.

He stood where she had stood when he was in the tub. And he tried to peer through the water exactly as she had done. He suspected he was less successful at seeing anything as her bath water had already clouded with grime.

"Stop looking at me!"

"What's the fuss about? If you've seen one woman's body, you've seen them all," he quoted. Smiling at her expression, he let her snatch the cup from his hand before he ambled to the stove and poured himself a cup of coffee, then took a seat at the table.

She threw back the whiskey, then closed her eyes, and a shudder of relief passed down her body. After a moment she opened her eyes and glared. "Get out of here, Stone. I don't want you here."

In case Lodisha also needed reminding, Stone smiled and said, "I'm your husband. Some would say I have a right to be here."

"Tha's a fact," Lodisha muttered. She advanced on Rosie with a cake of lye soap and a rough cloth. "We'll start with that filthy neck and work ourselfs down. Good Gawd, but you is a stinkin' mess, girl! Jest look at that dirt come rolling off'n you!"

There was no doubt. Rosie Mulvehey was blushing. Her face flamed to the color of red worsted. Stone sipped his coffee and let her see him watching. He took as much grim pleasure in her discomfort as she had taken in his.

But his smile abruptly vanished and his throat dried when Lodisha dragged Rosie to a standing position and began scrubbing her buttocks and thighs. Bowie stared in disbelief.

Rosie Mulvehey had the most magnificent body he had ever seen.

He hadn't even suspected. His coffee cup halted in midair, frozen between his mouth and the table. He could not have looked away from her if his life had depended on it.

Long golden legs curved up to small tight buttocks that angled sweetly to a tiny waist. Her back was smooth and muscled, the ridge of her spine sharply defined. Creamy ivory and gold emerged from the glistening soap and water.

Intent on her task and paying him no mind, Lodisha turned Rosie to face him. Bowie sucked in a sharp hard breath.

Her full breasts were high and firm, tipped with buds of cherry. Her waist flared into rounded hips and a taut flat stomach. Bowie's eyes dropped to the tawny triangle between her thighs, and he swallowed hard.

Good God. She was perfectly formed. Bowie Stone had seen his share of beautiful female bodies, but none had affected him as powerfully as Rosie Mulvehey.

He recovered his senses in time to watch Lodisha pull Rosie down in the tub and shove her head beneath the water. She came up gasping and wiping at her eyes while Lodisha lathered the harsh lye soap into her scalp.

Bowie stared helplessly. His intention to embarrass Rosie as she had embarrassed him had circled back on him. It was he who felt acutely uncomfortable. He would have left immediately except that she would have noticed his state of arousal. He remained at the table, powerless to look away from her.

When Rosie's face emerged from beneath the towel Lodisha

was vigorously applying to her hair, her cheeks were crimson and her eyes were wet. All Bowie saw was the luxuriant mass of long curling hair that Lodisha began combing over the back of the tub.

Rosie's hair was not the muddy brown that Bowie had assumed it was. Already he could see that her wet hair would dry to a shining tawny color, a splendid mix of gold and chestnut and flame that would glow like silk in the sunlight.

Lodisha helped her out of the tub, wrapped her in a large mended towel and gave her a gentle push toward the stove. "You stay there and keep yourself warm while I rustle up some clean clothes."

Rosie stood trembling in front of the stove, clutching the towel around her body, her head bowed. Wet curls fell forward against her scrubbed and glowing face. Her eyes were closed, her lashes a thick dark crescent against her cheekbones.

"You are absolutely beautiful," Bowie whispered, staring at her. "It's criminal that you let yourself look like you did before."

She swayed on her feet. Tears spilled down her cheeks. "You've had your revenge," she said in a strangled tone. "Now go. Please go."

"Rosie, I just—"

"If you touch me or come near me, I swear I'll claw your eyes out."

The torment pinching her features and grinding her voice told him that his presence was an injury to her. Her expression and the way she huddled in on herself reminded him of the terrified Indian women at Stone Toes. He didn't understand what he was witnessing, but he recognized that her anguish was deep and genuine.

"I made a mistake and I apologize," he mumbled, crossing the kitchen in four strides. Disturbed and ashamed, he closed the door behind him.

* * *

No one spoke during supper.

Rosie made herself swallow enough of the stewed chicken to appease Lodisha, but she wasn't hungry. Each time she remembered Stone's steady blue eyes scalding her body, she reached for the whiskey bottle beside her plate.

Stone caught her wrist. "Don't do that," he said quietly, looking at her across the table.

It was the first time he had deliberately touched her, and for one paralyzing instant Rosie could not move. Then she jerked her hand and the bottle away from him.

"Don't tell me what to do." When she noticed John Hawkins watching, she glared at him, too. "I need this."

Lodisha sailed into the silence. "Now don' our honey girl look pretty as a pumpkin?" She stroked Rosie's hair on her way to get more biscuits. "Prettiest little thing I ever did see."

John Hawkins nodded solemnly. Stone kept staring at her as though she were a prairie mirage.

"Shut up all of you!" There wasn't enough air in the room. She was suffocating.

"I wish you had a mirror," Stone said in that same quiet voice that made her feel nervous inside. "I wish you could see how beautiful you are."

"Stop it!" she screamed. Panic turned to acid in her stomach. Jumping to her feet, she faced them with a wild expression. "I know what I look like, don't lie to me!"

Stone started to rise. "I don't think you do, not if you don't realize how—"

A wild heat shot through her and she backed away from him. She scrabbled at her waist, searching for the revolvers she had left in her room.

"Stay away from me!"

She wanted to scream and howl and throw things. She wanted to hurt someone. She wanted to tear her hair and scratch her cheeks and roll in the dirt. A low moan began deep in her chest and built until it choked her. Strangling on a sob of panic, she bolted to her room, slammed the door behind her, and sat on her bed, holding her revolvers pointed at the door.

"We'll walk the fence lines and see how extensive the damage is." Rosie made the announcement at breakfast, keeping her gaze fixed on her plate.

Something was wrong with her this morning, but she couldn't identify the peculiarity. She wasn't positive if something were actually wrong or merely different.

Not until she was sipping her second cup of sugared coffee, marveling at how good it tasted, did she suddenly realize what was different. She didn't have a hangover. Her mouth dropped and her eyebrows soared in surprise. She couldn't recall the last time she had begun a morning without feeling wretched.

It was wonderful not to have a headache and to really taste her food and coffee, but it also felt . . . different. And it was Bowie Stone's fault.

She had slammed into her bedroom without realizing she had left her whiskey bottle behind. She had dreaded facing Stone more than she had craved a drink, which was saying a lot. Shaking all over, she had covered her head with a pillow and prayed she would fall asleep before she heard the squeak of *his* bedroom door.

Stone was staring at her again and she self-consciously touched the hair she had tied back with a piece of string. God she hated baths. Baths dissolved the layers of concealment and left her feeling exposed and defenseless.

"Stop looking at me!" Jumping up, she turned her back on him and strode to the pegs beside the door. After jamming a hat over her hair and pulling on a heavy shapeless coat, she felt a little more protected. "Are you coming, or are you going to calf around all day?"

Not waiting for him to follow, she stepped outside and breathed deeply of the cold translucent air. For once the sunlight bouncing off the melting snow didn't sear her eyes or sting her eyelids. The lack of pain and discomfort felt good, but she also felt disoriented, as if she had lost something important that she needed to have.

The instant she heard the kitchen door bang behind her, she took off walking toward the east section, talking to Stone over her shoulder.

"We have to decide how many acres we think we can plant. There's no sense killing ourselves repairing fence lines around acreage that's going to remain fallow. We'll only fence the acres we intend to plow. How many acres do you think we can do?"

Stone moved up beside her and she jerked away, increasing her pace, keeping her head down.

"You decide," he said. "It's your farm."

"I could use some help with this decision."

"I haven't made many successful decisions lately. You aren't planning to harness Ivanhoe to a plow, are you?"

She risked a look at him, glad his hat brim was pulled down far enough that she couldn't see his eyes. "I plan to harness you to the plow."

His head jerked up. "*I'm* your plow horse?"

"We both agree it would ruin Ivanhoe to work him on a plow, so what other choice is there?" Rosie moved ahead of him and entered the field, stepping around muddy patches of melting snow. "You pull the plow and I'll guide it. John Hawkins will follow behind and put in the seed." Dead silence greeted the announcement of her plan. "I don't know how else to do it."

Stone followed her into the field, walking on the other side of the fence they were tracking. In most spots the ground was still frozen; in other spots their boots sank an inch or two into cold slushy mud.

For three hours they walked the six acres Rosie finally decided they would plant, inspecting the downed areas of fence, checking the lay of the land.

They stopped to share a canteen of coffee at a section of fence that lay on the ground, half buried in melting drifts of snow.

"Today you look twenty-three," Stone commented, watching her lift her face to the winter sun. "Why won't you allow mirrors in the house?"

"Because I don't need to see myself," she snapped. "Leave it alone." They had been getting along fine, talking about the farm and planning for spring. Now he had to spoil it, just when she had begun to relax a little.

"There's a lot that I don't understand. Where in the hell did you get the idea that you're ugly?"

"Just shut up." Men picked and pushed and assumed they had the right to own a woman's thoughts as well as her property and her body. Grinding her teeth together, Rosie kicked through a snow drift and moved away from him. He crossed the fallen section of fence and followed behind her.

"Did Frank Blevins tell you that you were ugly?"

Her eyes darted involuntarily to the headstone between the house and the cottonwoods. She couldn't see it clearly from this distance, but she felt *him* watching and listening.

"Because if he did, the man was blind. He was lying."

"Damn it, shut up! Don't speak to me about him!" Beneath her coat her heart began to pound, and she could feel the sweat rising on her palms and throat. Pulling off her gloves, she wiped the moisture off her hands.

Stone stopped three feet away from her. "What did Blevins do to you, Rosie?"

Her throat burned and her chest was suddenly so tight that it hurt to breathe. Even the mention of *his* name made her mouth go dry and taste like ashes.

"Forget him. This is none of your business."

"Why can't *you* forget him?"

"I will *never* forget . . ." She had not spoken his name aloud in three years and couldn't do it now. "Him. Not ever!"

She struck out toward the house, pausing only to drag her boots out of the sucking mud. When they were a half-mile from the barn, Rosie laughed, a harsh bitter laugh that scraped her throat.

"You and me . . . we're a fine pair, aren't we?" Placing her hands on her hips, she tilted back and scowled at the sky. "You've got nothing, and I've got nothing. All we have is a tarred-black past, blasted reputations, no friends, no family, no future. You and me, Stone, we're standing outside looking in the world's window. I'm a drunk, and you're a walking ghost. Neither one of us has any reason to live."

When he moved to stand in front of her, she noticed his eyes had darkened to a stormy navy color.

"I can't change my situation, but you can change yours. You can stop drinking. You can walk away from this dirt farm and away from Gulliver County. You can start fresh someplace else. You don't have to stand outside of life looking in."

"You don't know what you're talking about." She clenched her fists and her jaw tightened. "Think about it. We're all people who used to be. That's how we define ourselves. John Hawkins used to be an Indian. Lodisha used to be a slave. You used to be a cavalry officer. I used to be clean and sober. None of us have a future. Going someplace else isn't going to change that. We'd still be people who used to be."

He caught her arm when she turned away and spun her back to face him. His eyes were clear and so intense they burned through her. Dark eyebrows slashed across his forehead. His jaw was clamped down tight.

"You're right. I don't know what's at the bottom of all this. So tell me."

The instant his large hands closed on her shoulders, panic leapt like fire in her stomach. "Let go of me!"

"Why don't you like yourself, Rosie? Did Frank Blevins do that to you?"

She drew back her fist and hit him in the jaw hard enough to rock him back on his heels. When she tried to hit him again, he caught her wrists, struggling to keep her from kneeing him in the groin. Suddenly they were fighting. Or rather Rosie was fighting, and Stone was fighting her off.

Wild with the need to punish him for all the things he had done since he came into her life, she lunged at him and they fell to the ground, rolling over and over in the mud and snow. Snarling and spitting, Rosie tried to claw his cheeks, tried to gouge his eyes and kick and incapacitate him.

Exhausted and panting heavily, Stone fought her down and pinned her to the ground with his body, clamping her wrists against the muddy ground. They both gasped for breath, their chests heaved.

"For God's sake, Rosie, stop this. I don't want to hurt you."

Sweating and shaking, she glared up at him. She saw two blue eyes staring down at her, saw the scratch marks welling blood on his cheek. She felt his breath on her lips and felt the hot weight of his body pressing her into the cold mud.

The weight of his hard male body.

Wild frantic panic surged through her and she bucked and heaved beneath him until her lungs screamed for breath. And in the terrible end it was all for nothing. Stone overpowered her and held her down with his thighs and torso. The heavy heat of his body scorched into her, and she thrashed beneath him, terrified and powerless. Tears of rage and helplessness spilled down her cheeks.

Stone stared down at her, panting for breath. "What did—?"

"He *raped* me," she screamed up at him, certain that it was about to happen again. "Three times a week for *four years* I heard the squeak of his door and he dragged me by the hair into his bedroom and he *raped* me!"

"Oh my God."

"He beat me, he broke bones, and he raped me! Is that what you wanted to know? Are you satisfied now?"

Abruptly Stone rolled away and sat beside her, drawing up his knees. He covered his eyes. "I should have guessed."

He wasn't going to rape her. Relief swept over her, sapping her strength. She lay like a rag doll in the cold mud, her fists clenched at her sides, so limp with relief at her escape that she couldn't move, couldn't even lift a hand to wipe the tears that continued to stream from her eyes.

When she spoke again, the words poured out in a flat, expressionless tone.

"It started after he beat Ma so bad that she died. Then he started on me. He made me do things . . ." She closed her eyes. "John Hawkins and Lodisha tried to help me, but there wasn't anything they could do. He said he would kill them if they interfered or told anyone, and he would have."

"I don't know what to say . . . I'm sorry."

"He told me I was ugly and no man but him would ever want me. After a while I didn't care that I was ugly." She rolled her head to stare at him. "I *want* to be ugly. Because I don't want any man to do that to me ever again. I don't want any man to look at me like that or touch me like that."

"Rosie—"

"I planned to kill him. I had it all figured. First I had to steal enough money to buy a gun. He kept his locked up. Then I had to get bullets." She looked up at the sky and her ragged fingernails dug into her palms. "Planning it kept me alive, kept me from going insane. He'd drag me into his room and I'd go away inside my head and plan exactly what I was going to say just before I shot him. I had it all worked out.

"Then, a week before I planned to do it, just a week, the creek flooded. He went down there to get some stupid cow up on the bank before it drowned. The cow lived, but he drowned. I thought I would lose my mind. The son of a bitch cheated me. He died before I could tell him how much I hated him. Before I could strike back and kill him. It eats me up inside that he never suffered one minute for what he did to me and Ma. I think about that every second of my life, except when I'm drunk."

She sat up and focused blazing eyes on Stone. "He has to pay for what he did to Ma and me. He has to know that I'm better than he was. I have to win, Stone, and he has to suffer!"

When Stone looked at her, she read a devastating pity in his eyes that was worse than a blow would have been. His voice was hoarse but gentle. "Rosie, Frank Blevins is dead. You can't take revenge on a dead man."

Her eyes glittered in the winter sun. "You're wrong. I can and I know how to do it. You're going to help me."

Chapter Five

Washington, D.C., 1880

A constant stream of callers flowed to the house off Pennsylvania Avenue to pay their respects and leave cards with the left corner folded to convey condolences. As etiquette forbade personal visits while the body remained in the house, none of the callers ventured farther than the foyer. Only the servants witnessed Susan's distraught state.

Red-eyed and tearing a black-bordered lace handkerchief between her fingers, Susan Bonner Stone paced across the flowered carpet of the drawing room, occasionally pausing before the senator's coffin to gaze at his face with consternation and bewilderment.

She didn't understand how this could have happened, how life could have turned so suddenly bleak and uncertain. Senator William Stone had been a rock, a forceful, vigorous man. When Bowie left her in his father's care, there had been no reason to doubt the senator's health or prospects for longevity. But now the senator was dead, and the comfortable protected future Susan had taken for granted had shattered into a frightening emptiness.

She didn't know what she was going to do. How could she live without a man to depend on? She had no surviving family of her own, and now, in stunningly swift succession, both her husband and her father-in-law were dead. She was utterly alone for the first time in her life and petrified by the prospect. Who would take care of her and Nate? Who would tell her what to do?

The questions were too large, too terrifying to face directly. Taking a seat across from the coffin, she smoothed shaking fingers across her black alpaca gown, touched the crepe collar at her throat. What was she going to do? The question hammered at her mind in a constant unanswerable refrain.

For one scalding instant, a surge of fury and resentment choked her. It was Bowie's fault that the senator was dead and that she was frighteningly adrift with no man to anchor her.

First had come the horrifying news of Bowie Stone's dishonorable discharge. The scandal swept Washington like wildfire, seized upon by the senator's enemies. Though the senator held his head high through the storm of scorn and condemnation, the disgrace to the family aged him overnight. He had lost two sons in uniform; one died in a foolish carriage accident, the other end in the bitter shame of a court martial. His private anguish sliced so deep that he had ordered all reminders of Bowie removed from the house. It became painfully obvious that the senator could hardly bear to occupy the same room with Susan and Nate. Their presence offered a living reminder of the son he could not forgive.

When the second blow fell, the news that Bowie had been

convicted of murdering a fellow officer and would hang in an obscure Kansas town, the shock proved too great. A week after Susan donned widow's weeds, the senator's heart failed. He died in his library, rereading the announcement that former captain Bowie Stone's sentence had been satisfied.

Now Susan had no one to guide her, care for her, take responsibility for her. A terrifying hole opened at the center of her life.

Because anger overwhelmed her with guilt, she could not bear to think about Bowie—Bowie whose selfish unthinking actions had cost his own life and the life of his father, Bowie who had promised to take care of her and Nate forever. Pressing her handkerchief to her eyes, Susan made herself focus on other things. She concentrated on small womanly details, tasks she could more easily manage.

She had stopped the clock in the drawing room at the hour of the senator's death. The mirrors were draped in crepe, and a black ribbon was tied to the front door latch. The funeral invitations had been delivered. Cook had begun to prepare the do-ahead portions of the funeral feast. Susan still had to see Mr. Dubage, the senator's lawyer, but everything else had been attended to.

Only the larger unanswerable questions remained. How would she manage? How would she raise her three-year-old son without a man's protection and guidance? She knew nothing about finance, nothing about carriages and equipage, nothing about the realm of men. She had no idea how to plan her son's future or her own.

Her social and personal identity had been swept away. She was no longer Captain Bowie Stone's wife or Senator William Stone's hostess and daughter-in-law. She was that most pitiable of creatures, a woman alone. Where would she fit into society once her two years of mourning were completed?

Tears of self-pity and fear spilled over her cheeks. The senator's house, now her house, had become a ship without a pilot or a destination.

"Mrs. Stone?" Mr. Johns entered the drawing room, bringing her a silver bowl mounded with calling cards. He cast a respectful glance toward the senator's coffin and blinked rapidly. "If I may have a word. . . . The stonecutter came by again. He insists he must know at once what you wish to have carved on the senator's headstone. The sexton sent word that he is still awaiting your decision regarding the pallbearers." He cleared his throat. "General Morley sent Captain Stone's books and papers that were left behind after the court-martial. Mrs. Halstead would like instructions as to what you wish done with the box. At present it's in the kitchen and Cook would like it removed."

Susan couldn't breathe, couldn't think. None of these problems should have been her responsibility to solve. She hadn't been trained to make major decisions; the idea of exercising an untried and unwilling authority made her feel queasy inside.

"Mrs. Stone? How shall I respond to the stonecutter and the sexton?"

"I don't know," she whispered. The anguish of indecision shook her voice. "I . . . Tell the sexton . . . tell him I . . . I need more time. I just don't know!"

Suddenly Mrs. Halstead rushed into the drawing room, her white hair rising in an agitated frizz around her head. "Come quickly, Mrs. Stone! Nurse says young master Nate got away from her and ran outside and the coal carter's horse knocked him down. He's scraped up and Nurse says we should send for Doctor Rickart; except Cook says that's nonsense because young master Nate isn't really injured, but he's crying as if he were. The coal carter is fighting with the coachman, and the coachman's livery got torn, and there's no time to mend it before he has to drive the senator's coffin to the church.

No one knows what to do! Mrs. Stone, come and tell us what to do."

Reeling, Susan wobbled to her feet. "We ... I just ... I can't do this," she whispered.

Spots danced before her eyes, coalesced, and carried the light away. She fainted in a billow of black wool.

Today was the first day since the funeral that Susan had felt strong enough to rise from her bed and dress to receive visitors. Somehow she had stumbled through the funeral and the feast afterward. The worst part had been the actual burial. The senator was interred between his sons, Major Nathan Abner Stone on one side and the grave that awaited Bowie's body on the other. The senator's and Bowie's stones were blank and uncarved. Susan had read the inscription on Nathan Stone's headstone and collapsed in sobs.

Mrs. Halstead rapped at her bedroom door. "Mr. Dubage is waiting in the drawing room, Mrs. Stone."

"Thank you. Instruct Mr. Johns to serve sherry and biscuits. I'll be down directly."

Should she powder or was she too pale already? The black untrimmed collar so near her face leached the color from her cheeks and lips. No powder, then.

A sigh lifted her bosom. It would be two long years before she could wear anything but black, gray, or white. But she needed color to bring her pale blue eyes to life and add a snap of contrast to light brown hair.

Gazing at her drab red-eyed appearance in the mirror, she found it difficult to recall that she had been considered a belle just a few short weeks ago. Had she really ever laughed and flirted with her fan and spun from dancing partner to dancing partner?

Was this the same woman who once had thrown caution and propriety to the wind to lie in the arms of an adoring lover, a man who had whispered endearments and compliments into her ear? It seemed so long ago, the memory a fading mirage.

Rising from her vanity table, she stepped into the room next to her own, nodded to Nurse Gassy, then stood over Nate's narrow bed, watching him dream the dreams of napping children.

Her small son resembled his father so closely that it squeezed her heart to gaze at him. He had the same beloved high forehead and firm stubborn mouth, the same dark unruly curls. Nate had inherited his father's berry-blue eyes, and he followed in the Stone tradition by already displaying a taste for exploration and adventure. This dear little boy was all that remained of the man she had loved so passionately and so unwisely. To say she adored him was to understate her love. Nate was the only thing in life left to care about.

She would have liked to take a seat beside him and remain there until he awoke from his nap, but Mr. Dubage was waiting to fill her head with confusing items of business that she didn't want to hear and wouldn't understand.

Mr. Dubage rose to his feet when she entered the drawing room and inclined his head in a stiff bow. The lawyer was a stern man, cloaked with authority and importance, his demeanor intimidating. The dark jacket and silver-shot waistcoat he wore were more formal than the hour decreed but well-tailored and cut in the latest fashion. His beard reminded Susan of the mode preferred by President Hayes, whose portrait hung in the library.

She noticed he had not touched the sherry on the tray beside his chair. "Perhaps you would prefer tea or coffee?"

"Thank you, no. I'm late for another appointment. Therefore, if we could proceed directly to business?"

"Of course." She took the winged chair facing his and folded her hands in her lap. "As I informed you at the services, I'm afraid I don't know anything about business. It's my fond hope that I may rely on you to continue representing the affairs of the Stone family on behalf of myself and my son."

"I believe you'll find our discussion simple enough to understand," Mr. Dubage said tersely. Lifting a tapestry case from the side of his chair, he opened it across his lap and withdrew a sheaf of papers.

"We'll begin with your husband's estate. As your husband inherited from his mother and his brother, the estate is considerable. Once the estate has been settled, I think you'll discover that you and your son can live quite comfortably." He frowned. "There is, however, a problem which has necessitated a delay in probate."

"I'm certain you'll solve any problems, Mr. Dubage."

"My office has been unable to obtain a death certificate from the authorities in Passion's Crossing, Kansas. Our first request was answered by a scribbled note stating that Mr. Bowie Stone was sentenced to hang and the sentence was satisfied. Further requests for the actual death certificate have been ignored. We have been equally unsuccessful in obtaining a satisfactory reply to our requests for shipment of the body."

Susan swallowed hard and lifted smelling salts to her nostrils. "Must we discuss this?" she inquired in a faint voice.

"It is important for you to understand that the probate court will not release any of your husband's monies or assets until the court is furnished with a death certificate. Do you understand, Mrs. Stone? You may not draw on your husband's funds until such time as his will is probated, and the court cannot proceed with probate without a death certificate. Frankly, I cannot guess how long it might take to obtain the certificate in view of the Gulliver County clerk's utter disregard of our requests."

Susan looked toward the window, wishing she did not have to hear any of this.

"If funds were available, I would send a man to Kansas to

collect the papers in person and arrange for shipment of your husband's body. But as I previously pointed out, you have no available monies to fund such an errand."

Bewilderment drew her brow into a frown. "I'm sure the senator provided for us. Couldn't some of those funds be used?"

Mr. Dubage occupied himself sorting his papers. To Susan's surprise, his stiffness momentarily dissolved toward an expression of acute discomfort.

"It is my unfortunate duty to inform you that Senator Stone left you and your son only forty dollars." He ran a finger around his collar. "His instructions are that you and your son are to vacate this house within a week of receiving this letter. You are to take with you only those items which belonged to you prior to your marriage to Captain Stone."

"I beg your pardon?" Shock immobilized her. She sat frozen in her chair like a lump of black marble, a polite half-smile paralyzed on her lips. "Could you ... ?"

Mr. Dubage repeated his statements.

"But there must be a mistake," Susan managed to whisper on her third attempt to speak. Her voice emerged thin and strangled. Pressing a hand against her corset stays, she struggled to breathe. "When Bowie went west, he left us in the senator's care. The senator promised to take care of us."

"Senator Stone indicated you would well understand why he saw fit to take these measures."

"But I don't! I don't understand at all!" She clasped her shaking hands tightly together and stared at Mr. Dubage as if she were drowning. Her teeth chattered and her fingers had turned to twigs of ice.

"Perhaps this letter will explain further."

Susan stared at the cream-colored envelope he extended toward her. For an instant she couldn't think what it was. Her mind refused to function, could not progress beyond the shock and disbelief of being ordered into the streets.

From the beginning the senator had held himself aloof, resisting her efforts to charm. And he had not permitted her to address him as Father Stone as she had wished. But he had honored his promise to Bowie. The senator had taken Susan and Nate into his home, had designated her as his official hostess, had provided generously and without an impolite word. She had attributed his distance and coldness to a reserved nature. It had never once entered her mind that the senator might actually dislike her or that he could detest her so deeply that he would banish her and his grandson from what she thought of as her home.

The shock of discovering that she had been hated glazed her vision and made Susan's heart pound. Even if she could have focused sharply enough to read, she was shaking so badly that she could not have held the senator's letter steady in her hands.

"Please. I can't . . ." Her voice was an anguished whisper. "Please read it to me."

Mr. Dubage studied her, then broke the red seal on the back of the envelope. "Are you certain, Mrs. Stone? Letters such as this are generally of a private and personal nature."

She inhaled deeply over her small bottle of smelling salts. Her mind whirled in drunken circles and she prayed to awaken from this nightmare. "Please. Tell me what the letter says."

Mr. Dubage shook out two pages covered closely with the senator's bold handwriting. He settled a pair of spectacles on the end of his nose.

Mrs. Stone,
    In keeping with my promise to my son, I have reluctantly provided you and your bastard with the

protection of the Stone name and the Stone fortune. Allowing the Stone name to be further sullied by a grasping adventuress becomes unconscionable now that my son is dead. Such heinous opportunism shall cease at once.

Susan gasped and the blood rushed from her face. "It *can't* say that!" Waves of shock stunned her mind.

It has been known to me for some time that Bowie Stone could not have fathered your child. An investigator hired to inquire into the circumstances informed me that my son met you exactly one week before you ensnared him into an opportunistic marriage. Seven months later the child you foisted onto this family was born. It is my assumption that being confronted by your deceit impelled my son to accept a posting in the west, and suggests why he chose not to take you and your bastard to share his assignment. I think it likely that discovering himself married to an adventuress of low moral character caused my son to suffer a brain fever which resulted in the series of dishonorable actions that ultimately led to his death.

"Oh, my God! This can't be happening! Mr. Dubage, I swear to you by everything I hold sacred! My son Nathan is Senator Stone's blood grandson!"

Mr. Dubage continued reading without looking at her.

While my son was alive I felt constrained to honor the promise extracted by him that I accept you into my home and provide for you though it pained me deeply to do so. It goes counter to every concept of decency that a woman of your ilk should inherit my son's estate. You shall not benefit from mine. I go to my grave consumed by regret that my son's gullibility has pinned a fine and respectable name on another man's spawn and on a woman of deceitful and loose character. You will vacate my home within the week. You will take nothing away with you but that which you possessed prior to entrapping my son.

Susan's eyes rolled up and she slid to the floor.

Gossip was the bread and drink that fed Washington, D.C. Almost at once rumors took wing that the senator had repudiated Susan Stone in his will and had cast his disgraced son's wife out of his house.

None of Susan's friends or acquaintances responded to her frantic notes and appeals. By mid-week she understood that Washington dined behind doors now closed to her, cutting, slicing and digesting her reputation. Her worst fear returned to haunt, that no one had believed the fiction that her eight-pound son had been born prematurely. It became clear that her acceptance in society had resulted solely from the senator's power and protection. With the senator's imprimatur withdrawn, Susan Stone became persona non grata.

Red-eyed and distraught, exhausted from lack of sleep, Susan paced back and forth across her bed chamber until Mrs. Halstead announced Mr. Dubage had arrived in response to her panicked summons.

"You must help me!" she cried the instant she entered the drawing room. "I don't know what to do! I have no place to go, no one to turn to! Mr. Dubage, I beg you. Help me!"

His eyebrows soared and he stepped backward. "Mr. Johns informs me that you have made no visible arrangements to vacate the senator's house." He cleared his throat with an uncomfortable sound, watching her pace and wring her hands.

"As much as it pains me, madam, as administrator of the senator's estate, it is my duty to remind you that you have but three days remaining in which to secure an alternate residence."

Susan collapsed into the nearest chair and sobbed into her handkerchief. "I can't support my son and myself on forty dollars! We'll be on the street in a week! We'll die! In the name of mercy, Mr. Dubage, I beg you. Tell me what to do!"

"There, there," Mr. Dubage murmured gruffly. Weeping women reduced him to a state of exasperated helplessness. He looked toward the door, wishing for rescue.

"No one will answer my appeals. Washington has closed its doors to me!" Susan watched her fingers pulling apart the lace on her wet handkerchief. "I have no one, Mr. Dubage. No husband, no father, no family. What will I do? Where will I go? Tell me how to save myself and my son. Tell me what to do, I beg of you!"

He said the first thing that jumped into his mind. "Go west, Mrs. Stone."

"West?" She stared up at him with streaming eyes.

"Forgive me for a hasty reply," Mr. Dubage said with a sigh, examining her delicate features and small stature. He lifted his hands. "I can't make decisions for you, Mrs. Stone. I can assist to the extent of granting you another week in the senator's home, but that is all I can do; and I do so with extreme reluctance knowing I act against my client's express wishes." He edged toward the drawing room door. "I'm sorry but I must insist that you and your son vacate the premises by the end of next week."

Before Mr. Dubage withdrew he reminded her to inform him of her ultimate destination so that he could send her notification should he obtain her husband's death certificate. He fled an outburst of fresh tears.

When she had cried until her eyes were dry and her throat burned, Susan dropped her head against the back of the chair and struggled to fix her thoughts on Mr. Dubage's advice. It was all she had. Summoning the strength to move, she rang for Mr. Johns and asked him to bring her the morning paper, which she opened across her lap.

Go west. Susan knew little about the territories, and what she did know discouraged further interest. But she remembered Washington's army officers decrying the scarcity of women on the frontier. The territories might lack theaters, opera houses, fine restaurants and fashionable promenades, but the territories had a plentitude of men. And she desperately needed a man to rescue her and decide her future.

Yes, here were the notices she sought. Running a shaking finger down the page of classified ads, she read notice after notice placed by frontier men seeking wives or housekeepers, men willing to pay travel expenses.

The ads themselves both repelled and fascinated her; the idea of responding to one sickened her. After closing her eyes and waiting for the queasiness in her stomach to subside, Susan drew a long shuddering breath and then carefully reread each ad.

There were commonalities. Whether seeking a bride or a housekeeper, most of the men advertised for a stalwart, self-reliant woman with an adventurous spirit and an eye toward the future. Some wanted women experienced in handling livestock, a qualification Susan could not believe any woman could fulfill. Some specified the ability to cook, which ruled her out. Some sought women who would not be unnerved by living in isolation and solitude, a situation that caused her to shiver with horror.

At the end of two days of vacillation and dread, Susan narrowed the column of choices to one ad:

Attorney and homesteader seeks educated woman for the purpose of marriage. Prefer sturdy maid unafraid of hard work, age twenty to thirty-five. Can offer small house in town and homestead in progress; will pay travel expenses. Respond to Gresham Harte, Owl's Butte, Wyoming territory.

For two more days Susan carried the notice, taking it out of her pocket at odd moments to read and agonize over. Mr. Harte's appeal was the only ad that requested an educated woman or sounded as if the man himself might be endowed with a modicum of learning. His request for a sturdy woman unafraid of hard work troubled her as she was slender, delicately formed, and had never performed a task more taxing than deciding the day's menus.

On the other hand, an attorney would be one of the town's prominent citizens and would surely employ servants to perform household tasks. Because she needed it to be true, Susan convinced herself that the line mentioning sturdy and hard work was a misprint, a line erroneously repeated from the ad directly above Mr. Harte's.

She gave herself a day of tears and resentment, mourning the unbelievable fact that she had been reduced to marrying a stranger in a distant and semi-civilized area. For two hours she wept and paced and railed against Bowie Stone, blazing with condemnation that he had left her and failed her and doomed her to a fate she could not yet quite imagine. If it had not been for Nate, she would rather have starved on the streets of Washington than give herself in marriage to a stranger.

She had no choice but to grasp the only lifeline extended to her.

The next day Susan and Mrs. Halstead took the senator's carriage to the telegraph depot. Clutching her smelling salts and with Mrs. Halstead supporting her, Susan dispatched a telegram to Mr. Gresham Harte in Owl's Butte, Wyoming, then sat with her head bowed, awaiting Mr. Harte's reply. She desperately prayed Mr. Harte would accept her as she had no other plan, yet she also prayed that he had already found a bride and would refuse her.

When the reply came, she opened the telegram with shaking fingers, afraid to read her future.

> To Miss Stone, Washington D.C. stop take the train to Denver, then the stage to Fort Washakie stop at the fort change to Eban Conner's Wind River Coach stop telegraph operator will give you tickets required for passage stop I await your arrival stop Gresham Harte, Owl's Butte, Wyoming territory end message.

"Oh, my," Susan whispered. The telegram fluttered from her suddenly boneless fingers. Her pale cheeks pinched in an expression of fright and dread. "I am to be married."

Mrs. Halstead pressed her lips together and cast a sidelong glance at Susan's widow's weeds. Disapproval quivered in every white hair frizzing out of her bonnet. But after she glanced at the dates on Susan's tickets, her voice was not without sympathy when she suggested they had no time to waste and should begin packing at once.

"But Mr. Harte didn't send a ticket for Nate!" Coping with distressing details was not Susan's forte; she couldn't think how to solve this problem.

Mrs. Halstead regarded her for a long moment. "As Nate is a toddler, he can ride on your lap, Mrs. Stone. He doesn't require a ticket."

Two exhausting days later, feeling overwhelmed, frightened, and disoriented, Susan and her son sat huddled together on a train heading west.

Chapter Six

The three-week journey was a nightmare. As Mr. Harte had not thought to provide for a sleeping car, Susan and Nate slept on the hard wooden train seat, trying to doze while being jostled and jolted until their bones rattled and their teeth chattered, while they choked on soot and thick fumes. At night Susan felt certain they would freeze before morning; during the long monotonous days she struggled to breathe sour air thickened by cigar smoke and the odors of tightly packed humanity.

Mr. Harte also had neglected to provide money for incidental expenses, so she had to use her own dwindling funds to purchase food at the stopover depots. These small wretched dots on the great plains were sink holes of exploitation and greed. The food offered for sale to the train's hungry passengers was outrageously priced, cold and greasy, and hideously overcooked or undercooked. Tea was unavailable and the brew that passed for coffee tasted like warm mud. The milk

94

she bought for Nate had been watered, thinned and leached of all substance.

Susan prayed for a day of rest in Denver to recover before continuing the nightmare journey, but her stage ticket revealed she had only four hours between the end of the train journey and the departure of the stagecoach she had been instructed to take. Fighting tears and staggering with fatigue, she managed to get herself and Nate from the train depot to the stage post with mere minutes to spare.

The harrowing ride in a nine-passenger stagecoach was a horror unlike anything she could have imagined. Her fellow passengers stank, and they cursed and argued violently for an inch of extra space. Boxes and mail sacks continually crashed down on her head and shoulders, passengers fell against her or splattered her hem with tobacco juice, and after the first hour Nate felt as if he weighed a ton. When she crawled out of the coach at night, she was covered with bruises and too exhausted to eat the execrable food offered at the overnight stops. The sleeping arrangements were horrifying. As sleeping on unwashed sheets in vermin-infested beds was unthinkable, she spent the nights sitting hollow-eyed before the post-house fire, cradling Nate on her lap.

In the midst of all this, Susan discovered she had previously had no notion how energetic and worrisome a three-year-old could be. With all her heart she yearned for Nurse Gassy. How did one entertain a bored child? Or restrain him when he wished to race up and down the aisles of a rocking train? How did one comfort him when he cried at night? Why had no one informed her that a three-year-old could vanish in the blink of an eye? Or that small boys resisted a wash as if they believed their faces would dissolve if brought into contact with water? Her beloved son frazzled her nerves and unraveled her patience; and when she listened to his endless chattering, she felt like screaming for a single moment of quiet.

At last the stage skidded to a halt and she heard the knight of the reins, as he was called, cry out the announcement she had been anticipating and dreading. "Owl's Butte! Those going on to Jackson be back here in twen'y minutes."

Susan's mouth dried and her heart pounded against her corset stays. After a moment of paralysis, she hastily straightened her crushed bonnet and cape, then tried to pull Nate's clothing into some semblance of order.

"Hold still, darling. Let Mama smooth your hair and wipe your face." She spat on her handkerchief and dabbed at his chin as he wiggled beneath her hands.

"Are we there yet?" he demanded, cranky with fatigue and boredom.

"Yes, darling," she whispered, watching the other passengers depart the cramped confines of the stage's interior. "Now remember your manners. It's very important that we make a good impression on Mr. Harte. Don't fidget and don't stare no matter what he looks like or what he says. Don't speak unless you're spoken to. Be a good boy for Mama." She gave him a quick kiss, then followed him out the stage door, stepping onto a snowy street turned rusty by mud, tobacco juice and frozen horse manure.

The air was so frigid that her breath plumed out before her and her cheeks turned fiery pink. The first thing she saw was the range of snowy mountain peaks rising like jagged teeth against an overcast sky. Susan gasped. For a moment she could not grasp that what she observed was real and not the majesty of imagination. The Wyoming Tetons took her breath away.

Then she lowered her gaze to Owl's Butte and her heart stopped altogether. The main street was sunk in mud and snow, flanked by two rows of unpainted buildings featuring square, ugly false fronts. She saw wagons and buckboards, carts and a one-horse gig, but not a single respectable carriage.

The only woman she spotted wore a mended coat that had gone out of fashion a decade ago. Susan gazed at the dismal rows of buildings and her heart plummeted to her toes.

"This all yer luggage, Ma'am?"

She turned to count the meager collection of boxes surrounding her trunk and nodded dully. Taking Nate's mittened hand, she picked through the mud and snow to stand beside her trunk and wonder frantically if she had enough money to climb back on the stage and run home to Washington.

A man rushed out of the hotel behind her and called to the stage driver. Watching him, Susan swallowed hard and gripped Nate's hand. Instinct warned her that this was her first glimpse of her husband-to-be.

Her first thought was that Gresham Harte wasn't nearly as tall as Bowie had been; Mr. Harte was only five foot six or so. Although he wore wire-rimmed spectacles, she guessed he couldn't have been much over thirty years of age, younger than she had expected. His dark broadcloth suit and coat were unfashionable and shiny with use, but the fit was good. He wore his hat at a slight tilt, almost jaunty but not quite. Except for heavy gloves and chunky boots, Gresham Harte might have been any one of the thousands of young men who scurried about all large cities, invisible even to those whose instructions they hurried to follow.

"I was expecting a young lady," he said to the stage driver. His glance passed over Susan and Nate then followed two of Susan's fellow passengers as they climbed into a waiting wagon. "Did Miss Stone miss the stage? Or has she wandered off somewhere?"

The driver jerked his thumb over his shoulder. "Don't know about no Miss Stone, but that there's Mrs. Stone and her boy."

When Mr. Harte turned toward her, Susan noticed that his eyes were as dark as his short hair and mustache. She decided Mr. Harte was not a handsome man; his nose was too prominent, his jaw too square. Lines of concentration divided his brow into halves above his thick eyebrows. But he had a pleasant face, and Susan thought she identified signs of good character. She desperately hoped the wrinkles fanning from his eyes were laugh lines and not an indication of bad temper.

He blinked at Susan with an incredulous expression as his gaze traveled slowly down her black traveling costume, then settled a moment on Nate's shy stare. He glanced at the trunk and boxes surrounding her hem before he lifted his head and met her nervous gaze.

"Mr. Harte?" Susan's voice quavered, sounding as if it belonged to an eight-year-old. "I am Susan Stone and this is my son, Nathan Stone."

"Mama, you're squeezing my hand too hard," Nate protested.

"I believe there's been a mistake," Mr. Harte said finally. "I specified a maid, a woman who has never been married. I specifically did not request a woman with children, and you said nothing about a child in your telegram."

"I'm a widow, Mr. Harte."

"I can see that, Mrs. Stone." Kneeling, he gazed into Nate's eyes. "Here's a nickel, son. Why don't you go into the hotel and ask Mrs. Alder to give you a slice of her famous mince pie? Your mother and I need to speak privately."

When Nate looked up for approval, Susan nodded. She watched him run into the hotel before she turned a white face to Gresham Harte.

"I know it was wrong of me not to mention my son, but I was afraid you might refuse me if you knew I had a child."

"During the winter I practice law, Mrs. Stone, a profession requiring study and quiet. During the summer, I live on my homestead outside of town where I'm building a residence. There is no room in my life for a child. I lack both patience and time to cope with an energetic young boy. I have no experience with children and don't wish to remedy that lack at this time."

Susan wrung her hands and fastened a pleading glance on his face. "Nate is quiet and well-behaved. I'll see that he never disturbs you or interferes with your studies. He won't be any trouble at all."

They both watched the knight of the reins crack his whip above the shoulders of his horses. The stage sped down Main Street toward the distant mountains.

"May I inquire how long you have been a widow?"

"My husband died nine weeks ago."

"Nine weeks!" Shock lifted Mr. Harte's eyebrows.

Susan bit her lips as a rush of embarrassed heat flooded her face. "I know it's indecently soon to remarry, but I have no choice."

He studied her hat and cape. Although crushed and soiled by travel, her clothing was well made from expensive fabric. "At first glance, it would appear that your late husband was not impoverished."

"My husband was a captain with the Eleventh Cavalry, but he . . ." She paused. Although she was distracted by the cold and trembling with nerves, still she sensed it was too soon to reveal the consequences of Bowie's disintegration. "Due to circumstances I don't fully understand, my son and I have been left destitute." The admission deeply shamed her, but there was no help for it. She lifted the fashionable little drawstring purse tied to her wrist and nodded toward her trunk and boxes. "What you see before you is all I own in the world."

"I see." Rocking back on his heels, he frowned at the range of mountains, watching the peaks disappear behind a wall of advancing clouds. "May I see your hands, Mrs. Stone?" he asked after a lengthy pause.

"I beg your pardon?"

"Your hands. Would you remove your gloves, please?"

Puzzled by the request, Susan did as he asked, feeling the cold plunge into her bones. Mr. Harte moved close enough to inspect her smooth white palms before he stepped away from her, shaking his head.

"Forgive me for being blunt, but those hands have never known a minute's physical work. I doubt you have ever scrubbed a floor, Mrs. Stone, or washed a tub of laundry. I doubt you have carried a bucket of water or hammered a nail or lifted an iron."

Suddenly Susan understood, and she hastily replaced her gloves. "I play the piano," she said in a low voice. "I paint a little and I'm skilled at fine needlework. I'm an accomplished hostess and I have experience managing a large household." She sounded defensive and desperate.

"Those are laudable accomplishments, I'm sure, but this is the frontier. I don't own a piano and I have no need of a hostess. I need a wife who can coax an old and cranky stove to produce a meal. I need a wife who will keep my house and office during the winter and help me build a permanent home in the summer. I need a wife accustomed to hard work."

"I can learn," she said desperately, wringing her hands together. "Whatever you want from me, Mr. Harte, I'll learn how to do it."

He shook his head. "I'm sorry. I can't marry the wife of a man only two months in his grave, a man who died in the service of his country. And the last thing I need is a wife who cannot clean, wash, iron or contribute any service of value. I'm afraid you have made a long journey for nothing, Mrs. Stone. I would advise you to return to your family."

He tipped his hat to her, turned, and walked toward Main Street.

"Mr. Harte!" Swallowing convulsively, Susan stumbled after him. "Please, I beg you! I have no family, no money, and no place to go. You brought me here, you can't just abandon me! Please, sir, you must help me!"

He turned back to her with a scowl. "You came to Owl's Butte under false pretenses, Mrs. Stone. I am in no way obligated to provide for your welfare or your future. I regret your circumstances, but I am not obliged to assume responsibility for you and your son." When he saw the tears brimming in her blue eyes then spilling over her lashes, a look of annoyance tightened his lips. "I will assist you to the extent that I won't require you to repay the cost of your travel. But that is all, Mrs. Stone. Our association ends here." He tipped his hat again and then strode away, not responding when she called his name.

Susan's shoulders collapsed and she covered her face. Dimly she was aware that her hem was sodden and filthy, her bonnet crushed and crooked, her hair straggling around her face. But she was acutely aware that she and Nate had been abandoned in the middle of nowhere without funds to flee, and there was no one to rescue her. She stared at the snowflakes beginning to fall, watching them with blank defeated eyes. She hadn't an inkling of what to do next.

"You there . . . Mrs. Stone!" Sliding her fingers down to her lips, Susan turned to see a tall, gaunt woman wearing a white apron standing in the doorway of the town's only hotel. "Come inside before you catch your death." The woman waved her forward. "Your son is calling for you, chattering up a storm. I'm Mrs. Alder, a widow like yourself," she said, peering through the snowflakes at Susan's weeds. Straightening, she called to someone behind her. "Fred, bring Mrs. Stone's goods inside. Shake a leg now. Mrs. Stone? Do come inside before your hem turns to ice."

Humiliation burned bright on Susan's cheeks. She wondered how much Mrs. Alder had overheard of her conversation with Mr. Harte. Exhausted and numb inside, unable to stop shaking, she swallowed her pride and lifted her hem over a freezing puddle of tobacco spit.

Mrs. Alder helped her up the porch steps and out of the falling snow. "Take Mrs. Stone's things to room three," she instructed a tall lanky boy who had the same narrow face and auburn hair as she did. "Your boy's in the kitchen," she said to Susan, leading her through a small homey parlor and past the registration table. "It's warmest there. I just made a big pot of fresh coffee, and there are biscuits left over from lunch. Here, give me your bonnet and cape. We'll hang them to dry."

Susan let herself be ministered to, silently following where Mrs. Alder led.

The hotel's kitchen, a large warm space at the back of the house, was the first clean room Susan had seen since beginning her journey. A row of cast-iron cookware hung above the stove; shelves of thick crockery lined the wall beside the back door. The air was rich with the yeasty aroma of baking and the dark fragrance of real coffee.

Nate had curled up on a bench and fallen asleep beside an empty milk glass and a crumb-covered plate. Mrs. Alder dropped a thick towel over his shoulders and smoothed dark curls away from his forehead.

"He's a polite little lad. Minded his pleases and thank yous. Take a seat at the table, Mrs. Stone. I'll have a meal in front of you faster than a cat can blink."

"I . . . I couldn't eat," Susan murmured, remembering how little money she had and how far it had to stretch. "But a cup of coffee would be welcome." Closing her eyes, she gripped her hands together and leaned back in a wooden chair until Mrs. Alder placed a clean thick mug of steaming coffee in front of her.

"Now then," Mrs. Alder said after she had poured coffee

for herself and settled across the table from Susan. "The next stage won't be in until the day after tomorrow and there won't be many customers for supper, not with a storm blowing in, so there's time to hear your tale." A basket of mending appeared in her lap and a needle that flew, applying patches to rips and worn knees and elbows.

The heat in the kitchen drained what little energy Susan had left. The good strong coffee warmed her inside. She wished she could curl into a ball like Nate and sleep and sleep and sleep until the world became benevolent again.

She blinked rapidly, looking into her coffee cup. "First my husband died, then a week later my father-in-law. There was no money and I had to leave, but there was no place to go. So I replied to an ad in the paper and came here to marry Mr. Harte, but he won't have me because I'm a widow and because of Nate and because I don't know how to cook or wash or iron or do anything of value."

"Well now," Mrs. Alder said. "Seems to me you're in a bit of a pickle. What are you going to do?"

Panic soured the taste of the coffee. "I don't know," she whispered. "Are there any other men in Owl's Butte who might have need of a wife?"

"Dozens." Before Susan could brighten, Mrs. Alder shook her head. "The territories are different from the states, Mrs. Stone. Out here a man needs a woman who can do the same work he does plus all the woman chores. A western man is long on dreams and short on ready cash. He expects his wife to do all the chores an eastern man hires out and then some. As for your boy—if young Nate was old enough to work, he wouldn't be a problem. And if you'd been married to anyone but a military man, recent widowhood probably wouldn't be much of a problem either. But every man in the west knows he owes his land and his safety to the brave soldiers who subdued the savages. No Wyoming man is going to marry a military man's widow until she's properly mourned his passing."

"There's no hope, then."

"There's always hope, Mrs. Stone. But you have some powerful points against you when it comes to finding a new husband."

Susan stared into her coffee cup and fixed her tired mind on the immediate problem. "How much does it cost to stay in your hotel?"

"A dollar a day. That includes breakfast and supper every day but Sunday. Board on Sunday is extra and laundry's extra. So is mending and ironing."

Susan tried to concentrate. If she spent only a dollar a day, if she gave up luncheon and didn't eat on Sunday, if she took no extras, she and Nate could live nineteen days before the Alders turned them into the streets of Owl's Butte. Or she could take the next stagecoach to Colorado and arrive in Denver with seven dollars in her purse.

It hardly made much difference if she starved and froze on the streets of Denver or on the streets of Owl's Butte.

She lowered her head and blinked at the tears that had become her constant companion. "It's so hard without a man to depend on and tell me what to do."

"Indeed it is. I miss my Henry every hour of the day."

Susan's head jerked up. "You run this hotel by yourself? Without a man?"

Mrs. Alder shrugged. "My boy Fred helps out, and my daughter Hettie. It's hard sometimes, but we manage. Owl's Butte is up to two hundred and thirty souls now. The community's growing, and some day this hotel is going to be worth something. I'm building for the future," she said proudly.

Susan stared in astonishment. "You make your own way? Without a man?"

"Sometimes a woman has to."

"You haven't thought about remarrying?"

"Pshaw, no. There's no man in Owl's Butte who could fill my Henry's shoes." Her wrinkled face softened. "I was never pretty like you, Mrs. Stone. But my Henry, he used to say I had eyes like a doe and beautiful hair." Her hand strayed to the bun on the nape of her neck. "Well. There must be something you can do to support yourself and your young'un."

Susan lowered her eyes. "I grew up with servants. Until I got on the train that brought us west, I'd never even arranged my hair or dressed myself." She raised her hands. All of her life she had creamed her hands and shielded them from sun and weather, had taken pride in well-shaped nails and smooth, unblemished skin. With bitter clarity she recognized that in Wyoming her hands were not considered beautiful. Here, calluses were beautiful.

Mrs. Alder's eyes widened and her needle slowed. "I don't believe I've ever met a woman who couldn't fix her hair or dress herself. That does put a Friday face on things. I guess it goes without saying that you can't cook or wash either? Well now, there's a pity. A woman can always put food in her mouth if she can take in wash, 'specially in a place like this. A man will pay right smart for a home-baked pie and to have his clothes washed every now and then."

Gently Mrs. Alder guided Susan to her feet. "What you need now is a good night's sleep. You take your boy and go on upstairs. Everything will look brighter tomorrow."

When no one offered to carry Nate upstairs for her, Susan did it herself, struggling up the stairs, carrying Nate's sleeping weight and dragging her soaked hem behind her.

The room Mrs. Alder had assigned them was high-ceilinged and papered in cheerful cabbage roses. It was cold in the room, but the sheets on the bed were wonderfully clean and crisp with starch. Too fatigued to cope with her trunk or boxes, Susan peeled Nate down to his underwear and placed him in the bed, then she stripped off her own travel-stained clothing, loosened her stays and fell into the sheets beside him.

When she awoke twelve hours later, Nate was gone. Flying out of bed, her heart pounding, she threw on her dress and ran downstairs, holding her bodice together with shaking fingers.

"Where's my son?" she cried, wild-eyed, almost skidding into Mrs. Alder, who was down on her hands and knees scrubbing the risers on the staircase.

"I sent Fred to the blacksmith's to repair a cracked iron. Your Nate wanted to tag along. The rascal said he had your permission."

Susan collapsed on the bottom step and buried her face in shaking hands. If anything terrible ever happened to Nate, she would die herself.

"I feel so inadequate and overwhelmed. Do you know what the worst of it is?" She knew it was a mark of low breeding and bad manners to complain or to confide in anyone but family, but the words poured out of her. "The worst is that I keep thinking about my husband and sometimes I hate him for dying and leaving us. Then I feel guilty for thinking ill of the dead and so I'm angry and guilty too and I start hating him again. How could he do this to us?" She struck the step with her fist. "How could he abandon us and leave us to suffer?"

Mrs. Alder dropped her stiff scrub brush in the bucket and pushed back a strand of auburn hair. She looked up at Susan. "It seems to me like you don't have much faith in yourself, Mrs. Stone."

Susan stared at her, then laughed. The harsh bitterness in her laugh shocked her. "Isn't it obvious, Mrs. Alder? I'm a woman who is nothing without a man. I need a husband to take care of me and tell me what to do. On my own, I can't *do* anything. I can't make decisions, I can't cope, I can't save my son or myself."

"Pshaw. You're selling yourself short. You're stronger than you think you are, Mrs. Stone. Never met a woman who wasn't."

"I don't think so. I've only done one daring thing in my whole life, and that was years ago."

"You got yourself out west, didn't you?" Mrs. Alder asked mildly. "What would your fancy Eastern friends say about a woman traveling alone all this distance with only a three-year-old for company? It's easier now than when Henry and I came west, but it's still an undertaking and that's a fact. You did it, and you managed without a man to help you, now didn't you?"

Susan blinked and sat up straight.

Later when she was dressed and Nate was tucked in for his afternoon nap, Susan slipped on her cape and stepped out on the hotel porch to have another look at Owl's Butte.

To an eye accustomed to grandeur, the single block of board buildings was an affront, as were the small, unimpressive homes that marked surrounding streets. Already she suspected the wind never stopped blowing in Owl's Butte.

But when she raised her eyes, the splendor and raw beauty of the Tetons filled her with awe. Shielding her eyes against the brightness of the sky, she watched tails of snow spin into the atmosphere, teased by alpine winds. These rugged mountains had endured since time began. There was serenity in their strength, beauty and timelessness.

Unexpectedly Susan felt something loosen deep inside, surprising her. She hadn't foreseen that she could find anything positive in these, the blackest moments of her life. But she found herself thinking about Mrs. Alder's comment.

By heaven, she really *had* come west by herself. She had managed it alone and without assistance. Wonder darkened her eyes, and she felt a tiny flash of pride.

She had been too sunk in fear and self-pity to recognize the enormity of her undertaking, too filled with panic to consider what she was doing. But Mrs. Alder was correct. She, Susan Stone, had accomplished something rather remarkable, especially for her. The realization took her breath away.

A tiny kernel of hope blossomed in her chest. Was it possible that she possessed capabilities she had never recognized? If so, she had eighteen days to discover what they might be; then her funds would be exhausted.

That thought smashed her small glimmer of optimism.

Chapter Seven

Fat wet snowflakes swirled beyond the lace curtains of Mrs. Alder's dining room. The corner stove occasionally made a cheerful popping sound above the subdued conversation of Sunday night diners.

Susan sat with her back to the room, her hands folded in her lap, watching Nate pick and push at his evening meal and listening while he chattered excitedly about the animals he'd seen in Owl's Butte. Bits of fried ham floated above the bed of potatoes and cream gravy covering his plate, and she bit her lip to keep from admonishing him to eat every single bite because Sunday supper cost extra.

"Mrs. Stone?"

Mr. Harte's voice startled her from a contemplation of all the food she had wasted during her life.

Gresham Harte stood beside her, turning his hat brim between his hands. Tonight his dark hair was parted down the center and curled on his forehead above the rims of his spectacles. He wore the same shiny broadcloth suit he had worn to meet her stage, and a boiled shirt that had begun to show signs of wear at the collar.

"Hello, young man," he said to Nate. Susan was surprised to discover he had a wonderful smile. His expression relaxed and his eyes crinkled. His mustache curved to reveal a full lower lip. "I hear you almost caught Mr. Stevenson's pig yesterday."

Nate grinned in delight. "Yes, sir." A detailed account of his muddy adventure would have followed if Susan hadn't shot him a mind-your-manners glance.

"Perhaps you would permit me to join you for pie and coffee, Mrs. Stone."

Crimson flooded her throat and her hands fluttered in uncertainty. A few weeks ago she would have turned aside with icy aloofness, indignant and outraged by an improper advance. But this was the west. As she was swiftly discovering, manners were different in the west.

"As you wish, Mr. Harte," she said stiffly. Unable to resist, she added, "I confess your request puzzles me. I was under the impression that our association had ended."

He touched his collar and frowned. "I assumed you would depart on the next stage. Since you did not . . . it's difficult to end an association in a town the size of Owl's Butte."

Hettie Alder appeared at the table, startling them both. She flipped a braid over her shoulder, grinned at Nate and poked him on the arm. "Ma has fresh taffy in the kitchen. Want some?"

Before Susan could voice an objection, Nate slipped from his chair and streaked toward the kitchen, Hettie skipping along behind. Susan glanced at the food left on Nate's plate and clenched her teeth together. If Mr. Harte had not been present, she would have finished Nate's supper herself.

Mrs. Alder appeared with a fresh pot of coffee. She gave

Susan a bland smile as if she'd had nothing to do with Hettie carrying off Nate. "More coffee?"

"I'll need another cup, I left mine at my table," Mr. Harte said. "And would you bring us some of that chokecherry pie I saw you serve Mr. Wessle?"

"I'm not hungry," Susan said quickly. "No pie for me."

Gresham Harte looked at Nate's plate, then at the solitary cup of coffee that sat in front of her.

"I'm paying for two slices of pie," he said to Mrs. Alder. Susan suspected he was actually speaking to her. "If Mrs. Stone doesn't want hers, I'll eat it." Mrs. Alder beamed at him.

"You didn't need to buy me a slice of pie," Susan whispered after Mrs. Alder had bustled away. Embarrassed heat flamed on her cheeks. "You made it clear that you don't feel responsible for me or my son."

"I haven't changed my opinion. Buying you a slice of pie is a gentlemanly courtesy, not an indication of obligation." They sat in silence for a full minute. "I've considered our situation, Mrs. Stone. I concede there may have been fault on both sides. I should have been more specific in my advertisement."

"I wouldn't have replied if you had excluded widows and children."

"Why did you reply, Mrs. Stone?" Leaning back, he waited while Mrs. Alder placed thick slices of cheese-topped pie in front of them both. "What I mean is, why did you respond to my advertisement instead of another?"

Susan noticed that Gresham Harte was the only man in the dining room who placed his napkin across his lap instead of tucking a corner into his shirt collar.

"You requested an educated woman. I may lack other qualifications of value, Mr. Harte, but I can read. I had excellent tutors, and I attended Miss Haversham's School For Young

Ladies." Her stomach rumbled audibly, mortifying her. It took an exercise in will power to make herself take dainty bites instead of finishing the pie in three gulping swallows. "I was impressed that you were an attorney. I assumed you would offer a way of life more familiar to me than that of a rancher or a farmer."

He studied his pie and his jaw set in a stubborn line. "I'm not insensitive to your plight, Mrs. Stone. I sympathize with your circumstance. But I'm not responsible for it."

"If you don't feel responsible for bringing me to Owl's Butte, Mr. Harte, then why did you seek me out tonight?"

"I did not seek you out," he said stiffly. "I've taken my Sunday supper at Mrs. Alder's for four years." He glanced toward his usual table beside the front window. "Encountering you was happenstance. It seemed rude to share the same dining room without some acknowledgment. Our situation is awkward, but we do share a small acquaintance."

"Oh."

For one brief but intense moment, Susan had dared to hope that he might have changed his mind about marrying and rescuing her. She had begun to persuade herself that his brown eyes were kind, that his prominent nose was noble and authoritarian.

"Mrs. Stone, I don't wish to mislead you. I accept no responsibility for your welfare." He watched her close her eyes and hold a bite of pie on her tongue before she swallowed it. After looking at the ceiling, he pushed his plate toward her. "I'm not as hungry as I thought."

She stared at him with horror, humiliated that her hunger was so obvious. "No thank you," she said coldly, feeling a hot pulse at the base of her throat. She tried to ignore the piece of pie he offered, tried not to imagine the cheese melting against the roof of her mouth or the sweet tang of berries.

"I would like to know your intentions regarding your future."

All she could think about was the pie he wasn't going to eat. Never in her life had Susan expected to suffer actual hunger pangs. Never again would she take food for granted.

"Mrs. Stone?"

"I'm sorry. What did you say?"

With a directness she found both rude and fascinating, he removed her empty plate and placed his pie in front of her. He stared into her eyes. "Eat that."

"If you insist," she said, releasing an elaborate sigh and hoping she sounded indifferent. "I guess it would be a shame to waste it." The pie filled her vision.

"I insist," he said, directing another glance toward the ceiling. Lowering his gaze, he leaned back in his chair and watched her struggle not to gobble the pie. "I thought you intended to return to your family back east."

"Even if I had the wherewithal to return to Washington, there would be no purpose. I have no surviving family, and I no longer have ties back east." The pie vanished and she politely blotted her lips with her napkin. "My mother died when I was a child. My father perished shortly before I married Captain Stone." The pie eased her lightheadedness, but didn't fill the hollow in her stomach. She made a quick count of the hours remaining until the breakfast that was included in her fare.

"Then you intend to remain in Owl's Butte?" The possibility appeared to alarm him.

"I have no choice," she said in a weary voice. She lowered her head. "I am praying for a miracle, Mr. Harte."

At once he placed his napkin on the table and rose to his feet. "I cannot stress too firmly that you must not look to me for your miracle or as a remedy for your difficulties. I have verified the law and the law is clear. An advertisement is not a contract. I am not obliged under law to provide for you in any way whatsoever."

As he finished speaking, Nate ran laughing into the dining room, his mouth sticky with candy and his blue eyes merry. "Here, Mama," he said, opening a fist to offer her a lump of taffy, "I brought this for you." He opened his other fist and extended a similar lump to Gresham Harte. "This is for you, sir."

"Thank you, young man." Gingerly, Gresham accepted the sweet, then placed his hat firmly on his head. "Good night, Mrs. Stone. If I don't encounter you again, please know that I wish you well."

"Thank you for the pie, Mr. Harte," she murmured, without looking up at him, as her son climbed onto her lap. She kissed the boy's head and pressed her face against his brown curls.

Gresham was out of the door and half-way down Main Street before he realized what a stupid thing he had said. Unless Mrs. Stone departed Owl's Butte—which she displayed no indication of doing—he most certainly would encounter her again. She was, in fact, as omnipresent and sticky against his conscience as was the bit of taffy that stuck to his palm. He could not shake her out of his thoughts.

Scowling, Gresham reminded himself, as he had repeatedly reminded her, that he was absolutely not responsible for her and her son. He was utterly clear on this point.

It was also true that she was stranded in Owl's Butte because of him. And she had not eaten all day.

Swearing, he kicked at a frozen clump of manure.

Had he remained back east, Gresham Harte might very well have courted Susan Stone. Certainly she was a pretty little thing, slender and well-formed with eyes the color of a pale spring sky. He liked the way her brown hair had shone in the dining room's lamplight. Had he remained in Connecticut, he was confident his law practice would have flourished and generated an income comfortable enough to afford a large home and servants, the kind of life to which Mrs. Stone was accustomed and in which she belonged.

But the west had exerted an irresistible appeal. At his core Gresham Harte was a pioneer spirit, a man who sought open spaces and the self-sufficiency now eroding from more civilized urban centers. He admired the honesty and directness of the frontier settlers. The idea of owning open land and building a home with his own hands thrilled him. He felt proud to join the men who would settle this wild country, proud to place himself at the leading edge of the future. And to do so while indulging his passion for order and law was to enjoy the best of all worlds.

All that he lacked was the pleasure of female companionship, of an ambitious woman to share his dreams and work at his side. He believed that two horses could pull a load faster and farther than one horse alone.

But advertising for such a woman had proved a dismal mistake. What he did not need was a clinging, dependent woman like Susan Stone. And he rejected the responsibility and distraction of raising another man's child during the crucial years of building and structuring his life.

Refusing her was the correct decision, the only decision possible. He needed a sturdy young wife with muscle on her bones and calluses on her palms. He needed a woman who knew the difference between a skillet and a wheel hub, who could hang a roof, sew a suit, grow a garden and butcher a hog and do it all cheerfully and without any fuss.

Shining brown curls, smooth white hands and helpless pale eyes had no place in his plans or dreams.

A week later, Mrs. Alder tapped on Susan's door. "You have a caller," she announced, leaning on her broom in the doorway.

She smiled at Nate, who was snuggled under Susan's arm, studying the pictures in the book she was reading to him. "Mr. Harte wishes to speak to you in the parlor."

Wearily, Susan set the book aside. "How odd." Bending to the vanity mirror, she patted her hair and smoothed down her skirt. Lines of worry and fatigue had appeared between her eyes and she pressed at them with her fingertips. Waiting for the final inevitable disaster was an exhausting and debilitating chore.

"I don't mean to pry, Mrs. Stone, but I can't help worrying about the telegram you received. Not bad news, I hope."

Susan almost smiled. Everyone in the west pried into everyone else's business. In the States such behavior was considered shockingly rude; here, they called it being neighborly.

"The telegram was from my attorney in Washington, D.C. I'd hoped to learn my husband's estate has been settled, but I was disappointed."

A dozen questions flickered in Mrs. Alder's eyes, but she didn't voice them. "Hettie's peeling potatoes in the kitchen. She'll watch over the young'un while you speak to Mr. Harte."

"Thank you."

When she entered the parlor, Mr. Harte was standing in front of the window, his back to her. Gresham Harte lacked the style and flair flaunted by most of the attorneys Susan had known. If he owned more than the one shiny suit he wore, she had yet to see it. He was also more compact than the soft-fleshed attorneys she had met in Washington. His stomach was tight and flat, his chest broader than that of most men his height. His thighs, arms and shoulders were all muscle.

After whisking her fingers through her bangs, Susan coughed into her hand.

Turning from the window, he swept his hat from his head, nodded, and spoke bluntly. "I'll come directly to the point,

Mrs. Stone. Am I correct in my impression that you intend to settle permanently in Owl's Butte?"

"I shall be equally direct," Susan decided, though it pained her. Although she found frank speaking a habit shockingly easy to adopt, she couldn't feel comfortable with it. An urge to apologize always followed an instant of directness.

"I lack the money to leave Owl's Butte. It doesn't matter. I've concluded that one place is much the same as another." She drew a long breath. "Seven dollars constitutes my entire fortune, Mr. Harte. When that is gone, I'll be penniless. Mrs. Alder has been kind enough to teach me many things throughout the last two weeks, but I don't deceive myself that I can earn my way. I haven't mastered a fire box and my one attempt to assist with the wash ended in disaster." She couldn't speak of these matters without feeling sick inside. Sudden panic threw a rush of bile into her mouth.

"I see. How and where will you live when you can no longer pay your hotel fees?"

She seated herself on the edge of a horsehair chair and silently vowed not to burst into a storm of helpless weeping. Not in front of the man who had rejected her.

"I don't wish to discuss this."

"I'm sorry, but I believe we must."

It was not in Susan's nature to challenge a male. All of her life she had taken direction from men and responded to their authority. Hating it that he forced her to humiliate herself, she drew an unsteady breath and lowered her head.

"I cannot let my son perish of cold and starvation. When my last dollar is spent . . . " she steeled herself to state the unspeakable, her voice sinking to an anguished whisper of shame. "I shall present myself to Mrs. Hawk and beg her to hire me."

Gresham Harte dropped his hat and stared at her in shock. "You would prostitute yourself?"

Her shoulders hunched inward and she cringed to hear her intention stated so baldly. "What else can I do?" she asked in a voice that sounded ancient. "Selling myself is the final solution, the only option open to a penniless woman with no skills and no man. The alternative is to let my son starve to death, and that I will not do." She turned her face so that Harte could not see the glimmer of her welling tears.

Gresham Harte stared at her.

"Mrs. Stone, there is someone I think you should meet. Will you come out with me for a drive?"

"I'm sure I've met everyone in Owl's Butte," she said, feeling exhausted and ill.

"You haven't met Mrs. Winters. She lives in County Creek, about fifteen miles from here. Mrs. Winters is a remarkable woman. She may be able to assist you."

Susan glanced toward the window. The weather outside was fine, cold and windy but dry. The sky was blue enough to make a person weep, and the air pure enough to drink. Susan couldn't recall the last time she had enjoyed a genuine outing.

She pressed the heels of her palms to her eyes, then looked at the floor. "Why do you interest yourself in my case, Mr. Harte?"

He scowled. "It's not because I feel an obligation toward you."

Under different circumstances, she might have smiled. His stubborn insistence that they were not joined in a subtle invisible way was sadly amusing. "If it will relieve your mind to hear it stated aloud, I don't hold you responsible for my plight. Others are to blame for my ruin, not you. I stopped blaming you a week ago."

His eyebrows clamped together. "I regret that you blamed me at all. There was error on both sides."

"I suppose." She lifted a hand and watched it fall back to her lap.

"Will you come out with me to call on Mrs. Winters?" When she just looked at him, he leaned to the floor to retrieve his hat and straightened with another scowl. "Although I am not obligated, Mrs. Stone, it seems you intend to remain in Owl's Butte and therefore I naturally take a neighborly interest in how you fare. In the west, people offer a hand to their neighbors when a helping hand is needed."

She turned her face to the window, thinking how lovely it would be to escape her room and her troubles for a few hours in the fresh air. Perhaps Hettie would watch Nate for her. A drive would give her an opportunity to air her cape and bonnet.

"May I assume you have arranged for a chaperon?"

He actually laughed, the lines around his eyes fanning into crinkles. "Forgive me, Mrs. Stone. I forget how new to the west you are, and how rude our manners and customs must seem. Out here, we have no time or patience for such nonsense as chaperons. Certainly not for mature adults. Your reputation will in no way be compromised by driving out with me."

The irony in his tone suggested how ridiculous her concern became in view of the fact that a week from now she would be selling her body to any man with fifty cents and an urge to buy an hour of counterfeit affection.

"That was stupid, wasn't it? To request a chaperon."

She wondered how many times she had made a fool of herself by blindly following etiquette instead of applying a moment of thought or reason. What a snobbish innocent she had been. It no longer puzzled her that Senator Stone had treated her like an irritating child.

Mr. Harte stroked his mustache and squared his shoulders. "Your honor is perfectly safe with me. My sole design is to assist you if I can. To speak frankly, Mrs. Stone, I'm desperate to remove you from my conscience and be rid of you."

She pursed her lips and lifted a surprised eyebrow. A tiny smile danced in her pale eyes.

He flushed and gripped his hat, crushing the brim. "I said I am not responsible for you. I did not claim that you don't weigh on my conscience."

"I'll have a word with Hettie about Nate and then fetch my things, Mr. Harte," she said, rising gracefully enough to have sent her old teacher Mrs. Haversham into spasms of delight. "I won't be a moment."

She sat far to one side of the wagon seat and Mr. Harte sat far to the other side. A lunch basket occupied the space between.

For a mile or two Susan occasionally peeked at him from the corner of her eye and daydreamed that his conscience would provoke him to offer marriage and save her at the eleventh hour.

By now she knew a snippet of gossip about every soul in Owl's Butte. She knew that Gresham Harte came from solid English stock, had no surviving family, and that he had put himself through law school by working at any task however menial or demeaning. What he lacked in powerful connections, he made up for in ambition and single-minded endeavor. He was respected in Owl's Butte, and the residents felt proud and fortunate to have an attorney of their own. Susan had overheard the owner of the general store explaining Gresham Harte to a stranger as if Mr. Harte were a local monument.

She also knew that he bathed regularly, something of a local curiosity; had better manners than most men in the west; and apparently he possessed an exacting conscience. She had not erred regarding his character.

"I am never going to marry you, Mrs. Stone," he said when they had traveled another mile in silence.

She lifted her head to the mountains, hoping to absorb some of their rocky strength. "I know." Her fantasy fluttered away with the breeze that plucked at her cape and bonnet.

"It occurs to me that you may be hoping I'll change my mind and spare you an unfortunate destiny." He faced rigidly forward, his gaze focused on the horse's heads. "I have plans, Mrs. Stone. I know exactly the type of wife I want and require. She must be strong, self-reliant, accustomed to hardship, and willing to lend her labor to the future. I would prefer an educated wife, yes; but I would relax that qualification if given a choice between education and self-reliance."

Susan turned toward the cold wind blowing off the snowy range.

"Are you crying again?" he demanded, leaning to peer into her face.

"I'm trying not to," she whispered, pressing her handkerchief to her eyes. Men hated tears, she knew that. When women cried, men either capitulated and resented it, as Bowie had done, or they turned coldly irritable as Mr. Harte did.

"Damn it! Whatever possessed you to come west? You don't belong out here!"

"My attorney in Washington told me to go west," she said into her handkerchief.

"Didn't you think about it or investigate? A client doesn't have to accept every word of advice that falls from an attorney's mouth! Ultimately, the decision belongs to the client."

"Go west. That's what Mr. Dubage told me to do."

"Mrs. Stone," he said after a minute, shaking his head. "I fear for your future."

"So do I, Mr. Harte." She sniffed into her handkerchief. "Oh, so do I."

County Creek was larger than Owl's Butte, boasting a court-house, a jail, and a church with an actual steeple. Mr. Harte exchanged nods with many of the people along Main Street while Susan examined the storefronts with cautious interest. The creek for which the town was named flowed behind the town and because of the water, there were more trees than she had noticed in Owl's Butte. But fifteen miles had altered the scenery and the County Creek residents did not enjoy as fine a view of the Tetons—a view that Susan was beginning to love.

Mr. Harte turned the wagon left off Main Street and clucked at the horses under his breath, his gaze fixed on a log house.

Susan waited until he stopped the horses before a hitching post. "I should have inquired earlier. Who exactly is Mrs. Winters?"

"Mrs. Winters is the superintendent of schools for this district."

Susan's eyes widened and her mouth dropped. "A woman is the superintendent of schools?" She couldn't imagine such a thing.

"Wyoming takes pride in being a progressive territory. The prevailing theory is that children are of great interest to women, therefore it follows that women should assume an active role in their education."

She stared at him. "But to place a woman in a position of responsibility and authority?"

He gave her a curious look. "Does the idea offend you?"

"No," she said slowly. "I've just never heard of it before."

She marveled that a woman had been found willing to shoulder such a heavy burden. The thought of it amazed her. She wasn't entirely certain that Mr. Harte wasn't testing her gullibility by inventing a wild tale.

"Is Mrs. Winters required to make important decisions?"

"I assure you, the lady is equal to the task."

After Mr. Harte handed her to the ground, Susan straightened her skirts and cape and looked at him. "Is this true? You aren't having a jest with me?"

"Certainly not."

"Why did you bring me here?" The idea of meeting such

an unnatural woman as Mrs. Winters unnerved her. Mrs. Winters was certain to be mannish and formidable, a virago. How could she be otherwise? She and Susan would have nothing to say to each other; she couldn't think why Mr. Harte had imagined they should meet.

"There is a schoolhouse in Owl's Butte," Mr. Harte explained, watching her expression. "It's a one-room building located a mile and a half outside of town. The last school teacher, Miss Abraham, married a horse trader two years ago and moved to Laramie. Owl's Butte hasn't had a teacher since."

Understanding slowly dawned, followed by a gasp of amazement. "Are you . . . ? You think I could teach school?"

"You're educated. Teaching seems a better way to earn your bed and board than by selling yourself at Mrs. Hawk's brothel."

Wetting her lips, Susan whirled to face the log house, clasping her hands tightly together. "I've never taught anyone anything. I've never even thought about it." She tried to swallow. "I don't know if I could do it. Will Mrs. Winters hire me?"

He touched her elbow lightly, leading her forward. "I have arranged an interview for you. What comes of it is up to you."

"But do you think I could do it? Should I?"

He frowned. "Mrs. Stone. Please do not look to me to make your decisions. You're a grown woman, quite capable of deciding things for yourself."

While they waited for a response to his knock at the door, Mr. Harte turned to look at her. "I consider that arranging this interview discharges any obligation you may imagine I owe you."

Tremors of nervousness ran through her body. This could be the miracle she had prayed for, the rescue she had abandoned hope of finding. Her heart banged against her rib cage and her mouth turned as dry as hot wool. She lifted her face to Mr. Harte. "Quick! Does my hair look all right? Did the wind pull my curls straight?"

His eyebrows shot upward in a startled expression. "Your hair looks fine. Sort of frizzy in front. I think it's supposed to be that way."

"Am I too pale? Black makes me look so pale!" Furiously she tried to pinch some color into her cheeks. "I do wish you had told me about this beforehand! I could have worn my silk instead of the alpaca! Oh dear, I'm so nervous I'm going to faint!"

Alarm darkened his eyes. "Don't faint! Mrs. Stone, you look lovely and I'm certain you'll perform splendidly in the interview." He didn't look at all certain.

The door swung open and a small woman smiled at them. "Mr. Harte, how pleasant to see you again. And you must be Mrs. Stone. Please come inside."

Susan couldn't help staring. Mrs. Winters was not at all what she had anticipated. Far from being mannish, Mrs. Winters was as petite and feminine as Susan. She wore a well-cut gown of dark maroon that was only a year or two out of fashion. An ivory cameo adorned her throat, and pearl ear drops hung from her ears. A luxuriant mass of ash-colored hair swept back from a rounded face, secured in a simple knot at the crown. The style was plain but elegant on a woman with presence. And Mrs. Winters had presence.

Without Susan noticing exactly how it was managed, Mrs. Winters whisked Mr. Harte into a side room and led Susan to a sunny room at the back of the log house, indicating a chair facing an ordered desk.

Mrs. Winters folded her hands together on the desktop and smiled. "I'm not a woman to mince words, Mrs. Stone, so we'll get to business, shall we?"

Susan clasped shaking hands in her lap. "Forgive me for saying so, but I can't get over the fact that a woman is the superintendent of schools!"

Mrs. Winters briskly brushed the comment aside. "Wyoming is desperate for teachers, Mrs. Stone. Unlike many areas, we don't require our teachers to be male or to be unmarried. We pay the highest wages in the west."

"Ah—what might those wages be, if I might inquire?"

"If I decide to employ you, Wyoming will pay you fifty dollars a month, plus we will furnish a place to live. That is ten dollars a month higher than teachers in Denver are earning."

"Oh my heavens." Tears of relief and gratitude brimmed in her eyes. "A place to live and fifty dollars a month would be a godsend!"

"You will be expected to provide books, slates, and materials for your students. The town will provide firewood and any repairs to the schoolhouse. Tardiness and non-emergency absences will not be tolerated. Should a scandal attach to your name, your contract will be terminated at once. I expect my teachers to be leaders in the community, Mrs. Stone."

"Leaders in the community?" Susan repeated uncertainly.

"If I decide to employ you, I will expect you to involve yourself in all community affairs and to protect the interests of your students by forcefully making your opinions known on any local issues involving children. Issues of a controversial nature may be referred to me, of course."

"Me?" Susan whispered incredulously. "You expect me to speak forcefully? To defend a position before the men on the town council?"

"If need be, yes, Mrs. Stone. I do," Mrs. Winters said briskly. "Now, I would like to hear more about your qualifications. While I am eager to provide Wyoming's children with teachers, I am not willing to place just anyone in such a position of high trust. You must satisfy me as to your qualifications."

Susan had never met a woman like Henrietta Winters. Mrs. Winters looked as if she might preside over a society table, but she was as brisk and businesslike as a man. Her smile remained pleasant and even charming, but the words that emerged from her soft mouth were crisp and to the point. Her direct gaze did not waver. It occurred to Susan that she could easily imagine Mrs. Winters commanding an army without anyone questioning her gender or authority.

Hugely intimidated, Susan drew a short breath and recited her educational background.

"Your educational qualifications are splendid," Mrs. Winters said, pleased.

"I've never taught school, Mrs. Winters, have never considered employment at all, let alone teaching. I don't have the vaguest notion how one begins; I'm not at all sure that I'm equal to the task. I assume there would be some instruction beforehand?"

"No, there would not." Mrs. Winters' sharp eyes studied Susan's twisting hands. "This is the wrong moment for modest disclaimers, Mrs. Stone. I urge you not to pretend doubt unless that is what you feel. This is the moment to assert yourself and speak frankly of your virtues. While I don't require previous experience in my teachers, I do require an indication that they will succeed. Shall we try again?" Her smile was kind. "Are you confident that you can handle a classroom and provide your charges with an education?"

"I just don't know," Susan answered in an anguished whisper.

Mrs. Winters sighed. "Tell me, Mrs. Stone, what would you do if an older student, let us a say a boy of fifteen, began to bully a younger boy of, say, age eight?"

Susan bit her lip in a torment of indecision. "I guess I would ask the older boy to stop," she said finally.

"And if he did not?"

"I . . . I guess I would have to speak to his father."

"Given a severe case, parental involvement might be necessary as a last resort. But you are the adult in your classroom, Mrs. Stone. The problem is yours to handle."

She couldn't think of an answer. Perspiration dampened her underarms.

"Let us suppose one of your students was bitten by a rattlesnake, Mrs. Stone. What would you do?"

Susan gasped in horror and shuddered. "Oh my heavens! Could such a thing happen?"

"Thankfully, none of our students has yet been attacked, but rattlesnakes have found their way into schoolhouses."

The very thought of it made her feel lightheaded and helpless. "I would probably faint," she blurted.

"I see." After a moment, Mrs. Winters rose behind her desk. Regret softened her words. "Thank you for calling, Mrs. Stone. I wish I could offer you the position, but a teacher must be tough and resourceful. A teacher must be confident, self-reliant, and exude the impression of being in control at all times." Coming around the desk, she placed her fingertips on Susan's shoulder. "I think you'll agree," she said gently. "Teaching would not be a fortuitous choice for you."

Susan bowed her head and battled a tide of hopelessness. Behind her stinging eyelids she saw the painted women sitting in the windows of Mrs. Hawk's bordello. Next week she would number among them. Her son would grow up in a whorehouse.

Numbed by a sense of her own inadequacy, she followed Mrs. Winters toward the front of the house. It wasn't until she observed Mrs. Winters exchange a disappointed look with Mr. Harte that Susan found her voice.

"No," she blurted, touching Mrs. Winters' arm. Crimson burned in her cheeks; desperation lent strength to her tone. "Please, Mrs. Winters, I urge you to reconsider. I can do this job, I promise you! If a snake came into my classroom, I would kill it." How, she didn't know. But if killing snakes formed part of a teacher's job description, then she would find the courage to kill snakes. "If the older boy did not stop bullying the younger boy, I would punish or expel him." She met Mrs. Winters' surprised gaze. "If you will give me the chance, I'll be the best teacher you ever hired! I'll try harder than anyone else!"

Mrs. Winters hestitated only a moment before she took Susan's arm and turned her back toward the sunny office. "Excuse us, Mr. Harte. I believe Mrs. Stone and I have not yet concluded our interview."

Two hours later, flushed and stunned with triumph, Susan floated out the door and allowed Mr. Harte to assist her up onto the wagon seat. She was shaking so badly that she could not hold her hands still in her lap.

"I'm going to be a teacher!" she whispered when Mr. Harte took up the reins beside her. Worry darkened her eyes. "If only I knew how." Drawing a long breath, she struggled to calm her anxiety. "I'll manage somehow. The position is only temporary."

"Temporary?"

She placed her gloved fingers on his arm, then hastily withdrew her hand. "Please don't tell Mrs. Winters that I don't plan to teach for more than a couple of months."

"What happens at the end of two or three months?"

Susan drew a breath of resolve. "I intend to save every penny I'm paid," she said softly, thinking about the primitive conditions in Owl's Butte. Now that she saw a way out, she could almost consider the raw little town as bearable, merely a distressing interlude. "When I have enough money saved,

I'll hire a man to ride to Kansas and take my husband's body home to Washington, D.C."

"That's a laudable goal, I'm sure," Mr. Harte said, frowning. "But I don't understand how achieving it would terminate your teaching contract."

Sunlight glowed in her excited eyes. "Don't you see? Then the probate court will have to release Captain Stone's estate. Once that happens, Nate and I will have the funds to leave this awful place! I'll have a home again, and servants. Plenty of food and no worries. I can have my life back!" She pressed her fingertips against her eyelids. "I want that more than anything."

Soon she would have the means to bypass Mr. Dubage and provide for Nate's and her own future. All she needed was a death certificate or Bowie's body. Now she had a way to get them both.

Chapter Eight

Gulliver County, Kansas

During daylight hours Bowie worked harder than he had worked since his early days in the army. He helped John Hawkins and Rosie repair miles of fence, shore up sagging roofs, clear the well and cut firewood, and he handled his share of the daily chores. When blizzards swept the plains, Bowie and John Hawkins mended tack in the barn, repaired Lodisha's pots, tanned hides, cleaned and fixed farm tools.

The work was a godsend, strengthening his body and numbing his mind. Hard physical labor provided an outlet for anger, frustration, guilt, and the unwanted return of sexual needs.

In the evenings after supper, Bowie and John Hawkins played checkers at the kitchen table while Lodisha sewed, mended or scrubbed her pans with sand and vinegar. Rosie read aloud to them, drinking steadily, until her words slurred and she slid out of her chair beside the lamp. Then Bowie carried her to bed.

Most Saturday nights Rosie rode into Passion's Crossing, drank herself into a stupor and shot up Harold's place. Then— as he was doing now—Bowie had to walk five miles into town and pay her way out of jail.

He hated seeing Rosie after a major bender, hated what she did to herself. But the part he detested most was encountering Deputy Carl Sands. Squinting his eyes, he spotted Sands standing in a patch of sun on the jailhouse porch, watching Bowie slog through the mud that lay ankle-deep across Main Street. When Bowie reached the jail, Sands moved a toothpick from one side of his sneer to the other.

"What's the matter, Coward? You ain't man enough to keep your drunk wife at home?"

"How much are the damages?" Bowie reached in his pants pocket for the money he'd taken from the fines-and-damages box. If it hadn't been for Lodisha's egg money, they would have had to leave Rosie in jail. Sometimes, he thought sourly, leaving her in jail sounded like a good idea.

He paid her fine and three dollars in damages, then walked to the stables behind the courthouse to fetch Ivanhoe and the wagon. When he returned around front, Deputy Sands was hauling Rosie outside by the scruff of her neck. Sands pushed her toward the steps, then lifted his boot and kicked her into the street, laughing when she sprawled on her hands and knees in the mud.

Bowie shot off the wagon seat like a flash of greased lightning. In two seconds he was up the porch steps and had Deputy Sands by the throat, slammed up against the wall of the jailhouse.

Eyes glittering, he leaned in close enough to smell Sands's rotten breath. "If you touch her again, I'll break both of your arms! That's a promise, Sands."

Sands hit him in the stomach and they fell to the ground, fists flying, gouging, doing damage until Sheriff Gaine pulled them apart and stood between them, his gun barrel moving from one to the other. "What the Sam Hill is going on here!"

"The son of a bitch attacked a deputy of the law!"

"That so? What do you got to say for yourself, Stone?"

Rosie stormed up the jailhouse steps, shaking clods of cold mud from her hands and boots. "Sands booted me down the steps and Stone came to my defense!" She shot Bowie a look that labeled him a damned fool and reminded him that she didn't want him messing in her affairs.

Lem Sorrenson, one of Rosie's drinking buddies, stepped out of the crowd that had gathered at the first indication of a fight. He shoved back his hat. "Ole Rosie's telling it straight, Sheriff." He considered Bowie with a thoughtful expression. "Ain't no man worth the name that's goin' to sit by while his wife's being flung in the mud. I don't like to side with no coward and killer, but tha's how it happened."

Bowie clenched his teeth, ignoring the irritation of a cracked lip. He spoke to the crowd. "This is not 'Ole Rosie.' This is Mrs. Stone. I'll thank you to address her properly and with respect."

"Well 'scuse me all to hell," Sorrenson said, staring. "Sometimes I plumb forget that yer jail-house wife's now a respectable lady."

"You will address her as Mrs. Stone," Bowie repeated, his eyes narrowed. "The day you start calling Preacher Paulson's wife Minnie is the day you can call my wife Rosie."

"Oh for Christ's sake!" Rosie wiped her chin, leaving a smear of gray mud. She glared at the sheriff. "Can we go home now? My head's banging like a drum on the Fourth of July."

"Watch your step, hear?" The sheriff leaned close to Bowie's face. "The ice under your boots is mighty thin, boy. I'll overlook this here incident," he shot a slitted glance toward Deputy Sands, "but I wouldn't go tangling with the law again if I was you. You hear what I'm saying, Stone?"

"I'm not looking for trouble." He stared at Carl Sands over the sheriff's shoulder. "All I'm asking is that my wife be treated with the same respect as any other woman in Gulliver County."

Sands laughed until the sheriff silenced him with a scowl. "I don't like you, Stone. You deserved to hang and in my opinion, you should have. But I guess what you're asking here ain't too unreasonable." He studied the dirty hair falling out of Rosie's hat and frowned at her soiled clothing. "Ridiculous, maybe, but that ain't the point." Sheriff Gaine faced the crowd wearing a look that said, I don't like this either but we've got to do it. "Ro—that is, Mrs. Stone, ain't much and we all know it. But there's plenty folks in this town who owe her, and that probably counts for something. And it's true she's got herself hitched now. So it ain't outta line for this town to call her by her married name. Now you all pass the word." To Stone, he added, "I don't want to see you in town for a while, you got that?"

Bowie tried to assist Rosie onto the wagon seat, but she reared back and gave him an incredulous look before she slapped his hands away. Tight-lipped, he walked around Ivanhoe and climbed up on the other side.

Deputy Sands spit off the porch and shouted after them. "This ain't over, Stone!"

"If you don't take the cake!" Rosie said the minute they were out of town and rolling across the prairie. "What the hell came over you?" Lowering her head, she pressed her fingertips to her temples and groaned. "God. The sun would be shining today! Bouncing off the snow like needles."

"It grinds in my craw that nobody in Passion's Crossing

feels it's necessary to address you by your married name, a courtesy they show every other woman in the county," Bowie said between his teeth. His ribs ached, and each time he spoke he opened the cut on his lip.

"Ha! Next thing you'll be wanting me to wear skirts and a little feathered bonnet! Well, it's not going to happen. And if you think this town is going to respect me just because you say so, well, that isn't going to happen either." She wiped her muddied hands against her pants legs. "Did you bring me a bottle?" When he didn't answer, she shouted and kicked him on the shin bone. "Damn it! I keep telling you to bring a bottle when you come to get me! I suppose you didn't bring any smokes either!"

"I'm not going to help you destroy yourself." He drew a breath and looked at her, trying to recall how she looked and smelled when she was fresh out of a bath. "Getting drunk won't change the past. It's time to forget the past, clean up your life and move on."

"I am so *sick* of your lectures! Stop drinking, stop smoking, stop swearing, stop remembering . . . I might as well stop living!" She stared at his tight jawline. "You just don't understand, do you? There's nothing in this whole miserable world I'd like better than to forget what he did to me! And I could forget if only I'd had the chance to say my piece and shoot the bastard. Everything would be different!"

"It's too late for revenge. You've got this crazy idea that Frank Blevins can still see you and hear you. He's dead, Rosie. Blevins has been dead for three years. I'm sorry you didn't get to say your piece, and I'm sorry that life isn't fair; but it's too late to change that. It's over now."

She shifted on the seat, squaring off for a fresh skirmish in the battle they had continued to fight ever since she had told him about Frank Blevins. A dark plum color pulsed in her cheeks.

"He worked that farm for eleven years, Stone. Eleven years! And he never once brought in a profit. Even so, he thought he was the best damned farmer who ever turned a line of sod. Well, I'm going to show him that I'm a better farmer than he was! That's how I win, Stone, that's how I end it! By showing him that I can run his goddamned farm better than hē ever could! That's my revenge! And you bet he can see and hear what I'm doing! I planted him right there in the yard facing the fields so he can watch me beat him!"

On this subject Rosie was as crazy as a June bug. The odd thing was, in his gut Bowie understood what drove her. Revenge was a powerful motivating force. And there weren't a lot of ways to take revenge on a dead man. Hell, maybe she was right. Maybe when she brought in a profitable crop her need for revenge would be satisfied and her hatred would die. Maybe she'd put away the bottle and begin to rebuild her self respect.

"What happens if you never bring in a profitable crop?"

"I will sooner or later, because I'm better than he was."

He came at her from a different direction. "All right, suppose you get your revenge . . . what will you do then?" The look she gave him was absolutely blank, as if she didn't understand his question. "You haven't thought about the future, have you?"

"Hell, Stone, I don't have any more future than you do." She turned her muddy face toward the patches of snow melting into the prairie. "The prairie dogs are out of their holes already," she commented absently, watching a village of dirt mounds pass on their right. She threw out a hand. "Maybe when it's over I'll go to California where it's warm all the time. Buy a little spread and raise lemons and oranges. There's no point thinking about it until it happens." She fell silent a moment, then fixed him with a penetrating scowl. "You can hit the trail after we get a profitable harvest, but not before. You aren't thinking about cutting out before-hand, are you?"

"I told you how it's going to be. I owe you one harvest. But once the wheat goes to market, I have to leave."

"And I told you how it's going to be. You aren't leaving alive until we get a profitable harvest."

Mud clogged the wagon wheels and they climbed down to pry out the heavy clods and ease the strain on Ivanhoe. As usual Rosie worked as hard as he did. Only her constant scowl and an occasional wince reminded him that she hadn't eaten since yesterday and her head must be banging. They climbed back into the wagon and he clucked his tongue over the reins.

"I thought you were starting to like me a little," Rosie blurted suddenly. An appalled look widened her eyes and she quickly turned her face aside, pulling her hat down to her ears in an effort to hide the color in her cheeks.

Bowie glanced at her in surprise. "Do you care if I like you?"

"Of course not!" She crossed her arms over her chest and jutted her chin, staring at the horizon. "The thing is," she said after half a mile had rolled under the wheels, "we've been married almost three months now, and I'm getting used to your ways. I don't even mind it so much anymore that you blab in the mornings. You pull your weight around the place, I'll give you that. If you'd stop lecturing me, we'd get on just fine. It riles me up when you talk about leaving, that's all. You're my husband and you're supposed to help me get my revenge no matter how long it takes. Besides, the army doesn't want you anymore and you don't have anything else. You're like me, Stone. You've got no place to go."

His hands tightened on the reins and he faced forward. "I have family obligations back east."

"From everything you've said about the senator, your father

wouldn't give a spit if he never saw you again. He marked you off the minute he heard you were dishonorably discharged."

It cut to the bone to hear Rosie repeat his private belief. Regardless of the reason for his dishonorable discharge, his father would never forgive him for it. The senator might accept the killing of Luther Radison, but never a dishonorable discharge.

"You're right," he said quietly. "But I have other obligations as well."

"Like what?"

"I can't explain, Rosie. Maybe someday."

"It doesn't matter," she said with an indifferent shrug. "You aren't going anywhere anyway."

The longer Bowie stayed in Passion's Crossing, the worse his dilemma became. It was unforgivable to allow Susan and his father to continue believing he was dead. Undoubtedly they had held a memorial service and Susan would be wearing weeds, denying herself the balls and entertainments she loved. She wouldn't grieve overmuch at Bowie's death—they hardly knew each other—but widowhood would be a hardship for her.

As for the senator . . . surely there was a small spot in his father's heart that could regret the death of his second son.

Bowie hated himself for causing them pain. But he could not notify them that he was alive without explaining why he couldn't return home at once. A bitter smile twisted his lips. He could well imagine Susan's horror and the senator's outrage when they learned he had added bigamy to his crimes. If a court-martial and a murder conviction hadn't tarnished the Stone name beyond redemption, the scandal of bigamy certainly would.

More often than he liked to think about, he lay awake at night pondering his situation and searching for a way to notify his family that he hadn't been hanged, while at the same time fulfilling his obligation to Rosie Mulvehey.

Whatever shreds of honor he still possessed prevented him from running out on Rosie. Regardless of her reasons, Rosie Mulvehey had saved his life. Most of the time he wished she hadn't bothered, but she had and he owed her. The least he could do was keep his promise to help her harvest a profitable crop.

The only thing that made keeping his promise to Rosie possible and bearable was the knowledge that Susan and Nate were safe and comfortable. The senator might despise Bowie for bringing shame and disgrace to the family, but he would honor his word. He would protect and care for Susan and Nate.

"That first day," he said, forcing his thoughts to the present as the house came into view, "I didn't think I'd ever find anything to admire about you."

"Just shut up."

"I've changed my mind. There are many things I truly admire about you."

"Is that right?" She lifted a boot, bent over it, and picked at the mud caked on the heel. "I don't want to hear this bunk. But I guess if you have to tell me, then I guess I have to listen." The side of her cheek turned bright red.

He focused on the house. Inside, Lodisha would be heating water for Rosie's jailhouse bath. Tonight her tawny hair would shine like silk in the light at the supper table. Her face would glow like ivory and strawberries, and her skin would smell a bit like lye soap and a little like the rose water Lodisha had taken to adding to her bathwater. It would be one of those nights when Bowie wouldn't be able to sleep, when he tossed and turned and tried not to remember how long it had been since he had lain with a woman.

"I admire how hard you work," he said finally. "Most men

I've known don't work as hard as you do. And you never complain about it. You have more will power than a dozen preachers, and you're a decent woman."

She rolled her eyes and made a strangled sound that might have been a gasp of pleasure or it might have been a choked laugh. "Decent? I doubt you'd find many who'd agree with that!"

"Rosie, look at me." She wouldn't do it. "Why did you take the wagon instead of riding to town on Ivanhoe?"

"You know why," she said. "I was going to get a couple of sacks of flour and some sugar for Lodisha."

He jerked his head toward the empty wagon bed. "So where are they? The sacks of flour and sugar?"

Heat flowed off of her in embarrassed waves.

"What?" he asked, leaning to peer at her face. "I didn't hear you?" But he could guess the gist of her answer. This wouldn't be the first time she had given away their provisions.

She scowled. "You remember the lard-belly who was standing next to you on the gallows? Josiah Willsy? A bale of hay fell off the barn loft and knocked him senseless. He wandered out in a blizzard and passed out cold with his feet in the creek. Shotshi Morris had to amputate one of his legs at the knee."

"Shotshi Morris? The barber?"

"Nearest thing we've got to a doc. Anyway, Mrs. Willsy spent all her ready on whiskey for the operation, then laudanum. And Shotshi doesn't cut off legs for nothing, you know."

"So you gave our flour and sugar to Mrs. Willsy. Isn't Mrs. Willsy one of those priggish tight-mouths who won't give you a nod or a hello on the street?"

"Hell, that doesn't matter." She laughed and waved a hand. "If I took offense every time somebody refused to say howdy, I'd never leave the farm, now would I?"

He caught her chin in his palm and made her face him, surprised by how firm her skin was, yet how soft and yielding.

"Listen to me, damn it. How is anyone going to respect you if you don't start respecting yourself? There's hardly a family in Passion's Crossing whom you haven't helped in some way or another. But you let them treat you like a disease! It's time you put a stop to it!"

She jerked away from his hand, her brown eyes blazing. "If you think Passion's Crossing is going to start doffing its hat to me just because you threaten to hammer anyone who doesn't call me Mrs. Stone, you're dumber than I think you are. This town has never respected me and they never will because I'm not going to change. And I don't care."

"You do care."

"Shut up, Stone! Just shut the hell up!"

"Stop talking yourself down and start holding your head up."

She grabbed the reins out of his hands and twitched Ivanhoe toward the barn. "I am so hell-fired sick and damned tired of your lectures! Just leave me alone!"

There was something perversely appealing about the way her small body appeared to grow when she was angry. Fire crackled in her brown eyes, and lightning seemed to flash and sizzle around her. Bowie could no more imagine a demure Rosie Mulvehey sitting meekly with her hands quiet in her lap than he could imagine her dressed in silk presiding over a tea table.

"Since the conversation has taken a turn toward your faults," he said mildly, watching her grind her teeth, "I'd like to register a complaint concerning your reading."

"Don't start on that again! I have to wet my whistle between pages. Reading aloud makes a person's mouth go as dry as a chip."

"I'm referring to the way you make up paragraphs the author never wrote. You know perfectly well that Romeo and Juliet were not magically resurrected by a sorcerer. They did not buy a villa on the Mediterranean and live happily ever after."

She shouted at John Hawkins to open the barn doors. "I like happy endings. If you've got a burr in your britches about the way I make stories end, then you do the reading and I'll play checkers with John Hawkins." Her lip curled. "I can beat him."

"The hell you can! Nobody can beat John Hawkins at checkers!"

Because it was a point of pride with her, she was out of the wagon before he was, unhitching Ivanhoe from the doubletree.

"Go up to the house," he ordered with a sigh, taking Ivanhoe's reins. "Lodisha's waiting for you." Rosie had to be craving a nip from the bottle and one of her stubby little cigars.

"Don't order me around!" she shouted.

Pride demanded a token resistance, but she allowed herself to be convinced. Bowie watched with a smile as she swaggered away from the barn with a casual bravado that wouldn't have fooled the town idiot.

Considering that Rosie was about as loveable as a stink bug, he didn't understand why he liked her; but he liked her more the longer he knew her. She was generous to bastards who did not deserve her generosity. She was fiercely loyal to Lodisha, John Hawkins, and even to him. No roustabout had ever worked harder than Rosie did. She groused about little things that didn't matter but didn't complain about the things that did. On those rare occasions when something tickled her, her laugh was light and infectious and transformed her scowl into something lovely that could steal a man's breath away.

Fresh out of the bath, she was the most beautiful and most desirable woman he had ever seen. And sometimes she was so painfully vulnerable that a child could have crushed her.

Shaking his head, he led Ivanhoe toward his stall and a rubdown. When he thought about Rosie blurting, "But I thought you liked me a little," a painful tightening stretched across his chest.

This strange wounded woman whom he'd had no right to marry was beginning to get under his skin.

Rosie leaned back in her scented bathwater with a pleasure that she would not have admitted to anyone. A strong black cigar dangled between her fingers. In her other hand she gripped a glass jar of whiskey. Smiling, she sniffed the fragrance of baking ham and buttermilk biscuits and decided this was one of life's good moments.

She didn't worry that Bowie might come barging into the kitchen. After that first awful experience, they had bent double to respect each other's privacy. They both maintained an eagle eye against accidental touches or an unexpected glimpse of bodies in the process of dressing. They tried to avoid excessive eye contact. After three months of tense vigilance, she had begun to relax and trust that Bowie was not going to appear in her bedroom doorway one night and attack her.

All in all, her marriage was working out better than she had dared to hope. She had herself the best damned roustabout in the entire state of Kansas, and he knew his place more or less. There were a few things she didn't like about marriage and Bowie Stone, but by and large they were small things that she could ignore. So why, with everything so rosy, wasn't she as happy as a hare in clover?

She released a long slow sigh. "Damnation anyway."

"Now you jest watch yor mouth," Lodisha said from the stove. "I ain't havin' no more swearin' in my house! The Cap'n don't like it, and tha's that."

Rosie sat up straight, splashing water on the planks. Swiveling, she strained to look behind her. "What's this all about? Swearing never bothered you before."

"It do now," Lodisha said, glaring over her shoulder. "The Cap'n don't like it. Tha's yor husband, honey girl. Got to polish up a bit."

"What?"

"No more swearin'," Lodisha stated stubbornly. "You keep on swearin' and you don't get no baths. Cain't fool me, you done started likin' yor baths. An' you don't get no clean clothes or no mended socks, you keep swearin'. No more shoofly pie or yor favorite chicken 'n dumplin's."

Sputtering, Rosie waved her cigar. "Is that why you let me smoke in the house this time? Because you were getting ready to spring a new rule on me? Son of a bitch!"

Lodisha pulled up straight, then she walked past the tub so Rosie could see what was going to happen. Looking Rosie straight in the eye, Lodisha turned a pie tin upside down and let the contents splatter across the kitchen table.

Rosie shouted and her eyes widened to the size of eggs. "You ruined our pie! I don't believe my eyes! You wasted food!" In fifteen years she had never seen Lodisha waste a single usable scrap.

"Cap'n don' like to hear ladies swearin'. So we ain't gonna have no more swearin', and tha's how it is from now on. You jest set yor mind to it."

Rosie dropped her cigar in the tub and hit the surface of the water with her fist. "Damn it, you and Stone are trying to change me all around! I won't stand for it, do you hear me?"

All the good thoughts about marriage flew out of her head. "I'm fed up to my eyeballs with all of you! I can't enjoy a little nip without feeling three pairs of eyes looking daggers at me! I can't have a little fun in town without the three of you drying up for a day and not speaking. I can't have a smoke in the house. Now, by God, I can't even talk!" She drew a deep breath that made her breasts quiver. "You gave

Stone his clothes, you gave Stone his room. What next? You think the Captain's so all-fired wonderful that you're going to give Stone his belt to beat me with?"

Lodisha's black eyes softened. "Now you know the Cap'n ain't goin' take a belt to yor hide."

"There's times he'd like to! Isn't anybody on my side?"

"We's all on yor side, honey girl." She started scraping the ruined pie into the slop bucket. "Only person here who ain't on yor side is you."

Rosie gulped the rest of her whiskey, then fell back in her tub, glowering and sputtering. There was no sense arguing with Lodisha. Once Lodisha made up her mind to something, she became as immovable as a city block. "Hell fire!"

Lodisha sighed, then walked around in front of the tub and ripped the patch off of Rosie's long johns. "You want this mended agin, you goin' have to find time to mend it yorself."

Rosie threw back her head and screamed, a mistake as Lodisha used the motion to grab her by the hair and shove her under the water. She came up spitting water and fury with Lodisha's strong fingers working soap into her hair.

"Now honey girl, real soon we gonna have to talk 'bout you and the Cap'n sleeping in different rooms. It ain't natural."

"What? *What*?" Twisting and turning, she tried to jerk out from under Lodisha's fingers, but Lodisha kept a firm grip on her. "I'll *starve* before I'll let him poke me! I'll put a gun to my head first!"

"Ain't natural for a man not to poke," Lodisha said, her fingers digging into Rosie's scalp. She shoved Rosie under the water to rinse off the suds.

Rosie came up yelping and spitting soapy water. "John Hawkins isn't out there poking every skirt!"

"John Hawkins is old and he ain't married no more. Besides, you don' know what John Hawkins does when he goes off to visit his friends in the Injun territory."

Rosie started shaking. "No man is ever going to hurt me like that again!"

"It don't always hurt. There's ladies what like pokin' jest fine, and I'm not talkin' jest 'bout no whores neither. The Cap'n strikes me as a man who'd know how to go about pokin' right. How you think you ever gonna git yorself a baby if'n you won't allow no pokin'? You jest think about that."

A shudder ran down Rosie's frame. "I'm barren. If I could catch a seed, I'd have had a baby years ago!" The thought of bearing *his* child sent acid pouring into her stomach.

"It ain't always the woman's fault. There's men what can't plant a seed no matter how hard they tries. Truth is, you don't know if'n you can catch a seed."

"I don't want a baby!" Rosie twisted to give her an incredulous stare. "You think I want a baby who has a whiskey-brain for a mama?"

"Well some of us 'round here does want a baby. We'll talk about that whiskey-brain 'nother time. Right now we's talkin' 'bout pokin'. Yor husband done showed more patience than a wooden saint. But the Cap'n's a man, honey girl. If'n you don't slide over in yor bed, then sooner or later the Cap'n he's gonna ride to town and pay a visit to one of them sorry whores up at Maud's place. You want ever flap-tongue in town knowing yor husband gots to go to Maud's place for his pleasuring?"

Horror widened Rosie's eyes. She could picture the sly glances and knowing smiles, the wildfire spread of ridicule and gossip. She could just imagine what the boys at Harold's would have to say. She'd never hear the end of it.

What compounded her horror was the secret admission that lately she had been thinking about poking every now and then. She detested such thoughts and didn't understand how in the hell she could think about a disgusting thing like that.

But more and more often she found it difficult to sleep, no

matter how much whiskey she poured down her throat. She'd lie on her bed feeling over-warm and itchy, restless inside and sometimes sort of tingly as she listened to the sounds of her husband tossing and turning a wall away. When Stone had first arrived, those sounds had made her feel panicked and nauseated. Now the same sounds made her feel tight-chested and hot inside. Her mouth dried and sometimes her heart pounded.

There was more. Sometimes when they were working in the sun, Stone would throw off his coat and she could see his shirt pull tight across his wide shoulders. Sometimes he'd brace to yank up a fallen fence post or shove back a sagging wall, and his thighs would swell against his denims. These glimpses of his body made Rosie feel peculiar inside, as if she were coming down with a fever. Once or twice she'd found herself staring at his mouth, tracing the shape of it in her mind.

Lately, she had amazed herself by wondering if all men poked the same, if all men had to wound and hit to get their pleasure.

Tears of bewilderment glistened in her eyes. Blevins had taught her about poking. She knew how hideous and painful it was. But when she watched Bowie Stone and when she saw the way ne looked at her sometimes, it occurred to her that maybe there were things about poking that she didn't know after all. Such crazy thoughts scared her and sent her reeling with confusion.

"Lawdy! Is you crying?" Lodisha peered into her eyes with an astonished look.

"No, I'm not!"

After hauling Rosie out of the tub, Lodisha wrapped her in a clean dry towel and enfolded her in a massive hug. "This all goin' work out, don't you see if it don't. We goin' take it one tiny li'l step at a time, and 'fore you know it, you goin' be skippin' around singin' Dixie, yes sir. Ain't nothin' to be scairt 'bout. Jest one tiny li'l step at a time!"

"I can't do it!" she groaned against Lodisha's strong broad shoulder. "Stone doesn't want me anyway, and I don't want him to!"

"Jest one li'l step at a time, honey girl."

Chapter Nine

"What are you staring at?" Rosie shoved the lamp to one side and glared at her husband across the supper table.

"You look very pretty tonight."

John Hawkins murmured agreement and Lodisha beamed.

"Lodisha put this ribbon in my hair. I didn't do it." She scowled at Lodisha, then filled her whiskey glass and turned back to Bowie with stony eyes. "I suppose you want to poke me now."

Bowie knocked over his coffee cup. John Hawkins lifted his head, his fork midway to his mouth. Lodisha jumped to get a towel and mopped it over the spilled coffee.

"Well, you're not going to. This stupid damned ribbon is not a signal that I want you climbing into my bed!" Her shoulders hunched, and she shuddered.

Bowie couldn't believe what he was hearing. Rosie glared as if she wanted to slice his throat. Lodisha and John Hawkins slid expectant glances in his direction.

Frowning and searching for a response, he drew a breath and blotted his napkin against the coffee on his shirt and denims.

"Just because you look pretty doesn't mean I'm going to attack you or make unwelcome advances."

"That's what it usually means. The only time a woman is safe from poking is when she's ugly."

"That isn't true," he said, staring at her. "Not all men are animals with no self-control. Most men can appreciate a lovely woman without being offensive or forcing himself on her."

"Just answer the question. Are you going to try to poke me?" she demanded, her narrowed eyes raking his face.

He looked at John Hawkins and Lodisha. Fascinated interest met his glance. "Of course not. I'm not going to poke you," he said finally, frowning. John Hawkins went back to eating. Lodisha released a disappointed breath.

"Not even if Lodisha keeps on hiding the twine and puts ribbons in my hair?"

Standing, he went to the stove and poured another cup of coffee. He didn't know what to make of this conversation except that it was excruciatingly uncomfortable.

"Not even if you wear a skirt and a lace waist and splash yourself with powder and perfume." He sighed. "Not even if you parade yourself wearing nothing but your long johns." Imagining her perfumed and powdered made his stomach go taut. He wondered again if Rosie had any idea how stunningly beautiful she was with her mane of silky hair and a freshly scrubbed face. Her skin glowed, and her fiery eyes were the same amber brown as a new saddle. Even a man's loose shirt didn't completely conceal the lush curve of her breasts.

She continued to eye him suspiciously when he returned to the table. Tension tightened her shoulders and jaw.

"I suppose sooner or later you'll be riding in to Maud's

place to poke one of Maud's whores." Crimson dots flared on her cheeks.

"Damn it, Rosie." He could see that John Hawkins was struggling not to smile. Lodisha slapped another chunk of baked ham on his plate in a manner that said she didn't care for the twist this conversation had taken. "Do we have to discuss this now?"

"I guess that means you are going in to Maud's."

A dark rush of color pulsed in his throat. "I haven't thought about it, all right?" He glared at all of them. "It's nobody's business anyway."

"Hell's fire! One of Maud's girls has the pox. Everybody knows it!"

There wasn't time to decide if Rosie's eyes were damp, because Lodisha came out of her chair like a thundercloud. She snatched away Rosie's supper plate, crossed the kitchen in three strides, and scraped Rosie's supper into the slop bucket.

"Ain't goin' have no swearing in my house. Cap'n don't like it."

Rosie threw back her head and howled. "He swore too!" she shouted, pointing a finger at Bowie.

"Nice young ladies don' go 'round swearin' like a cow man," Lodisha said, thrusting out her jaw.

"That isn't fair! I'm not a nice young lady, I'm . . ." Jumping up, Rosie kicked the table leg, then she grabbed her coat from the peg and ran out the door, banging it shut behind her.

Bowie put down his fork and the biscuit he had forgotten he was holding. "What in the hell just happened here?"

"This is good," John Hawkins said mildly, accepting another biscuit from Lodisha. "Rose Mary is beginning to think about becoming a wife."

Lodisha sighed and placed a bowl of stewed plums near

the lamp. "Still got a long ways to travel on this here road. But we's one step closer."

An alarm exploded in Bowie's head. "Lodisha, I appreciate your sentiment on this, ah, issue, but some things are better left alone."

"Ain't natural for a husband and wife to go sleepin' alone. Cain't git no babies that way, no-how."

Bowie stared at her, appalled. "Rosie has been brutally abused. You both know that. The last thing I want to do is hurt her." His shoulders stiffened. "I've done a lot of things in my life, but I've never forced myself on a woman."

John Hawkins spread butter on his biscuit, applying himself to the task as if the sun would not rise tomorrow unless every crumb was carefully covered.

"Do you remember the day after you came here, Captain Bowie Stone? You took the Winchester into the fields, and you killed two hares."

That act had removed him two shots from the shot that had killed Luther Radison. And now when he sighted down on a hare or a pheasant he thought about the last hare or pheasant that he'd brought to Lodisha. He no longer saw Luther Radison's face at the end of the barrel.

"It was good to shoot those hares," John Hawkins said. "Now you bring us meat often."

"I understand what you're saying, John Hawkins," he said finally. But he was not the man to replace Rosie's terrible memories with something better. He didn't have that right. He put down his napkin and stood. "Rosie and I can't live as man and wife. It would be wrong."

That's what he told himself every night as he lay staring at the ceiling, listening to her turn in her bed, thinking about the way she looked just out of her bath. Remembering how her pants molded her buttocks when she leaned into the chopping block. Remembering the soft womanly heat of her that day when he had pinned her to the ground. Remembering her cherry-tipped breasts and the tawny triangle between her legs that he'd seen when he had watched her rise out of the tin tub.

He swallowed hard. "That was a fine supper," he said, passing Lodisha on his way to the kitchen door. Taking his hat and coat, he stepped outside into the yard.

The days were longer now. Traces of pink and orange lingered across the western horizon. A few stars winked in the cold sky, looking close enough to scoop into his hat.

He found Rosie standing beside Frank Blevins' grave, her hands thrust deep into her coat pockets. She had flung away the ribbon and her hair rippled in the night breeze, hanging loose almost to her waist. Resisting an urge to sample a strand between his thumb and forefinger, Bowie pushed his own hands into his pockets.

"I'm not going to hurt you," he said in a quiet voice. "You're a beautiful, desirable woman, Rosie, I want you to know that. What you also need to know is that you don't have to hide your beauty under men's clothing or layers of dirt to be safe from me or anyone else. There are men in Passion's Crossing I don't like, but most of the men around here are decent and God-fearing. They aren't going to molest you if you let them see who you are. Neither am I."

"You can't speak for every man in Passion's Crossing," she said, kicking a loose rock toward Frank Blevins' headstone.

"I can speak for most of them. The most important thing is, you aren't to blame for what Blevins did to you. He didn't hurt you because you wore a skirt or because you dressed your hair a certain way or walked a certain way or because you looked pretty. Blevins hurt you because he was weak and brutal. He was a coward and sick inside. Maybe he was evil. But he was to blame for what happened, Rosie. Not you. It was never your fault."

In the fading light he saw that her cheeks were wet, and the sight of her tears clawed at his gut. Some women cried as a form of manipulation, or they cried in pain or out of self-pity, or over matters too insignificant for a man to comprehend. But he had watched Rosie Mulvehey rip a jagged splinter from her thumb without a tear, had seen her dismiss ridicule and Deputy Sands's rough treatment with a wave. She didn't attempt to manipulate anyone, and he had never heard a whisper of self-pity pass her lips. When a woman like Rosie Mulvehey wept, the pain was deep and real, and wrenching to watch.

"Do you . . . really believe that? What you just said?" she whispered, not looking at him.

"Everything I said is true. None of what happened with Blevins was your fault. I believe that utterly and absolutely. Deep down you have to know it too."

As if sensing that Bowie's instinct was to step forward and put his arms around her, she moved away from Blevins' grave and faced the dark fields.

"John Hawkins says we'll have one more hard frost. After that we can plow."

"Do you trust me, Rosie?" There was no reason why any living soul should trust him, considering how he had messed up his worthless life. But right now he needed her to trust him.

"Maybe," she said finally.

"Then believe what I'm telling you. You're not to blame for being victimized. You have nothing to be ashamed of; you can hold your head as high as any woman in this county. You're not dirty or ugly or anything else you might be thinking. You're fine and strong and decent. You're a worthwhile person, Rose Mary Mulvehey. You deserve respect and admiration."

The light was almost gone, but he saw her face when she

lifted her head. Her expression was so vulnerable and fragile that he knew he could destroy her with a single word.

"Oh God," she whispered in a strangled voice. Her eyes fastened on him in the dying light. "You can't believe all those good things, not about me."

Carefully, moving slowly so he wouldn't frighten her, he touched his fingertips gently to her cheek. She stiffened and trembled beneath his fingers, but she didn't jerk away from him.

"You're good and decent, Rosie."

"I drink and smoke and cuss. I'm ugly."

"You're not ugly. You're generous and loyal."

"Please," she whispered, moving back a step. "Don't say these things to me."

"I know who you are."

Because she was Rosie, she didn't react like another woman might have. She made a fist and hit him in the stomach, then she ran toward the house.

The blow was totally unexpected and it doubled him over. She was small, but she was strong and capable of hitting as hard as a man. Swearing and holding his side, Bowie straightened and shouted into the darkness.

"Think about what I said!"

When he returned to the house, moody and with his stomach aching, Rosie was nowhere to be seen. Lodisha was drying the supper dishes and John Hawkins pretended to read an ancient newspaper.

"Rose Mary left that for you." John Hawkins nodded toward a jar of whiskey sitting on the table.

"Must of said somethin' powerful strong out there in the yard, Cap'n," Lodisha murmured, holding a plate toward the light. "Our honey girl don' share out her blazer none too often."

This he knew. Rosie hadn't offered him a drink from her

stash since the day he had arrived. Silently he took two more jars from the broadshelf and poured the whiskey into three shares.

He raised his jar. "To women. I don't know a single goddamned thing about women."

"It is better that way," John Hawkins said before he tossed his share back.

Lodisha held her jar with her little finger daintily extended. "Now Cap'n, you gots to set a good example. Cain't have no more cussin' 'round here."

Suddenly he laughed, the first time he had laughed in eight months. He was drinking in a rude kitchen with an Indian and a black woman who knew the intimate details of his life, after being blindsided by a beautiful derelict who thought nothing about discussing sex over her supper plate and who was probably lying in bed right now getting drunk as a rat.

Never in his wildest flights of speculation had Bowie imagined people like these or a situation like this.

"You know," he said, grinning. "Right now there isn't another place in the entire world that I'd rather be."

Three weeks later, he had changed his mind. He would rather have been anywhere else on earth than pulling a plow across a hard dry Kansas prairie.

Blisters blossomed on Rosie's palms, burst, and spilled bloody fluid across the handles of the plow. Although the temperature was cool, by midafternoon the sun felt like an oven pulsing in the sky, sucking sweat through her pores and moisture out of the hard gray soil she stumbled over.

When Bowie stopped, she fell forward, narrowly missing the blade of the plow.

"Christ!" he said, mopping his brow. Tearing off his shirt, he flung it toward the rows already planted. "It's a hundred degrees out here!"

The instant they stopped working, Rosie felt the sweat turn cold against her ribs. "It's only about fifty degrees." She looked at Bowie's shirt, wondering if she had the energy to fetch it and make him put it back on. If Bowie took sick, the season would end in defeat before it really began.

"Rose Mary, this row is swerving too far to the left," John Hawkins called from behind.

Rosie shifted to squint at the turned soil behind her, then peered ahead, trying to see past Bowie. His shoulders were shaking beneath the leather straps that harnessed him to the plowshare and the veins stood up on his neck. The sweat on his torso glistened like oil beneath the pale sun.

"You're straying too close to the planted rows again," she cautioned, amazed that her words were coherent. Cold dust clogged her throat and nostrils. Her throat felt as dry as bleached bone. She would have given anything to tear off her own shirt and fling it aside. Sweat ran down her ribs in rivulets.

Bowie adjusted the leather straps at his waist and across his naked shoulders, closed his eyes for a moment, then steadied his legs. "I'm ready."

"Go ahead."

Pushing down on the handles, struggling to keep the blade even and steady, Rosie stumbled after him. Her boots caught in the freshly turned clods, sweat dripped into her eyes. It was excruciatingly hard stop-and-go work.

An hour later John Hawkins shouted that he was out of seed grain. They all stopped, falling to the ground where they stood. Rosie shaded her eyes and studied the sky, gauging the hours of remaining daylight.

"Too soon to quit," Bowie said. He pressed his lips together and silently eased out of the harness straps, then limped past her, heading across the field toward the storage shed next to the barn. It was a mile walk to the shed and back.

"I can get the grain," John Hawkins announced in a sullen tone.

"We've been over this before," Rosie snapped. "A bushel of grain weighs sixty pounds. You're an old man, John Hawkins. I don't want you keeling over on me before we get the crop in."

She worried about him constantly. John Hawkins complained that his job was the easiest, but bending over all day, dragging the bushel of seeds and pushing them one by one into the ground, was not easy. He couldn't straighten his back at night and his knees twitched and made popping sounds at the supper table.

They sat on the chill ground, feeling the cold now, waiting. There were buds on the cottonwoods lining the banks of the creek, and hints of green on the prairie, but spring was late this year.

When Bowie returned, he placed the bushel of seed grain beside John Hawkins and touched his fingertips to the old man's shoulder. He looked at the sky, then moved past Rosie and bent for the straps.

"Want to lend a hand here?"

She helped strap him into the harness, her fingers leaving smears of dirt across his wet upper body. A trickle of blood leaked down his back where the strap had abraded his flesh.

"I'm sorry," Rosie mumbled. "Maybe we should get Ivanhoe."

Bowie's eyes jumped to life and blazed in his face. "Ivanhoe is the only good thing you own. We're not going to ruin a fine animal by harnessing him to a plow!"

She stared up at him and felt a lump form in her throat. Swallowing, she returned to her place at the handles.

The turned rows crept from fence to fence, from acre to acre. They lost one day to a wet spring snow that was good for the seeds in the ground but bad for further plowing. They waited another day for the snow to melt and the mud to dry. Then the agony began again.

In the field they measured speech like drops of water, too battered and exhausted to utter an unnecessary word. Despite Lodisha's frantic efforts, the weight dropped off of them, shrinking their flesh to muscle and bone.

At the end of each day, they staggered back to the house and collapsed on the kitchen stoop, too bone-weary and numb to speak.

Rosie's hands looked like raw meat. So did Bowie's shoulders and back. He slept sitting up, unable to tolerate even a sheet against his bruised and broken skin. John Hawkins ate his meals doubled over on a low stool, unable to straighten his back. Rosie drank her supper from a bowl; her hands were too cramped and blistered to grip a fork or spoon. There were nights she didn't have the energy to drink more than a single cup of whiskey.

Lodisha treated them with spring tonic and she rubbed healing balm into their wounds. They fell mindlessly into their beds immediately after supper, shaking with exhaustion and dreading the next day.

"Hooee, won't you look at that!"

Rosie let go of the plow handles to wipe the blood off her palms and the sweat out of her eyes. She squinted across the rows of turned sod.

Deputy Sands and two of his cronies stood at the edge of the field, leaning on a fence post and passing a bottle among them. Rosie had been too numb, too fatigued to register the sound of their horses.

"I'm ready," Bowie said quietly. "Take up the plow."

"In a minute." She reached inside for the strength to shout. "What do you want? You got no business here."

"Heard you got yourself a new draft horse . . . Mrs. Stone. Wanted to see the beast fer myself," Sands said, grinning. The men laughed.

"Get out of here!" Clenching her fists at her sides, she cursed herself for leaving her revolvers back at the house.

"Yer new horse looks kinda skinny and puny to me. Whatta you think, boys? Should we shoot him and put him out of his misery?" Sands sighted his Colt on Bowie, then shifted the barrel and fired a bullet into the ground in front of Bowie's feet. "Fancy that, boys, I missed."

Bowie adjusted the harness over his shoulders. "Come on, Rosie. We aren't going to get this done by standing here."

Rosie was shaking with fury. "They're shooting at you! Don't you care that those sons of bitches rode out here to laugh at you?"

"No."

"Hey Stone! Hey coward! How's it feel to be a horse?" Sands poked one of his cronies and laughed. "Does your old lady ride you in bed too?" The cronies slapped their knees and doubled over with laughter.

Rosie shouted. "You go to hell, Sands!"

"Giddy up, boy! Give us a neigh." Sands fired another bullet into the field a few feet in front of Bowie's boots.

"All right, Sands. You've had your fun. Now get your butt off my property!"

"Or what . . . Mrs. Stone? You'll sic your horse on us?" Sands's cronies hooted and hollered and wiped tears of mirth from their eyes.

Bowie planted his feet and leaned forward. "Come on, Rosie. It's almost supper time. Let's finish this row."

Shaking with rage, trying to ignore the shouted comments and hoots of laughter, Rosie gripped the plow handle and watched Bowie strain forward, watched a thread of blood zigzag down his spine. She didn't look at Sands or his cronies again, didn't realize Sands had gone until they quit for the day and stumbled across the fields toward the house.

They sat on the stoop, searching for the energy to wash up and go inside. When Rosie could breathe and think again, she turned to look at Stone, who sat on the step beside her, holding his head in his hands.

"You honest to God really didn't care that they were laughing at you, did you?"

He lifted his head and stared toward the fields in the fading light. "I can't believe you even thought about trying to do this alone. Jesus."

"I wanted to kill them!"

He looked at her. "What difference does it make what Sands thinks?"

"They were *laughing* at you! Ridiculing you! I know what that feels like!" She stared hard at him. "The difference is, I tell myself that it doesn't matter, but with you . . . it really doesn't."

"Just forget about it."

"They took a couple of shots at you, for Christ's sake." When he didn't reply, she leaned forward to look into his face. "You're punishing yourself. That's it, isn't it? That's why you grit your teeth and smile all strange when Lodisha rubs the balm on you and it hurts like fiery hot hell. That's why you don't give spit about Sands. You think you deserve to be humiliated. Why, because you're alive? Because you didn't hang that day?"

She hadn't thought about it for a while. It shocked her to realize that Bowie still didn't care if he lived or died. He'd fight anyone in town if they ridiculed his wife, but he wouldn't lift a finger on his own behalf. She could work him to death in the fields, and he wouldn't murmur a protest or a word of complaint. Dying didn't matter to him.

"Any decent man would have done what you did at Stone Toes! And killing Radison was self-defense! So you aren't in the Cavalry any more. So what? You're needed here."

"Stop it, Rosie," he said, running a hand over his face.

"Suppose Sands had meant business . . . would you have just stood there and let the bastard kill you? Like he was doing you a favor? That's what it looked like. You didn't even flinch."

She watched him push to his feet and limp toward the barn.

Finally the day arrived when they hauled the plow out of the fields for the last time. The plowing and planting were finished. They stood at the edge of the rows inspecting their accomplishment and looked up as a fat spring snowflake tumbled out of the clouds.

"Snow!" Rosie shouted, waving her bandaged hands at the sky. "Come on, snow like a son of a—" she stopped and looked around for Lodisha. "Snow like crazy! Big wet flakes! Come on, snow!"

"This is good," John Hawkins said. Grinning, he placed his hands in the small of his back and tried to stand up straight.

"I'll be switched," Bowie said softly, watching a mantle of white slowly settle over the planted rows. A wide smile curved his lips. "We did it." He looked down at Rosie. "Damnation, Rosie! We did it!"

"Damned right we did! Seven whole acres!" Throwing back her head, she laughed out loud, shouting with pleasure when Bowie grabbed her by the waist and danced her across the yard. John Hawkins forgot that he was no longer an Indian. He also danced through the snowflakes, yipping and chanting a song of victory.

Coming out on the porch to watch, Lodisha wiped her hands on a dish towel. "Come in this house right now, you pore fools." She grinned broadly. "We gon' wash that Kansas prairie off'n you once and fo' all, feed you good, doctor you up, and put you t'bed for a whole day."

"We did it!" Rosie shouted, trying not to bang her bandaged hands against Bowie's shoulders. Laughing, she spun around and around in their mad dance through the falling snow until she tripped on a stone and fell forward against his body.

Bowie caught her, his hands hard and firm on her waist. When he looked down into her upturned face, the smile faded from his eyes. His gaze dropped to her parted lips.

The laughter died on Rosie's mouth. She felt his body hard against hers, felt the sudden tension that scorched past her exhaustion. Her eyes widened and her breath stopped in her chest.

Bowie's hands moved from her waist and framed her face, tilting her chin up. "Congratulations," he said quietly. Leaning forward, he kissed her mouth, gently and lightly. A warm brush of lightning, then gone.

The kiss was so unexpected, so abruptly confusing, that Rosie froze, unable to jerk away from him. She stared up at him, paralyzed, her heart beating wildly.

"You were magnificent out there," he said softly. Taking her wrists, he raised her hands to his lips and kissed her bandaged fingers. "I don't know another woman who could have done what you did. I'm proud to know you, Rose Mary Mulvehey. I hope to hell that you get the crop you deserve."

He thought she was magnificent. He felt proud to know her.

Hot tears pricked at her eyelids and she couldn't breathe. No one had ever said anything like that about her. The sentiments and the sincerity in his eyes made her feel strange and almost sick inside. Joy and pain and disbelief built a searing pressure behind her chest.

"I couldn't have done it without you," she whispered. She

stared at his mouth and listened to her pulse thundering in her ears. They stood so close that she could feel the male heat of his body. Her mind reeled, telling her to hit him and run away, telling her to kiss him again. Horror clouded her eyes that she could have such a terrifying thought. But she also marveled that a kiss could be soft and gentle. She hadn't known that was possible.

His hands slid down to her waist and he leaned forward again, slowly, looking into her wide eyes.

This time when he kissed her, he held her lightly against his body. Again his kiss was benign, so soft and gentle that it made her feel like weeping. She stood on the balls of her feet, poised to hit and run, but she did neither. She accepted his kiss, her eyes wide open and fixed on his expression, waiting for the ugliness of animal passion to transform his familiar features into something swollen and alien.

It didn't happen. Bowie remained Bowie, handsome, deliberate, the man who insisted that Gulliver County show her respect by addressing her by her married name. This was the man who had acted as her plow horse, who had bled for her. A man who had never made an offensive move in her direction. This was a man who thought she was magnificent, who was proud to know her.

She felt his mouth soft and warm on her lips and a strange feverish earthquake erupted deep inside. A violent tremor swept from her head to her toes.

Confused, Rosie stumbled backward a step and wiped his kiss off her mouth with her forearm. "Please don't do that again," she whispered.

Her heart slammed against her rib cage; her knees felt weak. She hadn't dreamed that a man's mouth could be tender and exciting. It terrified her to realize the extent of her own rush toward self-destruction; she wanted him to kiss her again and hold her close.

Horrified and swallowing convulsively, tasting panic at the back of her throat, she whirled and bolted for the house.

"This is good," John Hawkins said, moving up to stand beside Bowie in the thickening snow. "Rose Mary did not black your eye or try to kill you."

Bowie clenched his hands and kicked at the accumulating snow. "I didn't mean to kiss her. I forgot myself."

Closing his eyes, he reminded himself that Susan, not Rosie, was his legal wife. Eventually, like it or not, he would have to return east and resume his obligations. It would be a kindness to everyone if he kept that thought uppermost in his mind.

Lifting his head, he peered through the snow, watching Rosie pass by the kitchen window. In the light of the kitchen lamp, her hair reminded him of flame and sunlight.

Swearing, he kicked at Frank Blevins' headstone, then followed John Hawkins toward the house.

By the time supper was ready, Rosie had already retreated into her bottle of Brown Blazer. Staring at him in silence, she drank one jar of whiskey after another until her strange look of confusion and apprehension relaxed and she fell unconscious on the rug.

Bowie picked her up and held her in his arms.

"You break my heart," he said softly. Then he put her to bed.

Chapter Ten

At some point each day, each of them interrupted his or her chores and walked out to the fields to stare at the tiny green shoots and silently coax them upward. Life revolved around rain—the possibility of rain or the lack of rain.

While the prairie freshened and the cottonwoods unfurled silvery green leaves, Bowie and Rosie put in a kitchen garden, slapped a coat of whitewash on the house and most of the barn, cleaned out the root cellar, and helped Lodisha make up a fresh batch of lye soap and cast some tallow candles.

Today they cleared dead limbs away from the creek banks, collecting firewood and opening a path for the livestock.

"Are you going into town tonight?" Bowie asked, stopping work to wipe the sweat from his forehead and throat.

"Maybe," Rosie said defensively.

Spring seemed to have bypassed the prairie this year. The temperature had jumped from cool to hot with no intermediate stage. She glanced up at the sun, blazing white in the sky. There was no sign of rain.

"It's been nice having you home on Saturday nights, not having to walk into town to bail you out of jail."

Rosie thrust out her jaw, feeling circles of heat leap to her cheeks. "I don't always end up in jail."

"Most of the time you do."

"I'm going to town tonight," she said, deciding on the instant. Too often lately she'd been making small changes to please Bowie. When she recognized what she was doing, it made her feel as if she were giving up little bits of herself. Occasionally she needed a reminder that she was still her own person.

Bending, she wrapped her arms around a bundle of dead willow branches and carried them toward the house. Irritated, she flung the twigs into the kindling box.

Now she would have to go. The thought of wasting an evening listening to Lem, Shotshi, and Acey while they swapped stupid jokes bored her already. For some reason, the idea of shooting up Harold's place no longer held the appeal that it once had.

Leaning against the side of the house, she watched Bowie carry up the last load of dead limbs and dump them beside the chopping block. He ladled a drink out of the water barrel, then splashed water over his face and throat before he took up the axe and started chopping the cottonwood limbs into firebox lengths.

He hadn't tried to kiss her again. Neither of them had mentioned the day they finished the plowing.

But Rosie thought about it. A lot. She could hardly function for thinking about Bowie kissing her that day. When she looked at him across the supper table, she thought about him kissing her. She watched him riding Ivanhoe, inspecting the fields, and she thought about him kissing her. She listened to him turn over in his bed and she burned with thoughts about him kissing her.

"You have a mirror in the barn, don't you?" she asked abruptly. One of the first things he did every morning was walk out to the barn. When he returned, he was clean shaven.

He glanced up from the chopping block, but he didn't answer.

She had intended to kick up a ruckus about the mirror, but to her annoyance, the words that came out of her mouth were, "Just don't ever bring it up to the house."

She looked at his mouth and thought about him kissing her.

Furious with herself for thinking such nonsense and for making concessions she really didn't want to make, Rosie turned to watch a curl of dust following a buckboard toward the house.

She didn't know what was wrong with her. A dozen times each day she started to say something sharp to Bowie, but the words and the tone came out milder than she intended, softer than she wanted. Sometimes she thought her brain was turning to pudding.

"Are you expecting anyone?" Bowie asked, mopping his brow and looking toward the approaching buckboard.

"That's Miss Evaline Buckner." Rosie frowned as the buckboard stopped in front of the house. After pushing her hat firmly down on her head, she hitched up her pants and walked forward, hearing Stone's boots behind her.

"Howdy Rosie, Mr. Stone." Evaline dimpled at Bowie from beneath the protective wide brim of a straw bonnet. She wore a print skirt and a shirtwaist that picked up the amber color of her eyes. A charming array of wildflowers lay scattered across her lap.

"Howdy Evaline," Rosie said. "What brings you out this way?"

Bowie removed his hat and smiled. "I believe Lodisha made some lemonade. Would you care for a glass? It's a hot day for a drive."

Rosie scowled at him. She didn't like the way he and Evaline were smiling at each other. Watching them look each other over made Rosie feel like she'd swallowed some bad pork.

"Why thank you, Mr. Stone." Evaline cast down her lashes and looked flustered. Rosie rolled her eyes and frowned. All Bowie had done was offer the silly twit some lemonade, he hadn't asked her to elope to Hayes City. "I'd purely adore to have a lemonade with you, but I'll just have to postpone that pleasure." Long blond eyelashes swept up and down over pink cheeks. "I have a half-dozen other stops to make before I can rest these old bones."

Rosie noticed Bowie's grin. Evaline's bones were only twenty years old and overlaid by abundant soft curves. Suddenly and inexplicably, Rosie yearned for blond ringlets and a pouty mouth and tiny little yellow slippers. She would have very much liked to drag Evaline off the buckboard and pound her pretty pink face into the dirt.

"What do you want, Evaline?"

Evaline ran a slow glance down Rosie's sweat-stained shirt and man's pants. She restrained a shudder; but her nostrils pinched, and she cast Bowie a conspiratorial look that suggested they were united in their disapproval of Rosie and her attire.

"The Ladies' Society is sponsoring a calico hop to celebrate getting the crops in. I've come to invite you to attend. It's next Saturday night. The ladies will provide punch and lemonade, and cookies."

"We'll be pleased to attend, Miss Buckner." Bowie accepted for them, still smiling. His voice sounded warm and deep.

Evaline clapped her gloved hands together as if he had granted her fondest wish. Her eyes sparkled flirtatiously. "You won't change your mind, will you? I can count on you? That's wonderful. We'll have two extra men!"

Rosie pulled a cigar from her pocket, lit a match against her boot heel, and blew smoke at Evaline Buckner while Evaline gushed at Bowie. A grim smile curved her lips each time Evaline coughed and waved the smoke away. She didn't return Evaline's wave when Evaline finally took up the reins.

"How come you said we'd go to that stupid dance?" Rosie demanded the minute Evaline turned the buckboard out of the yard.

Bowie watched the dust trailing the buckboard with a thoughtful expression. "I never met a woman who didn't like to dance."

"You're looking at one now," Rosie snapped. They walked back to the chopping block. This time it was Rosie who picked up the axe and swung it down on the cottonwood limbs.

"What was that remark about two extra men?" Bowie asked, watching her. "Exactly what did that mean?"

Raising the axe above her head, she swung it down hard. "The only reason the Ladies' Society invites me to their dances is because there aren't enough men in Passion's Crossing to make up a dance unless some of the women wear a blue armband and dance the men's part."

His eyebrows met across the bridge of his nose. "That's what I thought it meant. Miss Buckner expects you to attend the calico hop as a man."

"That's why they invited me." Feeling Bowie's stare, Rosie swung the axe up and brought it down. "I don't care," she said, lifting her chin. "I get to hear the music."

That night Rosie took her usual place at the bar beside the cigar stand and the jars of brandied peaches. Harold slid a bottle across the counter and actually smiled at her. Harold was happier to see her now that she didn't shoot up his place as often.

"You jest ain't the same since you got yourself hitched," Lem commented sadly, peering down the bar at her.

Rosie touched her fingertips to the dirt she'd smeared on her face before she entered the saloon. "Shut up. I don't want to talk about my marriage or my husband."

"This town's dying," Shotshi offered, leaning his head back to stare at the dusty chandelier overhead. "Used to be we could at least count on old Ro—Mrs. Stone—fer a little excitement. Now there's plum nothin'."

Rosie looked into her shot glass and imagined she saw Evaline's face floating on the surface. "You boys think Evaline Buckner is pretty?"

"Pretty as a new pup!"

"Prettiest gal in Gulliver County."

"Shotshi ought to know. Follows that gal around like a sick cat," Acey said. He and Lem laughed.

A hot dark taste surged in Rosie's mouth. Because she had never before experienced jealousy, she didn't recognize what she was feeling. She only knew that cramps gripped her stomach and she suddenly despised Evaline Buckner. She turned her shot glass in circles on the bar and remembered Evaline fluttering her lashes at Bowie and Bowie standing there in the yard looking tall and handsome and smiling back at Evaline all sappy and soft-like.

"Well I don't think she's much to look at," Rosie snarled.

She sighed and clapped her hands on her gunbelt. Harold was going to be upset. It looked like this was a shoot-'em-up-night after all.

"What's going on here?" Rosie demanded, her eyes widening.

The minute Lodisha cleared the supper dishes, Bowie and

John Hawkins rose to their feet. The three of them stood looking down at her with tight determined expressions. Rosie gripped the edge of the table, apprehensive about the look in their eyes.

Bowie glanced at Lodisha and John Hawkins. "Now!"

They came at her in a rush, pinning her between the table and the kitchen wall. A half dozen hands grabbed at her. Rosie didn't know what the hell they were trying to do, but instinct told her not to let them do it. She fought and hissed and battled not to be captured. Before Bowie caught her feet, she landed a kick in his mid-section, then John Hawkins' iron grip closed over her wrists and the fight was finished.

"What are you doing? What the hell is this?" Rosie screamed as they dragged her into the center of the kitchen.

"You jest stop that cussin'," Lodisha said calmly. While Bowie and John Hawkins held her immobile, Lodisha pulled off Rosie's clothes, peeling her down to her long johns. She gave Bowie a nod. "I've got the rope and padding."

"What? What rope?" Rosie twisted and bucked against Bowie and John Hawkins, but she couldn't break free. They carried her by her feet and arms into her bedroom and swung her up on her bed, holding her down while Lodisha padded her wrists and ankles then tied them to the bedpost. Terror rose in her eyes and she thrashed against the restraints.

"Now honey girl, stop pulling against the ropes lest you hurt yourself. Ain't nothin' bad goin' happen here."

After checking the knots and slipping extra padding next to her skin, Bowie straightened over her with a frown of determination. "You are going to be sober at that dance tomorrow night."

Rosie kicked and yanked at her restraints. She screamed. "You got no right to do this! Untie me this minute! I want a drink!"

John Hawkins examined the ropes. "This is good," he said,

pleased. "You will enjoy the dance, Rose Mary." Smiling, he and Lodisha left her room.

Rosie screamed after them, calling them traitors and worse.

"Here's our plan," Bowie said, watching her throw herself against the knots. "You're going to stay right here, tied up until tomorrow afternoon when it's time for your bath. This is one night that you are not going to ride into town and get foxed. And in case you think you'll get drunk the minute we untie you . . . Lodisha and John Hawkins are right now going through the house searching every little cranny for any liquor you may have hidden away. An hour from now there won't be a drop of whiskey on this farm."

Murder burned in her eyes. She screamed the worst curses she could think of until Lodisha stormed into the room and stuffed a handkerchief into her mouth.

"I's sorry, honey girl, but we ain't goin' have that kind of talk! This here is a respec'able house." She bustled out of the room in a whirl of apron and dark skirts.

Tears of fury and frustration brimmed in Rosie's eyes.

Bowie leaned over her and wiped the tears away with his thumb. "I'm sorry this was necessary, Rosie." He collected the bottle off her side table and checked under her bed. "But you're going to that dance sober, and you're going as a woman. Now, get some rest. I'll see you tomorrow."

Her rage was too powerful to permit rest. She fought the ropes half the night before she fell into a fuming, exhausted sleep.

When Rosie awoke it was early afternoon. Bright sunlight flooded her small room.

"Untie me!" she demanded, opening her eyes and glaring at Lodisha, who sat in a chair next to her bed.

Then she saw the gown spread across Lodisha's lap and she sucked in a hard, deep breath. The gown was the prettiest she had ever seen, made of crisp blue calico sprigged with tiny white flowers. It had a rose sash and real lace at the throat and cuffs. An explosion of petticoats hung on the wall pegs, as billowing white as sea foam.

Rosie's mouth dropped open and she stared in disbelief.

"They's more," Lodisha said happily. "Look here at these dancing slippers, blue to match yor dress. And lookee at these new drawers and shimmy. An' tha' ain't all. Jest feast yor eyeballs on this! This is a gen-u-ine French corset!"

Rosie was speechless. She stared at the confection of silk and satin that Lodisha was proudly holding up for her inspection. Pink ribbon threaded the boning and tiny embroidered roses outlined the bodice. It was the loveliest garment Rosie Mulvehey had ever seen.

"I'm not going to wear a stupid corset!"

"Yes, you is! No respectable young lady goes off to a dance without wearing a corset, now you knows that. Yor goin' to this dance dressed right and proper from yor skin on out!"

"Where did all this come from?" The blue slippers glowed in the sunlight, looking magical. A person's feet would fly in such slippers, barely skimming the floor.

"The Cap'n ordered everything special from Kansas City, yes sir. Arrived on the train." Seeing the question in Rosie's eyes, she added, "No, the Cap'n didn't take no money from yor fines-and-damages box. They was money in a pouch in the trunk. In his bedroom."

"When did he do all this?" Rosie asked, wetting her lips. She didn't let herself think that the money had belonged to Blevins. She couldn't take her eyes off the calico gown. Every time Lodisha moved, the calico made a crisp rustling sound.

"Went to town the very day Miss Evaline came callin'. 'Spect he telegraphed his order then."

Rosie ground her teeth together and made herself look away from the calico gown. "I'd feel like a fool wearing all this frippery. I'm not going to do it." She closed her eyes. "God, I need a drink!"

She desperately wanted a shot of blazer. She couldn't cope with French corsets and crackling calico ruffles. If she showed herself in public rigged out in petticoats and shiny blue slippers, she'd never hear the end of it. The town would still be laughing on Judgment Day.

Standing, Lodisha produced a knife out of her pocket and cut the ropes binding Rosie's ankles and wrists. "Ain't no liquor on this here property. We found the bottle under the loose board. Even found the jug in the corn crib." She cocked a dark eyebrow. "And you ain't ridin' into town to git any, lest you's prepared to ride down Main Street in yor long johns."

Sitting up and rubbing her wrists, Rosie turned her head this way and that. "What happened to my clothes? What did you do with them?"

"All yor clothes is tucked aside where you'll never find them. This here is all you got to wear, honey girl." Lodisha held up the blue calico gown. The ruffled hem danced around her ankles. "You gonna look like a dream come true in this here dress! You gonna make that Evaline Buckner look like a tired old sow, gonna put that Evaline in the shade, yes sir!"

Rosie reached out a hand and touched her fingers to the material. Back in the days when she had worn dresses, years ago, they had all been cut down from her mother's gowns. As far as Rosie knew, she had never owned a brand-new gown all of her own. She eyed the petticoats and silk corset from the corner of her lashes, feeling a melting sensation in her stomach. She wondered if Evaline Buckner owned a real French silk corset and layers of fresh new white petticoats.

"I'm not going to wear all that," she repeated weakly. She wet her lips and wondered if the blue slippers would show beneath the hem of the gown.

"Yes, you is. Now you come along. Yor bath is waitin'."

"Not going to wear it." Standing, she surveyed her new finery, and lust exploded in her heart. Without knowing it until this minute, she had craved a lace-trimmed, blue calico gown since the moment of her birth. In some hidden corner of her heart she had been perishing to own blue dancing slippers. Just looking at the French corset sent a shiver of curiosity and possessiveness through her frame. Never in her life had Rosie expected to own such finery. She felt like a miser examining a wondrous hoard of gold. This new clothing was hers.

"Did he remember to order stockings?" she asked in a low voice, hating the rush of heat that flooded her cheeks.

"Cap'n didn't forgit nothin'. Even got ribbons for yor hair and little blue earrings made out of shell. Even got you a li'l bottle of lilac water." Lodisha smiled. "I got a surprise fo' you too. Got some Spanish red fo' yor cheeks and lips and made you some powder fo' yor nose."

Rosie made a show of dragging her feet into the kitchen where her bath was waiting. She would have sold a portion of her soul for a smoke and a little whiskey courage. She would look like an idiot dressed in all that frippery, she just knew it. John Hawkins could put on that rig and look better than she would.

"Do you think Evaline Buckner has a new dress for the dance?" she asked, after she was settled in the warm fragrant tub.

Good God. What was happening to her? She hadn't asked such a silly girly question since she was twelve years old.

"Well?" she demanded as Lodisha lathered soap into her hair. "What do you think Evaline will wear?"

Lodisha was grinning too broadly to answer.

Bowie brushed the sleeve of a crisply ironed shirt across the brim of his hat, then touched the scarf at his throat. He inspected the toes of his boots, polished to a high-spit shine, then glanced at John Hawkins and Lodisha, who gave him a beaming nod of reassurance.

"Jest you wait, Cap'n. You ain't gon' believe yor eyes." Lodisha called out again. "Honey girl? You got to show yorself sometime. Cap'n's waiting to take you to the dance."

A stream of muttering issued from behind Rosie's bedroom door. Bowie's eyebrows arched and he blinked at Lodisha and John Hawkins, then repeated the ladylike swear words he heard coming from Rosie's bedroom. "Drat? Chicken feathers? Thunderation?"

Lodisha grinned and made a shushing sound. "Somethin' 'bout a corset and petticoats make a lady out'n a woman. Our honey girl cain't work up a good cuss, all gussied out like she is. Rose Mary? You come on out here! Cap'n's gettin' mighty impatient."

The bedroom door opened an inch, closed, then opened again. Finally Rosie stepped into the living room, her face as crimson hot as cherry jam. "I feel like a durned fool!"

A long, low sound came out of John Hawkins' chest. Lodisha beamed and smiled from ear to ear. Bowie gasped, then fell speechless.

Rosie Mulvehey looked like an illustration on a fashion card. She was absolutely and utterly lovely.

Lodisha had drawn her tawny hair away from her face, up into a silky twist at the crown. Rose and blue ribbons fell among long fat finger curls that bounced flirtatiously around her shoulders and the delicate shell earrings in her ears. The bodice of the gown fit like a second skin, molding her breasts and narrowing to a tiny waist. Lace followed the scoop of the neckline, curving over the tops of her breasts. The skirt belled over her hips and swayed above slender ankles encased in thin white stockings.

"You've laced me so tight that I can't breathe," Rosie said, looking everywhere except at Bowie.

"I knew you were lovely," Bowie said, finding his voice. "But I didn't imagine you would be this beautiful." The fragrance of lilac water and powder reached him. He suspected she had tinted her lips and added a touch of shaping to her eyebrows.

"Don't say that to me!"

"Rosie, look into my eyes and see the truth. You're so lovely you take my breath away."

Apprehensive and almost shy, she finally made herself look at him. She studied his expression for a long moment, then dropped her lashes, and the color in her cheeks deepened. "Everyone's going to laugh at me!"

"Believe me," Bowie said in a husky voice. "No one is going to laugh at you." He signaled John Hawkins.

"I am sorry Rose Mary, but this is necessary." Stepping forward, John Hawkins brought his hands from behind his back and held Bowie's shaving mirror up in front of her face.

"It's Mama!" Rosie gasped and recoiled backward a step. The color drained from her cheeks, and she started shaking.

"No, honey, that ain't yor mama," Lodisha said, taking the mirror from John Hawkins and pressing the handle into Rosie's trembling hand. She brought hand and mirror up again. "That there is you, honey girl. And ain't you a pretty thing! Prettier than yor mama ever was."

"Oh my God," Rosie whispered. Staring, she touched her shaking fingertips to the image in the glass. "That's *me*?"

Bowie cleared his throat. Her amazement was painful to witness. "When was the last time you looked into a mirror?" he asked gruffly.

She turned wide eyes toward him, then gazed back into the

mirror, frowning as if she didn't trust what she saw. "I don't know. Maybe seven or eight years." She touched her chin and lips, watching in the mirror. "Oh my. I grew up."

Lodisha laughed and wiped the tears in her eyes with her apron hem. She leaned against John Hawkins. "That you did, honey girl. You shore did grow up."

"And . . . " the next words emerged in a blurted rush. "I'm not ugly!" Doubt clouded her vision. "I'm not—am I?"

"Good God, no. You're definitely not ugly!" Smiling, Bowie stepped forward and offered his arm. "If Lodisha will fetch your fan and parasol, I'd be proud to escort the most beautiful woman in Gulliver County to the dance. That would be you, Mrs. Stone."

"I have a fan and a parasol?" After years of avoiding mirrors, Rosie now seemed loath to release his shaving mirror. She tilted the glass to inspect her hair and then the blue shell earrings. "Oh Bowie," she whispered, lifting shining eyes. "I can't believe this. I look . . . I look . . . "

"Beautiful," he supplied softly, wrapping her hand around his arm. "You look absolutely beautiful!"

"Suddenly—oh God—I feel beautiful!" she said in a wondering voice, as if she were confessing to something both thrilling and frightening. "John Hawkins! Are you crying?"

"I have a speck in my eye, that's all!"

"I's cryin' enough for both of us," Lodisha said happily, dabbing her eyes with her apron hem. "Now off you go, and have yorselfs a wonder of a time! I don' 'spect to see you home 'til sunup."

Bowie led Rosie outside and handed her up onto the seat of the buckboard. She looked dazed and moved like a sleepwalker. He climbed up and settled his hat on his head while Rosie pulled on white lace gloves then opened her parasol above a spring bonnet.

"Are you all right?" he asked when they had traveled half a mile without speaking.

"I thought I was looking at my mama," she said finally, speaking in a choked voice. She turned her face toward the waves of pale green rippling over the prairie. "Mama was a vain, silly woman, Stone. I don't think she liked me much. But I loved her. She was so pretty, and she always smelled good."

"I'm sure she loved you too." Bowie took her hand.

"No." She was rigid on the seat beside him. "She might have loved me if I'd been a boy."

Bowie clenched his teeth and flicked the reins across Ivanhoe's back. There had been too many destructive forces in Rosie Mulvehey's life. Glimpsing her today, as the young woman she might have been, made him gnash his teeth and seethe inside over the injustices that had been done to her. If hell existed, then he fervently hoped Sadie Mulvehey and Frank Blevins were roasting there.

When they drew up among the crush of wagons in front of the hall, the light had faded to purple shadows. Rosie suddenly gripped his arm with icy fingers.

"I'm scared," she whispered. Panic flared in her clear brown eyes. "I can't do this without a drink." Licking her lips, she darted a glance down Main toward Harold's place. "A person feels things too much without the blazer, you know?"

He turned to her and tilted her face up to his. "Listen to me, Rosie. All you have to do is walk in there and enjoy yourself. You do harder things every day of your life."

"No, I don't," she said simply, anguish in her eyes. "Please, Bowie. If you care for me even a little bit, then turn around and take me home! I'm begging you. I can't go in there looking like this. They'll—"

He gave her a shake. "You're going to this dance if I

have to throw you over my shoulder and carry you inside kicking and screaming. Now listen. You're the bravest woman I know. Do you really care what those people think?" He waved toward the hall.

It was unfair to use her pride against her, but they had come this far and he was willing to do whatever was necessary to get her inside. Once Rosie walked into that hall looking as beautiful as she did now, Evaline Buckner and others like her would never again dismiss Rosie Mulvehey with a smirk of disdain.

"Rosie? You've always said you didn't care what people thought. Did you mean it?"

"Drat! Damnation! Joe's holy beans!" She bit her lip, and he felt her trembling.

This was a Rosie Mulvehey Bowie had never seen. Suddenly shy, blushing, frightened and uncertain. She was all woman and mystery, vulnerable yet powerful in her beauty.

"No," she said in a low voice. "I'm not going to this stupid dance. I'm not going to exhibit myself like a—"

When she reached for the reins, their hands collided. The sudden touch of her electrified Bowie, caused an instinctive and immediate response. Catching her arms above the elbows, he pulled her into his arms and his mouth came down on hers hard, hungrily. He could no more have stopped himself than he could have changed the fate that had thrown them together. He needed to taste her mouth under his, needed to feel her body against his chest. There was nothing gentle in his kiss. He forgot her history and his own. He kissed her as a man powerfully drawn to a beautiful and desirable woman.

When he released her soft mouth, the heat in his groin scalded him. Right now he wanted this woman as he had wanted no other woman in his life.

"I'm sorry," he murmured hoarsely. "I took advantage."

But she wasn't fighting him. She remained frozen in place,

leaning toward him and staring at his mouth with wide round eyes. Her lips trembled.

"I'm so confused," she whispered. "I never thought I'd ever want a man to kiss me. But I like it when you kiss me. It makes me feel strange and hot inside, but a good kind of strange. And it makes me think of . . . other things. Other things that used to . . . that I never thought I'd . . . "

With her hair pulled back from her face, she looked so open and vulnerable, so puzzled and anxious and achingly lovely. Bowie glanced at her moist parted lips, then clenched his jaw. He made himself pat her hands in a reassuring gesture before he jumped to the ground.

After taking a moment to cool his thoughts, he helped her down from the wagon, catching a glimpse of slender ankle, inhaling her light fragrance and the womanly scent underneath.

Wrapping her hand around his arm, he pressed her close to him as they walked through the twilight toward the sound of fiddles floating from the door to the hall. He heard her draw in a sharp deep breath and felt the tremble that shook her body.

When she straightened her shoulders and walked through the door, Bowie understood he was witnessing an act of courage as great as that required to plow seven acres with bleeding hands.

Chapter Eleven

It wasn't until Rosie had stowed away her parasol and bonnet that she heard the first gasp of recognition.

"Oh my stars! I don't believe it. *That's* Rosie Mulvehey!"

"By God, it is! Look, that's *Rosie!*"

Whispers and nudges swept the hall like a firestorm, confirming Rosie's worst fears. Her face flamed and she shook so badly that she couldn't move. The fiddlers scraped to a halt in mid-reel. Dancers faltered on the floor. In dumbstruck silence, everyone present froze like statues and stared at her. Rosie tried to spin and flee, but Bowie clasped her arm in a viselike grip, forcing her to face the gaping crowd.

"Evening, folks," Bowie said in a pleasant voice. His blue eyes pierced the faces nearest him, daring anyone to snicker.

Minnie Paulson, the preacher's wife, was first to recover her manners. She stepped forward, speaking into the silence.

"Rosie?" Flustered, she glanced at Bowie, then made a birdlike movement with her hands. "I mean Mrs. Stone. It is you, isn't it?" She stared into Rosie's face as if not quite certain. "You look lovely," she said softly. Gently, she dislodged Bowie's grip and wrapped Rosie's arm around her own. It was impossible that she didn't feel the tremor shaking Rosie's body. "Come join the ladies for a cup of lemonade."

Rosie cast Bowie an imploring look. "I don't think—"

"Don't be afraid, dear," Minnie Paulson said in a low voice, patting her hand. "Passion's Crossing has waited years for this moment." She too looked at Bowie, sending him a warm smile of gratitude. "I don't believe any of us guessed you would be a beauty. What a wonderful surprise you are."

Following Minnie Paulson's lead, the respectable ladies of Passion's Crossing rallied to the occasion and surrounded Rosie with a barrage of encouraging compliments. Rosie found herself the center of attention in a way that had never happened to her before. In her entire life she had never received as many flattering comments as she did in the next ten minutes.

So began the most magical evening in Rosie Mulvehey's life.

When the fiddlers resumed, Shotshi Morris and Lem Sorrenson materialized before her, begging for the first dance.

"Son of a bitch, Ros—Mrs. Stone! You plum look like an angel! I had no idea!" Shotshi appeared so thunderstruck that Rosie laughed. "You got bosoms! And a little tiny waist!"

Lem seemed equally as dazzled. "Damn, but I never seen a more beautiful woman, and that's the God's honest truth. I can't believe my eyeballs! You been hiding your light under a bushel for years and years! Woman, a little soap, a curling iron, and a dress does amazing things for you!"

While they vied to outdo one another with compliments, the widow James's boy, Billy, bowed before Rosie, then spun her onto the dance floor. He held her like she was made of fine china and might break apart in his hands. He couldn't take his eyes off her.

Rosie stumbled once or twice, not accustomed to dancing the female part, then she got the hang of it. Gradually she steadied, amazed and thrilled to discover every man at the dance wanted to claim her for the next set. And through all the fuss, she was aware that Bowie stood against the wall, grinning and watching her. After a few minutes she no longer needed his nods of encouragement, but she couldn't help sneaking peeks at him anyway. Just to see if he was watching.

When Bowie cut in on Lem Sorrenson, Rosie leaned breathlessly into his arms, her eyes shining like starry beacons.

"They all want to dance with *me*! I never dreamed a dance could be so much fun!" she whispered, trembling in his arms. Excitement and pleasure blazed on her cheeks and throat.

He grinned down at her, watching her curls and ribbons flying around her flushed cheeks. "You're the belle of the ball."

"Oh Bowie, I really am!" A laugh of sheer happiness made her vibrate in his arms. "It's a miracle!" When he spun her around, she laughed like a young girl, giddy with her success. "This is the most wonderful night of my entire life! I owe it all to you."

"There isn't a man here who doesn't envy me," he said truthfully, gazing down at her. A light dew of perspiration made her face shine. Her lips were moist, curved in an excited breathless smile. She blazed and sparkled like an exploding star.

"You're the best dancer," she confided the next time he claimed a dance, leaning her rosy mouth close to his ear. For an instant their breath mingled and Rosie missed a step. A violent blush rose on her cheeks and she trembled like an autumn leaf.

Bowie's arms tightened around her. Fascinated by her beauty and by her joy, he gazed into her eyes, unable to look away from her. She was radiant tonight, incandescent. Wonder glistened in her expression; she was as much of an amazement to herself as she was to everyone else. He could feel her resonating in his arms.

"Every third dance is mine, Mrs. Stone," he reminded her in a husky voice. "In the meantime, don't break too many hearts. I don't want to have to fight my way out of here."

Rosie tossed her curls and laughed with delight. She looked at him as if she were seeing him for the first time, almost flirtatiously. Tonight they were different people. He was tall and handsome and powerful in his self-assurance, proud of her; she was small and feminine and enchanting as she awakened into a new and surprising self.

"Thank you for tonight," she said softly. Tears of gratitude glistened in her wonderful clear eyes as she lifted her head to meet his steady admiration. She looked at his mouth and blushed.

Gazing into each other's eyes, Rosie and Bowie waltzed around the hall, oblivious to anything but each other. Sixty people smiled from the sidelines as Rosie Mulvehey fell in love with her husband.

Bowie glared at Deputy Sands when the man cut in on him, but, since Sheriff Gaine was watching, he decided not to make a scene. The hostility between Bowie and Sands was thick enough to slice, but neither man wished to disrupt the first social of the summer. Reluctantly Bowie surrendered Rosie and grinned as she turned her back on Sands, cutting him dead, and pulled Shotshi onto the floor. Embarrassed, Sands flushed bright red, then cut in on another couple.

As Bowie moved off the floor, he noticed a row of hopeful

female faces watching him expectantly, but there was no woman he wished to dance with except his wife. Compared to Rosie, the women of Gulliver County paled to dim shadows.

He leaned against the door jamb, not taking his gaze from her flushed smiling face as one man after another whirled her across the floor. Pride and pleasure expanded his chest.

Rosie Mulvehey was experiencing the first real triumph of her life. She would not have believed him if he had told her, but her success would have been equally as sweeping in Washington, D.C. or anywhere. Sober and properly gowned, she possessed a beauty so unique and vivid that she easily eclipsed other women. And tonight, dazzled by her success, she blazed like a column of flame, drawing every eye. The evening belonged to her alone.

When he saw that she had been claimed for a Virginia reel, Bowie ducked outside for a breath of cool air and a nip from the barrel of hard cider set out by the old cottonwood. Fingers of lightning probed the prairie along the horizon.

"Mr. Stone!" Evaline Buckner followed him out to the side porch. She was a pretty thing in a pallid sort of way, dressed in yellow calico with an amber sash. "Aren't you dancing?"

He inclined his head but politely declined her thinly disguised invitation. "Not at the moment, Miss Buckner. And then only with my wife." He met her eyes. " I believe Mrs. Smiley is available." Mrs. Smiley wore a blue armband to designate her as a male partner.

Blushing furiously, Miss Buckner spun on the heels of her slippers and darted back inside the hall. Bowie took a tin cup from the back of Cord Blute's wagon and helped himself to a splash of cider.

The air was thick and heavy tonight. Lightning opened the sky at increasing intervals, and thunder rumbled in the distance. It amused him that he had become enough of a farmer to hope the lightning augured rain.

A man wearing red suspenders over a boiled shirt eyed Bowie, then ambled forward to stand beside him in the pool of light falling from the door to the hall. They could hear the music from inside and the thumping of heels against the puncheon floor.

"The name's Clive Russell. When I ain't killing myself trying to get a crop out of the cursed ground, I'm the clerk over at the courthouse."

"Pleased to make your acquaintance, Mr. Russell. I'm Bowie Stone."

"I know who you are. I been getting inquiries about you."

Bowie's head snapped up, and he focused hard on Clive Russell. "What kind of inquiries?"

"From a lawyer fella back east, name of Dubage. Wants your death certificate and wants your body."

Bowie tilted his head and swallowed the cider, watching lightning dart across the prairie sky. Alexander Dubage was Senator Stone's attorney. Dubage would be trying to settle Bowie's estate.

"Have you informed Dubage that I'm alive?"

"Told him your sentence was satisfied. Since then I been throwing away his inquiries. Figure it ain't my problem." Clive Russell shrugged. "This Dubage fella is starting to sound right peevish. Might be something you want to take care of." Russell rocked back on his heels and studied the sky. "If you've a mind to."

Bowie watched Rosie flash past the doorway inside the hall, her face shining with excitement and pleasure.

"If you receive further inquiries, I'd be obliged if you'd throw them away too."

"Gotta say one thing, Stone." Clive Russell hooked a thumb inside his suspenders. "Heard you got Rosie's crop in. Folks around here don't always treat Rosie right. She's different. But she's one of ours, and she ain't had an easy time of it.

Folks in this town are glad she's got herself a husband and some help out at her place. Some folks say it's good you didn't hang."

After Clive Russell drifted away, Bowie checked on Ivanhoe, then returned his thoughts to Alexander Dubage's efforts to close his estate. Had there been any possibility whatsoever that Susan and Nate suffered financial want, he would have telegraphed Dubage at once. He wouldn't have had a choice. But their well-being was not an issue, thank God. Susan didn't need the money from his estate. His father would take care of her and Nate.

Scrubbing a hand over his face, he turned a frown toward the streaks of lightning unzipping the warm night sky.

At Nate's age, children grew rapidly, changing every day. Bowie doubted he would recognize the boy when he saw him again. And Susan . . . he could no longer picture her. They had been married for only a short while before he was posted out west. He had returned to Washington only once between then and now. It had seemed better that way, easier on them both.

Moving closer to the door of the hall, he watched two men arguing over who would have the next dance with Rosie, while Rosie peeked at them over the top of her fan. An unconscious smile curved his mouth, then faded.

He'd created a hell of a mess by marrying her. In the beginning the situation hadn't seemed so unmanageable. He intended to repay her by remaining through harvest, then he'd return to Washington and resume his obligations there.

He had never intended to fall in love with Rosie Mulvehey. Hell, in the beginning he would have sworn that it was impossible for any man to fall in love with Rosie Mulvehey.

The thought constricted his chest and a frown shut his expression. *Christ*. He didn't need the complication of loving Rosie, didn't want it. But he looked at her and he wanted her.

He wanted to protect her, wanted to tear apart the bars of the cage she had built around herself. Sometimes he saw her smiling at him, and he wished he were more than a shell of a man, wished he could give her more than he could.

Swearing, he kicked the wheel on the buckboard. It would have been better for everyone concerned if Rosie had let him hang.

The evening was magical, a shimmering dream that Rosie wanted never to end. This was what her life might have been like if her mother had never married Frank Blevins and brought Blevins' poison into their lives. Maybe this was what it could be like from now on. Such thoughts amazed her.

The true enchantment was Bowie Stone and what he had done for her. It was Bowie who had bought the dress and the slippers and the flying petticoats that made her feel so feminine and pretty. It was Bowie who had tied her in bed to make sure she was sober to enjoy her triumph. It was Bowie who had brought the mirror to the farm and made her look at herself for the first time in years, made her see that just maybe she was not ugly as she had believed she was.

Since arriving in her life, Bowie Stone had taken a chisel to everything Rosie thought she was and thought she believed. He was shaping her into something new and sometimes exhilarating. He was changing her life.

And tonight, flushed with the excitement of her triumph as a woman, she loved him for it.

Every dance was a pleasure, but the dances with Bowie were the moments her heart yearned toward. She felt him watching while she danced with other men, and she laughed and tossed her curls for his benefit, and prayed that he thought she was pretty and that he felt just a little jealous. To know that he hadn't danced a single dance with anyone but her made her heart pound.

And when Bowie took her in his arms and the music began, she felt as if Lodisha had laced her corset two sizes too small. She couldn't breathe, couldn't speak. A strange heat flowed through her limbs, and her skin tingled where he touched her.

All she could do was respond helplessly to the thrill that shot from her scalp to her toes when his strong arms claimed her. And when she remembered the kiss he'd given her on the seat of the buckboard, her knees turned to liquid and her pulse ran amok. Strange thoughts disturbed her mind.

Since his first kiss, Rosie had begun to secretly wonder about how his body would feel up against hers. What confused and appalled her was the realization that the idea didn't terrify and disgust her as much as it once had. Thinking about physical intimacy still frightened her, but not to the extent that it had before. Before Bowie had kissed her.

Rosie recognized that she was undergoing profound changes, and it mystified her as to why that should be so. She didn't understand how her long-held beliefs could suddenly start to crumble.

How could she have been ugly yesterday and be pretty tonight? How was it possible that she had danced for hours without craving a sip from the barrel of hard cider out by the cottonwood tree? How could she find such joy in a silly constricting corset and a pair of dancing slippers?

Most stunning of all, how was it remotely possible for her mind to circle around the idea of letting Bowie into her bed—an act she had sworn never to allow another man so long as she lived?

Yet tonight as she floated in Bowie's arms, she couldn't help remembering his naked body in the tub and she felt a feverish heat rise inside her. Instead of disgusting her, her memory and speculation about Bowie ignited a slow flame in the pit of her stomach, and her breath quickened.

"Thank you," she murmured to Reverend Paulson, who requested the next dance. "But I need to catch my breath."

She needed a moment to sort through the strange heated confusion that whirled her mind in a frightening direction. Lifting her skirts, Rosie slipped past the refreshment table and moved toward the door leading to the ladies' porch. Outside a flash of lightning lit the sky and pulsed, then the night went black again.

She blinked, pausing in the doorway to let the glare of lightning fade from her vision.

"She's a disgrace! An embarrassment, that's what she is!" Evaline Buckner's furious hiss came from the chairs bunched to the right of the door.

"My, my," someone commented. "Do we sound a bit jealous?"

"Jealous? Of that drunken cow? Don't make me laugh! Mark my words. You can't make a silk purse out of a sow's ear! Tomorrow Rosie Stone will be falling down drunk again, as filthy and disgusting as she ever was. Does she really think a few ribbons and a new dress are going to fool anyone? What a joke! She's still a no-account, just making a fool of herself, that's all!"

Rosie gasped and a hand flew to her pounding heart.

"Who does she think she is, anyway?" Evaline's voice lashed through the darkness. "The only reason we invited her was because we needed extra men and she agreed to come as a man! Why else would anyone want her at a party? Then what does she do? She comes dressed and painted up like one of Maud's whores! And takes all the men for herself!"

"I've only had two dances all evening," a sour voice agreed.

"They're only dancing with her out of pity. Having a little fun with her, but she's too stupid to know it. She thinks she's the belle of the ball, but she isn't and never will be! She's trash. And her husband's no better!"

Rosie reeled backward a step, the color draining from her face. Humiliation iced her veins.

Oh my God. She covered her face with her hands. They were all laughing at her. Everyone shared the joke. They had watched her flirting and laughing and behaving as if she were the grande dame of the evening; and all the while they were snickering behind their hands, ridiculing her for the fool that she was.

"Shut up, Evaline! She's standing in the doorway!"

"I don't care if she hears. She was supposed to come as a male, and she didn't! She should be ashamed of herself, rigging herself up like that and ruining everything for the rest of us."

Bleeding inside, dying, Rosie raised her skirts and ran pell mell off the side porch into the darkness. Lightning opened the sky as she dashed through the wagons parked in front of the hall. She saw Bowie's startled face and heard him call her name, but she didn't stop.

Blinded by tears and mortification, Rosie ran down the road into the blackness. One of her slippers flew off and she left it behind. Swearing, she yanked the stupid ribbons from her hair and flung them into the rising wind. She would have thrown away the dress and corset too if she could have managed it.

When a stitch opened in her side, she stopped running. Pressing a hand to her ribs, she staggered from one side of the dark road to the other, swearing and weeping with humiliation. When she thought how she had actually believed she was pretty and having a success, she wanted to die of embarrassment. All the time they were laughing at her.

God, she wanted a drink! She would have sold her soul for a jug of blazer, for even a cup! She wanted to get so drunk that she couldn't feel the pain, so drunk that she didn't give a damn what anyone thought, didn't care that she had made herself a foolish object of scorn and ridicule.

As the first fat raindrops tumbled out of the blackness, she heard the sound of hoofbeats pounding up the road behind her.

"Rosie!"

Damn the prairie. There was no place to hide. Crumpling in despair, she sank to her knees at the side of the road, slapping at a billow of calico as she dashed humiliated tears from her eyes. She wanted to curl on her side and die rather than face Bowie.

Ivanhoe loomed out of the quickening raindrops, skidding to a halt as Bowie jumped off his bare back. Bowie ran to her and pulled her to her feet, throwing his arms around her.

"Clive Russell's wife told me what happened. Rosie, look at me." His fingers grasped her chin, forcing her face up to his. Raindrops pelted her cheeks. "Evaline Buckner is a petty, jealous, small-minded bitch! Nothing she said was true. No one was laughing at you. No one danced with you out of pity. Do you hear me, Rosie? You were beautiful and wonderful tonight. You captivated everyone!"

She swayed in his arms, feeling sick inside. "I just want to go home. Please, Bowie. We'll get the wagon tomorrow."

"It's raining hard."

"I don't care. Please take me home. I can't go back there."

He mounted Ivanhoe, then swung her up in front of him. "Goddamn Evaline Buckner!" Cradling her with his body, he dug his heels into Ivanhoe's flanks.

Rosie wrapped her arms around his neck and leaned against the solid warmth of his chest, closing her eyes. This was real, she told herself. The cold rain and Bowie's strong arms around her. The dance had been an illusion, not what she had believed. The magic had eroded, like an apple devoured by a worm.

By the time Bowie slid from Ivanhoe's back to open the barn doors, they were both drenched and shivering. The calico dress hung like a lead sheet from Rosie's hips. Her curls were gone and her hair dripped down her back in wet strands. Bowie's shirt lay plastered against his skin.

Bowie led Ivanhoe into his stall, then lifted his arms for Rosie. Limp as a piece of straw, she slid off of Ivanhoe's back and into Bowie's arms, pressing her forehead against his chest.

"I made a fool of myself," she whispered. "They said I looked like one of Maud's whores."

"The hell you did! You were beautiful!" His hands framed her wet face and his blue eyes blazed down at her. "Don't let one jealous bitch ruin your triumph! And Rosie, it was a triumph! You were magnificent!"

Frustrated by the inadequacy of words, he kissed her then, his mouth hot on her rain-chilled lips, his hands warm on her wet back and waist.

When his mouth covered hers, suddenly, miraculously, it didn't matter what Evaline Buckner thought, or the people of Gulliver County. What mattered narrowed to Bowie Stone and this minute, to the strange wild heat racing through her body and the hard thighs and strong arms of this man. This wonderful giant of a man who was changing her in ways she didn't understand, ways that thrilled and frightened and excited and appalled.

When Bowie slowly released her lips and drew back to look at her in the rain-washed dimness of the barn, a nervous thrill shot through Rosie's body. Her mouth dried and she trembled violently. Something unique and profound flashed in their locked gaze. When he lightly touched his fingertips to her throat, Rosie closed her eyes and a low moan issued from her lips. She swayed on her feet.

Then she did the unthinkable. She raised his hand to her lips and kissed his palm, trying to express her gratitude for his loyalty. But it was more than that. A powerful and restless heat pulsed through her, demanding expression.

"Rosie." Bowie groaned, then folded her into his arms and covered her face and temples and eyelids with kisses. Shaking like an aspen leaf, she stood within his embrace and felt the strange heat rise like sap inside her, felt her blood turn molten, heard the pulsebeat hammering in her ears. "You're cold," he said in a hoarse voice. "You're shivering."

"I know what you want," she whispered, shaking. She could feel his erection through the layers of soaked petticoats. "I want to, but I'm afraid," she whispered, holding on to him in case her knees collapsed. He made a low pained sound and crushed her against his body. Feeling his desire frightened her and excited her at the same time. She had never felt as confused.

"Do you trust me?" He spoke against her lips, kissing her. His mouth moved over her face, kissing cheekbones, temples, then her lips again. The warmth of his probing tongue made her feel faint. Wave after wave of sensation broke across the walls of her resistance and she felt herself sinking in a tide of conflicting emotions.

"Yes."

Her last small defense crumbled and flowed away. She did trust him. Bowie had never lied to her, had never broken his word, had never injured her. For the first time in Rosie's life, she looked into a man's eyes and surrendered her trust. She felt vulnerable and exhilarated, raw and vibrantly alive. She was frightened and shaking all over.

"Then trust that I won't hurt you," he said in a low, thick voice. Taking her by the hand, Bowie led her to the hay loft and followed her up a wooden ladder into the warmth near the roof. He threw a blanket over a pile of straw, then drew her to him.

"Relax," he whispered against her lips, running his hands up her arms, then down the curve of her back, bending her into his body. She felt his fingers opening the hooks that ran down the back of her bodice and she stiffened in his arms, clutching handfuls of his wet shirt.

"I'll stop if you tell me to," Bowie promised hoarsely. His palms cupped her buttocks and pulled her close to him as he kissed her, slowly, deeply, deliberately, until she moaned and began to relax in his arms and return his kisses, shyly at first, then with growing heat and hunger.

Hands gentle and slow, he removed her wet gown and petticoats, then turned her toward a shimmer of lighting to look at her in her corset and drawers.

"You are so beautiful, Rosie," he breathed. "A perfect hourglass figure. Lush and lovely."

Holding her gaze, he opened his shirt, then slid her hands inside, pressing her palms against his damp taut skin. Rosie gasped and swayed. His skin was warm and firm. She could feel the pounding beat of his heart against her palm, could feel the crisp mat of hair curling over his broad chest.

Guiding her down on the straw beside him, he jerked off his boots and tossed them aside. Then he opened his denims, paused to look at her, and pushed them down his long legs and away.

Rosie stared at his erection, full and hard, then gasped and tensed to run away. Part of her screamed that she didn't want this. Part of her wanted to strike out, to incapacitate him and then flee. But this was Bowie. He wasn't brutal or demanding. He was slow, deliberate, gentle with her and patient. And, God help her, part of her wanted to lie in his arms and know him. Part of her needed to know if a man's poking could be more than pain and humiliation.

Weak with indecision, shaking with apprehension and fear, she dropped back on the straw, covered her face, and curled away from him. She couldn't do this. She wanted him, but she . . .

Bowie spooned himself around the curve of her body, moving her hair aside to kiss the nape of her neck, her shoulders. His warm breath flowed over her skin, following his fingertips. Gently he traced the curve of her shoulder to waist to hip, his fingertips delicate on her skin, and warm.

Infinitely patient, he stroked her trembling body while Rosie ground her teeth and battled an instinct to run. She gasped when she felt his fingers at her laces. After a moment the French corset came free.

Face flaming, she swiftly raised her hands to cover her breasts. And she listened to the rain hammering against the roof of the barn, as loud in her ears as her own heartbeat.

"I can't," she whispered, wondering how much of her he could see in the liquid flashes of lightning. "I'm afraid."

"Shhh." Turning her in his arms, he clasped her nakedness against his bare chest and Rosie sucked in a sharp breath as skin ignited against warm skin. Kisses brushed across her forehead, her eyebrows, her nose, the corner of her lips, while his hands moved over her back, warming her, molding her. His erection throbbed between them, a thick hot weight against her belly.

Tensing, she clenched her fists and squeezed her eyes shut, expecting him to thrust into her. But he didn't.

"Lie back," he murmured against her throat, gently pressing her against the straw. To Rosie's amazement, he continued stroking her, caressing her. His hands slid up from her waist and cupped the weight of her breasts. He teased his thumbs across and around her straining nipples until she couldn't restrain a cry of surprise and pleasure.

This was new and strange and wildly exciting, unlike anything Rosie had experienced before. Blevins had ripped off her pants and rammed into her, tearing against dry resistance. Occasionally he had mauled her breasts through her shirt, his ruthless grip making her cry out in pain.

She'd had no idea, not an inkling, that a man's touch could be gentle, or could arouse this wild restless wanting, this strange hot emptiness that boiled to the surface of her skin and followed his touch. Moaning and twisting on the straw, she arched to him, wanting something, but not knowing what it was until his mouth closed over one nipple and she felt him gently suck her, rolling his tongue across her nipple until it rose hard and quivering.

"Oh, my God," she whispered, panting. Twisting her fingers in his hair, she moved his head to her other breast and felt the thrill of his lips on her skin shoot through her like a flaming arrow. Felt his hand slide to the waist of her drawers, then slip within. His fingers on the soft skin of her lower body made her gasp and twitch.

Something like a sob constricted her chest as his hand slid between her legs and cupped her, not moving, just letting her feel the pressure and the heat. Then, to her amazement, her hips arched and she pressed up against the mystery and strength of his hand, embarrassed when she realized she was wet against his fingers. But not too embarrassed to frantically push down her drawers and kick them away.

Bowie lifted above her. "You are so beautiful!"

"You can do it," she whispered, quickly before she changed her mind. "You can poke me now."

Smiling, he kissed her quivering mouth. "Not yet."

Then he was kissing her until she burned with longing from his deep scalding kisses, until she could not restrain herself and found her arms wrapping around his neck, found herself returning passionate kiss for passionate kiss, frenzied touch for frenzied touch.

He moved down her naked body, kissing her breasts, teasing her with his tongue, kissing her waist, her hip bone. Then his fingers began to trace up and down along the inside of her thighs, drawing recklessly near her center before teasing away and leaving her gasping.

Then, stunningly, shockingly, his mouth followed where his fingers had been and she screamed and tried to wriggle away, but Bowie cupped her buttocks and held her tightly while he explored her center with his lips and tongue.

The world shattered and flew out of her consciousness. Rosie no longer heard the rain pounding the barn roof or the sound of the livestock shifting in the stalls below them. Her universe contracted to sheer sensation, to moist dark heat and shudders of tension and ecstasy. Wave after wave of hot pleasure rocked through her body. She thrashed and arched and moaned mindlessly as Bowie stroked her and teased her and awakened her body to the explosive miracle of satisfaction.

"Oh, my God," she murmured again, drowsily, as he moved up her shaking body, kissing her, licking droplets of perspiration from between her breasts. "Bowie, something happened to me. I . . ."

But he covered her lips with his mouth, letting her taste the liquid heat of herself. And when his erection stirred against her belly, hard and insistent, she felt herself shamelessly aroused again, suddenly needing the fullness of him inside her.

"Yes," she moaned against his throat. "Yes, yes, yes!"

She opened to him, wrapping her legs around his perspiring torso, and when he guided himself into her, she cried out with the miraculous pleasure of feeling herself close around him and draw him deep inside.

He would have been gentle with her. She saw his effort in the eyes above her. It was Rosie who needed the release of hard thrusting passion, Rosie whose body had flamed violently and passionately to life. Perspiring and moaning, her head thrashing back and forth, she rocked beneath him, meeting thrust with thrust, crying out as her hands frantically flew over his nakedness, pulling him closer, harder, until he shouted her name and his shoulders convulsed and she felt him explode inside her.

Bowie's wet head dropped to her shoulder, and he panted to catch his breath. Finally he dropped to one side of her and guided her into his arms, holding her until they could breathe normally again.

"Are you all right?" he finally managed to ask, his voice deep and concerned against her ear.

Rosie pressed her face against the hair on his chest and inhaled the earthy male scent of him.

"I feel like I've had a ride on a bucking mustang," she whispered, smiling. "I didn't know it could be like that between a man and a woman. I didn't even guess." She closed her eyes, trying to press closer to the warm heat of his skin. "You made me feel . . . wild and crazy inside. Hot and empty and . . . just crazy with wanting you. I never thought that could happen." She swallowed, truth coming hard. "And it was wonderful."

"*You* were wonderful!" he murmured, stroking her. She heard the smile in his sleepy voice. "You tasted like summer apples."

Rosie rested with her head on his chest, listening to the sound of the rain on the roof and to the thump of his steady strong heartbeat.

What had happened was a miracle. Not just that she had submitted, but that she had touched the face of rapture. The realization that she had responded, had returned his passion, awed her. That together their bodies and spirits had soared to splendid heights made her feel like shouting and weeping with joy. What they had created together had been magical, wonderful, thrilling. She was too filled with her discovery to sleep.

An act she had believed to be only ugly, painful, and demeaning, could be exciting, blissful, and fulfilling.

The realization spun her world upside down.

Quietly, careful not to disturb him, Rosie slipped from Bowie's arms. Rising on her elbows, she gazed at his sleeping face and gently touched her fingertips to his cheek. A tear slipped down her face.

"You are the best thing that ever happened to me, Bowie Stone," she whispered. "And that scares me. I'm happy right now and that scares me most of all."

She wrapped her arms around her drawn-up knees and tried to make sense out of everything that had happened to her today. But she couldn't. Confusion overwhelmed logic. And she discovered that happiness could be painful too, because she didn't fully trust something she had experienced so seldom.

There was only one way to cope with the confusion blowing through her thoughts, the same way she always coped with the pain and tough questions. The only way she knew.

After covering Bowie with the blanket, she stole away from him, pulled on her chemise and drawers, and then climbed down the loft ladder. Taking a poncho from a hook on the barn wall, she dropped it over her head, then picked up a shovel and slipped out of the barn door, ducking her head against a chill steady drizzle.

Her bare toes sank into cold mud as she crossed the yard to the grave between the house and the creek. Because the ground was soaked and soft, it required little effort to dig up the jug buried in front of Blevins' headstone.

"You were wrong," she said, speaking to Blevins while she dug. "A man did want me. A wonderful man. And he thinks I'm pretty! I'm winning, you filthy pig! You'll see!"

She carried the jug to the stoop and sat there drinking steadily while she watched the horizon lighten and while she tried to make sense out of a blizzard of emotions.

Eventually, as her mind started to fuzz, Rosie looked down at the jug she held between her legs. It occurred to her that she wasn't going to find any answers in a jug of whiskey. If she was honest with herself, she had to admit that whiskey had never solved any of her problems. In fact, getting fox-faced usually added new problems.

And it didn't require much thought to conclude that whiskey was a poor substitute for what she had just shared with Bowie in the barn. That was real. So real that she still felt warmed by the excitement of his caresses, still radiated with the glowing and unexpected satisfaction of fulfillment. A jug of blazer had never done that for her.

She started to lift the jug to her mouth for another pull, but she hesitated, then lowered it instead. Tonight's revelations were too new and too fragile to permit huge changes, therefore she didn't empty the jug over the edge of the stoop. But she pounded the cork back in place and pushed the jug away from her. Right now, she didn't seek oblivion. She wanted to bask in the memory of what had happened between herself and Bowie.

She had an idea that her life had changed tonight in ways she would be discovering for a long time to come. Oddly, the realization didn't frighten her as she would have thought it might. And that was because of Bowie.

Wrapping her arms around her knees, Rosie sat and watched the rain diminish as the sun pushed aside the clouds and edged above the horizon.

She watched a new day dawn and wonder filled her eyes. Bowie Stone was her husband. Her husband until death parted them. They had a whole lifetime ahead, a lifetime filled with wondrous nights like last night. For the first time in longer than Rosie could remember, she had something to look forward to, something to live for. My God. She was healing. And she owed it all to her husband, Bowie Stone.

She loved him so much that it hurt her inside. For an instant the idea of loving terrified her. But she ground her teeth together and willed her pounding heart to steady. Bowie would not hurt her. They were man and wife and she trusted him.

Tears of hope and happiness glistened in her eyes as she watched the sun rise in the sky.

Chapter Twelve

Owl's Butte, Wyoming

Susan's days were anxious and nerve-racking, but the evening hours were often terrifying. The back of her neck prickled at every coyote's howl; she heard every small unexplained sound within miles of the cabin. Once the sun sank behind the mountain peaks, she became acutely aware of how isolated and alone she was. The town of Owl's Butte, a mile and a half from the cabin, might as well have been in another country.

"Did you hear something?" Tilting her head, she looked up from the alphabet blocks she was helping Nate arrange on the floor. There—she heard it again, a scraping noise just outside her door. Her heart leaped behind her corset stays.

The worst was the necessity that she appear brave for Nate's sake. She, who was the most cowardly person she knew. Standing, Susan grabbed the broom, which was a poor defense but all she had; then she crossed the one-room cabin in four strides, drew a deep breath and flung open the door, praying she wouldn't find a bear on her doorstep or a hungry coyote or a bandit bent on raping and murdering his way across the countryside.

She stumbled over a basket of food that had been placed in front of her door.

Relief sagged through her body, and she experienced a giddy urge to laugh at her fears. Instead, she peered through the evening shadows at a figure striding rapidly toward a horse tied to the post in front of the schoolhouse next door.

"Mr. Harte!"

Pushing the broom inside the cabin, Susan hastily smoothed her apron and tucked a strand of hair into the coil on her neck. At this moment she wished she still possessed the time and patience to curl her hair and do something more than wrap it in an uninteresting bun.

Gresham Harte stopped near the hitching post, and she heard him swear before he turned reluctant steps back in her direction.

"Good evening, Mrs. Stone." He smiled at Nate, who was peeking around her skirts. "Hello there, young fella."

"I suspected it was you who was leaving the food. Thank you," Susan said, bending to lift the food basket. "This isn't necessary, but your generosity is appreciated." More than he knew—or maybe he did. After purchasing school supplies, her funds had sunk to a perilous level, and she wouldn't receive her first salary payment for another eight days.

"I thought you could use a little help getting started," he said, looking uncomfortable. He stepped into the light falling across the porch and pulled his hat from his head, leaving his dark hair tousled.

They looked at each other, then Susan remembered the iron-shaped scorch mark on her sleeve and tucked that arm behind her.

"You didn't have to leave the food on the doorstep," she said. "You could have knocked and said hello."

He fussed with the watch fob that dangled across his waist-coat, a habit Susan had noticed he indulged when he felt uncomfortable. "I didn't want to disturb you."

The basket was heavy. The smell of chicken and ham wafted past the napkins, making her mouth water. If this basket was like the others he had left on her step, there would also be freshly baked bread inside, and maybe a raisin cake, plus a jug of milk for Nate. She assumed Mrs. Alder assembled the baskets for him.

Gratitude relaxed her shoulders. "Nate and I were about to sit down to supper." She drew a breath and glanced toward his horse tied in the dark road. "Will you join us?"

"I don't want to intrude . . ." Gresham let his voice trail, watching Nate, who continued to peek around her skirts.

"I'd be grateful for the company," Susan said truthfully.

"In that case . . . the basket should contain ample provisions for three."

"I'll save the basket for tomorrow. I already made a stew." With annoyance she noticed Gresham Harte's step falter, then continue toward her. Clearly he didn't think she had learned to cook. Well he was in for a surprise.

Stepping from the door, but leaving it open for the sake of propriety, Susan turned inside, trying to see the one-room cabin as Gresham would see it. Thankfully, she had strung sheets across a line, screening off the sagging bed she shared with Nate. She wouldn't have dreamed of inviting a man inside if the bed had been exposed and visible. Her standards had not sunk that low.

The entire cabin was only a smidgeon larger than the bed-room she had enjoyed at Senator Stone's house. There was room for a stove, a broadshelf, and a wooden table. She had two mismatched chairs flanking a scarred side table, and a braid rug to cover the planks. Mrs. Alder had given her white lace curtains for the three windows.

"You've made it very homey," Gresham said solemnly, looking around at the jugs of sage and dried foliage she had placed here and there, at the family pictures she had hung on the walls.

"In my spare time I'm making doilies for the chairs and the side table." Susan closed the lid of Nate's toybox and moved a stack of books from one of the chairs. "Please sit down."

"Is this a portrait of your husband?" he asked, inspecting one of the wall hangings.

"Bowie is in the middle, standing between his brother and his father."

For an instant her eyes lingered on the frame, and she suppressed a sigh. Already she recognized that saving money was going to be more difficult than she had supposed. It would take longer than she had hoped to hire a man to ride to Kansas.

Gresham sat down, balancing his hat on his knees until she remembered to take it and hang it on one of the pegs beside the door. Immediately Nate climbed into his lap.

"Will you read to me?" Nate asked, placing a book in Gresham's hand.

"Maybe later," Gresham said, blinking behind his spectacles.

Embarrassed, Susan plucked Nate from his lap. Her fingertips brushed his waistcoat and she inhaled the pleasant scent of the pomade he wore on his hair. Occasionally she considered how remarkable it was that initially she had not thought he was particularly handsome. Actually Gresham Harte was a very good-looking man.

"It's time to wash for supper," she said to Nate. After dropping a quick kiss on top of his head, she gave him a gentle push toward the wash basin behind the screen, noticing that he had an iron-shaped scorch mark on the back of his shirt. A sigh lifted Susan's bosom. There were days when she despaired of ever mastering household chores.

Gresham cleared his throat and touched his collar. "Well. You seem to be settled in. I imagine this cabin is a far cry from what you're used to."

Feeling self-conscious and trying to hide the scorch mark on her sleeve, Susan went to the stove to check on her biscuits. "People have been very kind. I think everyone in Owl's Butte donated something, either materials or labor to repair the schoolhouse, or the items I needed to set up housekeeping."

"It's small," he commented, looking around.

She met his eyes. "It's better than a crib at Mrs. Hawk's." When he smiled, she blushed and looked away. "It's true that I miss the comforts of my previous life, but, oddly, I like it here," she said slowly, realizing it was true. "Sometimes I'm frightened at night . . . but I'm earning the use of this cabin through my own labor." The wonder of making her way gave her pause and widened her eyes. She had honestly believed she would perish without a man's protection, but it didn't seem to be working out that way. "I didn't know I could provide for myself. That makes this cabin special. It's mine in a way no other home has been. Does that make sense?"

Gresham Harte smiled and glanced toward the splashing noises coming from behind the line of sheets. "I'd say you've caught the pioneer spirit, Mrs. Stone."

Pink bloomed on her cheeks and she laughed, turning to stir her stew. When she noticed the stew was the color of dishwater and smelled a little peculiar, she paused and frowned, wondering if it had been a wise idea to invite Gresham to share her table.

"So. How is teaching working out?" he asked, watching her glare at the stew with a puzzled expression, then turn away to set another place at the table.

"The responsibility terrifies me. I have five girls and two

boys, and I have no idea if I'm teaching them anything. I'm trying, and sometimes it feels exhilarating and wonderful and sometimes it's frustrating and maddening. I sent Mr. Dubage my mother's brooch. I asked him to sell it and use the proceeds to buy any books he can find about teaching and send them to me."

"Who is Mr. Dubage?" Gresham asked, glancing up at the picture of Bowie, Nathan, and Senator Stone.

"Mr. Dubage is the family attorney." Starting, she spun toward wisps of smoke leaking from the oven door. The biscuits she removed were flat, odd-sized, and black on the bottom. She stared at them as Nate ran to the table and pulled out a chair with a scraping noise. Pressing her lips together, Susan pried the biscuits off the pan and pushed them into a basket.

"Mama burned her hands," Nate announced as they sat down at the table. "Show Mr. Harte, mama."

She narrowed her eyes at Nate. "Let me have your bowl," she said, reaching for the ladle in the tureen. One of the biscuits showed beneath the napkin covering the basket. It looked like a blackened lump of charcoal.

"What happened to your hands?" Gresham Harte inquired, studying the angry red blotches that covered the backs of her hands and wrists and disappeared into the cuffs of her sleeves.

"I scalded myself doing the laundry," she said shortly, not looking at him. The pain had left her wet-eyed and breathless. Even smearing peppermint oil on the burns hadn't helped a lot. "It doesn't hurt as much now."

She wished to high heaven that she wasn't wearing the blouse with the iron-shaped scorch mark, wished with all her soul that her biscuits were light and fluffy and golden on the bottom. She loathed parading her inadequacies in front of Gresham Harte, of all people. Her heart sank as she ladled stew into Nate and Gresham's bowls, then into her own. The liquid part was gray and thin. Her stew smelled a bit like the laundry tub.

Nate pushed a spoon into his bowl, but Gresham just stared at his with a stricken expression.

"Biscuit, Mr. Harte?" she asked grimly, extending the basket.

He selected one of the smaller biscuits, hefting it in his hand. The biscuit was charred and heavy, too thin to slice in half. Susan looked away, feeling circles of embarrassment pulse in her cheeks.

"I'm going to school," Nate announced happily, spooning up the stew. "I'm learning my ABC's and I'm learning to count. I'm almost this many." He held up four fingers. "Mama says I can have a party for my birthday. You can come too. What I want most of all is a puppy. Do you have a puppy, Mr. Harte?"

In agony, Susan watched Gresham set aside the biscuit, then push his spoon into the stew. He fished a lump of meat out of the gray liquid.

"I had a puppy when I was your age," he said, inspecting the piece of meat on his spoon. "His name was Othello."

"That's a funny name," Nate said, laughing. "I'm going to name my puppy Wolf. Or maybe Bunny. I don't know yet."

Gresham Harte put the piece of meat into his mouth and chewed. And chewed and chewed. "I wonder," he said after a minute. "Do you have any salt, Mrs. Stone?"

Susan placed the salt dish within his reach. Heat blazed on her cheeks. The stew mortified her. The meat tasted like erasers and was about as tender. The potatoes and turnips had cooked to a mushy consistency. The gray liquid had a gluey texture that was absolutely bland and tasteless.

"I'm sorry there's no wine or dessert," she said tonelessly. Not even Nate tried to eat the black biscuits. They all tactfully ignored the basket and the dish with the pat of butter.

When Gresham had eaten half the contents of his bowl, he pushed back, patted his stomach, and managed a smile. "I'm too full to eat another bite. That was, ah . . . it was . . ."

"Terrible," Susan supplied, meeting his eyes. "The meat was tough and the vegetables were overcooked. The stew was terrible."

"True," he admitted after a minute. Then he smiled. "But the coffee was weak and the biscuits were really awful."

She stared at him, then burst into laughter. "I'm sorry. I keep telling myself I've conquered the art of cooking, but I haven't. You should see the pie I'm hiding from you."

He grinned at her. "Please . . . no pie!"

They smiled at each other across the table, and suddenly Susan liked him very much and was glad he had come. The stew really was awful, there was no point pretending it wasn't. More importantly, he had made her laugh, which she hadn't done in a long time.

"I'm trying so many new things, Mr. Harte, and I'm doing rather badly at all of them." She plucked at the scorch mark on her sleeve, inspected the burns on the backs of her hands. She sighed, then smiled again. "Believe it or not, I'm making progress of a sort."

"I'm sure you are," he said softly. "It takes a lot of courage to try new things, Mrs. Stone, and to keep trying when we don't meet with immediate success."

"You think I'm courageous?" She stared at him with amazement. Never in her life had Susan thought of herself as courageous, not once. Her former friends in Washington would have laughed in disbelief to hear such a description of her.

But the west was shaping her into something new, a woman very different from the woman she had been.

"Yes, I do think you're courageous."

Discovering that Gresham Harte recognized her efforts and attributed them to courage brought sudden tears to her eyes.

She hadn't realized how much she had wanted someone to notice what she was trying to do and how hard it was. Rising abruptly, she cleared the table, taking the bowls and utensils to the broadshelf and standing over them until she could see without tears blurring her vision.

Behind her, she heard Gresham asking Nate about his toys. Then he said, "Come over by the lamp and I'll read to you while your mother does up the dishes."

When Susan turned around, surprised, Nate was curled into Gresham's lap, his head on Gresham's shoulder. Gresham settled his spectacles on his nose, then began to read aloud, pausing so Nate could examine the pictures before he turned the page. He glanced up and met Susan's eyes, smiled, then continued reading.

Susan swallowed hard and turned back to the broadshelf. As she scraped the uneaten stew into the slop bucket and washed the dishes, her heart opened to the domestic scene behind her. It was a scene she had imagined without much hope of seeing it happen.

While she had always trusted Bowie to take care of her and Nate, she hadn't been certain about Bowie's attitudes toward fatherhood. In fact, at the time of their marriage, neither had displayed any leanings toward real domesticity. She now understood that she and Bowie had begun and ended as strangers to one another, seeing only that which lay on the surface.

Pausing with her hands in the dishwater, Susan looked out the window and let her thoughts roam. Sometimes it frightened her to realize that she would never have known her son, really have known Nate, if Bowie hadn't died and left her without a nurse or a maid. It was sad that she knew her son only because her husband had died. But if Bowie had lived, someone else would have taught Nate his ABC's; someone else had always tucked him into his bed at night. Now she was the central figure in her son's life and he in hers, and it was the joy of her existence.

After she finished the dishes, she looked a question at Gresham, but he shook his head and continued reading, Nate snuggled in his arms. Filled with quiet happiness, Susan took the chair beside them and worked on her lesson plans for the next day. Eventually she became aware that Gresham had stopped reading.

"He's asleep," Gresham whispered.

"I'll take him," Susan offered, standing.

"Let me."

Gresham carried Nate behind the line of sheets and placed him carefully on the bed. Moving backward a step, Gresham watched as Susan removed Nate's clothing, then eased a night-shirt over his tousled head. Nate roused briefly to give Susan a kiss, then he smiled sleepily and extended his arms to Gresham. Gresham looked startled, but he leaned over the bed and submitted to a kiss.

Suddenly and acutely conscious that they were standing together beside a bed, Susan and Gresham hastily returned to the lamplight.

"It's a warm evening. Would you care to take a turn outside?" he asked, examining his watch fob.

Nodding, Susan fetched her shawl and they stepped off the porch into the cool darkness. "For a man who dislikes children," she said, sliding him a glance, "you're very good with them."

"I never said I disliked children. I said I wasn't ready to assume responsibility for a child." After a minute he added, "I like Nate very much."

They walked along the path that led from Susan's cabin to the porch of the schoolhouse. Moonlight threw the shadow of the bell steeple out before them. Crickets hummed in the darkness.

"Mrs. Winters dropped by during my first week. She's coming again sometime next week." Susan watched her hem kicking out in front of her boots. "After her next inspection, she'll decide whether or not to offer me a permanent contract."

Gresham rocked back on his heels and studied the one-room schoolhouse. "Since you're planning to stay in Owl's Butte only temporarily, do you really want a permanent contract?"

She looked up at him. "Yes, I do. I suppose pride is a factor ... but it's also crossed my mind that I need to protect myself in case I never receive my inheritance." The possibility made her feel queasy inside.

Gresham frowned. "Surely the estate will be settled eventually."

"Something is very wrong," Susan said finally. "It shouldn't be so difficult to obtain a death certificate." Tilting her head, she gazed up at the bell steeple. "Actually, I'm enjoying teaching. The children have been wonderful." A frown touched her brow. "But I'm going to have trouble with Eddie Mercer."

She explained Eddie's reading problems, then asked how Gresham thought she should handle Eddie's growing frustration.

"I believe we decided you would solve your own problems, Mrs. Stone," he answered gently.

Susan kicked at a loose stone. Once again she had turned to a man to rescue her. Her cheeks burned in the darkness. There was something about Gresham Harte that drew her inadequacies to the surface. On the other hand, she thought with a sigh, at least she had progressed to the point where she understood that looking for a man to solve her problems was indeed in inadequacy.

"I need this teaching position, Mr. Harte. I don't know what will happen to us if I fail. I worry about it day and night.

I want to succeed at teaching more than I have ever wanted anything in my life. I *must* succeed."

"Then you will, Mrs. Stone."

They paused beside Gresham's horse, stroking his neck. When their hands accidentally touched, they both jumped as if suddenly scalded and moved away from each other, placing a good distance between them as they continued walking down the road, looking at the lights of the town in the distance.

"I took the opportunity to learn a little about your husband," Gresham commented as they cut back toward Susan's cabin. "I sent for clippings from the *Rocky Mountain News* and from the *Gulliver County Tattler*."

Susan stopped and turned toward him, feeling a rush of heat in her throat. That Gresham Harte had learned of her husband's disgrace embarrassed her and struck at her pride. "Why would you pry into such matters, Mr. Harte?"

He shrugged and looked down, watching his fingers move across his watch fob. "Curiosity, I guess." He lifted his head. "Your husband was a remarkable man."

Susan stared in surprise. Admiration was the last sentiment she would have expected him to express. "My husband was dishonorably discharged for disobeying a direct order from a ranking officer. Afterward, he murdered a man, Mr. Harte, for which he was hanged."

"In the same circumstances, I too would have disobeyed that order. Your husband shouldn't have been discharged, Mrs. Stone; the officer who issued the order should have been. He's the son of a bitch who should have been court-martialed."

"I beg your pardon?" Susan peered at him through the darkness. "Mr. Harte, what are you talking about?"

He returned her stare. "Is it possible that you don't know what happened at Stone Toes Gulch?"

"All I know is what Senator Stone told me. He said that Bowie threw away his career and dishonored the family."

Taking her arm, Gresham led her to the small porch in front of the cabin. After seating her on the step, he told her the full story of the ambush at Stone Toes, about the slaughter of Indian women and children.

"Oh, my heavens," Susan murmured at the end of the story. She pressed the hem of her shawl against her eyes. "I thought . . ."

Anger shook her frame. The Senator had known exactly what happened at Stone Toes Gulch but he had focused only on the disgrace of a dishonorable discharge, the slur on the family name. The Senator had never admitted that Bowie had acted with conscience and honor.

After a silence, Susan touched Gresham's sleeve, then withdrew her fingertips. "Tell me about the murder."

"Captain Stone did kill Luther Radison," Gresham said quietly. "Radison tracked Captain Stone to Gulliver County, Kansas. He had sworn to kill your husband. In the transcript of the trial, two witnesses swear that Captain Stone surprised Radison and shot him down in cold blood. They swear Radison was unarmed at the time."

Susan hung her head and bit her lip. That was the story she had heard from the Senator.

"The case seems straightforward enough, except . . ."

"Except?"

"The two witnesses were friends of Radison's. Both men were also at Stone Toes, were also tarnished when your husband's court-martial brought out the truth. In addition, Stone had been shot in the thigh." Gresham frowned. "It's possible there was a conspiracy against your husband. There's no way now to know the truth, but I suspect Captain Stone was sentenced to hang for an act of self-defense."

Susan dropped her head and pressed the heels of her palms against her eyes. "I had no idea," she whispered.

"I also agree the matter bears further investigation."
Gresham paused. "Newspaper accounts end with a notation
that Captain Stone's sentence was satisfied. The reports don't
actually state that your husband was hanged."

"Of course Bowie was hanged," Susan said, blinking at
tears. "Otherwise he would have come for Nate and me." She
peered at a point in the darkness. "I just accepted what the
Senator said. I thought Bowie had lost his senses."

Gresham dropped an awkward arm around her shoulders
as she turned into his chest, weeping softly. "You should be
proud of your husband, Mrs. Stone. Captain Stone was an
extraordinary man, a man of honor."

When she became aware that Gresham Harte's lips were
against her hair, Susan blushed and made herself straighten
and move away from him. She drew a deep breath and placed
a hand on her breast, surprised to discover that her heart was
racing and the side of her face tingled where his lips had
brushed.

"Bowie was more extraordinary than you know," she said
after a minute, glad for the darkness that surrounded them.

Then, drawing another deep breath and speaking in a halting
voice, she confided the circumstances of Nate's birth.

Gresham sat on his horse for several minutes, looking through
the darkness at Susan Stone's cabin and thinking about the
evening.

He knew Susan believed her story had shocked him, but it
had not. Surprise was a better description, and that of a mild
form. Few things shocked him, although he'd come close to
shocking himself by his reaction to learning about Captain
Bowie Stone.

He had wanted to dislike Captain Stone, to condemn him
for leaving his wife and son destitute. Instead, he had ended

by admiring Bowie Stone and feeling outraged by the injustice done the man. He also felt a burst of unreasonable jealousy toward Stone when he remembered how Susan's voice softened when she spoke of him.

As far as Gresham knew, no female had ever referred to him as extraordinary. No blue-eyed woman hung his picture on her wall.

She had felt so small and yielding when she turned to him in her distress. He had felt the electrifying softness of her breasts against his chest, and her hair had smelled like lemon and sunshine.

Sighing, he turned his horse toward Owl's Butte and touched his heels to the horse's flank.

Why couldn't he push Susan Stone out of his thoughts once and for all? What was it about her that made him feel responsible for her and drawn to her?

He thought about the burns on her hands and wrists, the scorch marks on her sleeve and on the back of Nate's shirt, about the stew, that remarkably tasteless stew, and the charred biscuits. He thought about her soft brown hair drawn back into a new plain hair style, thought about the tiny cramped cabin she actually seemed proud of. He tried to imagine her exerting authority over a room full of restless children.

Susan Stone fascinated and irritated him. He pitied her plight and admired her for trying to overcome it. He thought she was hopelessly inadequate at everyday tasks but too courageous to concede defeat. She had a capable mind, but wanted a man to do her thinking for her. Her fragility annoyed him no end. He suspected that confronting Henrietta Winters was the first and only act of assertiveness that Susan Stone had ever attempted. She was absolutely the wrong woman for him.

So why couldn't he stop thinking about her and worrying about her? Susan Stone was driving him crazy. She had the bluest eyes he had ever seen, and a soft ripe mouth that begged for kisses. She had a shapely form and a tiny waist. Her hair smelled like sunshine. He even liked her son, young Nate.

"Damn it, anyway!"

Susan stood behind her oak desk, drawing a ruler down the chalk board as Hettie Alder read the paragraph Susan had earlier inscribed there. Except for Eddie Mercer, the mayor's son, the students worked on assignments at their desks. Eddie was frowning out the window, watching a hummingbird that darted in front of the glass. Nate napped on a blanket on the floor near the water pail. Except for Eddie Mercer's wandering attention and dark expression, all was going smoothly.

That was good because Mrs. Winters sat on a stool at the side of the room, observing and judging, her sharp eyes watching everything. She wore a flat straw hat and a severely cut green waist and skirt. Both hands were folded primly atop the handle of a green and yellow parasol.

Susan wet her lips and thanked heaven that she'd worn the white waist without a scorch mark. She hid a nervous tremble by tucking her hands within the folds of her dark skirt. She smiled at Hettie.

"Thank you, Hettie, that was well done. I'd like you to work on your arithmetic problems now. I'll check everyone's slates after Eddie reads." This was the moment she dreaded. "Eddie? Please read your history composition aloud. You may stand by your desk."

Eddie Mercer glanced at Mrs. Winters, then looked back at Susan. A dull red flush climbed his throat.

"No," he said, dropping his head.

"I beg your pardon?" Susan stared at him, her heart skipping a beat. Silently she begged him not to defy her, not now with Mrs. Winters watching.

"I ain't going to read aloud," he mumbled.

Susan swallowed hard and resisted looking to Mrs. Winters

for direction. Instinctively she understood that seeking help would sink her.

"If you could read perfectly, you wouldn't be here," she said gently. "No one expects perfection, but you must try. That is how you learn, through practice."

With a sinking heart she watched the crimson deepen in Eddie's face, and her sympathy went out to him. Eddie Mercer was fourteen, her oldest student, but he read at third-grade level. It was bad enough that the younger students teased him, but to display his incompetence before a visitor would be agony for him. If she could have spared him, she would have. But Mrs. Winters, who missed nothing, would never have made an exception or displayed favoritism for whatever reason.

"Eddie?"

"I ain't going to do it." His fists clenched and his mouth set in a stubborn line. He hunched over his desk with his head down.

An abrupt silence opened around her, and Susan realized that the other children were watching with intense interest. Abandoning their studies, they shifted in their chairs, cutting glances back and forth between Susan and Eddie.

At once she saw with terrible clarity that her future as a teacher depended on the next few minutes. Either she established her authority and credibility or she lost her students' respect, her teaching position, and what little security she had. There would be no cabin, no salary.

"Eddie," she said quietly, her face pale. "I order you to read your composition aloud. Do it now, please."

"No," he whispered, his voice miserable. He didn't look at her.

But Mrs. Winters did, Susan noticed from the corner of her eyes. Mrs. Winters waited with an expressionless face.

Only one arched eyebrow suggested the crucial importance of this moment.

"If you don't do as I've instructed, I'll have to punish you."

She gazed at Eddie with pleading eyes, silently imploring him to comply. He was two inches taller than she was and outweighed her by thirty or forty pounds. If she couldn't make him read, how was she going to force him to submit to punishment? The situation horrified her, spiraling rapidly from bad to worse.

He lifted his head. "Please. Don't make me read aloud."

"I can't make an exception, you know that. Please read your composition." Please, please, she repeated silently, begging him. Don't let this incident escalate; please do as I ask.

Eddie wadded his composition into a ball and dropped it at her feet. When he looked up at her, his gaze was a mixture of misery and defiance.

Time seemed to stop. In the motionless silence, Susan felt tiny beads of perspiration appear on her brow and beneath her arms. She imagined she could hear the accelerated heartbeat of everyone in the room. She felt the weight of watching eyes and expectations.

"Very well," she said quietly. The corners of her lips trembled, and her hand was shaking. The blood had drained from her face and she swayed on her feet, dizzy with the enormity of a necessity she hated. She hoped to heaven that she could see this through.

"Hold out your hands."

Eddie frowned up at her, unsure what she meant.

Frantically, Susan tried to remember what Mrs. Winters had told her that day almost a month ago. She was the adult in the classroom, she was in control. If her students did not respect her authority, then she could teach them nothing. She had to exert herself and manage the situation and she had to do it immediately. The key was to remember that Eddie was accustomed to obeying adults.

"Hold out your hands! Now!"

The anger shaking her voice was deep, despairing, and genuine. She was furious with Eddie Mercer for creating this situation, furious with herself for fearing it. She was furious at Mrs. Winters for remaining calm and removed, for not stepping forward to solve the problem. She was furious at the other children for watching with smirks of curiosity and pleasure, furious that a fourteen-year-old could only read at third-grade level. She was furious at Bowie Stone for dying and furious at Gresham Harte for not marrying her as he should have and sparing her this deeply upsetting experience.

She slapped her ruler down on Eddie's desk. The sharp crack caused everyone to jump, including her.

"Stand up, Eddie, right now, and hold out your hands! Do it!"

Whatever blazed in her eyes and on her expression brought him to his feet. When he thrust out his hands, they were shaking as badly as her own.

Susan drew a deep breath, struggling against an urge to faint; then she, who had never raised an angry hand in her entire life, swung the ruler across the back of Eddie's hands as hard as she could. The cracking sound and the resultant flare of red across his knuckles appalled her.

"For God's sake, Eddie," she whispered between bloodless lips. Her hands shook violently. "Read the damned composition!"

His face was as white as her own. Clouds of freckles rose on his cheeks like dots of brown paint.

"No."

Wincing inside, fighting tears, Susan again cracked the ruler across Eddie's hands. Dimly she was aware that Nate had awakened from his nap and was crying beside the water pail. She was shaking so violently she could hardly stand.

"You've placed us in an impossible situation," she whispered to Eddie, her voice quivering. "Do you want to tell your father that I had to expel you? That's what will happen next. Please, Eddie. You must read the composition."

He blinked at her through watering eyes, then slowly, thank God, he bent and retrieved the wadded composition. With trembling and reddened hands, he smoothed open the page. Then in a mumbling, nearly inaudible voice, he read his composition aloud.

The composition was inaccurate and badly written, riddled with grammatical errors. Susan stood beside him, shaking, and said nothing, uttered no corrections. Silently she vowed to offer Eddie private tutoring.

"Thank you," she said when he finished and sat down, hanging his head. She walked to the front of the room and placed her ruler on her desk, noticing that the edges had bitten into her palm and left deep depressions. Turning, she faced her students, who stared at her with wide, rounded eyes. "We'll dismiss early today," she announced in a choked voice. "Hettie, would you take Nate outside and watch him for a few minutes, please?"

The instant the children filed outside, Susan sank to the chair behind her desk and dropped her head into her hands. She felt as if it were she who had been publicly struck and humiliated. After a moment Mrs. Winters pressed her shoulder.

"The next time—if it's necessary—will be easier. You don't realize it now, but today you became a teacher."

"That was the hardest thing I have ever done." Tilting her head back, Susan stared unseeing at the ceiling. "I've never struck anyone in my life. I've never even spanked my son."

"Spare the rod and spoil the child," Henrietta Winters commented crisply. "You did exactly the right thing. Your students must know that you are in control and must accept your authority. I'm confident you will experience little trouble with young Mr. Mercer in the future." Mrs. Winters consulted the pocket watch that hung from a gold chain at her waist.

"I hope not," Susan said fervently.

"It's painfully obvious that a two-year absence of instruction has seriously retarded your students' abilities," Mrs. Winters continued. "Would you be amenable to continuing classes throughout the summer?"

Susan had not permitted herself to think about the looming summer or about losing her salary and the use of the cabin for three months. She had decided to cross that bridge when she reached it. Now Mrs. Winters was offering a solution that would benefit everyone.

"I agree the children are badly in need of further education." Gradually it dawned on her that she had successfully passed her probation period. Her shoulders lifted in shy pride and she straightened in her chair.

"Excellent," Mrs. Winters said, smiling. "Then I'll expect you to persuade the town council to accept our decision."

Susan blinked and her mouth dropped. "You want *me* to address the town council? And persuade them to keep the school open?" The starch melted out of her posture. Her throat dried. She couldn't conceive of herself giving instructions to the men on the town council. It was unthinkable, beyond her powers of imagining.

"You may expect some resistance," Mrs. Winters cautioned, standing and drawing on her gloves. "Parents will want the children home to assist with summer chores. The council may resist extending your salary for an additional three months. I'm confident you will overcome these objections."

"You are?"

"I'll arrange for you to meet with the council a week from tomorrow." Mrs. Winters reached across the desk and gave Susan's hand a shake. "Good day, Mrs. Stone. I'm quite pleased with how well you've taken to your post."

Susan felt too stunned to rise. She remained seated as Henrietta Winters sailed out the classroom door and across the yard to her gig.

Address the men of the town council. Persuade them to keep the school open during the summer. Dazed, she stared at the dust motes dancing in the air.

She couldn't possibly do it. Just the idea sent her heart pounding against her stays and made her feel light-headed.

Chapter Thirteen

"Hello there! Mrs. Stone?"

"Look Mama, it's Mr. Harte!" Nate streaked across the yard toward the buckboard Gresham was tying in front of the cabin. He chattered at Gresham's side as Gresham walked to the cabin's side yard. "Mama hit Eddie," Nate said, still awed by the event. "Mama didn't want to but she had to. She hit him with a ruler. You should have heard the sound it made. It was awful."

"I heard about the incident."

"You did?" Susan shoved back a lock of hair and rested against the handle of a shovel. Why was it that Gresham always seemed to happen along when she was looking a mess? Today she wore a scorched apron over her oldest dress and a pair of man's boots that she had found in the cabin. Her face was flushed with exertion and long tendrils dripped out of the bun at her neck.

"Your stock has risen, Mrs. Stone. Most of the townspeople

didn't think you had the grit to discipline a student. Frankly, neither did I." He studied the ground she had been hacking at with the shovel. "What are you doing?"

"I'm putting in a kitchen garden," she explained, running a thumb across the calluses rising on her palm. "It's like trying to dig a trench in a slab of marble."

Kneeling, Gresham inspected her packets of seeds. He squinted up at her. "The peas, beans, and squash should go in the ground during a new moon. You can plant the carrots and turnips now. They go in when the moon is waning."

She stared at him. It continually discouraged her to learn that nothing was as simple as it ought to be. "What does the moon have to do with my kitchen garden?"

"The theory is that a rising moon encourages crops grown above ground. A descending moon drives root crops down."

"That is the most ridiculous nonsense I ever heard!" She bit her lip and gazed at the shallow earth she had turned. "That can't be true . . . can it?"

He dropped his hat on Nate's head and smiled. "I'm driving out to my homestead. I thought you and Nate might like to come along. I have a picnic in the wagon."

"Thank you, but—"

"There's a stream filled with fish just waiting to be caught," he added with a wink for Nate. "And I happen to have two fishing poles in the buckboard."

Excitement danced in Nate's eyes as he caught her hand. "I've never been fishing! We can go, can't we, Mama? Say we can!"

Susan sighed. "This garden isn't going to plant itself, Mr. Harte. I need the food it will provide." Nate's face fell.

"I'll come by tomorrow and finish the spading for you."

She touched her calluses again, noticing one had swelled into a blister.

Nate pulled on her skirt. "Please, Mama?"

"Please, Mrs. Stone?" Gresham echoed, smiling.

Laughing, Susan threw up her hands. "It seems I'm outnumbered. You won't forget your promise?"

Gresham placed his hand over his heart. "You have my word, ma'am." He grinned at Nate, who beamed at him.

"Give me a few minutes to change my dress and find my hat. If you feel inclined, you could begin spading now." She pushed the shovel toward him and a blush warmed her cheeks as their fingers brushed. A tingle shot down to her toes and for a moment Susan felt paralyzed. They gazed into each other's eyes, then she turned, stumbled, and hurried inside the cabin.

When she returned, Gresham had tossed his jacket aside, rolled up his sleeves, and had spaded nearly half the ground she had marked out. Susan focused on the muscles swelling his arms and a sigh lifted the lace trimming her blouse. Men made things look so easy.

"I have a cake in the house," she said, letting the suggestion trail.

"I have everything we need," Gresham said hastily, smiling.

The center of her cake had sunk like a crater and the icing remained sticky, refusing to set. Susan was relieved she wouldn't have to show him the awful thing. More than anything, she wanted Gresham Harte to think well of her.

Gresham handed her up onto the seat of the buckboard, and they settled Nate between them. The day was clear and fine, warm but not too hot. Opening her parasol, Susan decided an outing was exactly what she and Nate needed. What made the day perfect was the opportunity to share it with Gresham. Lately it seemed to Susan that she thought about him all the time.

They spoke of inconsequential matters, the fine weather, the acting troupe that had passed through Owl's Butte, the lake outing planned for the Fourth of July celebration next month. When Nate leaned against Susan's side and dropped into a doze, Gresham mentioned that everyone was impressed by how she had handled the situation with Eddie Mercer.

"It was terrible," she admitted quietly, looking down at her gloves. "I felt so sorry for Eddie. And for me too. But in a strange way, I'm glad it happened."

Though she hated corporal punishment and always would, Susan recognized that the incident with Eddie and the ruler had strengthened her confidence and established her authority. Nothing in the future would be as shattering as that moment when she had decided to strike Eddie and knew she would do it. Something had changed. Perhaps she had finally learned that her problems were hers to solve, that no one would help her.

"Everyone's talking about the meeting next Saturday night," Gresham said, glancing at her above Nate's sleeping head. "I feel I should mention that opinion is running against you."

"Is that why you asked us out today? To inform me the council has already made up its mind?"

Susan's good mood vanished in a twinkling. Her shoulders slumped and she stared down at her hands, disappointed that Gresham's invitation was motivated by more than a desire to see her and Nate.

Being reminded of the upcoming meeting sent her spirits plummeting further. Whenever she thought about the meeting, her stomach went sour and she felt sick. She wasn't going to sleep a wink this week from worrying about it.

"Mrs. Winters didn't say so, but I feel certain my future depends on keeping the school open," she said, ducking her head.

It required every ounce of willpower not to beg Gresham to help her prepare her presentation. Some men might have been flattered by such an appeal, but Gresham Harte would have viewed a plea for assistance as a sign of weakness and a mark against her. The women he admired were self-reliant.

He would have been surprised to know how often Susan recalled his remark praising her courage. The comment strengthened her because she wanted him to think well of her. Moreover, his belief actually seemed to instill a little courage.

As for the town council, their reaction was unlikely to be favorable. In her heart, Susan knew she would fail to persuade them to keep the school open. How could the result be otherwise?

Gresham touched his watch fob, cleared his throat and gave her a sidelong glance. "You look very pretty today. I especially like your hat." His gaze lengthened. "The sun makes your cheeks look pink."

Instantly, Susan's mood lifted. She shifted on the seat to stare in pleased astonishment. "Gresham Harte! Are you courting me?"

Her blurted question caused them both to blush the color of dark plums. Susan's hands fluttered and she would have given half her life to take back the impulsive question.

"I was merely stating an observation," he said irritably, "offering a compliment as any gentleman would do." A long pause opened before he spoke again. "I believe we're becoming friends, and I've come to value that friendship. I enjoy your company and admire a few of your qualities. I would hope that I might occasionally utter a compliment without being misunderstood."

Crimson burned on her cheeks. "I apologize for mistaking your meaning," she said stiffly. She thanked God that Nate was napping and not awake to witness her disappointment.

After puffing out his cheeks, Gresham shifted the reins in his hands. "I'd like to hear your opinion regarding the brief I'm preparing for the Clausen dispute. May I tell you about it?"

"Please do," Susan said in a small voice. But she didn't hear a word of his lengthy explanation.

Why couldn't she accept once and for all that Gresham Harte was not going to return her growing affection for him or jump on his white horse and ride forth to save her? Nor was any man. She and Nate would have to make their way without a man to guide and provide for them. Why couldn't she accept that?

"We're on my land now," Gresham announced thirty minutes later, turning the wagon onto a rutted lane. Gently rising hills flanked a sunny valley, then rapidly climbed upward. High above them rose lofty peaks still wearing sugary caps of snow. Gresham's chest expanded with pride but when he spoke his voice was almost shy, seeking her approval. "Do you like it?"

"Oh Mr. Harte, it's beautiful!" Releasing a breath, Susan clasped her hands together and gasped at scenery so lush and lovely that the sight tightened her chest in a painful grip.

A rushing stream tumbled out of the high mountains to meander along the east side of the valley, shattering the sunlight into diamond-like sparkles. Pine, spruce, and aspen grew down to the wildflowers that carpeted the meadows. On the far side of the valley, a herd of elk lifted their heads, gazed at the buckboard, then sprang toward the trees.

Gresham reined in the horse and the buckboard came to a rolling stop in the lane.

"Are we there yet?" Nate sat up and rubbed his eyes.

Gresham laughed and helped them down from the wagon. "This is my house, such as it is."

He led them toward a grove of leafy aspens and the foundations of his future home, showing them where the chimney would be, and the bedrooms, and the kitchen and larder.

"You'll have a fine view," Susan remarked in a soft voice, standing where the front windows would be. She gazed at the distant snowy peaks, at the lush meadow below, and her heart felt at ease, as if she had come home.

Dipping her parasol to shade her expression, she turned back to the house proper and drew a breath. "Your home will be larger than I expected."

Gresham tangled his fingers in his watch fob and looked toward the well stones. "I hope to have a large family some day."

Sorrow struck deep in Susan's heart, and she ducked her head. She wished things were different, wished Gresham were thinking of her as he spoke of his house and the family he wanted. She wished that she and Nate could be part of his future.

Nate broke an awkward silence by running up to Gresham waving the fishing poles. "Where are the fish?"

Laughing, Gresham let himself be dragged to the banks of the stream, leaving Susan to follow with the picnic basket.

She spread a blanket on the meadow grass and pushed the handle of her parasol into the ground to shade her. Gradually, for the first time in weeks, she began to relax. She'd remembered to bring along a book and her sewing bag, but they lay untouched on the blanket beside her.

Instead of reading or working on her doilies, Susan watched Gresham teaching Nate to cast and eavesdropped as man and boy discussed topics of interest to the male species. They spoke of guns and the Indian wars, wagons and trains, hunting and fishing, school and animals.

"So when are you going to get this puppy you're so excited about?" Gresham asked, casting his line out into the stream. He had discarded his jacket and waistcoat and rolled up the cuffs of his trousers and sleeves. Susan studied the fascinating way his suspenders stretched across the muscles on his back.

"My birthday is . . ." Uncertain, Nate glanced over his

shoulder. Already he had lost his hat, and sunlight teased auburn highlights from his tousled hair.

"In August," Susan supplied, smiling at them. Her heart swelled. There was something truly wonderful in the sight of a man and a boy fishing on the banks of a summer stream.

"Is August a long time away?" Nate asked Gresham, his small face anxious.

Gresham smiled. "I suspect it will seem that way. Tell me more about this birthday puppy. What will he look like and have you decided on a name?"

A heavy weight filled Susan's chest, and she dropped her head. With all her aching heart, she wished she could be the kind of woman that Gresham Harte wanted.

It would have been wonderful to spend the rest of her life with him, to live on this site in the home he was building, to fill the rooms with mischievous boys and laughing girls, to watch his warm dark eyes smile at her across the supper table. It would have been so wonderful to be loved by a man like Gresham.

Tears glistened on her lashes as she lifted her face to the warmth of the sun.

She should be worrying about her speech instead of thinking about broad shoulders and smiling eyes, about a firm mouth and elegant hands. She even dreamt about Gresham, strange romantic dreams that left her feeling breathless and over- heated. Somewhere along the way she had made the disastrous mistake of falling in love with the man she had intended to marry but never would.

Susan paced across the porch of Mrs. Alder's hotel and watched with growing consternation as dozens of people filed into the town hall down the street. It was hideous to think about addressing the men on the town council; it made her physically ill to realize she would do so in front of a large audience.

"I can't do this," she whispered, wringing her hands.

"I'd like to be encouraging, but . . ." Mrs. Alder stepped onto the porch and adjusted a fringed shawl around her shoulders. She inspected Susan's bloodless face. "However, I'm willing to listen to what you have to say." A look of concern narrowed her gaze. "Are you all right? You're swaying on your feet."

"I'd rather eat spiders than walk into that town hall!"

When Susan spied Gresham Harte walking toward her up the middle of Main Street, she closed her eyes and released a breath of relief. She'd never been so happy to see anyone in her life. Instinct promised that Gresham was on her side. She'd have at least one sympathetic face in the crowd.

"Evening, ladies." He tipped his hat to them, then placed a nosegay of tiny wildflowers in her gloved hands. "For luck."

"Thank you," she whispered as Mrs. Alder attached the nosegay to the shoulder of her jacket. For tonight's momentous event, she had chosen her gray linen traveling suit, which seemed more businesslike than anything else she owned. Her hair was pinned beneath a flat straw hat with a gray and white band and she wore the gray boots she had purchased just before leaving Washington.

"Ready?" Gresham asked, extending an arm to each woman.

Susan darted an anxious glance toward the hotel doors and chewed her lip, which was already raw. "Maybe I should . . ."

"Hettie has Nate well in hand," Mrs. Alder said briskly, taking one of Gresham's arms.

Slowly Susan stepped forward and wrapped a shaking hand around Gresham's sleeve. As they walked down Main Street toward the lights in the windows of the town hall, she felt as if she were walking to her own execution.

"Is your speech prepared?" Gresham asked, looking down at her. He hugged her arm close to his chest.

"Yes." The folded speech was tucked inside her glove where she couldn't misplace it. Although she had rewritten it a dozen times, she had no faith that her presentation would be successful. Her speech was too short, she realized, and too meek and apologetic. An expectation of failure underscored every word.

Her feet dragged as they approached the hall. Voices buzzed inside, sounding like a hornet's nest. In an instant Susan's heart was pounding so loudly she could no longer hear the conversation spilling from inside.

"Good luck," Mrs. Alder called, moving away from them toward the door. Her voice was cheerful but the words were merely polite. Mrs. Alder wanted Hettie helping at the hotel during the summer, not in school.

"I can't breathe," Susan murmured, pressing a hand to her side. She shouldn't have laced so tightly. "I think I'm going to be sick."

Gresham cast a quick glance up and down the darkened street. When he was certain no one watched, he tilted her face up to his.

"The secret of public speaking is to speak from the heart. If you truly believe the school should remain open throughout the summer, then let them see and hear that belief. Speak from the heart, Mrs. Stone, not a piece of paper. Let them see and hear your conviction and your passion!"

His fingers on her cheek paralyzed her. They stood so close that she could feel the warmth of his breath flowing over her lips, experienced the solid impression of his body. She hadn't thought it possible for her heart to beat any louder or faster, but standing so close to him made her pulse accelerate to dizzying speed.

She felt an insane impulse to fling herself into Gresham's

strong arms and cling to him. With all her faltering spirit, she wished Gresham would carry her away from here and save her from the humiliation of tonight's failure.

His hand dropped from her cheek and he smiled into her eyes, his gaze warm and steady with his unfounded belief in her. He pretended not to notice the bluish circles under her eyes or the ashen tone of her skin.

"You look lovely; your speech is prepared, and you believe in your objective. Have faith in yourself," he advised her.

"This is the hardest thing I've ever done."

His laugh made her frown and stare at him. "Mrs. Stone, you claim everything you do is the hardest thing you have ever done." His expression sobered. "But that's what life is, isn't it? Attempting and accomplishing one hard thing after another?"

Her eyebrows snapped together and she moved backward a step. "I do not need a lecture about character building. Not now!"

He laughed again and turned her toward the door of the town hall. "Now don't get your dander up. I only meant to remind you of all the hard things you have already accomplished. You'll succeed again tonight."

She stopped and twisted her hands together. "Don't say that," she implored him in a low voice. "I don't want you to be disappointed in me."

"Would that matter?" he asked, lifting a surprised eyebrow.

"Yes," she whispered. When she lifted her head, Gresham was staring at her with an intense expression that she couldn't read.

He opened his mouth to say something, but Mrs. Alder leaned out of the doorway. "They're waiting for you, Mrs. Stone."

Flustered, she smoothed down her skirts, patted her hair,

and gingerly withdrew her speech from her glove. Dying inside, beginning to perspire, Susan forced herself to turn away from Gresham and place one foot in front of another.

"You will prevail," he said from behind her.

She paused, then entered the hall. She was on her own.

Chapter Fourteen

Gulliver County, Kansas

Loving a man was a new and not altogether pleasant experience. Loving changed a person.

In many ways loving endowed Rosie with greater strength and a feeling of weightier substance. Her days seemed fuller and calmer as if she had found an answer she hadn't known she was seeking. What surprised her most was the joy of merely being in the same room with Bowie, just to look at him. Hearing his voice made her feel good, and his smile sent a thrill shuddering down her spine.

In other ways, the ways that irritated her, she was weaker than she had ever been, soft at the center and more vulnerable. Her image of herself had turned spongy and malleable. On occasion she curled her hair, and on Sundays she had taken to wearing the new skirts and waists that Lodisha sewed for her. She bathed regularly, and it was she who now insisted on adding a few drops of rose oil to her bathwater. Now and then she even wore her corset.

The problem was, the man whose approval she sought praised the changes she was effecting and complimented her appearance . . . but he hadn't attempted to make love to her again.

Stopping work, Rosie straightened her aching back and mopped the sweat out of her eyes. She leaned on her hoe and squinted across the rows of wheat, past John Hawkins, to study Bowie's naked back. Sweat poured out of him like water out of a sieve, wetting the waist and crotch of his work pants, staining his hat band. Watching the lean, hard muscles move beneath his sunburned skin made Rosie feel liquid inside, as if warm honey poured through her body.

Sighing, she blotted her throat and glanced up at a heat-white sky. The July sun blazed like an oven, baking the moisture out of soil and human skin. Heat waves shimmered over the fields.

Pulling her sweat-soaked shirt away from her ribs, she gripped her hoe, ignoring the blisters bubbling up on her palms. The fight to keep the thistles and crouch grass out of seven acres was a merciless and hopeless battle, but they had to try. What galled her soul was watching the weeds thrive while her wheat wilted and died in the relentless, dry heat.

Frowning, Rosie stared at the stalks and tried to guess why Bowie hadn't wanted her again. Worrying and wondering about it was draining the snap out of her.

That was another change. Her ideas about poking had leaped from North to South in the span of one blissful night. Considering her history, Rosie regarded as miraculous the fact that that night in the barn with Bowie had been the single most wonderful experience in her life, better even than being the belle of the ball.

Although the admission shamed and embarrassed her, she

longed to try it again. The possibility that being with a man—the right man—might be wonderful each time was an idea that intrigued and staggered her imagination. The trouble was she lacked the grit to brazenly demand another poke and Bowie didn't seem inclined to instigate a repetition on his own.

The rock-bottom worst problem about loving someone was the awful helplessness it caused. She wanted Bowie to love her back but she didn't know how to make him do it.

Reaching for the strap around her neck, Rosie opened her canteen and swallowed. The lukewarm water did not diminish the heat of the sun burning her skin or alleviate the backbreaking labor of hoeing the fields. Behind the buzzing in her head she imagined the sound of Frank Blevins' laughter as he watched her wheat stalks dying for want of moisture.

Bending at the waist, Rosie attacked a tough spread of wild mustard, swinging her hoe like a weapon and feeling more nettled and helpless by the minute.

It wasn't fair that Bowie should vanquish her fear and revulsion and show her how rapturous and exciting poking could be, then turn around and keep her at arm's length for weeks afterward. He could at least acknowledge that something wonderful had happened between them.

And it wasn't fair that he kept her nerves quivering and her brain feverish with his brief touches and occasional hugs and all those compliments about staying clean and spruced up a little, then he didn't follow through with another poke. Consequently, poking ran a close second to rain as the subject uppermost on her mind.

By the time Lodisha rang the bell beside the door, signaling supper would be on the table in an hour, Rosie felt as mean and resentful as a scalded cat. She threw down her hoe and followed John Hawkins toward the cottonwoods lining the creek.

Falling into step beside her, Bowie wiped his throat and glanced at the sky. "If we don't get some rain, we're going to lose the crop."

"You think I don't know that?" Rosie snapped, bending to pull off her boots before she walked into the creek. She lowered herself into the water, resting her back against a tumbled row of stones. A weak current flowed over her sunburned arms and bare feet, carrying away the sweat on her clothing and the scalding ache in her muscles.

"Some days I regret leaving the Indian life," John Hawkins groaned, sighing and sinking into the water beside her. Bowie splashed down on her right. "I would rather hunt than farm. This farming breaks the spine and roasts the spirit."

Leaning his head back against the rocks, Bowie fanned his face with his hat, examining the first stars appearing in a twilight sky. "Not a single cloud."

"It will rain tonight," John Hawkins announced wearily.

"I hope to God you're right, but I don't think so." Rosie slid down until her hair was in the water and she felt the cool flow against her scalp. She could hardly bear to utter the next words, but they were all thinking the same thing. "It's starting to look like we won't get a harvest this year." The possibility seared her.

Frank Blevins, God rot his black soul, would win again. Her chest constricted and her hands curled into fists beneath the sluggish current. The panicked thought of losing another crop made her want to drown herself in liquor.

With a groan, John Hawkins pulled himself out of the creek, gave them a tired wave, then limped toward the barn and dry clothing.

Bowie shifted and his thigh brushed hers beneath the water. Rosie jumped as if he had prodded her with a pitchfork.

"All right," he said quietly, "let's talk. You've had a burr in your bonnet for weeks. Are you anxious about the crop?"

"Of course I'm worried about the crop, worried sick. But that isn't what's sticking in my craw," she said, keeping her eyes on the darkening sky.

"Contrary to what most women think, men are not mind readers. If you have something to say, just say it."

She let a silence linger long enough that Bowie started to rise, looking toward the house.

"It's about poking," she blurted.

He sat back down in the water and studied the flush beneath her sunburned cheeks. "What about poking?" he asked. Knots rose along his jawline. He didn't look at her.

She needed a few minutes to find the words and the nerve to speak them. She couldn't look at him either. "I don't understand," she said finally. Her face burned with humiliation. "I thought you understood that I liked that poke we had. It wasn't like before. You didn't hurt me and I didn't feel sick or dirty afterwards. I felt . . . good all over. It was wonderful."

Oh God. She didn't know if she could talk about something like this. Cursing herself for starting something, she sucked in a breath and kicked herself forward, blundering on.

"So if you're thinking that I'm still afraid or repulsed or anything like that—well, I'm not."

"I'm glad, Rosie."

"I just thought you should know. In case you were supposing that nothing had changed." She took a peek at his bronzed face, surprised to notice he was frowning and looked sad. Maybe she hadn't explained well enough. "I used to say I'd cut my throat sooner than let a man poke me. That isn't true anymore. Least I don't think it is. I need more experience to know for sure."

Bowie removed his hat and raked a hand through his hair. Rosie sensed his discomfort, and she didn't blame him. Some things were hard to talk about. Leaning forward, cheeks hot, she focused intense attention on her toes beneath the water. When Bowie still didn't say anything, she realized she was going to have to say it right out. Hell-fire and damn.

She ducked her head. "What I'm trying to say is that I'm willing to be poked again." The mortification of actually asking a man for a poke was killing her by inches.

"I'm sorry, Rosie," Bowie said after a minute. "We can't make love again."

She went as still as a rock inside. The reason seemed obvious, but she asked him anyway. Her voice sounded small and far away. "I wasn't any good at poking, was I? You don't want me any more."

Reaching for her, Bowie grabbed her chin and tilted her face toward his blazing eyes. "I want you all the damned time. I can't sleep for remembering how you looked and how you felt beneath me. I'll never forget that night, Rosie," he said in a low intense voice, staring into her eyes. "Not as long as I live."

The air flew out of her body in a rush. His admission sent her heart soaring. "So why can't we do it again?"

He scrubbed a hand over his face, then turned his head toward the deepening darkness. "There are reasons," he said finally.

"What reasons?" Sometimes he stiffened and turned inward, looking at something that Rosie couldn't share. At such times he became as much a stranger as the day she had first seen him. "Bowie? I need to know."

"Some of it I can't tell you."

"Tell me what you can."

He turned his head to look at her. "That night in the barn . . . you were sober. I'm sorry, but there's nothing desirable about a drunk woman."

"I'm hardly ever drunk anymore! I'm sober now."

"It's true that you haven't been falling-down drunk in weeks, and I'm glad. But Rosie, not a day goes by that you don't have several drinks."

"Just little ones!"

"You may not be drunk, but you aren't entirely sober either."

"Wait a minute," she said, frowning, working it out. "Are you saying you won't poke a woman with whiskey on her breath? Is this some kind of ultimatum?" When he didn't answer, she sat up in the water and stared at him.

"I'm not asking you to completely quit drinking. I don't have that right."

"The hell! It sure sounds like you're saying I can have my blazer or I can have a poke, but I can't have both!"

"Drinking yourself into an occasional stupor is your choice, and I don't dispute your right to make that choice." Standing, he splashed through the darkness, wading toward the bank.

"I haven't passed out in over a month!" she shouted. "When's the last time you had to walk into town and bail me out of jail?"

After stepping out of the water, he bent for his boots, then looked back at her. "If you want to kill yourself with drink, fine. That's your choice. If I prefer to make love to a woman who will remember it in the morning, that's my choice."

Seething, Rosie watched him stride toward the house and enter the kitchen door. Then she laid her head back on the rocks and stared at the stars through the high branches of the cottonwoods.

Loving a man was damned hard, almost as hard as living with one. Love twisted a woman around inside, forced her to think about things she had never thought about before. Love undermined a woman and left her vulnerable to her man's every stupid whim.

Her whiskey or her husband. Now that was a hell of a choice, and damned unfair. The thought of never again lying in Bowie's arms tore at her as much as the thought of never again finding relief and comfort the only way she knew.

Whiskey was something she could rely on. A bottle of blazer lifted her on a golden ride that left behind memory, pain and worry. She knew exactly what liquor could and couldn't do for her.

But trust a man? Trust an elusive glimpse of happiness? That was entering unknown territory, akin to leaping into an abyss.

Bowie had no right to demand this of her, Rosie decided, standing up and shaking the water out of her hair. She'd been friends with a jug a lot longer than she had known Bowie Stone.

"Damn you," she muttered, glaring after him, not sure if she cursed him for his ultimatum or for making her love him.

On her way to the house, she stopped in front of Frank Blevins' headstone as she always did, and kicked rocks at the granite slab. If only Blevins had been a different kind of man, if only she'd had her revenge while the bastard was alive, then maybe she wouldn't have needed to hide in a bottle of whiskey, maybe she wouldn't have been poisoned by fear and a deep need to best him.

"You don't scare me anymore!" she hissed between her teeth. Sometimes she almost believed it. She spat at the headstone. "You failed as a farmer, failed as a husband, failed as a stepfather! You were rotten and mean and shriveled inside. I'm not worthless like you said, and I'm not ugly. There *is* a man who desires me!"

Except that her husband didn't want her the way she was. He demanded more changes, the biggest change of all. He wanted her to give up her shield against the world. Cutting back wasn't enough for him. No, he wanted her to quit drinking entirely.

The thought scared her half to death.

A roll of thunder woke her. Bolting up in bed, Rosie blinked and shook her head as a flash of lightning pulsed through her room, then faded, followed by another shimmer and crash of thunder. A light patter on the rooftop increased in intensity, deepening into a hammering noise that announced a steady soaker.

Elation expanded her chest, choking off her breath. Flinging back the covers, cursing the tangling hem of the nightdress she had recently taken to wearing, she ran into the hallway and pounded on Bowie's door. The door opened beneath her fist.

"Wake up! Do you hear it? It's raining! The crop—"

Lightning illuminated the window and revealed a figure propped against the pillows. Rosie froze and the hair rose on the back of her neck. Fear dried her mouth and her heart slammed against her rib cage. Him.

"I'm awake, come inside." The figure spoke in a low voice.

Eyes riveted to the form on the bed, Rosie stumbled backward. In a minute he would stand and reach for his belt. Already she imagined she could hear the steady menacing slap of leather against his palm and anticipated with dread the sight of his hairy nakedness, the angry rising of his weapon. Foreseeing the degradation and the beating to come sent her reeling backward.

"No!" Her throat closed on a surge of fear and panic.

Thunder crashed overhead, shaking the planks beneath her bare feet. There was nowhere to run; no place to hide. Trying to escape would make it worse for her. Acquiring that knowledge had cost her a cracked rib and a broken arm.

"Rosie?" It was Bowie's voice. Confused, she cast a frantic

glance behind her, searching for him, before she returned a terrified stare to the figure on the bed. "Frank Blevins is dead. He's not in this room."

"He is!" A strangled sob tore out of her chest. Blevins was here. She felt his dark presence, smelled his rankness, heard the belt slapping his palm.

Bowie's deep voice penetrated her fear. His urgency and intensity thrust against the powerful forces of memory. "Fight it, Rosie, bury the bastard once and forever. Walk into this room and push the ghost out. You can do it!"

Oh God, she craved a drink! Frank Blevins' evil passion wrapped around her, shriveling her skin and burning her insides. Acid memories assaulted her like blades, slicing at brain and body.

"I can't," she gasped, grasping the door jamb.

But it was Bowie's voice that called to her, not Blevins'. Blevins was dead and buried in the yard. She had put him there herself. He couldn't hurt her ever again. But damn it, he was *here*. She could hear him panting, waiting for her. "I'm not strong enough, I can't," she whispered on a sob. Fear doubled her over.

"You're the strongest woman I've ever met."

"I'm not. I can't do this!"

"I can't help you, Rosie, you have to walk in here yourself." His voice was low and urgent. "Do it, come to me, Rose Mary."

Panic clawed down her spine. He didn't know what he was asking. The battle to walk into this chamber of horrors was titanic, overwhelming. On some level she comprehended that Bowie was right. She couldn't hope to be whole until she reclaimed this room and wrested it away from Frank Blevins. But God, how could she face him again? Fear and indecision split her in half.

"Rosie, there is no one here but me."

A flash of lightning lit the room, tinting it ghostly white. She saw Blevins' bed and bureau, his trunk and the row of pegs where his belt had hung. A violent tremor ripped down her body, leaving her shaking and feeling sick inside. Her fingernails shattered against the wood of the door jamb, but she didn't notice.

Noise roared in her head, the boom of thunder and crack of lightning, the steady hammering of rain against the roof, the slap of leather striking flesh, the memory of screams and pleas and a man's grunts and low laughter.

"Fight him, Rosie. He's no match for you. You can beat him. Make new memories in this room."

"I . . . can't!"

"You're strong and courageous. You can win."

The voice of her husband called to her, a man she loved and trusted. Bowie would not betray her; he would not injure her.

"Do it now, Rosie."

Shaking uncontrollably, her heart like a wild animal kicking in her chest, she fastened desperate eyes on the bed, waiting for the next pulse of lightning to prove that it was Bowie waiting there. When the next flash opened the sky, she saw him, saw his steady intent gaze, saw his sympathy and caring. She saw his familiar naked chest and his arms open to her.

"Bowie!"

Plunging deep in search of a sliver of courage, shaking all over, Rosie tightened her body, then bolted forward. Her bare feet skimming the planks, she flew forward and dived onto the bed, feeling sick inside and faint. Bowie caught her in his arms and enfolded her in a crushing embrace.

"You're safe," he murmured against her hair. His hands stroked her back, fighting the chills that racked her body. "You're with me, and you're safe. No one is going to hurt you."

Shock glazed her eyes. She was in Frank Blevins' bed. His bed. Bile flooded her throat. She couldn't breathe. Her heart lurched and stopped beating. Gripping Bowie's shoulders, she pressed her face into the crease of his neck and frantically tried to hide by melting into him. Silent screams echoed in her ears.

"It's you," she babbled over and over, shaking. Not him. Not him. "It's Bowie. It's you."

"You're safe." His hands moved over her nightdress, stroking, soothing, caressing. His body half-covered her, shielding her.

She didn't know how long she clung to him, concentrating on Bowie, just Bowie, his hands, his voice, his scent. Only gradually did she become aware that her nightdress had hiked to her waist and she lay pressed hip to naked hip against her husband. His erection rose hard and hot against the softness of her belly.

Instantly a wild tearing panic overwhelmed her and she tried to twist away from him. Then she heard his soothing murmur in her ear, recognized his calm eyes and sunburned face above her. This was Bowie, her husband, and she loved him.

Wrapping her arms around his neck, she held on to him until the panic subsided, gratefully accepting a gentle rain of kisses that showered over her temples, her eyelids, her brow, her cheeks. When Bowie's warm hands followed the curve of her back to cup her buttocks and press her closer against his body, she sucked in a breath, then pushed her hips hard against his, letting her body choose present over past, opening herself to a deep need to dissolve into him.

Never had this room known tenderness or whispers of comfort or endearments. No love had flourished here, no kindness, no gentle caresses.

Trembling, Rosie thrust the dark memories aside. She

squeezed her eyes shut and concentrated fiercely on the gentle strength in Bowie's hands, on his tenderness, on the arousing magic of his lips kissing her throat.

Watching her, Bowie saw the moment when her terror began to abate. Her fingernails released their painful grip and her hands opened and relaxed against his back. A long shudder rippled through her frame as her body surrendered the abominations of memory. Gradually he felt a new tension gathering beneath her skin, and when she moved against him, he recognized it as the healthy tension of desire, not fear.

Moving slowly and deliberately so he wouldn't startle or frighten her, pausing often to examine her eyes and assure himself of consent, he eased the nightdress up her body and over the mass of tawny hair, then he drew in a breath and gazed at her in a flash of lightning that forked past the window.

The burning sun had darkened her skin to form a collar-shaped arrow that pointed to the pale creamy globes of her breasts. Awed by the perfection of her beauty, Bowie gently brushed his palm across one breast and felt the nipple rise hard and strong. Feeling his breath catch in his chest, he dropped his hand, stroking his fingers along the contours of her waist before he paused at the crisp triangle between her thighs. A low groan sounded in her ear as she twisted beneath his hands, the movement an involuntary invitation signaling building urgency.

She was so perfectly formed, this small strong woman, so beautiful in her female power and mystery. In a burst of painful insight, Bowie understood he would never tire of listening to her unique point of view, never grow weary of looking at her or of making love to her. He knew he was not truly free to take this woman as his wife, but tonight he could not resist her. He needed her as much as she needed him.

"Slowly," he murmured, as her body bucked against him and her fingernails dug into his shoulders. "Slowly."

Grasping her hand, he kissed the calluses on her palm, then

guided her hand down his chest. She hesitated and he heard a sharp intake of breath before she permitted him to draw her hand down to him. Looking into her eyes, he folded her fingers around his erection, fighting a powerful urge to claim her immediately. But it was important that she understand she need not fear him. For an instant she stiffened in his arms, then slowly, tentatively, she relaxed her hand and moved her fingertips over him, stroking, exploring. Beads of sweat rose on his brow, and Bowie felt himself grow harder as her fingers gently enclosed him, applying a wildly arousing pressure.

"It's soft," she whispered in a wondering voice.

"I hope not," he said hoarsely, smiling into her eyes.

She laughed, then her eyes widened in amazement as if it had never occurred to her that laughter and sex might be compatible.

He kissed her then, long and deep, again and again, excited by the taste of her, responding to the fire that burned on her lips and skin and the pressure of her firm smooth body against his.

Only when his fingers confirmed that she was ready for him did he enter her, gasping as her womanly heat enclosed him and guided him down into liquid mystery. Concentrating on restraint, he moved slowly and rhythmically, stopping when she soared near the edge, teasing her, carrying her with him on spiraling tides of sensation until they both were sweating freely and panting and she thrashed beneath him like a wild thing, sobbing his name.

Only then, when her fingernails raked his back and buttocks, when pulses of lightning revealed the perspiration glistening on her throat and breasts, when he felt himself trembling on the brink of uncontrollable passion, only then did he drive into her with a man's power and urgent need.

But not until she thrust up against him with a scream of joy did he relinquish control and let himself explode within her.

Afterward, she lay in his arms and together they listened to the rain pounding the rooftop and inhaled the warm musky scent of their cooling bodies.

"The demons are gone," Rosie marveled softly, watching as lightning briefly illuminated the bed and bureau. Her fingers tightened on his forearm and she gazed around her in wonder. "This is just a room. Nothing more."

"Yes." Her hair smelled clean, like sunlight and creek water. She fit into his arms as if her body had been custom-made for his.

Leaving her was going to be the hardest thing he ever did.

"What are you thinking?" she murmured, shifting to rest her cheek against his chest.

"I was thinking about the crop," he lied. "Once we bring in the harvest, you'll be free of that son of a bitch forever."

"Bowie?" she asked quietly, rousing him from a light doze. The urgency in her voice brought him fully awake. She was leaning over him, gazing into his eyes. "I'm never going to drink again. Not one drop."

He studied the earnestness pinching her expression. "This is a promise to yourself, Rosie, not to me. If you mean what you're saying, then you have to do it only for yourself. No one else."

She hesitated and licked her lips. "I know."

Just thinking about going dry made her crave a shot of whiskey with all her heart and soul. But whiskey could offer only temporary relief. With Bowie she had a chance for something permanent. Before she changed her mind Rosie told him where all her jugs were stashed and asked him to destroy them. Never again would she come to his bed smelling of liquor.

The shaking began before noon and continued for days. A headache settled like an axe at the base of her skull; her stomach twisted and cramped. Rosie's hands shook so violently that she couldn't hold food on her fork, couldn't drink coffee or a lemonade without slopping the liquid down the front of her shirt. Too sick to sleep, she wandered around the yard at night, hurling stones at Frank Blevins' headstone or walking through the wheat fields, fighting demons that whispered seductively in her ear, urging her to jump on Ivanhoe and ride into town to Harold's saloon.

Keeping busy helped, but she lacked concentration and focus. Her hoe dropped from trembling fingers. The sun pounded her brain to parched pulp. She should have taken joy in the rain-fed green of the wheat stalks but she hardly noticed them.

Every cell in her body screamed for a taste of blazer, demanded comfort. Her stomach rejected food and cramped so badly she could hardly stand upright. Every tormenting moment was a battle against pain and denial.

John Hawkins took over the errands to town, Lodisha prepared her favorite foods, Bowie picked up the slack when she couldn't perform her regular chores. Engrossed in a struggle of epic proportions, Rosie didn't notice.

She couldn't eat, couldn't sleep, couldn't read, couldn't work. Whiskey dominated every waking thought. The only task she accomplished was a complete and frantic search of the farm, but Bowie had been thorough. Not a single jug remained. The night she finally accepted the fact that there truly was not a drop of liquor on the farm, Rosie sat in the creek and sobbed in the moonlight until her eyes ran dry and she was too weak to move. At that moment she hated Bowie Stone as much as she had ever hated anyone.

That she endured amazed her. Somehow she found the willpower not to jump on Ivanhoe and ride in search of relief. If a jug had been handy she would have celebrated her triumph with a good stiff drink. Instead she made herself work harder and she drank gallons of Lodisha's lemonade.

Loving Bowie carried her through those terrible first days. Sometimes the contest was close, but love rose more powerfully in her mind than her craving for a drink.

When the need gnawed at her insides, when she found herself running toward the barn to saddle Ivanhoe, Rosie made herself stop, turn around and go in search of Bowie.

When she found him, she stood off by herself, watching him work and struggling to contain a swirling contradiction of emotions. Resentment, love, anger, admiration. If he glanced up and sent her a smile of encouragement, she found strength in his confidence. But more often it was enough just to see him and know he was hers and be assured that she hadn't invented him. There was comfort in knowing when night fell they would sleep in each other's arms. And her breath and skin would be untainted by liquor.

Their nights together made the days bearable. Loving him replenished her determination and strengthened her resolve to win this battle. Recognizing the pride and encouragement in his eyes stiffened her fortitude and added muscle to her willpower.

During the moments of hard thought, and there were many such moments, Rosie conceded she would never have decided to dry out on her own. She waged this battle and endured this suffering solely because she wanted to share Bowie Stone's bed and she wanted him to love her. She yearned to hear him say the words, and she longed to say them herself—without spewing whiskey fumes in his face.

Slowly the days passed, dropped away and became weeks. The wheat ripened in the fields and shaded into tones of rippling gold.

Eventually the moment arrived when Rosie straightened over her hoe and realized she hadn't thought about liquor for several days. Or a smoke. Smokes didn't taste good since she'd quit drinking.

Everything else did. Lodisha's suppers were manna from heaven. Even water sparkled with a taste she hadn't noticed in years. The sun no longer shot splinters into her eyes in the mornings. She didn't wake with a sour stomach or a brown taste in her mouth. Her brain no longer careened against her skull when she moved quickly.

At the three-week point, Rosie waited until everyone else was occupied, then she slipped into the barn and searched until she located Bowie's shaving mirror.

Summoning her courage, she raised the mirror to her face. Bright alert eyes peered back at her, circles of clear chocolate surrounded by bluish white. A hint of rose bloomed beneath her tan. Her mouth looked soft and pink. A healthy glow suffused her skin and golden highlights shone in her hair.

Lowering the mirror, she covered her face and breathed deeply, then entered Ivanhoe's stall and leaned her forehead against his sleek black flank.

She had beaten the demons. The battle was almost won.

When Bowie rode back to the barn the next afternoon, a small deer lashed across Ivanhoe's flanks, Rosie was waiting for him. Smiling, he reined beside her.

"You look lovely," he said, his blue eyes traveling slowly across her hips and molded waist, then up to the wisps of hair teased from her bun by a hot breeze.

"I need to go into town," Rosie said, looking into his eyes. She drew a deep breath and wet her lips. "I have to go to Harold's saloon."

Chapter Fifteen

Bowie stared at her. "You've come so far. Why are you giving up now?"

"It's not what you think," Rosie explained, twisting her hands together. "I'm afraid to ride into town; can you understand that? I'm afraid my boots will turn into Harold's, and I'll find myself standing at the rail reaching for a shotglass as I've done a thousand times before. I can see myself doing it. I dream about it." She gazed up at him, the appeal in her eyes overshadowed by admitting there was still something she feared. "I have to know. I have to walk in there and sit down, surrounded by the sight and smell of whiskey, and I have to say no. Until I discover if I'm strong enough to do that, I won't know for sure if I've won."

"This is your war," Bowie said after a lengthy silence. "You have to fight it your way."

They didn't speak during the ride into Passion's Crossing,

but the tension drawing her shoulders was recognizable. Bowie had observed this kind of progressive anxiety a hundred times before as soldiers rode toward a battle they knew would be bloody. First came bravado, then silence, and finally a reckless confidence. He felt Rosie's nerves winding tighter with every roll of the wheels. By the time he tied Ivanhoe to the hitching rail in front of Harold's, she was rigid with strain and her fingers trembled.

After helping her from the buckboard, he clasped her shoulders and held her back a minute. "Whatever happens . . . I want you to know that I'm proud of you, Rose Mary Mulvehey."

Gratitude leapt in her eyes, followed by a flicker of disappointment. She wanted more from him and he knew what it was. She wanted what he had no right to give.

She licked her lips and swallowed, unaware of the wagons passing in the street behind them. The Widow Barnes called a greeting, but Rosie was too preoccupied to notice or respond. She cut a nervous glance toward Harold's swinging doors. "I might go loco in there and fall off the wagon."

"You might." He felt her trembling beneath his hands. "But I don't think you will."

"Thank you for believing in me," she whispered. "Sometimes that's all that keeps me going." Dressed in a dark skirt and white waist, her tawny hair pouffed up under a straw hat, she looked fresh and lovely, ten years younger than she had looked the day Bowie had met her. The soiled derelict had vanished.

"Ready?" he inquired softly, examining the moist shine in her eyes. She blinked rapidly, then pressed her lips together and nodded. Taking her arm, holding it tight against his side, Bowie pushed through the swinging doors and stepped into Harold's place. They paused inside the door, letting their eyes adjust to the dim interior. The sweet dark smell of whiskey and fresh sawdust rolled over them. The overhead chandelier glowed down on the tiers of bar glasses, making them sparkle and shine.

Earlier in the summer one of Harold's two bargirls had packed up and drifted on down the road. The other, mistaking Rosie for a respectable lady, jumped to her feet in surprise and clapped a hand over her cleavage. When she recognized who it was, she smiled, then returned to her seat beside the unused piano and resumed picking at the holes in her stockings.

Near the stairs a card game progressed, and a pair of dust-weary drovers leaned on the bar; but Acey James was the only regular with his boot on the rail. Seeing them, he grinned broadly and beckoned them forward.

"Well if you ain't a sight for sore eyes, Rosie gal! Long time no see."

"Howdy, Mr. James." She steadied a smile on her lips. "Being as how I'm a respectable married lady now, I expect you meant to call me Mrs. Stone."

A look of loss tugged Acey's mouth as he swept a glance over her hat, gloves and neat dark skirt. "I 'spect I did, Mrs. Stone. No offense intended."

"None taken." A look passed between them, acknowledging times past, times shared. "Times change," Rosie said softly. "And people too."

Staring at her, Bowie led her to a table near the bar and held out her chair. As far as he knew, this was the first time Rosie had insisted on being addressed by her married name, the first time she had asked for the respect she had never believed she deserved.

Harold came out from behind the bar and placed a bottle of cheap whiskey and a shot glass in front of Rosie, then jerked his head at Bowie. "What'll it be for you?"

Rosie licked her lips and stared hard at the bottle in front of her. The contents glowed warm and amber-colored, seductive with whatever promise she wanted to see there. Her hands opened and closed in her lap and a trance-like glaze flattened her eyes.

Clenching his jaw, Bowie watched her breath come faster and saw a glisten of perspiration slick her brow. He discovered his hands had curled into fists on the table. He wanted to sweep the bottle to the floor, wanted to carry her out of this place. But he couldn't help her, Either she would step forward or backward, but she had to decide her direction alone.

Swallowing convulsively, Rosie eased back in her chair and closed her eyes. She fumbled a handkerchief out of her sleeve and wiped it across her forehead. "I'll have a sarsaparilla, Harold," she said in a voice no louder than a croak. "Take this away."

Bowie opened his fists and pressed his palms flat on the table. He hadn't realized he'd been holding his breath. "Make that two sarsaparillas."

Harold's eyebrows shot upward. "You don't want your usual, Ro—Mrs. Stone?"

"Just sarsaparilla. Ginger pop if you have it. I'm dry as a hide and I mean to stay that way."

"My Gawd!" Acey's eyes bulged in his head. "Now I done seen everything." He waved a hand at the drovers, who were engaged in deep conversation. "You boys hear that? Hell jest froze over. Rosie Mulvehey went on the wagon." He continued to stare at her. "Ain't smoking neither. What the hell is this world coming to? A man can't count on nothing no more."

"Are you all right?" Bowie asked, watching her inspect the foam topping her sarsaparilla. Her mouth curled in disgust.

"I want a drink and I want one bad," she answered in a low tight voice. "Saying no is damned hard, but it isn't as hard as I thought it would be. I'm doing it." She lowered her head and gripped the glass of sarsaparilla with both hands.

Bowie let himself relax and tried to offer the impression

that he had never doubted her resolve. Leaning back in his chair, he stretched and crossed his ankles. Public saloons had never appealed to him. He preferred private clubs where a man could drink and engage in a friendly game with reasonable confidence that a brawl wouldn't erupt at his back, although occasionally that happened. He recalled an incident at the officer's club outside his last post when Evan Dugan had torn up the place and . . .

A knot appeared between his shoulderblades. Those days were gone forever, ended in a military courtroom.

Rosie lifted her head and swiveled to look toward the bar. "Do you hear what those drovers are talking about?" A frown tightened her brow.

"I wasn't listening."

Before he guessed what she meant to do, she stood and walked to the bar, automatically hooking her heel on the rail. "Excuse me, gentlemen, but am I overhearing you correctly? Surely you aren't planning to bring a herd of longhorns through Passion's Crossing?"

Bowie sighed and pushed to his feet. Rosie had effected enormous changes, but she was still Rosie. There wasn't a reticent bone in her small body. Following, he moved up behind her, crossed his arms over his chest and glared at the drovers until the leering smiles vanished from their lips.

"Yes ma'am, you heard right."

"Well, you better change those plans. Passion's Crossing isn't on the drive trail," Rosie said, shaking off the hand Bowie placed on her arm. "You can't bring a herd through here. This is a farm community."

"Well now, I'm the trail boss on this here drive and I 'spect we can do whatever we want. Me and Buck here, we figure we can cut 'bout eighty miles off the drive if we come through this way. Don't see where you got anything to say about it, ma'am."

Rosie's dark eyes narrowed. "Show me where you plan to leave the trail," she demanded. "Draw me a map."

Both drovers straightened and removed their boots from the rail, sliding angry glances from Rosie's flushed face to Bowie. The only sound in the saloon was that of Acey James sliding closer so that he wouldn't miss out on whatever was about to happen.

"My wife inquired after your new route, gentlemen. You have any objection to a peaceful discussion of your plans?"

The drovers returned Bowie's tense inspection while everyone in Harold's place estimated his chances in the event a fight should prove necessary.

The trail boss slid a glance around the room, then shrugged, and the tension eased. "Hell, I guess we can show 'em the route we're discussing." A sighing sound came from the card table and the game resumed.

He tipped a puddle of whiskey out of his glass onto the bartop, dipped a fingertip, then drew a wet line. "This here is the Arkansas, and this is Passion's Creek coming off of it. Here's the trail up from Texas and here's the railhead at Dodge City. This bump on the bar, that's Passion's Crossing."

The sweet curling smell of whiskey rose in tempting waves. Squeezing her eyes shut, Rosie swayed on her feet. Her jaw clenched, and a shudder ran through her body. She spoke through her teeth, holding her arms stiff at her sides.

"Where do you boys plan to leave the trail?"

The instant the trail boss's fingertip came down on the wet trail line, Bowie saw what he should have suspected before, but he'd been too concerned about Rosie to fully focus on the drovers. When he heard Acey James suck a breath through his teeth, Bowie knew he wasn't mistaken. Acey pushed back from the bar and walked rapidly toward the swinging doors.

Drawing to his full height, Bowie narrowed his eyes. "If

you run a herd along that line, you'll destroy the crops of a half-dozen families on both sides of town."

"Well now, that ain't our concern."

"Make it your concern," Bowie growled.

Rosie swallowed and tore her gaze from the puddle of whiskey. "How big is your herd?" she demanded. Her hands moved over her hips, searching for the gun belt she wasn't wearing.

" 'Bout seven hundred head more or less, depending on how many strays we pick up along the way." Moving casually but making a point of it, the drovers edged back their dusters to expose their gunbelts and provide rapid access.

Rosie thrust blazing eyes inches from the nearest cowman's face. "My wheat is just days from harvest, do you understand that? Two pissants like you aren't going to ruin everything I've worked for. I'll shoot any cow that tries to trample my fields!"

A thin smile tightened the nearest drover's lips. "You ever seen a controlled stampede? If you can shoot one of our steers before he plows you under, well ma'am, you can have him for your supper. That's how hard it is to shoot a stampeding longhorn."

The one called Buck grinned. "Seeing how much money we'll save by taking this route, we can afford to lose a critter or two."

Bowie stepped between Rosie and the drovers. "Sorry boys. You're not going to run that herd through my wife's fields." The weight of the plow lay behind his words, the memory of the harness abrading his skin, weeks of laboring in the scorching sun and the torment of watching the stalks wilt and sag. In his mind's eye he saw blisters leaking blood across Rosie's hands and John Hawkins so stooped he couldn't stand upright, saw sunburned skin peeling in sheets from faces and arms.

"Who's going to stop us, sodbuster? You?"

A rustling sound spread behind him and Bowie turned to see the audience Acey had collected off the street and brought back to the saloon. A half-dozen people stared at him.

"You heard what they're planning," Bowie said, recognizing several neighbors. "Are we going to let this happen?"

"You're talking a range war," said a tall woman, holding a child by the hand. The child gazed around the saloon with wide eyes.

"Unless we're willing to lose all we've worked for, we need to send a message that men like these have to keep their herds on the trail. They can't be allowed to destroy our crops just to save a few dollars." Slowly, Bowie moved his gaze from face to face. "Someone has to make a stand. Are you with me?"

These were farmers, not soldiers. No one met his eyes.

"Looks like you're standing alone," said one of the drovers, grinning. "Never met a sodbuster yet with any real guts for a fight."

Crimson flooded Rosie's face. She whirled on the drovers, her skirts spinning. "We don't need help. If you try to bring your herd across my land, you're going to end up with a lot of dead cattle! You hear me? You are not—not!—going to destroy my one good chance at a decent crop! I won't let you!"

"We'll just see about that, little lady, now won't we? Jest so's you'll know we're fair sorts, here's a bit of advice. You best lock up your livestock 'bout four days from now lest they get swept up in our herd. No point adding insult to injury."

"If you're looking for a fight," Bowie said, his voice no louder than a snarl, "you've found one." Taking Rosie's arm, he pulled her though the small crowd and out onto the boardwalk. "We'll start with the sheriff."

"It won't do any good," Rosie said angrily. "The sheriff won't do anything." A tide of helplessness crashed over her.

Seven hundred stampeding longhorns. Her wheat didn't stand a chance.

Sheriff Gaine sat on the edge of his desk and listened to their story, then he lifted his belly, shot a wad toward the jailhouse spittoon, and sighed heavily.

"Exactly what do you expect me to do, Stone?"

"Ride out to their camp and quote the law about staying on the drive trail. Or you could arrest them."

"I got one deputy." The sheriff tipped his hat brim toward Carl Sands, who leaned against the wall wearing a thin smile. "In a pinch maybe I could scrape together a half-dozen men to form a posse, but not with harvest right on top of us and not without them cowboys doing something illegal which so far they ain't done. So far all they done is spew out some big talk about saving their employer a few dollars. Maybe they'll drive them longhorns down Main Street and maybe they won't. Until they run them steers over private land they ain't broke no laws that I know of."

A silent scream ricocheted through Rosie's mind. She stopped pacing and pressed a palm against the pain in her side. "You know what this crop means to me!" Flinging out her hand, she pointed toward the cells. "How many nights have you listened to me screaming curses at Frank Blevins? Now I finally have a decent crop and a chance to beat him! Are you telling me you won't do anything to stop that herd?"

"If I told you once I told you a hundred times. You can't get no revenge off a dead man."

Despair began at her toes and seared upward, pushing the breath out of her body. "You're going to let them destroy my crop and the crops of a dozen families before you'll do anything?"

"Your fields are fenced, ain't they?"

"Not all of them. The acres nearest the house are open," Bowie said, grinding his teeth. "But what difference does it make? How long do you think a wire fence will hold against a stampede?"

"I'm sorry, Stone, but the law is the law. Best I can do is promise I'll go after them boys if they run their herd across private property."

"By then it will be too damned late!" Shaking, Rosie covered her face with her hands. "I won't have enough wheat left to make a stack of flapjacks!"

The sun was setting by the time they returned to the farm, sinking into the horizon in a brilliant fan-shaped burst that transformed dry, brown prairie grasses into a twilight sea of pink and gold.

Rosie tumbled from the buckboard and stumbled toward the edge of the fields, staring at seven golden acres of the healthiest crop she had ever wrested from this hot dry land.

"One week," she whispered, pulling a kernel free from a yellow stalk. When the kernel was soft enough to dent with her thumbnail, the wheat would be ready for harvest. She couldn't make a dent yet, but the kernel had softened since her last test. Experience told her the fields would be ready to cut in a matter of days. "We're one week from harvest, maybe less." The drovers would stampede their cattle through her fields in four days. When it was over, all she'd have left would be chaff and crushed stalks.

Feeling hollow inside, she stared at her fields with dry eyes. Despair this profound stabbed too deep for tears.

"Have you ever seen a stampede, Stone?"

"Once." Grasping her shoulders, he turned her to face him. "How much of this crop can you lose and still make a profit?"

A bitter laugh choked her. "I keep forgetting that you aren't a farmer. You look out there and seven acres seems like it goes on forever. I look out there and I see seventy, maybe eighty bushels. I need every grain of it to bring in a profit and then we're only talking a few dollars. Already there's news of a bumper crop in Iowa and Missouri that will bring down the price. I need it *all*!"

Frowning, Bowie released her shoulders. He jammed his hands in his back pockets and studied the fields in the dying light. "You go on inside. I'll be along in a minute."

The weight of Rosie's despair continued to press him even after she returned to the house. His instinct was to ride to the drovers' camp and force them at gunpoint to return to the trail. What stopped him was knowing a man would promise anything while looking down the barrel of a gun. The minute Bowie rode out of the drovers' camp, thoughts of profit would turn the herd back toward Passion's Crossing.

Bending, he snapped off a stalk of wheat and rubbed the kernels into his palm. Sweat and blood and tears had nourished this grain. Broiling sun and breaking backs. Bloody blisters and burning muscles. Equal portions of love and hatred, hope and anxiety. The falling price of wheat didn't concern him. Whether or not the harvest yielded a single grain of salable wheat didn't matter because money would never again be a problem for Rosie Mulvehey. Establishing a generous trust for her was the first thing Bowie intended to do when he returned to Washington, D.C. Never again would she or Lodisha have to decide between affording coffee or sugar. He would ensure that Rosie could buy whatever luxury she wanted. A house far away from the dry plains of Kansas, a carriage, fine horses, jewels and Paris gowns if she wanted them.

Turning, he gazed back at the house, and the headstone gleaming in the starlight. After a moment, he flung the kernels of wheat away from him.

Rosie didn't want fancy carriages or Paris gowns. The single thing she wanted was revenge. He had never heard her mention anything else. And to have her revenge, to make herself whole, she needed a profitable harvest.

Planting his boots wide apart, Bowie crossed his arms over his chest and listened to the night breeze whispering through the wheat. The sound of the stalks brushing together was a sound that ran through his head day and night, a sound he had learned to hate because of the pain it represented to Rosie. He doubted he would ever forget the whisper of the wheat. Soon he would leave it behind.

The harvest was almost upon them and his time in Gulliver County neared an end. He hadn't promised Rosie that he would stay until she brought in a profitable harvest; he had promised to stay until she brought in the next harvest. This harvest.

At odd moments he found himself thinking about the telegram he would send to Alexander Dubage explaining that he was alive and when he would arrive in Washington. It seemed kinder to ask Dubage to break the news to Susan and the Senator rather than subject his family to the shock of receiving a letter from a dead man. They would be outraged and justifiably furious that he had allowed them to believe him dead for all these months. He could hardly expect a warm welcome.

Susan would despise him; her fragile nature would not withstand the knowledge of his bigamy. The greater pain rested in his conviction that his father had undoubtedly considered hanging a fit end for a son who had brought disgrace on the family name through a court-martial.

Finally, painfully, there was Rosie to think about. Rosie, whose love for him glowed in every shining glance, in every laughing smile. Rosie with her heart-aching bravery and unbending willpower. Rosie, who finally trusted a man and was beginning to trust herself.

When he let his thoughts edge up to saying good-bye to her, betraying her trust, a painful vise gripped his chest. Rosie Mulvehey wound through him like an additional artery, infusing him with her ambitions, her purpose, her reason to rise in the mornings and live. When he thought of leaving her behind, he thought of standing on the gallows with the weight of the noose on his shoulders. Rosie would have done everyone a favor if she had let him die that day.

Now he would wrong her again, as he wronged her each time he surrendered to weakness and welcomed her into his bed.

Bowie could argue a thousand times that teaching her the joy between a man and woman outweighed the betrayal to come, but his was the argument of a moral coward. He despised himself for such deception. He took her to bed because Rosie was his life's passion, the woman he desired above all others. Because of his weakness for this woman, he had worsened a situation that was insupportable to begin with.

"Damn it to hell!"

Rosie deserved someone who could love her with all the vibrancy and wholeheartedness that she herself was willing to give. She deserved a whole man who embraced life, a man with a future, and a man she could trust. Bowie could offer her nothing but pain. Thinking about betraying her trust sliced away a little portion of his soul.

As for himself, he saw nothing ahead but a hollow void stretching across the rest of his life. Without the cavalry, he had no future and no prospects, no ambitions or goals, no rock on which to build his life or pride. The blight on his spirit penetrated so deeply that he seldom thought beyond today and didn't much care in any case.

Right now, the only thing that mattered was Rosie. Her pain flowed through his blood and became his. He found himself almost wishing she hadn't gone dry yet. Liquor might have helped her through the devastation to come.

The only thing Rosie wanted was to harvest her seven acres. It seemed like such a small wish. Surely he could find a way to give it to her as his farewell gift.

* * *

John Hawkins cupped both hands around his coffee mug. "You're saying we should fill bags with creek gravel and build a barricade that's three acres long?"

Leaning forward, Bowie pushed aside the lamp and smoothed a piece of paper flat on the kitchen table. "We're most vulnerable here, along the three acres nearest the house." He pointed to a box he had drawn to represent the house and barn. "The fences on the back four acres might hold."

"Against a stampede, Cap'n?" Lodisha's black eyes filled with doubt. She slapped a mosquito sampling the side of her neck.

"You're right," Rosie said, studying Bowie's crude map, "If I were those drovers, I'd run the herd through the point of least resistance. Part of our fences are wire, part are rail. Why risk injuries when you can avoid the fences and bring them through here?" A fingernail tapped the area nearest the house. "Where there are no obstacles."

"Assuming the drovers told the truth about their schedule, we have three days left to create some obstacles."

Rosie gave him a damp look of gratitude. His eyes seemed impossibly blue against his sun-bronzed face. She swallowed hard, wanting to trace her fingertips along the lines framing his mouth.

"I don't know if your plan will work, but it'll give us something to do besides just sitting here and letting it happen." Sitting here and fighting a raging urge for a drink. It had been years since she had faced a crisis sober and without her trusty jug near at hand. Swallowing again, Rosie tried to concentrate on the conversation instead of yearning toward the false comforts shining in a bottle of blazer.

"First thing we gots to do is figure where we's gonna git 'nuff sacks to build ourselfs a barricade," Lodisha said, removing the supper plates from the table.

"There are five bundles of feed sacks in the loft." John Hawkins pursed his lips in thought. "Not nearly enough."

"Them sacks can git us started." Lodisha dropped the dishes into a basin of sudsy water. "I'll rip up the old clothing in my sewing box and stitch bags out'n 'em. Got a pile of fabric scraps too." She chewed her lower lip. "Don't reckon I got 'nuff goods to make three acres' worth, not no-how. How high you figure this here barricade gots to be, Cap'n?"

"Three feet high would be best."

"Hoo-ee. Goin' need all the sacks in this here county!"

They contemplated the hopelessness of building a wall three feet high and three acres long.

"When we run out of gravel sacks, we can use brush and wood scraps," Rosie said. "We could cut down the cottonwoods if we have to."

"But we agree in principle?" Bowie examined their faces in the lamplight. "We'll do whatever we can?"

"This is good," John Hawkins said finally, speaking for them all. "A futile effort is better than no effort at all."

Rosie pushed away from the table and squeezed her hands on Bowie's shoulders. "Give me two minutes to change into my pants and boots, then I'll join you at the creek for a moonlight gravel dig."

They labored until three in the morning shoveling wet gravel out of the creek bed and piling it on the banks. After three hours' exhausted sleep, they wolfed down Lodisha's platters of bacon, mush and eggs, then began filling the sacks John Hawkins brought from the barn and those Lodisha had sewn during the night.

Swiftly it became apparent they had enough sacks to cover no more than about thirty yards. And the work was frustratingly slow and laborious. Lodisha held the bags open while

Rosie shoveled gravel into them; John Hawkins pushed them in a wheelbarrow to Bowie, who built their wall. By mid-morning the pile of empty sacks was gone.

After their noon dinner, Rosie pulled down the tin boxes above the stove and spilled them open over the broadshelf, counting out the coins she found there. "You have any more of that money you found in Blevins' trunk?" she asked Bowie. He produced a couple of dollars, and she shoved them in her pocket. "I'm taking the wagon to town. Keep digging gravel."

Rosie bought extra bullets and every sack offered for sale at Mrs. Hodge's General Store, then she posted a sign in the window saying more sacks were urgently needed, payment to follow later.

"Lordy, Mrs. Stone, why on earth would you need more feed sacks?" Mrs. Hodge pointedly refrained from glancing at Rosie's pants and soiled shirt. Rumor insisted Rosie Stone was a changed woman, but Mrs. Hodge didn't see much evidence of it. She still dressed like a man and did crazy things. Sacks indeed.

"We're building a barricade, Mrs. Hodge," Rosie explained between trips out to the wagon. "To stop those longhorns from coming through Passion's Crossing. At least we're going to try."

"Oh." Mrs. Hodge considered the answer. The feed sacks didn't seem so crazy after all if they were destined as a barricade to save the crops. She peered through the window at the bundled sacks stacked in the back of Rosie's wagon. "How much area are you trying to cover?"

"Three acres. What do I owe you?"

"Three acres?" Mrs. Hodge stared. "There isn't enough sacks or gravel in the entire county to enclose three acres."

"We aren't trying to enclose anything. We want to protect the outer perimeter."

"You got any help out there?"

"The best help there is. My husband, John Hawkins, and Lodisha. Please, Mrs. Hodge. I'm in a hurry."

"You need more sacks and more time and more help. Your plan ain't going to work, Mrs. Stone."

Rosie's eyes answered that she knew it. "We have to try," she said softly, hearing the desperation in her voice. "We can't let a handful of cowmen destroy our dreams without putting up some kind of fight."

"Seems to me this ain't your fight alone. If them steers get past your farm, they'll trample through the other farms between your place and town like a hot knife going through butter."

"Here." Rosie pushed her money across the high counter. "If that isn't enough, put the rest on my account and I'll pay the balance when I can."

Mrs. Hodge went to the door of her store and watched with a thoughtful expression as Rosie drove her wagon hell-bent for leather past Harold's place without giving the saloon so much as a howdy-do.

She called to her daughter. "You high-tail it over to Mayor Bill's smithy and you tell him your mama demands a town meeting before sundown, so he better put out the word. If old Bill even looks like he's resisting, you tell him what stores are left in Passion's Crossing are going to close down if the farmers can't pay and the farmers can't pay if they can't bring in their crops. Don't dawdle, girl. Cows are coming and that's bad for everybody. Some folks ain't thought this through or they're too beat down to put up a fight. We got to light some fires under some butts! Get moving, girl."

Chapter Sixteen

Owl's Butte, Wyoming

The mayor waited behind a table facing a packed audience. Two members of the town council sat on either side of him. They watched Susan walk down an aisle between a sea of benches, and Mayor Mercer indicated she should take the chair to the side of the council's table.

"I guess we all know why we're here," the mayor said, after calling for silence. "Our new teacher, Mrs. Stone, is going to ask the council to keep the school open over the summer." A swell of noisy protest erupted from the audience. "It's only fair that we hear what Mrs. Stone has to say. You can object afterwards."

Susan's heart fluttered behind her corset and plummeted to her toes. Her throat dried to dust. The council had made up its mind; there would be no summer school. She might as well have stayed away and spared herself the agony of speaking in public.

"You have the floor, ma'am."

Panicked, Susan touched the nosegay pinned to her shoulder, wishing she had the courage to examine the crowd and find Gresham. But a single glance at her audience would have shattered her completely.

Remaining seated, she swallowed, then smoothed her one-page speech across her knees before she read it aloud. Her choked whisper reminded her of Eddie, inaudible and painfully uncertain

"Can't hear!" someone shouted from the rear of the hall.

Susan wet her lips, tried to quiet her shaking hands, and raised her voice to a murmur.

"Louder!"

There was no reason to speak louder because she had finished her speech. When she lifted her head to glance at the men on the town council, she saw their closed, almost bored expressions, understood that they waited to cast a vote already decided.

The tragedy of failure pierced her heart. The children of Owl's Butte had not had any educational instruction for two years. They lagged in their studies and would fall farther behind during the summer. The earnest faces of her seven students rose behind her eyes. They wanted so badly to learn, even Eddie. It broke her heart that they would not have the chance.

Biting her lip and frowning, Susan examined the men on the council. Suddenly she realized they didn't grasp that she had completed her presentation. There was still time to change their minds. If that were possible. And if she was equal to the task.

Blood rushed into her head, and she ground her teeth together. Closing the school was wrong. If nothing else, the residents of Owl's Butte should at least understand what their decision would do to the children.

Abruptly, and without planning it, Susan sprang to her feet. Red-cheeked and shaking with the depth of her conviction, she faced the audience, forgetting her fear in the necessity of convincing them. Her heart opened and words poured out.

"I know you want your children home to help with the summer chores," she said, speaking loudly enough that her voice carried to the back row of benches. "But have you considered what a three-month break will do to your children? They will forget everything they've learned in the last month, just as they have forgotten almost everything they learned two years ago!"

Gaining strength from her utter belief in what she was saying, she moved to the head of the aisle, gazing into the faces turned up to her. "The children of County Creek are years ahead of our children in their studies. This means the children of County Creek are better prepared for the future and better equipped to make a success of themselves than our children. Is that what we want? To place our children at a disadvantage?"

No one spoke. They watched her and exchanged uneasy glances, sensing something had changed.

"Mrs. Alder," Susan said suddenly, finding her friend's startled face in the center of the crowd. "Did you know that your Hettie has a wonderful head for figures? Unfortunately, she's had very little instruction in arithmetic. If Hettie knew her sums, she could do more than clean and change linens at the hotel. She could keep your books and manage your budget, could register guests and make correct change. Hettie would like to work with accounting, but right now she can't. She lacks the skill."

She turned toward the mayor. "I had to discipline your son because he refused to read aloud. Do you know why he refused? Because he can't read, your honor. Eddie is a bright, resourceful young man who wants to be a doctor someday.

But he can't read. The years are passing and soon it will be too late for Eddie to pursue his dream. He'll have to settle for a vocation where reading isn't necessary. This breaks my heart, sir. Does it break yours?"

She moved down the aisle pointing to the parents of her students, telling them about their children and watching appalled expressions appear in the parents' eyes as she translated their children's ignorance into practical terms.

"Only one of my seven students understands why we will celebrate the Fourth of July next week," she said, her voice ringing with the passion that filled her heart. "Is that what you want? Do you want your children to remain ignorant?" Pausing, she cast flashing eyes down at a row of faces. "All of you have children, but they aren't in my classes. By denying your children an education, you're keeping them ignorant and vulnerable to those who *are* educated. Is that how we will conquer the west and civilize it? With a new generation that cannot read a land contract or a kitchen receipt? With sons and daughters who cannot figure profits or losses?"

She spied Gresham then, leaning against the back wall. He wore a wide proud grin and his dark eyes glowed.

"If you want an educated generation to follow in your footsteps and build on your labor, then I urge you to keep the school open and send me your children. If you can't spare them five days a week, then send them three days a week or whenever you can. The children of Owl's Butte are so far behind that any education at all will help them. But don't, I beg you, don't abandon your children to a life of ignorance and vulnerability. Give them the opportunity to develop their skills and talents!"

Susan stood at the front of the aisle, her blue eyes blazing, her hands shaking with emotion. In dead silence she slowly gazed up one row of benches then down the next, meeting the eyes of every person in the room.

Then she turned and walked to her chair, the tapping of her heels the only sound in the large room. Face flaming, she sat down and clasped trembling hands in her lap.

Mayor Mercer leaned over the table and stared hard at her. "My boy told me he was disciplined because he didn't want to read out loud."

"Your Eddie can hardly read at all. The other children laugh and tease him."

A voice that sounded suspiciously like Gresham Harte's shouted from the back of the hall. "I say we keep the school open!"

The silence ended and another voice took up the cry, then another.

". . . damned shame that our children can't . . ."

"Without an education, my boy isn't going to—"

"—finally get a teacher, and now they want to close the school. If that don't beat all!"

The tide of opinion had swung; without an education, a person was easy pickings for every sharp-tongued slicker who came down the pike, a waiting victim for every snake-oil salesman. Moreover, it was an outrage that the children of County Creek were more advanced than the children of Owl's Butte. When a lone voice objected to the expense of extending Susan's salary for an additional three months, he was shouted down.

Mayor Mercer glanced at the council members seated beside him. They didn't need to confer to know that Mrs. Stone had carried the day. The school would remain open throughout the summer.

After the meeting adjourned, Susan rose, straightened her shoulders, then floated down the aisle in a triumphant daze. Hands reached to pat her arm; voices called congratulations and urged her to continue her endeavors on behalf of Owl's Butte's children. Outside, knots of people congregated around her, wanting to hear more about her ideas on education, telling her how grateful they were that she had decided to make her home in Owl's Butte.

It was nearly midnight before Gresham took her arm and eased her away from the scene of her triumph. "Who brought you into town?" he asked, leading her back toward the hotel.

"Mrs. Alder," Susan answered absently, still dazed by the evening's events. The glorious ring of congratulations pealed in her head. She continued to see the residents of Owl's Butte looking at *her* with respect and admiration, not because she was a senator's daughter-in-law or because she was a captain's wife, but because she was herself, a schoolteacher and a champion for the town's children. For the first time in her life, Susan Stone had won respect in her own right.

The amazement of it dazzled her and lent wings to her feet. She floated up the darkened street, Gresham's arm her only anchor to the earth.

Without Susan remembering how it happened, it was decided that Gresham would see her home. Holding Nate on her lap, her nose snuggled against her son's sweet-smelling hair, Susan relived her victory, trying to recall exactly what she had said to the good citizens of Owl's Butte. The passion of the moment blurred her memory. She had spoken from her heart.

Gresham carried Nate into the cabin, received a sleepy kiss for his effort, and laid the boy carefully on the bed behind the screen of sheets while Susan lit the lamps.

"I could warm some coffee," she suggested hopefully, reluctant to let the evening end.

"It's late, and I'm driving out to the homestead from here. I hope to get some work done on the place tomorrow."

Regretting that he had to leave, wanting to discuss the miracle of her success yet again, Susan walked with him out onto the porch, inhaling the cool night air. A sliver of moon hung in the starry sky. Though the air was moist and smelled like rain, nothing could dampen her elation.

She placed her fingertips on Gresham's sleeve. "Thank you for your advice, Mr. Harte. Speaking from the heart made all the difference."

Gresham gazed into her glowing face, lit by the light that fell from the doorway. "I was as proud of you as you should be of yourself. You were wonderful tonight!"

They stood as still as statues, gazing into each other's eyes, and time stopped for them. It seemed the most natural thing in the world when Gresham stepped forward and drew her into his arms. He studied the sweet curve of her mouth, then he groaned softly and kissed her. And his kiss was exactly as Susan had imagined it would be. Warm and slightly moist, tender with a hint of restrained passion. She fit into his arms as perfectly as a cup in a saucer, exactly as she had dreamed she would.

He drew back and blinked at her. "Good God. You have the softest mouth in the world!"

He grabbed her and kissed her again, holding her tighter, his mouth harder on hers, his body tensing against her, his hands tight on her waist. Susan wrapped her arms around his neck and kissed him back until they were both reeling and breathless.

When he released her, Gresham stared down at her and she noticed his spectacles were fogged. "I'm deeply sorry, Mrs. Stone. I apologize," he said hoarsely, moving back from her. "I don't know what came over me, I—"

He fell down the last step of the porch, hastily picked himself up and dusted off his trousers.

"Please forgive me. I've acted like a cad."

Turning, he strode rapidly through the darkness toward his wagon, mopping his brow with a snowy handkerchief.

Good Lord. He had kissed her. Twice. And he hadn't wanted

to stop kissing her. He wanted to scoop her into his arms and carry her to a deep feather bed and make love to her until she was covered with dewy perspiration and rosy with satisfaction.

Halting beside the wagon, he looked back at the porch. She stood in a pool of soft light, her fingertips pressed to her lips. And she was looking after him with one of those secret woman smiles that he could never decipher. The light behind her outlined the seductive curve of her small perfect body.

Swearing, Gresham kicked one of the wagon wheels. Then he walked back to the porch steps and gazed up at her.

"Will you and Nate go with me to the Fourth of July lake social?"

"Yes." She dropped her fingertips to the nosegay pinned above her small lovely breast. And she gave him another of those soft-eyed enigmatic smiles. He had to restrain himself from leaping up the porch steps and grabbing her for another kiss.

"I'll bring our picnic," she said in a dreamy voice.

"As you like," he agreed, uneasily sensing that he would have consented to anything she said.

They stared at each other until the air crackled between them, and Gresham realized he either had to leave this instant or he was going to run up the steps and behave very badly.

"Well. Goodnight then."

"Goodnight, Mr. Harte."

Giving the horse his head, Gresham slumped over the reins and swore softly into the dark night. He was lost. The minute he had wrapped her small body within his arms, he had realized that he'd been daydreaming about kissing her for weeks. And kissing her had been as exciting as he had feared it would be.

She couldn't cook, couldn't wash or iron. She didn't know anything about building a house or fishing or livestock. He couldn't imagine her wringing a chicken's neck and preparing it for supper.

But by God, Susan Stone had courage. She had walked into a hostile audience, frightened and not believing she had a chance in hell to win them over. But she had opened a room full of closed minds. She had been magnificent in the passion of her convictions, striding up and down the aisle like a young queen. Like everyone else, he hadn't been able to take his eyes off her.

Although the thought was unworthy of a gentleman, he wondered if she were passionate in other areas as well.

He sighed and shook his head. God help him, he was indeed courting her.

"Gresham Harte, you are an idiot," he said aloud. As a lawyer he knew as well as anyone that the heart knew no reason. When it came to contracts and women, a man's judgment focused on all the wrong things.

But when she lifted those blue eyes and smiled at him, he felt ten feet tall. Her mouth was as ripe and sweet as a summer peach, and her hair was as soft and fragrant as he had known it would be.

A long sigh collapsed his shoulders. He had kissed her. Now he would never be able to forget her. He was a doomed man.

The breezy surface of McCairn's Lake reflected rippling images of distant mountain peaks framed by the cottonwoods and willows that grew down to the shore on the north side. To the south a tree-shaded promontory jutted into the water; children waded and swam off one side of the land spit, a flotilla of rowboats and sailboats launched from a jetty on the other side.

Children laughed, shrieked and chased one another through

the picnic area, waiting to watch the black powder shoot scheduled for later in the afternoon. Men played horseshoes in the shade and women gathered near the refreshment tables to visit and compare needlework. At five o'clock the Fourth of July speeches would begin, delivered on the steps of a bandstand draped with bunting. A fireworks display was promised as soon as darkness fell.

Nearly all the residents of Owl's Butte and a few from County Creek played or relaxed on the shores of the lake, exchanging greetings and sharing jugs of lake-cooled cider and lemonade.

Susan straightened and shaded her eyes, looking across the meadow toward the shore, trying to find Nate among the children racing through clusters of adults. After she spotted her son near the bandstand watching the older boys playing marbles, she returned her attention to the croquet game and made a face as Gresham knocked his ball against the post and won the game. He removed his straw hat in a jaunty salute and grinned at her.

"Having thoroughly trounced you ladies, I feel I owe you a turn around the lake. Will you join me in a sail?"

Henrietta Winters placed her fingertips on Susan's sleeve. "Perhaps later." They watched Gresham stride toward the checkers tournament as they opened their parasols above their hats. "Gresham Harte is a good man. You could do worse," Henrietta murmured, sliding a knowing glance toward Susan's sudden blush.

"He ate my picnic lunch," Susan answered softly, her gaze following him. Smiling, she recalled the moment when Gresham had opened her basket and spied the charred lumps of fried chicken. He had earnestly assured her that he preferred his chicken well cooked, and he had praised her hard-boiled eggs to the skies when even Susan knew there was no knack to boiling an egg.

It was when he complimented her watery over-sugared lemonade that Susan had lifted her head, gazed into his eyes, and realized Gresham loved her.

At that moment the summer day blossomed into the most thrilling and wonderful day of her life. Suddenly the sky was bluer, the air sweeter and brighter. The trees and freshly mowed meadow glowed in tones of emerald green, the wildflowers along the shore caught the sun like scattered jewels.

Her heart soared and sang with the wonder of discovery, of being loved, and her cheeks lit from within. In a blaze of happiness, she had caught Nate in her arms and buried a smile of joy against his wind-tousled hair. Gresham Harte loved her.

Gresham Harte, educated, mannered and thoughtful. Reluctant, stubborn, set in his ways. Gresham Harte, sturdy, bespectacled, handsome, the man who sent her woman's heart racing when she gazed into his warm dark eyes. Gresham loved her.

Smiling, hugging her secret knowledge to herself, Susan gripped the handle of her parasol and watched the sailboats billow across the lake. Daydreaming, she wondered how long it would be before Gresham admitted to himself that he loved her and guessed that she loved him too.

"I can't tell you how pleased I am with all you have accomplished in so short a time," Henrietta said after they had refreshed themselves with a cup of Mrs. Alder's excellent cherry cider. Arm in arm, they strolled toward the shore. "I'd like you to consider running for election as Superintendent of Schools."

Susan halted abruptly. "Me? Surely you have more experienced teachers better suited to such a responsible position!"

"I'm speaking of the future, perhaps four or five years from now," Henrietta explained, smiling and patting Susan's arm. "By then you will be ready. I'm mentioning the possibility now so you can begin developing administrative skills."

Frowning, Susan lifted her hem and stepped over a rock.

She could not imagine declaring herself as a candidate for election, exposing herself to the possibility of public humiliation . . . or public triumph. Still, since coming west she had thrown herself into many daunting projects that she would not have been able to imagine herself attempting only a short time earlier.

Twirling her parasol, trying to visualize herself assuming Henrietta's role and responsibilities, Susan watched Eddie Mercer and the older boys tilt their sails to the wind and shoot across the surface of the lake, earning shouts of angry protest from the occupants of lazily drifting rowboats.

"Your progress has been remarkable, Susan. I've watched you develop into a confident woman and a dedicated teacher, and you've done so in a shorter period of time than I would have thought possible. You aren't the same woman who knocked on my door. You speak with more conviction, you even walk differently. You carry yourself taller."

Susan laughed. "I walk differently?"

"You stride forward like a woman with a purpose, a woman who knows where she is going. You carry your head high and you look people squarely in the eyes. There's a new strength in your carriage and in your expression."

Many of these changes Susan had sensed, but it startled her to hear them confirmed by an independent observer.

"You've carved a place for yourself in Owl's Butte. You have proven your character and your worth, and you've earned the respect and esteem of the community."

Men tipped their hats to her in the streets, women greeted her warmly and solicited her opinion about child-related issues. She had overheard the owner of the general store proudly inform a stranger, "That's Mrs. Stone, our teacher."

"Mr. Dubage, my attorney in Washington, sends me trunk-loads of books on child care and teaching," she admitted with a smile, recalling the endless nights of reading after she put

Nate to bed. "But I still don't know a fraction of what I need to know."

"You will. Dedication such as yours will be rewarded."

Susan tilted her head to watch a kite flirting with heaven. "When I came to Owl's Butte, I was at the lowest point in my life. I felt cast out and abandoned, unable to cope. I honestly did not believe I could survive without a man to care for me. If it hadn't been for Nate, I might have done something very foolish." She drew a tremulous breath, recalling the nights she had wept in the darkness and considered taking her own life. "That first day, I stood on Mrs. Alder's porch and looked down Main Street and I thought Owl's Butte was the smallest, ugliest, most unappealing town I had ever seen. I thought the people were primitive and rude and lacking even the rudiments of culture or refinement. All I could think about was escaping from this place."

Henrietta smiled but said nothing.

"I was wrong about everything." Susan glanced fondly at her neighbors strolling along the shores. She knew all their names and the history of most. "These are good, honest, hard-working people. I'm proud to call them friends. Now I have the eyes to see Owl's Butte's virtues, and the vision to understand that time and growth will soften the town's rough edges."

"Do you miss a more sophisticated society?"

"For a while I did. But I'm building a life now that is full and satisfying." Sometimes she felt as if she had awakened after slumbering through most of her life. Emerging into true wakefulness was occasionally terrifying, but also exhilarating. "I've had an opportunity to know my son in a way I never would have if my husband had lived and my life hadn't changed." She fell silent a moment, searching the picnic area for Nate. That she didn't immediately spot him was not a concern. The residents of Owl's Butte kept an eye on everyone's children.

"I'm accomplishing something good here," she said, hearing the shy pride in her voice. "I'm making a difference in the children's lives. I'm earning my way in the world. I used to sleep late and awaken wondering how I would fill the hours until the evening's social events." She smiled. "Now I wake with the roosters and there isn't a wasted moment all day. By ten o'clock at night I'm so tired I can't keep my eyes open. But it's a good and satisfying kind of tired. I know I've accomplished something or learned something new."

A small frown disturbed her brow. One of the things she most wanted to learn was why she could not obtain the death certificate necessary to settle Bowie's estate. Either her inquiries to Passion's Crossing went unanswered, or the telegraphed replies were vague and puzzling.

Hettie Alder ran up to them, followed by two younger girls wearing new white aprons over their holiday dresses. She clasped Susan's hand.

"Mama says we can go on the lake if you'll take us. Will you, Mrs. Stone? Please?"

Susan smiled at Henrietta. "Only if Mrs. Winters agrees to share the rowing." When the girls protested that they wanted to sail like the boys, Susan shook her head. "I don't know anything about sailing. It looks dangerous to me." The ever-present Wyoming wind cupped the canvas of the sailboats and shot them across the surface at what looked to be thrilling but perilous speeds.

Mrs. Winters surrendered to the entreaties and let the girls pull them toward the jetty. She and Susan chose a sturdy rowboat and helped the girls inside, then seated themselves beside the oars, trying not to overturn the boat in the process.

Their initial efforts to coordinate their oar strokes sent them all into spasms of giggles and laughter. Not so long ago Susan wouldn't have dreamed of attempting to row a boat. She would have sought a man to accompany them and manage the rowing. Now she accepted the challenge that even on holiday there were interesting new difficulties to experience and master.

As they approached the racing buoys, they shipped the oars and drifted with the lake currents, opening their parasols and lazily calling greetings when other boats floated nearby. They were too far from shore for Susan to identify Nate among the children that romped around the bandstand or napped in the shade. She thought she spotted Gresham near the buckboards lined along the meadow, but she wasn't sure.

It was a perfect and wonderful day, the best Fourth of July she had ever celebrated and one she would never forget.

Tilting her head back and counting her blessings, Susan smiled at the clear cloudless sky, so filled with happiness that she wondered how her small body could contain it all. Her darling Nate was strong and healthy, tanned and happily thriving. For the first time in her life, Susan was beginning to feel confident in herself and worthwhile in her own right. She was surrounded by people who liked and respected her. And Gresham Harte loved her. The future was no longer a frightening concept; it looked bright and splendid, a gaily wrapped package promising joyful surprises.

And then, in one terrible moment everything changed.

It happened so swiftly that afterward she couldn't remember the exact sequence of events. She remembered Henrietta rousing from a sun-soaked reverie and suddenly gripping her arm, remembered Hettie shouting that their boat had drifted past the buoys and into the racing area.

When Susan dropped her parasol, she saw two sailboats bearing down on them, one on either side, heard the shouts and screams. There was no time to react, nothing she could do except watch in helpless horror as Eddie Mercer's sailboat struck the bow of her rowboat at almost the same moment as Jimmy Cathcart's sailboat crashed against the stern.

Suddenly she was pitched into the water, chill waves closing over her head, desperately fighting the weight of her skirt and petticoats as she struggled to the surface and gasped for air in the midst of the wreckage of the boats. Heads bobbed in the water around her. Screams for help shouted in her ears. Hettie Alder was nearest, terrified and tangled in the canvas of one of the overturned sailboats.

Later Mrs. Alder told Susan that she had disentangled Hettie from the canvas and lines and swum nearly half a mile to shore, pulling Hettie with her. She didn't remember kicking out of her boots, tearing off her skirt and top petticoat and returning to the overturned boats. But apparently she had. She had stayed in the water, gripping the overturned rowboat and holding Ellen Marsh's head above water until help arrived.

Jimmy Cathcart's father pulled Ellen into a rowboat that appeared like an answered prayer, and he asked if Susan had the strength to swim back to shore.

She remembered almost nothing of that final swim toward the anxious crowd shouting on the shore, except that she had been unsure if she would make it. Exhaustion shook her frame. The deep chill of the lake water seeped into her bones and turned her arms leaden. Tangled petticoats wrapped around her legs and threatened to drag her down.

Then she was struggling to stand and walk out of the water, gasping, shaking, her hair streaming into her eyes, her feet dragging through the mud on the lake bottom.

"Susan!"

Pushing back the hair dripping across her face, panting for breath, she lifted her head and watched Gresham run into the water, unmindful of his boots or pants. His arms opened to her but it was his devastated expression that froze her in place. Sunlight flashed on the tears filling his eyes.

For a moment Susan stared at him without understanding.

Tears? Gresham? Then her heart lurched painfully and ceased to beat. Suddenly she became aware of the terrible stillness of those who watched as she struggled to pull herself out of the lake. She saw Mrs. Alder cover her eyes and bend away, saw Henrietta, soaked and shaking, gazing at her with tears streaming down her white face.

And finally, she noticed the three bodies laid out beneath the cottonwood, covered by tablecloths. One of the covered bodies was so small.

Cold black terror bored through her heart.

"Susan." Gresham reached her where she stood paralyzed in knee-deep water. He would have pulled her into his arms, but she pushed him away in panic, trying to jerk her feet out of the mud, trying to reach the shore.

"Nate!" She screamed his name, not recognizing the strangled voice as her own. "Nate? Where are you? Nate!"

The small still body could not be Nate. Not her Nate. No.

He was playing marbles with the boys near the bandstand. He was napping. He was playing hide and seek with the Wilsons' girl.

Gresham caught her shoulders and turned her to face him. Tears rolled down his cheeks but he seemed unaware of them.

"No," Susan moaned, swaying and staring at him. "Oh God, no. No."

"Nate was in Eddie's boat, Susan." Gresham stared at her through wet eyes. "There's a gash . . . he must have struck his head when he was thrown out at impact. Eddie tried . . . they were both lost and Jane Olsen too."

"No." Anguish closed her throat, clawed her skin. Her fingernails dug into Gresham's arms. Throwing back her head, she opened her lips, but no sound emerged. "No. No! Nonononono!"

Floundering in the water, she collapsed against Gresham's

chest, felt his arms fold around her. The smell of sun-heated starch and male perspiration rose in her nostrils. The warm smell of summer and meadow, cider and fried chicken.

When Susan opened her eyes Mrs. Alder and Henrietta stood in the water beside her. She heard their voices, felt their hands on her shoulders, but she saw nothing.

She stared at scenes that only she could see: Nate with a book in his hand, eagerly asking her to read him to sleep. Nate, flushed and rosy with dreams. Nate, carefully pushing seeds into the warm soil of her kitchen garden, tumbling after Hettie Alder's cocker spaniel. She saw him learning to fish, learning his ABC's, struggling not to interrupt when she was teaching. She saw him playing in the sunshine, running after the bigger boys, counting the weeks until his birthday.

The puppy. Nate would never have his own puppy.

"Oh, God! Oh, God! Oh, God!"

Gresham's arm slid beneath her knees and he carried her out of the water and onto firm ground. The sky and overhead branches spun above her and Susan thought she would faint. She prayed to faint, begged God to take her away from this horror and let her faint, but the horror continued. The instant Gresham placed her on her feet, she spun toward the bodies laid in a row beneath the cottonwood. Gresham caught her arm and for a panicked moment she thought she couldn't jerk free.

"That isn't Nate," she explained, her lips wooden and blood-less. She couldn't breathe, the air had disappeared. "I'll show you. That isn't my Nate!"

"Let her go to him," Mrs. Alder advised Gresham in a low voice. "She has to see and know for herself."

Strangling, unable to fill her lungs with a full breath, Susan lifted her petticoats and sprinted toward the smallest form beneath the cottonwood. Dropping to her knees, shaking vio-lently, she whispered a prayer of denial. As if from a great distance, she watched her trembling hand reach, then draw the tablecloth down.

Not until she saw Nate's small still face did she believe that he could be dead. The knowledge plunged like a dagger into her heart, her pain building into a scream. Blinded by tears, she smoothed his wet hair from the gash on his forehead, dropped her shaking fingertips to his mouth. She clasped his hands in hers and rubbed them vigorously as if by love and will alone she could restore heat and life to those tiny fingers. Far away she heard someone sobbing and screaming "no" over and over again.

When she felt Gresham's hand on her shoulder, Susan bent over Nate and lifted him in her arms, clasping him close to her breast. "I have to go home now," she said, not caring if she made sense or not. Gresham helped her stand and would have taken Nate from her arms, but she made a low growling noise deep in her throat and clutched Nate's small body closer to her own.

A sea of stunned faces parted as Gresham led her toward the row of buckboards. Hands reached to touch her, but Susan felt nothing. Murmurs of sorrow and sympathy rose around her, but she didn't hear. She was dying, drowning by slow inches in an ocean of pain.

Throughout the seemingly endless drive from the lake to Owl's Butte and then to her cabin, she leaned against Gresham and rocked Nate in her arms, crooning to him and wiping her tears from his silent face.

Before they reached the cabin, she clasped Nate to her breast, then threw back her head and screamed and screamed, howling in pain.

Shock insulated her during those first hideous days of loss and agony. Somehow she moved through the hours, dead inside, doing what had to be done.

In the west kindness vanquished the rigid etiquette of the east. Instead of politely evading her grief, the women of Owl's Butte appeared at Susan's door early in the morning, bringing covered dishes of food, and they stayed to grieve and cry with her.

The Ladies' Aid Society sewed lightweight mourning clothing for her. Someone brought a packet of black-edged handkerchiefs. Susan's students composed poems in Nate's memory and presented them in a booklet bound in blue ribbon. The volunteer fire brigade took up a collection and bought gold funeral lockets for the parents of the drowned children. Mrs. Alder placed a lock of Nate's hair inside Susan's locket and pinned the locket to her breast.

Businesses closed and everyone in Owl's Butte turned out for the children's funerals, forming a long line of gigs and buckboards along the dusty road to the cemetery. When the service ended, a blanket of flowers covered the new graves.

And through it all, Gresham never left Susan's side.

He was there, holding her hand, when the women prepared Nate's body for burial, and it was Gresham who arranged for the coffin and Nate's headstone. He kept the coffee pot filled on Susan's stove and watered the horses of the visiting women. He made her eat though she had no appetite, walked with her when she had to move or go out of her mind. He packed away Nate's books, toys and clothing and he carried the box down to the cellar, placing it out of sight until Susan was ready to go through the things herself.

In the evenings, they sat on the porch steps, their shoulders touching, and he listened as Susan reviewed Nate's short life, remembering their train trip west, the meals in Mrs. Alder's dining room, and all the gestures, the smiles, the tiny things that had made Nate so unique and special.

Susan buried her face in her hands. "Why did I tell him that he had to wait until his birthday? Why didn't I get him the puppy when he first asked?" She tortured herself about the puppy, wishing desperately that she could turn back the clock.

When she lifted her face, she saw that Gresham's eyes were wet too. Blindly, she turned into his arms.

"Oh Gresham. The only thing he ever asked for was a puppy! And I made him wait. Now he'll never have a puppy!"

Gently, Gresham folded his arms around her and laid his cheek against her hair. "There are puppies in heaven," he promised in a thick voice. "It wouldn't be heaven if there weren't puppies for little boys to play with and love." His arms tightened around her. "I loved him too, Susan."

Holding each other, they wept.

On the night of the fifth day after the funeral, Gresham stood up from the porch step where they had passed the evening and extended his hand to help Susan to her feet. "It's almost midnight. You need some rest," he said, examining her face in the starlight. "You're exhausted."

"You must be tired too." Gresham had been sleeping in the chair by the window, there if she needed him. Raising a hand, Susan lightly touched the circles beneath his eyes, too weary to wonder where he had left his spectacles. "You should go home. Sleep in your own bed and get a good night's rest."

If occurred to her that if Gresham stayed with her much longer, people would begin to talk, if they weren't gossiping already. Until yesterday Mrs. Alder had also stayed over, but tonight she and Gresham were alone. They became aware of that fact at the same moment.

"I suppose I'd better return to town," he said reluctantly, studying her pale face. "Will you be all right?"

The question seemed ludicrous. Susan would never be fully all right again, would never feel entirely whole. Nate had been the focus of her life, her reason to live and go on. Now a vast emptiness spread through her heart, eating away at the space Nate had occupied. Nate's unthinkable death had hollowed her out, leaving her empty inside.

"Yes," she lied, blinking back tears.

Gresham cupped her chin in his palm and tilted her face up to meet his eyes. His voice sank to a whisper. "Do you really want me to leave, Susan?"

For an instant her world narrowed to the warmth in his dark eyes. For days she had relied on that warmth to keep the horror at bay, to make the deep chill inside bearable. She didn't know how she would go on when he left her.

Her fingers tightened on his sleeves. "Oh Gresham, I want you to hold me and make the cold go away. And the pain, the terrible emptiness. I want you to bring Nate back to me! I want to go back and watch the two of you fishing again. I want you to explain why this happened. Why, Gresham? Why did it have to be Nate? Why?" Tears blinded her.

In one fluid motion, he swept her into his arms. He held her against his chest for a moment, then he carried her into the cabin and behind the screen to her bed. Gently, he placed her on top of the quilt, then lay down beside her, smoothing tendrils of hair away from her wet cheeks.

"There is no answer, dearest Susan, I think you know that. We only torture ourselves by asking why." Drawing her into his arms, he kissed her temples, the tears at the corners of her eyes. "All we can do is accept God's will and go on."

Susan turned and pressed herself against him, drawing his warmth into her body, seeking comfort in his strength, in the familiar scent of him, and the tenderness of his kisses.

"I'm so cold." The summer night was warm, the heat of the day trapped within the cabin, but she couldn't stop shivering. She hadn't felt warm since the moment the lake waters closed over her head.

Gresham pulled the extra quilt over them, then folded her

in his arms, holding her tenderly against his chest, stroking his large warm hands down her back. His lips moved over her hair, her forehead, her eyelids, her mouth.

Susan couldn't identify the exact moment when holding and touching each other altered from gestures of comfort and shared sorrow to the caresses of lovers exploring a new and growing awareness.

One moment she was lying in Gresham's arms, quietly weeping, then she was responding to the building heat as his kisses changed character and became the expression of a man's love and passion for a desirable woman.

To her amazement, her body slowly returned to life. First her skin warmed for the first time in days. Then sensation flooded back as Gresham opened her high collar and kissed her throat. For the first time in days she drew a full deep breath and felt her pulse beat again. Something new and strong battled against the pain and pushed it to manageable levels, allowing her to focus on what was happening between them.

"Yes," she whispered as Gresham's hand gently cupped her breast. "Don't stop." Moving beneath the quilt, she pressed her hips to his, blindly seeking a reaffirmation of life. Wrapping her arms around his neck, she offered her lips and returned his kiss with a force born of desperation and sudden overwhelming need. She needed this moment, needed Gresham, but more, she needed to emerge from the death of feeling, the deadening of her senses. If she was to survive, she had to welcome life back into her spirit and body. She had to believe that life could be worthwhile.

Gresham drew back slightly, studying her face in the shadows. "Susan, are you sure?" he asked hoarsely. "I don't want to take advantage of—"

She smothered his words with her mouth, drawing him back to her. When her lips released his, they stared at each other in the darkness. Then suddenly they were pulling and tugging at each other's clothing, seeking the comfort and warmth of skin against skin, needing to see each other's bodies and touch without obstacles.

"Help me," Susan murmured urgently, sitting up and turning her back, presenting her laces for assistance.

His fingertips trembled along the curve of her shoulders. "You are so lovely!" After pulling the pins from her bun, he caught a cascade of silken hair in his hands, then lifted it aside to kiss the nape of her neck. A shiver of feverish pleasure rocked through Susan's body and she silently urged him to hurry.

Finally they lay naked before each other, suddenly shy. When Susan made herself steal a peek, she inhaled deeply and held her breath. Gresham was more muscular than she had guessed. His thighs were heavier, his chest broader than his clothing suggested. A fiery blush heated her throat as she inspected the triangle of dark hair that narrowed across a tight hard stomach and pointed to the urgency of his desire.

"I . . . I like the look of you," she whispered, amazed by her brazenness, but sensing that he needed her approval. Her blush deepened and spread a rosy glow as far as her breasts.

"You are the loveliest woman I have ever seen," he said in a thick hushed voice. Leaning over her, he studied her body with an expression of love and awe. "You are so small and perfectly formed, so beautiful! I could span your waist with my hands. I'm afraid I'll hurt you."

"You won't," she whispered. Lifting her arms, Susan drew him to her, gasping with pleasure as the heat of his body covered hers and his lips moved down her throat to her breast.

As she had expected, Gresham was a tender and civilized lover, his touch gentle and skilled. She had not expected that he would be a thrilling lover as well, had not expected to lose herself in a fever of urgency and excitement. Certainly she had not anticipated that their lovemaking would last until dawn or that they would discover a thrashing glorious passion that left them both perspiring and panting.

She had turned to Gresham instinctively, hoping to find renewal and comfort in his arms. But she had also found a new and unexpected self, a passionate and uninhibited woman who could take joy in giving as well as receiving pleasure. In Gresham's arms she discovered solace and rapture, warmth and joy and an explosive release that filled the terrible hollow space inside. She found life again.

Holding each other in a quiet happiness made poignant by their grief, they watched the light turn pale blue and then glow pink against the windowpanes.

"I love you, Susan."

"I know," she said softly, smiling against his naked chest. "I love you too."

Gently he raised her until her head was on the pillow beside his. Beneath the quilt his legs wound around hers; he touched his fingertips to her cheek and gazed into her eyes.

"Will you marry me? There's nothing I want more."

Tears brimmed behind Susan's lashes. She had waited for this moment, had dreamed of it, had yearned for it.

She gazed into his dark eyes and thought it amazing that once she had believed he was ordinary-looking. Gresham Harte was the handsomest man she had ever met. No one had eyes like his. Warm and intelligent and reflective of a strong decent character. And she loved his nose and chin, and the way his mouth quirked when he was annoyed about something.

"No, Gresham," she said softly. "I won't marry you."

Flinging back the quilt, he sat up in bed and frowned down at her. "I don't understand. Is it too soon after—?"

"Nate loved you too," she said softly. "It isn't that."

"Then what?"

Reaching, she pulled him back down beside her and wiped

her eyes before she peered into his. Suddenly she thought of the frustrating telegram she had received from a clerk in Passion's Creek, Kansas, in response to the query she had sent. The telegram informed her that a death certificate for Captain Bowie Stone was unavailable. The wording was so peculiar that for one startled moment, Susan had wondered if Bowie might be alive.

But that was impossible. Her refusal to marry Gresham had nothing to do with a fear of committing bigamy. Still, a niggling doubt persisted . . . but now was not the time to be thinking about Bowie or any man but her dearest Gresham.

"I'm better at household tasks than I was when we met, but I still can't cook very well . . . there are a lot of things I don't do well yet."

"For God's sake, Susan. I don't care if you scorch an occasional shirt or if there's dust under the bed," he said, staring into her eyes. "If that's what this is about—"

"You do care about scorched shirts and dust under the bed." Tenderly, she placed her fingertips against his lips, hoping she could make him understand what she needed to say. "Time and practice will improve my domestic skills, but I'll never be the kind of woman to pound nails or build a home from the ground up."

"We'll compromise. We'll make marriage work for us."

"The most important reason why I can't marry you is because I need you."

A frown of confusion puckered his brow. "Susan, I *want* you to need me."

"I couldn't have gotten through these last terrible days without you." For a minute she closed her eyes. "That isn't the kind of need I'm talking about."

He passed a hand over his eyes. "I love you and you love me, but you won't marry me because you need me."

She touched his beloved face and gazed into his eyes, wrapping her legs around his. "All of my life I've believed a woman is nothing without a man to protect her, care for her, and tell her what to do and think. I don't believe that any more. Because I didn't have a man, I've had the chance to learn that I'm stronger than I ever dreamed I could be. I can make it on my own. It isn't easy, but I can do it. I'm learning to trust my own judgment and decisions. I don't want to lose what I've gained."

She wound her arms around his neck. "Part of me is still that same terrified woman who needs a man to save her. When I marry you, Gresham Harte, I want to be confident that I'm marrying you because I've chosen to spend my life with you, not because I'm desperate or afraid or needing someone to take care of me. Right now I'm struggling and shaky inside. It would be so easy to revert to the person I used to be. I don't think either of us wants that. I don't want to be clinging and dependent, and that isn't what you want in a wife. I need time to be sure of the changes I've made."

He stroked her cheek, thinking about what she had said. "May I hope that someday you'll marry me?"

She smiled and kissed him. "I hope you'll keep asking me."

Holding each other, they watched the sun come up on another day without Nate. The pain of losing Nate would remain with Susan always, but this morning she could believe that someday the pain would be balanced by happiness. It wouldn't happen soon, but for the first time she sensed that it would happen eventually.

"How long will it take before you stop needing me?" Gresham murmured against her hair. "A few weeks? A year? A decade?"

She imagined his mouth quirking into an expression of amused bewilderment. "I think I'll recognize the moment when it arrives. Right now, dearest Gresham, I need you with all my heart."

A shine of tears appeared in her eyes. It was time to rise and dress and face another empty day.

Dear God, if only she had gotten him the puppy.

Chapter Seventeen

Gulliver County, Kansas

Lem Sorrenson and his oldest boys drove Lem's wagon into Rosie's yard at sunup, bringing a piled load of tree limbs and scrap lumber. By eight o'clock a column of dust hung over the road from town to Rosie's place, and a half-dozen boys had their hands full directing wagons and watering the livestock.

Reverend Paulson arrived with smoked hams and bushels of early corn on the cob; Mrs. Paulson commandeered Lodisha's kitchen and organized the ladies who would prepare the noon meal and supper. The Widow James and elderly Miss Bartlett headed to neighboring counties in search of additional sacks. Evaline Buckner and her sister Edie kept a dozen children occupied and out of the way so their parents could work on the barricade. Shotshi Morris and Accey James headed additional digging crews farther up the creek. A cheer went up when Clive Russell arrived bringing Harold's contribution, three barrels of whiskey and cider. Mayor Bill followed on his heels with a wagon full of extra wheelbarrows.

By nightfall on the third day after Rosie had confronted the drovers, the barricade formed a three-acre line along the outer edge of her fields. The hastily built wall wasn't a thing of beauty, and no one knew how effective it would prove to be; but it was there, a patchwork of dun-colored feed sacks and sacks sewn from colored scraps of old clothing, the gaps plugged by stacks of brush and branches and scrap wood.

Deputy Carl Sands stepped up beside Rosie to watch the wagons leaving her farm. Here and there voices called through the twilight, hearty with bravado, bolstering hopes of victory for tomorrow's showdown. Sands settled his hat on his head, adjusted his gun belt, then curled his lip.

"You think that puny barricade is going to stop seven hundred stampeding steers? Tomorrow that herd is going to bust through here like greased lightning. You see if they don't. You and the son of a bitch you married ain't going to be such big heroes then!"

"We aren't heroes. We're just trying to protect what's ours."

"Yeah? Well that ain't how I hear it. There's some fools saying Stone is trying to save the town, trying to save every damn farm between here and kingdom come. Seems some folks can't tell the difference between a genuine hero and a coward with blood on his hands." Sands spit a wad of tobacco juice inches from the tips of Rosie's boots before he stalked off toward his horse.

Rosie frowned, watching him mount up. Sands was like a clock ticking toward an explosion, and she didn't need a fortune-teller to predict the focus of the blast would be Bowie. She hadn't been too busy to notice that Sheriff Gaine had kept Sands occupied and well away from her husband. Sheriff Gaine heard the ticking too.

After a late supper, she stepped outside with Bowie, walking the barricade, following the ragged line across the dark prairie.

"I saw one of the drovers about noon, sitting on his horse on top of the rise," Rosie said. "Did you notice?" Bowie glanced at the knoll and nodded. "Maybe he got a good look at what we're doing and changed his mind about bringing the herd through."

Bowie wrapped his arms around her, resting his chin on top of her head. "This barricade wouldn't stop a herd of cats."

"That's what Carl Sands said." She pressed her forehead against his chest, feeling his solid strength.

"For once I agree with Sands. But building a barricade was better than doing nothing. When it's over we can say we tried. We did something more than just stand aside and let it happen. But Rosie," he tilted her face up in the moonlight. "You have to prepare yourself. The barricade isn't going to stop them."

"I know." Easing out of his arms, she snapped the head off of a stalk and stroked the whiskery spikes across her cheek before she picked off a kernel and pressed her thumbnail into it. The ripeness yielded, leaving a dent. "Next year," she whispered. The kernel in her palm disappeared behind a glisten of tears.

How many years had she stood where she was standing now, looking at a failed crop and promising herself that next year the harvest would be bountiful? Next year she would win. Next year, always next year. Next year was the opiate of fools. The cottonwoods rustled near Frank Blevins' grave, smothering a low ghostly whisper of laughter.

"Maybe next year you'll be in California raising lemons and oranges," Bowie said, straightening one of the sacks sagging atop the barricade. "Or maybe up north someplace, where it's cool."

Rosie wiped a sleeve across her eyes and shook her head.

"I swore on Frank Blevins' grave that I wouldn't leave this farm until I brought in a profitable harvest and rubbed his stinking nose in it. If it takes the rest of my life, Bowie, that's a promise I mean to keep. I don't have a choice. If I walked away from here without bringing in a profitable harvest, it would be the same as saying what he did to me didn't matter."

"That's not true, Rosie."

"If we lose this crop tomorrow—and maybe we won't— " She paused, giving herself a dose of the only medicine she had. "There's always next year. Next year I'll beat him; I'll win."

Bowie watched her walk away in the moonlight, her shoulders bowed. Before she went inside the kitchen door, she stopped beside Frank Blevins' grave to tidy the outline of whitewashed stones. He was too far away to catch more than a few of the words she spoke to Blevins. But he heard her say "next year."

Next year she would be alone.

Everyone who owned a gun and was old enough to use one arrived at Rosie's farm at sunup. A double row of wagons and traps surrounded the barn, well back from the house, which didn't speak highly for the level of confidence regarding today's outcome. Today the children had been sequestered in the town hall under the uneasy care of the Misses Buckner, who fully expected to see a herd of Texas longhorns thundering down Main Street before sundown.

Sheriff Gaine, Mayor Bill, Reverend Paulson and Bowie held counsel and decided to position the men at the far end of the barricade and the women closer to the house and safety. Since women outnumbered men, many would be perilously near the estimated point of break-through. Sheriff Gaine was appointed to set fire to a brush pile as a signal to cut and run, and he would fire the brush in plenty of time to allow everyone to reach safety.

Strategy agreed, Sheriff Gaine climbed on the back of a wagon and addressed the assemblage. "When I see the herd top that rise," he shouted, pointing, "and if it don't look like they're going to veer off, then everybody runs like hell for the house and barn. The creek flattens out at mid-point across the barricade so the creek ain't going to slow 'em down much. You ain't going to have a lot of time to get your hides to safety. When it turns bad, get your butts off the barricade line. We don't want no dead heroes here. You hear me, Mabel Simpson? This ain't facing down old Bill coming home with a snootful. You head for the house, hear?"

A ripple of nervous laughter eased the tension.

"I sent a rider out last night to have a look-see. Can't tell you when them longhorns are going to arrive, but they're off the trail and coming our way. Near as I can figure, and I ain't no expert on cows, we're gonna see them critters long about noon."

Mayor Bill climbed on the wagon. "Before you take your places on the barricade, I just want to say good luck and God bless you all. If nothing else, we're making a statement today. We're telling them Texas cowmen to stick to the trail or they're looking at trouble. Most important, we don't want nobody getting hurt." He stared hard at his wife, Mabel.

Bowie scanned the crowd until he found Rosie, her face grim, her fists resting on top of the revolvers strapped to her waist. They exchanged a long look while Reverend Paulson offered up a prayer, then Bowie shouldered his Winchester and followed John Hawkins to their appointed place on the line.

Everyone settled in to wait, growing bored and restless as the sun climbed in the sky and heat rose off the prairie in scorching waves. There wasn't a person present who didn't curse the grassy ridge that blocked their long view. To ease nerves that were growing ragged, the sheriff sent Deputy Sands to sit on the rise and act as lookout.

The sheriff watched Sands cross the creek and start up the ridge before he walked over to Bowie. "A word to the wise, son. If I was you, I'd steer well away from Sands. He's carrying half a snootful and he's wearing a layer of mean that's just looking to rub off on someone. Hear me?"

"Sands is your problem, not mine."

"He's your problem, Stone. This whole town knows it. All I'm saying is: not today. You boys save any tangle for another time."

Bowie watched the sheriff walk down the barricade line, offering a word here, a caution there. Turning aside, he opened the cap on his canteen and extended the canteen to John Hawkins. "This reminds me of a campaign in the Dakotas. The waiting is always the worst." He took back the canteen and raised it to his lips.

The heat intensified as the sun climbed. An argument broke out down the line. One of the women suffered sunstroke and was carried to the house. Some people played cards to pass the time, others talked in quiet groups.

"There's something I've been wondering about, John Hawkins. How did you stop being an Indian? How does a man stop being what he is and still live?"

John Hawkins sat on the ground, leaned his back against the gravel sacks and stretched his legs in front of him. "I have a question for you, Bowie Stone. Does it benefit a butterfly to dream of his days as a worm?"

Bowie turned his face into the hot breeze, looking past the wheat fields at a prairie that rolled toward forever.

Memory sounded the bugle call to boots and saddles. He could almost hear the rattle of wheels and harness, the creak of saddles and jangle of spurs as his regiment moved out. A hundred field camps took shape in his memory, he remembered a dozen bloody battles. Even the long winter months of boredom spent languishing in an isolated post seemed appealing when glossed by the pain of loss. The military was a world he had understood, a world of men and horses and duty.

"One life ends; another begins," John Hawkins said.

"I had the only life I wanted."

"That life did not want you. That life is finished. You are free to begin another."

"My father heads a committee for the Department of the Interior. My brother was a major with the Fourth Cavalry. I graduated from West Point Military Academy. Stones have served their country since this country was founded. It's what I do and what I am."

Several minutes passed before John Hawkins spoke again. "Once I knew a man who could see game where others saw only grass and rocks. When he passed the people said: there walks Gray Smoke, the great hunter. When he rose to speak, he said, 'I am Gray Smoke, the hunter.' Every day he hunted, and every day he brought meat back to the village. Women sang his praises; no one had ever known such a great hunter. Then a white curtain grew across his eyes and one day Gray Smoke could no longer see to hunt. He sat in his tepee and dreamed of the past. He refused to accept his portion from the pot because he had not given meat to the women."

"Go on," Bowie said, frowning.

"That is the end. Gray Smoke died. He starved."

Bowie returned his gaze toward Sands, who sat on the rise drinking from a flask and twirling his revolver.

"Do you define yourself only as a cavalry officer, Captain Bowie Stone? If you do, then I think you would have done better to accept the noose."

"There are people in this town who agree with you."

"Deputy Carl Sands will kill you one day, but I think dying does not trouble you. When Rose Mary went to your bed, I hoped your life flame would burn brighter. But you are like Gray Smoke. Your life flame burns low."

Bowie's laugh was harsh. "When you look at me, John Hawkins, you see a ghost. A man who should be dead but isn't."

"Rose Mary saved your life. Only you can choose to live it."

"Live it how?" He jerked his head toward the fields. "To be a farmer a man requires a strong dream to carry him through the dust storms, the insect infestations, the lack of rain and the back-breaking labor. He needs to love this god-awful land and be able to feed his family on promises of next year. My calling is the military, not the land. Without my commission, I have no future."

"A man chases life or he chases death. He eats from the pot or he starves. You will continue to die, Bowie Stone, until you decide to live."

A vibration tingled against their feet, faint at first, then building until the tremble in the earth was unmistakable. Carl Sands jumped to his feet on the ridge and shouted a warning. A cloud of dust rose behind him, spreading to fill the southern sky.

Sands sped down the rise like a jackrabbit chased by a coyote; he covered the half-mile to the creek in record time, not stopping to remove his boots before he ran splashing through the shallow water.

"Good Christ Almighty!" he shouted, waving at the barricade. "There's longhorns as far as the eye can see, an ocean of them! Nothing short of a goddamned miracle is going to stop them! Get the hell out! Go!"

Those on the line could hear the cattle now, a menacing rumble of hooves and grunts that built in volume until it shot terror into the brain. The earth shook beneath their feet, and dust swelled over the ridge like a ominous gray mushroom.

"I can smell them." A woman's nervous voice carried in the heat and awed silence that stretched along the barricade.

Sands vaulted the gravel sacks and spun, screaming at them. "Are you idiots insane? In about three minutes, seven hundred steers are going to stampede over that rise and shortly after that they are going to trample you into pulp!" The people on the line stared at him, then at each other. Mabel Simpson leaned to one side and vomited on the shaking earth, pulling herself upright with an apologetic and wobbly smile.

"If you want to stay here and get yourselves killed, fine," Sands shouted. "But I've got better sense." Bolting, he cut through the wheat fields, running for the house.

Rosie materialized at Bowie's side, gripping a revolver in each hand. Her face was white, staring up at the dust cloud. "He's right. This is crazy."

"Get the hell out of here!" Bowie shouted. He wasn't sure she heard him above the noise building around them. "Go back down the line with the women!" He tried to push her away, toward the safety of an easy dash for the house.

"I'm staying with you," she said, dropping to one knee behind the barricade and cocking her revolvers over the top of the gravel sacks. "I've never been so scared and mad in my whole life! There's going to be some dead cows today."

The earth shook, and a mooing, snorting, thundering din filled their ears. Every anxious eye was riveted to the top of the ridge, and no one saw Sheriff Gaine dash the sweat off his brow, then light the brush pile.

The longhorns stampeded over the rise like a wedge-shaped brown tide that nothing on God's earth was going to stop. Dust billowed up around them like a unearthly halo; sunlight gleamed on wickedly curving spikes of horn. The noise of nearly a thousand raging cattle assaulted the mind as if the gates of hell had opened to release a roaring thundering rampage of four-legged demons.

Shock paralyzed those crouching along the barricade line. No one moved or dared to breathe. Wide-eyed and frozen, they stared in horror as a force of awesome unstoppable destruction swept up and over the ridge, pounding down on them.

"Lawdy, Lawd! Bless me Jesus!"

Bowie spun to find Lodisha clutching the back of his shirt, her black eyes as wide as stove lids. An iron skillet dangled in her fingers. He swore and glanced quickly at Rosie, but she was staring at the rise in horror. Despair had leached the color from her face. John Hawkins was the only one to look away from the oncoming destruction and meet his eyes.

There was no need to think, no time to make plans—just time to react, time to give meaning to a life that should have ended months ago.

Bowie jumped the barricade and ran toward the creek then through it, firing at the lead longhorns as fast as he could snap the Winchester's lever. One of the longhorns dropped, then another. The tide veered a few feet, widened, then other longhorns stumbled over those he had shot.

"Bowie!" Rosie screamed. "You goddamned fool!" She sprang to her feet behind the barricade, her heart slamming hard in her chest. He was running straight into hell, running up the west side of the ridge, firing steadily, trying to turn the stampede east by building a barrier of dead longhorns. She grasped his idea in an flash, knew that one man alone couldn't bring down enough longhorns to make a difference, knew he didn't have one chance in a thousand of walking out alive.

She knew he would die and he didn't care.

Screaming curses, Rosie flung herself over the barricade and ran after him through the chaotic dust and heat and noise, her boots sliding on the trembling earth, her revolvers blazing at the longhorns. Gunfire sounded beside her and she saw John Hawkins from the corner of her eye, running beside her. And then, God help them, Lodisha, stumbling through the swirling dust and din, banging a long spoon on her skillet and screaming at the top of her lungs.

The paralysis broke. Sheriff Gaine was the next over the barricade, then Mabel Simpson and Mrs. Hodge, followed by a wave of cursing men. Shooting, screaming, a hundred and forty-eight terrified farmers poured over the barricade, gave themselves up for dead, and charged into the heart of the stampede, their guns blazing.

Dust billowed into Rosie's eyes and burned her throat. The smell of heat and gunfire and cowhide clogged her nostrils. Beneath her boots, the earth shook so violently at the impact of pounding hooves that she could hardly keep her footing. The dust opened, and she saw Bowie planted in front of her, one boot on a dead longhorn, firing steadily into the brown wall that rushed toward them. She saw Reverend Paulson jerk Lodisha to her feet, then both of them ran at the longhorns. Mrs. Hodge paused near Rosie to reload, then, nimble as a girl, she ran on, firing into the brown tide.

Rosie's revolvers slipped in sweat-damp palms and the barrels grew hot. The dust was so thick that she couldn't see what was happening, but she could smell blood and cowhide all around her.

She didn't realize the worst was over until she heard a raw cheer erupt from the dust swirling below her. Didn't believe it until she rubbed her eyes, squinted hard through the swirling chaos, and saw the longhorns running past her instead of toward her. The herd had turned east.

When she saw Bowie walking toward her through the dust, his Winchester dangling at his side, she shouted, then ran forward and flung herself in his arms, unmindful of the long-horns sweeping past them twenty yards above on the rise. Her hands flew over his dirt-caked face, assuring herself that he was uninjured. Then Rosie drew back her fist and hit him on the jaw as hard as she could, hard enough to send him reeling backward. She kicked his legs out from under him and stood over him when he sprawled on the chewed up ground.

"Don't you *ever* do such a stupid damned idiotic thing ever again!" she screamed, tears streaking her cheeks. Reaching down, she jerked him to his feet, then threw herself against him, sobbing. "Oh, God, I thought you were going to die!"

Dust-dark hands caught her by the waist and flung her down on the trampled ground. Before Rosie could pull to her hands and knees, Bowie had her over his lap. His hand came down hard on her buttocks, once, then again, then he dragged her up into his arms and held her so tightly that she couldn't breathe.

"What the hell is the matter with you?" he demanded, burying his face in her flying hair. "Don't you have more brains than to go running straight into the middle of a stampede?" His mouth found her lips in a fierce burning kiss. "Christ, Rosie! When I saw you coming after me, I figured we were both going to die!" He jerked a thumb toward the longhorns thundering past above them. "I want something better for you, you damned fool!"

Rosie stared into his dust-reddened eyes, her hands flying over his hair, his shoulders, his face. She clasped his cheeks between her palms, thanking God they were each still in one piece. A slow grin curved her lips.

"We're a pair to draw to, aren't we? Neither one of us has enough sense to fill a shotglass."

They stared at each other, then suddenly they were laughing, laughing until their sides ached and tears poured from their eyes, rolling on the trampled ground while longhorns pounded past them.

"Here they is!" Lodisha shouted, running up on them out of the dust. "You done scairt the stuffin's out'n us! Thought you was both mincemeat." She glared at them. "Git yourselfs off this here ridge and away from them cows! You got nothin' to laugh at!"

When Rosie crossed the creek and walked out of the worst of the whirling dust, she sucked in a breath and stopped dead. Lodisha was right.

The longhorns had veered to the east, had been deflected from cutting through the other farms between her place and Passion's Crossing. But their eastward curve had taken them across her back three acres. They had gone through her fences like milk through a baby. She watched for twenty minutes until the last of the herd swept out of the fields and ran east on the prairie. Her back acres looked like a rough dirt floor strewn with straw, pocked here and there by tufts of stubble.

Sheriff Gaine splashed through the creek and came to stand beside her. Rivulets of sweat cut through the dust caked on his face, leaving a grid of muddy lines.

"Clive Russell guesses you lost 'bout two and a half, maybe three acres. But you got four standing, which is four acres more than I thought you'd have left."

Rosie stared at her back three acres. She couldn't speak.

Bowie sat on the barricade and rested the Winchester on his shoulder. He tilted his hat brim toward Rosie's stubbled acres and his eyes narrowed. "What are you going to do about this?"

"Me and a volunteer posse are going after them drovers. Figure they'll need at least an hour to get their herd in hand and calmed down. Then we're going to arrest them boys, throw 'em in the hoosegow for a week or two, and then we're going to fine the living shit out of 'em. They ain't going to see a profit for the next two years. When word gets out, and we'll see that it does, there ain't never again going to be no Texas trail boss pondering over bringing a herd through Passion's Crossing!"

Bowie's eyes glittered in the heat and dust. Standing, he crossed his arms over his chest and planted his boots. "That's all fine and dandy, but how is arresting those bastards going to help Mrs. Stone? Seems like a lot of farmers have cause to be grateful that her wheat went down and theirs didn't."

The sheriff smiled and hoisted his belly. "Wouldn't surprise nobody if this town voted to allocate a portion of them boys' fine to compensate Mrs. Stone here for her trouble."

"Seems the least they could do," Bowie agreed.

Rosie turned dulled eyes toward the knots of excited people waving, pointing, exchanging experiences. The Fourth of July celebration hadn't contained this level of excitement and elation. Even John Hawkins was strutting around, his backbone as stiff and proud as a flagpole. Lodisha was still banging a spoon against her skillet, leading an impromptu parade toward the house.

"Was anyone hurt?"

"We got a broken arm and some scrapes and bruises up at the house. Miz Levenson got herself shot in the leg, and some durn fool shot off Clem Zook's ear. But nothing serious." Sheriff Gaine stood aside as Bowie swung Minnie Paulson up and over the barricade, setting her on her feet beside her husband.

"This is a glorious day indeed! Thank you, Lord," Reverend Paulson shouted. Staring at the mounds of dead longhorns scattered from the ridge down to Rosie's back three acres, he raised his palms toward heaven. "Thank you for giving us a decisive victory over the forces of profit and iniquity. Thank you, Lord, that no one was seriously injured. And thank you, Lord, for providing us with the fixings for a fine barbecue!"

The sheriff nodded. "Amen to that!"

Shotshi Morris shouted, pointing to Bowie' and Rosie. "There they are!"

Heads turned, then a surge of people ran toward them, cheering and shouting their names. Dozen of hands reached, lifted them onto sturdy shoulders, and bore them in triumph toward the house, where Lodisha was supervising the skinning of the first longhorn and the building of a spit to roast him on.

Covers came off the backs of wagons to reveal platters of food and ears of roasting corn and bushels of potatoes and snap beans. The ladies who had earlier run up the rise, firing revolvers and screaming fury, washed their hands and faces at the rain barrel, then cheerfully set about creating a feast worthy of the occasion.

The Sorrenson boys departed for town to fetch the children and the Misses Buckner. Acey James said he'd pay for a fiddler if one could be found. A dozen men rode off with the sheriff to capture the drovers. A dozen more popped the bung of a cider barrel and sat in the shade under the cottonwoods, swapping excited stories and beginning the legend that would grow around this day and a man named Bowie Stone who had walked into a stampede as coolly as if he were taking the air on a summer's eve, followed by his lady, her guns blazing at his side.

Rosie and Bowie abandoned trying to help with the celebration preparations. They couldn't move two steps without someone pushing forward to pump their hands and thank them and review what was being referred to as The Day of the Longhorns. Arms wrapped around each other's waists, they stood on the steps of the front porch and finally stopped protesting that they were not heroes. No one wanted to hear it. The people of Passion's Crossing recognized gumption when they saw it, besides which it had been a long time since the county was in a position to claim any bona fide heroes as their own.

Later, when mounded platters of barbecue were served and the toasts began, Rosie was able to laud Mrs. Hodge for galvanizing the town, and Bowie used the occasion to applaud Sheriff Gaine and Mayor Bill for organizing the barricade. But everyone knew who were the heroes of the hour. Without Rosie and Bowie Stone jumping the line, the longhorns would have pounded through Passion's Crossing, and a new trail would have been established, wiping out a dozen families and the shopowners who depended on them.

After the debate over how the dead longhorns would be removed and how they would be apportioned throughout the community, the fiddler arrived and the young people danced under the stars while others stowed away the extra food and dirty dishes, and gossiped on the sidelines.

"Mrs. Stone? Could I speak to you a minute?"

Rosie spun off the earthen circle designated as the dance floor, laughing and holding her side, trying to catch her breath. She hadn't sat out a single dance. Her smile faded when she saw Evaline Buckner standing before her.

"I . . . I owe you an apology, Mrs. Stone." Evaline looked down at her hands. Her cheeks burned as fiery red as Rosie's old long johns, which were now filled with gravel somewhere on the barricade. "That night at the dance . . . I was jealous and I said some things I oughtn't have said. I'm real sorry if I hurt your feelings. I hope you saw it for what it was, nothing to my credit, and didn't pay no mind. I'm hoping you'll forgive me for being mad that you were prettier than me."

"I'm not prettier than you," Rosie said softly. Evaline's remarks had led to that first night in the barn with Bowie. She bore the girl no malice. "I just know you're going to get a husband soon."

Evaline's expression lifted. "Do you think so?"

They both turned toward an eruption of shouting near the

cottonwoods. The fiddler stopped playing and everyone turned to peer toward a bonfire under the trees.

"Who are you calling a coward?" The shout belonged to Deputy Sands.

Clem Zook, drunk and flushed with the events of the day, a bandage covering his shot-off ear, shouted back. "Last anyone saw of you was your cowardly butt running for the house and safety. We got women here who were up on that ridge shooting cows, but where was our sniveling deputy? Taking his ease while the real men and the women and widows did the work!"

Snarling, Sands fell on him, fists flying.

Bowie and Mayor Bill arrived to pull the men apart before any serious damage was inflicted. When Sands saw who had interrupted the fight, he bucked against the restraining arms holding him and spit at Bowie, spewing venom.

"There's your coward! Stone rode away from an Indian fight and he gunned down an unarmed man! We should have hanged him!"

Reverend Paulson stepped forward. "Now son, you read the old articles from the *Rocky Mountain News* that Clive Russell passed around town last week. We all did, and now we know the truth about Stone Toes Gulch. Stone did nothing that any honorable man wouldn't have done. Are you saying you would have drawn down on women and children, even if they were Indians?"

"Maybe those articles about Stone Toes Gulch are true and more likely they ain't. But it's for sure true that Stone gunned down an unarmed man! Or are you claiming that Judge Rivers sentenced an innocent man to hang for murder?"

"I don't think the full truth came out at the trial." Reverend Paulson looked past the bonfire and regarded Bowie with a thoughtful expression. "I think Judge Rivers believed the wrong witnesses. Mistakes happen. This town has seen Captain Stone's true colors, and this man is a genuine hero."

Sands wrestled free of the hands holding him. He shook his arms and jerked back his shoulders. His eyes blazed hatred. "You think you got this whole town bamboozled, don't you, hero? Well, you ain't reckoned with me yet. You and me, we got a score to settle."

"Pick your time, Sands." Bowie's eyes were as narrow and glitter-bright as the deputy's.

"Now's as good a time as any!"

Sheriff Gaine pushed forward, having just arrived from jailing the drovers. "Come on, Carl. It's time to go home and sleep it off. You're standing on the wrong side of the fence this time." He lifted his chin and stared around the circle of wary faces. "There ain't a man here who didn't want to cut for the house. If Rosie Stone and her Indian hadn't followed Stone over the barricade, we'd all have been right behind Carl."

"That's Clem's point," Lem Sorrenson sneered. "A *woman* went over the sacks while Sands was running away."

The sheriff did the only thing possible to prevent Carl Sands from going for Lem Sorrenson's throat. He cold-cocked Sands, caught him as he fell, slung him over his shoulder, and carried him toward the wagons. "Looks to me like this party's over, folks. It's been a long day. Time to load them wagons and head on home."

After the last wagon departed, Rosie, Bowie, Lodisha and John Hawkins looked at each other, then, as if they had discussed it, they walked down the barricade to inspect the trampled acres.

The devastation looked worse in the white and gray light of the moon. Deep shadows accentuated the clods of earth gouged by stampeding hooves. The litter of destruction and pulpy straw extended out across the prairie. Eventually the tough prairie grasses would recover; Rosie's wheat would not.

Turning into Bowie's arms, she dissolved in helpless tears against his chest.

"Next year."

Although the wheat left standing in Rosie's fields wouldn't reap a profit, it would sell for enough cash to scrape through winter's expenses. But the heart had gone out of a harvest that had earlier promised excitement and the cold satisfaction of revenge.

Even after Clem Zook lent them the use of the only McCormick Reaper in the county, Rosie couldn't generate any enthusiasm for cutting. What should have been the happiest moment in recent years was nothing more than an extension of the back-breaking labor that had gone before. As she strapped sheaves in the fields, she continually looked toward Frank Blevins' headstone, gleaming in the hot sun. Hatred and helplessness bubbled inside her.

When she wasn't thinking about Blevins or consumed by her loss, she worried about Bowie.

On The Day of the Longhorns she had felt closer to Bowie than ever before. Together they had faced death and choked on its fiery breath. Together they had triumphed despite terrible odds.

But there was a vast difference between the motives that had sent each over the barricade and into the nightmare midst of the stampede.

Rosie had thrown herself in the path of destruction because she would have followed Bowie Stone into the maw of hell itself, because her love for him resonated so powerfully that she would rather have died at his side than live a life without him.

Bowie had charged into the stampede seeking release from

a life with no future and no meaning, challenging death to claim him and not caring if it did. When he walked out of the dust, in that moment before he saw her watching, Rosie had seen his disappointment. Fate had cheated him.

"I love you," she whispered, looking across the fields.

He stood tall and lean, as solid and strong as the earth beneath his boots. He was magnificent, this miracle of a man, this husband of hers.

Because of him, Rosie had awakened from the slumbering stupor of liquor. Because of him, she no longer feared mirrors or her own womanhood or a room with fading memories. Because of him, she was no longer an object of ridicule or scorn. She was earning the respect of the town and beginning to respect herself. Because of Bowie, she knew what it was to open her heart and risk the gift of trust, knew what it was to love a man, and had learned that sex between a man and woman could be something beautiful and joyous. Because of Bowie, Rosie had changed and grown into a woman she was beginning to accept and like.

What puzzled her and stabbed at her heart was the apparent fact that she had not touched Bowie as he had touched her.

She had overheard him refer to himself as a walking ghost, and that he was. An elemental spark was missing. When he thought no one was watching, an emptiness stole over his eyes and his shoulders settled into a posture of hopelessness or indifference.

When Rosie pressed, he spoke of a hollow future; but she didn't understand, and what he said hurt her. His future was here, and they had each other. It was enough for her; why didn't it satisfy him too?

John Hawkins stopped beside her to rest a moment and followed her frown across the fields.

"Will he ever love me, John Hawkins?" Rosie asked softly.

"An act of honor destroyed this man's vision and all he

held high. Before he can live, Rose Mary, his head must forgive his heart. He must believe that he deserves life and happiness."

A shine of tears appeared in her eyes and she clenched her fists in frustration and bewilderment. "No man ever deserved more to live and be happy."

On the last night of the harvest, as Rosie's exhausted household finished their supper, she was still worrying and puzzling. She was so absorbed in her thoughts that she didn't hear the horses in the yard until Carl Sands and two of his cronies fired their pistols in the air and shouted for Bowie to come outside.

"We're going to string you up, Stone! Ain't nowhere you can run. Tonight you're gonna die, hero!"

Chapter Eighteen

Rosie lowered her fork. "They'll go away if we don't pay them any mind." Turning from the table to look behind her, she saw a horseman canter past the kitchen window. Gunfire blasted and bullets smacked into the roof. They all jumped and Lodisha ducked to her knees, smothering a scream with her apron hem.

Bowie set aside his napkin and exchanged a look with John Hawkins. "This has been coming for a long time."

The resignation in his tone riveted Rosie's attention. She didn't know what the glance meant between Bowie and John Hawkins, but she suspected it concerned more than Carl Sands. When Bowie started to rise from the table, she leaned forward and grabbed his arm. "You aren't going out there!"

"It's me they want." Standing, he leveled a steady gaze on John Hawkins. "Rosie isn't part of this."

John Hawkins nodded.

"The hell I'm not. Whatever concerns you concerns me too!" Jumping to her feet, Rosie followed him to the front door.

"I mean it, Rosie. Not this time. Stay here."

Because his expression offered no room for argument, Rosie muttered, but she stopped at the door, leaning over the sill to watch as Bowie stepped into the patch of light spilling onto the porch. He raised his arms to show Sands that he wasn't armed.

One of Sands's henchmen had built a bonfire near the cottonwoods while Sands and his other crony raced their horses across the starlit yard, shooting at the sky or the roof of the house and shouting drunken threats. When Bowie appeared, Sands reared his horse and charged forward, spraying the steps with bullets.

"Ain't scared of bullets, Stone? Well, you're right. Shooting's too quick an end for a big hero like you. Gonna kill you slow so's we can all enjoy it."

"Get off our property!" Rosie yelled from the doorway. Regardless of Bowie's instruction, she would have rushed forward to stand at her husband's side; but John Hawkins clasped her shoulders, holding her back, and she couldn't shake him off.

"You're drunk, Sands. Go on back to town. We'll tangle some other time."

The speed with which the noose flew out of the darkness startled Bowie. He didn't see the rope until it looped over his head and pulled tight around his neck.

Snarling in triumph, Sands whirled his horse and jerked Bowie off the porch steps, dragging him across the yard toward the fire burning beneath the cottonwoods. The whole thing happened and was over in seconds.

"Oh my God! Where are my guns?" Rosie spun to dash

back into the house, but John Hawkins' hands slid to her forearms and clamped down like cuffs of steel, holding her immobile.

"This is not your fight, Rose Mary," he said calmly.

"They're going to hang him!" she screamed, kicking and fighting to free herself. Panic poured down her throat and burned her stomach like acid. If Sands and his men killed Bowie, they killed her too. "Let me go, damn it! We have to help him!"

"No."

Sobbing, weak with fear, Rosie stopped fighting only long enough to cast a frantic look toward the cottonwoods. Sands slid from his mount, then threw the long end of the rope toward one of the high thick branches. The rope sailed over on the second throw, dangling near the fire, before Sands caught it again. He bullied Bowie to his feet.

"Bowie! Oh my God! John Hawkins, I'm pleading, I'm begging you! Let me go, please let me go! You don't know what you're doing. You have to let me go. Please, if you ever cared for me, please let me go! I can help him!"

"Captain Bowie Stone must decide alone." John Hawkins' hands tightened on her arms.

With a detached sense of indifference, Bowie watched Sands test the rope against the cottonwood branch, listened to his drunken shouts and insults and the laughter of his men.

"Some hero! Look at him, boys, jest standing there like the coward he is, waiting to eat the noose!" Sands spat at him. "Should of done this a long time ago."

Bowie peered at the rope through the smoke curling off the bonfire, following it up and over the cottonwood branch, inspecting it with a dulled sense of curiosity. This was the fate destiny had allotted him, a rope with his neck at the end. Until now, he hadn't let himself hear the inner clock ticking off the minutes, moving toward this piece of unfinished business.

Ten minutes from now he wouldn't be staring into an empty future, would never again suffer the shame of knowing he had sullied the Stone name and disgraced his family. His father's voice would no longer disapprove and condemn in his inner ear, no longer would he drown in guilt when he thought about Susan and Nate.

There would be no more Rosie.

There hadn't been time to say good-bye.

Turning his head, he saw her in the patch of light on the porch, sobbing, screaming, fighting to break John Hawkins's grip.

Rosie Mulvehey had never been his to keep, had never been more than a temporary solace along his path to this moment. He would have had to leave her in any case. Sands's rope would spare him the pain of riding away, would spare Rosie the anguish of betrayal.

Rosie had exploded into his life like a shooting star, illuminating his spirit with her vibrancy and quiet courage. Long before he had earned her trust or loyalty, she had defended him. She had believed in him, based only on his word and whatever she saw in his eyes. To please him, she had faced a regiment of private terrors and had battled the pain and fear of change. She had shown him humanity's capacity for growth, and had done it without asking for help or asking that he make changes in return.

Rosie accepted him as he was, a flawed and hollow man, and she loved him.

In return for her love and trust, he was going to let three drunken vigilantes hang him in front of her eyes; and he was going to do it because he was so consumed by self-pity that he couldn't find anything worth living for.

Disgust cramped his stomach.

Other men had ridden away from the military and carved a new life for themselves, men without families who cared about them, men with missing limbs or blinded eyes, men in far worse shape than he. What the hell kind of a man was he—had he ever been?—if he could not face the consequences he had caused? If he could not accept his obligations? If he could not find something to appreciate in each God-given day? Was he really willing to end his life because life was not exactly as he wished it to be? Was he willing to die in front of Rosie Mulvehey? Was that Bowie Stone's concept of courage?

Courage was giving up liquor when liquor was the only thing that made the pain bearable. Courage was walking into a den of horrors, and, by will alone, turning that chamber into an ordinary room. Courage was offering in love a body that had known only violence and abuse. Courage was challenging the prairie and the elements and wresting a crop from this dry, inhospitable land.

To be worthy of a woman like Rosie Mulvehey, a man had to grab life with both hands, hog-tie it, and lay the package at her feet.

Shame and fury pumped through his body. He knew she loved him but he hadn't done a damned thing to make himself worthy of her love. Or worthy of his own respect.

"Tie his hands behind him," Sands ordered. He pointed at the second man. "Bring up your horse and heave Stone in the saddle."

Dying was the same as running away. Except for Stone Toes, Bowie Stone had never run away from a fight in his life. And he had been right to lead his men away from Stone Toes Gulch. Even knowing the consequences, he would do the same again. And in the same circumstances, he would again kill Luther Radison.

He clenched his teeth. All this time he had brooded over the past, believing he might have acted differently if fate could turn back the clock. But that wasn't true. Bowie regretted nothing. He could not have acted differently in either incident and still be a man he could face in the mirror each day.

He stared at Rosie, fighting and sobbing on the porch.

The time had come to show his wife and remind himself that his courage was equal to hers. It was time to reclaim his life.

When Rosie realized that Bowie wasn't resisting or attempting to escape, that he just stood there staring at the rope with fatalistic indifference, she sagged against John Hawkins and covered her face with her hands, unable to watch him die. Lodisha sobbed beside her, her head buried in her apron.

"That isn't a hanging. It's a suicide!"

"This is good." John Hawkins smiled, and his fingers dug into her arms. "Captain Bowie Stone has made his choice."

"What?" Rosie's head snapped up, and she dashed tears from her eyes, blinking frantically and trying to peer through the dark and the smoke drifting from the bonfire.

While she was shoveling dirt on his grave, Bowie had jerked the noose from his neck and had broken the jaw of the man who tried to rope his hands behind him. One hell of a fight had erupted under the cottonwoods.

"Yes!" Rosie shouted, her heart blazing. "Let me go, John Hawkins! I have to help him. He's outnumbered."

"Don' look like the Cap'n needs our help, honey girl," Lodisha said, dancing up and down on the porch.

Bowie had found a fallen branch and wielded it like a club. As Rosie watched, he swung the limb and sent Sands's gun spinning into the creek. Sands's henchmen fell on him from behind.

She burned to go to him, needed to be part of it. But in her heart Rosie understood that John Hawkins was right. This was Bowie's fight and he had to fight it alone. What lit her like a flame was the certain knowledge that Bowie Stone had chosen to live. When he walked out of the cottonwoods, he would emerge a different man, a man willing to grab life and stride forward.

"He eats from the pot," John Hawkins murmured.

"He goin' win!" Lodisha shouted, waving her arms. "See if he don't!"

To anyone else the outcome would have appeared uncertain, but not to those who watched and cheered on the porch. Even from a distance they could see that Bowie Stone fought like a man possessed. It wasn't only Sands and his cronies that Bowie raged against, but the court-martial of an honorable man, an unfair trial, and a state of mind he now saw as an appalling display of weakness. Bowie Stone had awakened from a long, numbing slumber and the result was awe-inspiring to observe. The fight under the cottonwoods exploded into a ripping, gouging, no-holds-barred, all-out, bust-'em-up dirt fight.

By the time it ended, Rosie, John Hawkins, and Lodisha were sitting on the porch steps, drinking coffee, shouting advice, and cheering when their man drew blood.

At the finish Bowie was the only man left standing. Staggering, he wobbled forward a step, then bent over and pressed his hands against his knees, gulping deep breaths of air while a stream of blood ran from the gash over his eye to the ground. Both eyes were blacked and swollen, his lips were cracked and maybe a rib. A bloody lump rose behind his forehead, and one wrist was sprained. A dozen nicks and scrapes leaked blood.

"Can we help him now?" Rosie demanded, staring at John Hawkins, itching to run out to the cottonwoods.

"If Bowie Stone requires help, he knows we are here."

After he caught his breath, Bowie lifted each man by his

boots and, staggering, dragged him to his horse, then heaved him up and over the saddle. Cursing and limping, he slapped the horses into motion, then kicked dirt over the bonfire.

Rosie stood to watch the horses trot past the porch toward the road to town. If anyone in Passion's Crossing was still awake, they would be treated to the sight of three violently battered, unconscious men who weren't likely to soon forget tonight's business.

Bowie limped toward the porch, cradling his wrist in his hand.

"Lawdy, Lawd!" Lodisha studied his face and the blood thick on his shirt, then she hurried into the house. "I'll fetch the doctorin' box!"

Rosie ran off the porch and wrapped her arms around his waist, looking up at him. Except for the lack of a hedgehog beard, the beating made him resemble the man she had married.

"I love you," she said simply, tears shining in her eyes.

She thought he might say the words back to her, hoped maybe she had been part of whatever made him decide to live.

He held her so close that she could feel the hard pounding of his heart. He buried his bloody face in her hair. "Rosie."

His whisper was low and filled with a strange anguish that she didn't understand. But he held her; she was his anchor.

"I want some soap and water, and some of Lodisha's spirits of turpentine," he said, pulling back to examine her eyes. "Then I want to take you to bed. Afterward I'm going to sleep for ten hours. Unless you've got something you want me to plow or plant or weed, or cut, or shoot."

Rosie laughed and dropped his arm over her shoulder, helping him up the porch steps.

There were some men who just couldn't say the words. She had to trust what she felt in her heart.

* * *

Bowie moved with new determination and purpose that gladdened Rosie's heart. This was a change she had hoped to see. Instead of deferring to her, he returned the McCormick Reaper to Clem Zook, and he rode into town despite his battered face and brought back a money pouch containing a portion of the drovers' fines. Ordinarily Rosie was the one to tie up loose ends. It felt strange but comfortable to trust Bowie to do it for her.

The fight had also changed him in ways that caused Rosie deep anxiety and kept her awake long after Bowie slept at her side.

Physically, they had never been closer. Their nights were long and rapturous. Bowie made love to her with such exquisite tenderness that tears filled her eyes, and she didn't think her body could contain such love and joy without flying apart. He could not pass her in the house or the yard without wrapping his arms around her and holding her if only for a moment.

Yet, every day he withdrew a little further, moving to that place inside himself where Rosie could not follow. Several times she caught him looking at her with such pain and unbearable sadness that her heart lurched and stopped beating.

Something terrible was coming.

Rosie cursed herself for being stupid and foolish; she didn't believe in premonitions, but something was coming. Lodisha and John Hawkins sensed it too. They followed Bowie with their eyes, frowning and exchanging uneasy glances.

Now, he had assumed the task of loading and driving their wheat to the depot. She accompanied him to deal with the broker.

"You're awfully quiet today," Rosie said, shifting closer on the seat of the buckboard. She liked the sight of her skirt overlapping Bowie's knee and the heat of his hip tight against hers. "What are you thinking?"

"While you're bargaining with the wheat brokers at the depot, I need to stop by the telegraph office." He sat hunched forward, focused on Ivanhoe's ears, his hat brim low over his eyes.

Eyebrows lifting, Rosie stared at his profile. In all the months she had known Bowie Stone, he had never sent or received a communication of any kind.

"Who are you sending a telegram to?" she asked, unable to contain her surprise.

When he turned to her, she sucked in a breath and her gloved hand flew to her throat. Never had she seen such sadness in a living person. His cheeks were drawn and tight, his jaw clenched. Even his eyes had turned pale, more gray than blue.

"We'll talk about it tonight."

A chill bounced down her spine. What was she seeing in his eyes? Regret? Sorrow? Determination?

"What is it? Are you sick? I don't want to wait until tonight. If you have something to say, say it now!"

But he didn't speak again until he set the brake in front of the depot. Lifting his head, he examined the boxcars mounded with grain and the frenzy of activity buzzing around the platform. Then he took her hand in his, pulled off her glove, and studied her work-hardened palm, rubbing his thumb over the line of calluses.

"Bowie? What's wrong? Something's wrong."

"I need to say something to you. I want you to remember it."

The saliva dried in Rosie's mouth, and she swallowed with difficulty. For the last half hour she had sat beside him rigid with anxiety, her mind flying over possible reasons for his sorrow, trying to guess what he wanted to talk to her about but wouldn't discuss now.

"Is this what you planned to tell me later?"

"It's what I want to tell you now." He pressed her palm flat against his own larger hand. "I've never met anyone like you, Rosie, and I doubt I ever will again. I admire you as much as anyone I've ever known. You're strong and courageous, generous and tender. You care about people more deeply than anyone I've known." He said this looking down at her hand.

"Bowie, please. You're scaring me."

"I will never forget you. Wherever I am, whatever I'm doing, you'll be with me, a part of me as strong as my heartbeat. Don't ever doubt that, Rosie. I didn't mean this to happen—I didn't want it to—but I love you. I want you to remember that, and I want you to believe it because it's true."

She stared at him. For months she had yearned to hear him speak those three words. Never had she imagined he would say them while the sun was high overhead or in the midst of people and the noise of commerce.

Not for an instant had she imagined her heart would freeze with dread when he finally spoke the words she had longed to hear.

"No," she whispered, staring at him with sudden heart-stopping understanding. He held her glance a moment, then turned away. When he came around the buckboard and swung her to the ground, Rosie's fingernails dug into his shoulders. "You're leaving!"

"I don't know how long I'll be at the telegraph office. When you've finished selling the wheat, take the buckboard back to the farm. I'll walk."

Behind them rose the yells and curses of men loading wheat into creaking boxcars. Grain brokers bellowed prices on the platform. Wagons rattled, horses whinnied, men shouted. Rosie heard none of it.

"You can't go! We didn't get a profitable harvest!" Right now revenge didn't matter. The wheat didn't matter. Tears of fury and panic brimmed in Rosie's eyes, then spilled down her cheeks. She was making a scene and didn't care. "We've been through so much, shared so much! You made me love you and you love me too. Bowie, you can't leave me behind! Please, I don't understand!"

Briefly he closed his eyes, then removed her hands from his shoulders and gripped them tightly against his chest. "There are things I have to tell you. After you hear what I have to say, you'll be glad to see the last of me."

"Never!"

He gazed into her eyes with that terrible frightening sadness. "We'll talk tonight. Just please, Rosie. Remember what I said to you. None of it was a lie." Turning, he walked away from her toward Main Street.

Reeling and confused, Rosie stumbled forward a step, then ducked her head so her bonnet covered her face while she struggled to breathe. For the first time in her life, she felt as is she might faint. Sagging, she leaned against the wheel of the buckboard.

Bowie couldn't leave her. She was his wife. She wouldn't let him go. But he would. The pain in her chest raised black specks in front of her eyes. She was shaking so badly, she didn't think she could stand upright.

"Mrs. Stone?" A hand steadied her elbow. "Mebbe you best come in out'n the sun."

Blindly she turned toward Clem Zook and crumpled in a faint.

After he sent the telegram to Alexander Dubage, Bowie crossed the street and entered Harold's Saloon to await a reply. He stood at the rail near the brandied peaches and the jars of cigars where he couldn't see into the mirror over the back bar. Right now he couldn't stand to look himself in the face.

"Howdy, Stone." Shotshi Morris studied the bruises on Bowie's face. The swelling had abated and the nicks had scabbed over, but his eyes presented a palette of yellows and purples. "Heard Deputy Sands left town to try his luck in Denver. He didn't say what train he walked in front of, but must have been the same train what hit you. You look like cow flop, boy."

Bowie poured another shot and tossed it down. "She's going to need help, Morris. She might come here."

Shotshi puckered his lips and moved closer. Before he could speak a boy from the telegraph office leaned over the swinging door and called Bowie's name.

"In a minute," he said, then stared into Shotshi Morris' eyes. "If she stumbles, make sure someone is there to catch her. She's come too far to throw it all away."

"What in blue blazes are you talking about?"

"Just do it. And pass the word. Help her stay off liquor."

Pushing his hat down, he crossed the street and entered the telegraph office, not looking toward the depot. Leaning against the wall, he read the long telegram Alexander Dubage had sent in reply to his.

Shock exploded like a bullet in the pit of his stomach and he sat down abruptly. He read the telegram again, then again before he leaned his head back and closed his eyes.

His father was dead. Susan and Nate were living in Wyoming, in a place he had never heard of. Strangers occupied the house where he and his brother Nathan had grown up. His father's estate was still in probate; his own estate was intact. As if he cared about that right now. His father was dead.

All this time he had pictured the three of them in Washington, D.C., going about their daily lives, sometimes thinking about him or maybe not. He had imagined them frozen in time until the moment when he was prepared to pick up his life.

Memory showed him the senator, stiff and judgmental, tall

and proud. Susan, fluttery and eager to please. Nate, just learning to walk when Bowie had seen him last.

Leaning forward, Bowie rested his elbows on his knees and rubbed the numbness that deadened his face. His father was dead, and Susan and Nate were living in the Wyoming territory. There were so many questions.

"I want to send another telegram to the same party," he said, when he could stand and speak again.

In a trance, Rosie walked through the motions of selling her wheat. She followed the grain broker to the mound that was hers, watched him eye it, measure it, then check his weight sheets. She amazed him by accepting the first price he named. What did money matter when her world was ending? What did anything matter?

By the time the paperwork concluded and she had her money in hand, the afternoon was gone. Still moving like a wind-up toy, Rosie climbed onto the seat of the buckboard and turned Ivanhoe toward Main Street, braking in front of the telegraph office. Inside, she could see Bowie leaning against the wall next to the counter, his head down, his face covered by the brim of his hat.

She peered inside until the late afternoon sun shot a glare off the window and made it impossible to see. Then she turned her head and stared at Harold's Saloon, watching the doors swing open and shut, unconsciously licking her lips and swallowing.

The bad thing was coming; and even though she couldn't imagine anything worse than Bowie leaving her, a cold knot behind her ribs told her there was more, and it would be devastating. The joy of Bowie finally telling her that he loved her did not make up for the despair his leaving would cause. If he left her, everything he'd said at the depot became a mockery.

When Bowie emerged from the telegraph office, his face was tense and pale beneath his sunburn. When Rosie called his name, he looked up as if he didn't recognize her, then he climbed onto the seat beside her, closed his eyes, and tilted his face toward the dying sun.

"You can't leave," she said between her teeth.

When he didn't answer, she flicked the reins over Ivanhoe's back and drove out of town, frantically trying to think of something other than her husband's dulled eyes.

She hadn't taken the grain money and settled her accounts around town, hadn't treated herself to the hat in Mrs. Hodge's display window. She hadn't bought John Hawkins the pocket knife he wanted, nor Lodisha the German chocolates she'd been lusting after since learning Miss Crandall had received a shipment. She hadn't bought Bowie the new boots she had wanted to surprise him with.

"Please, Bowie," she whispered when the silence became unbearable. "Talk to me."

"My father is dead." He turned his face toward the prairie, his hands dangling between his legs. "It was the court-martial and the hanging. The scandal killed him."

"Do you know that for a fact?" God help her, she felt relieved. With his father dead, there would be no family obligations in Washington to take him away from her. The air rushed out of her body and her arms went limp.

"It was there between the lines." He tilted his head, looking up at the vast sunset sky. "I wanted to tell the senator about Stone Toes Gulch myself. He wouldn't have understood or forgiven, but I wanted to tell him how it was that day and why I did what I did. I wanted him to know the newspapers were wrong about Luther Radison and why I had to kill him." He fell silent, watching the prairie roll by. "I wanted to tell him that I admired him."

"I'm sorry your father is dead," Rosie said carefully. "But that means you don't have to leave."

"I've always had to leave, Rosie. I told you that the first day. I stayed through the harvest as I said I would."

John Hawkins was standing beside the barn when Rosie brought the buckboard flying into the yard. One look at their faces and he silently came forward to take Ivanhoe.

"No," Rosie said, when Bowie came around to help her to the ground. She didn't know why she didn't want him to touch her, but she didn't. Intuition whispered that she hadn't heard the worst yet. Without discussing it, they walked out on the prairie grass, moving away from familiar sites.

Bowie stopped and gazed back at the farm. The fading light was kind, overlaying the dilapidated outbuildings with shining pinks and golds.

"Tell me before I explode," Rosie demanded, trying to hold her voice steady in these last minutes before the world ended. He glanced at her, then looked back at the barn and house.

"You remember my telling you about my brother Nathan. We were inseparable as boys," Bowie said, frowning, gazing down the years. "I idolized Nathan, wanted to be like him. He was a good, decent man."

Rosie stood apart from him, clasping her shawl close to her throat though the evening breeze was dry and hot.

"He died as a result of an overturned carriage?" She didn't understand this unexpected line of conversation, couldn't guess where it might lead; but the rigidity turning Bowie's muscles into curving rock told her the answer would be the terrible thing she dreaded.

"It was a stupid accident," Bowie said, kicking a stone. "Nathan had risked his life in a dozen campaigns, then he died after a carriage collision not three miles from home. He lingered for days in agonizing pain before the end came."

Jamming his hands in his back pockets, he fixed his eyes on the distant horizon. "Before Nathan died, he told me about a woman he loved. They planned to marry."

Rosie ducked her head and clenched her jaw and fists against the bad thing that was almost upon her. A tremble began at her toes and swept upward. She held her breath until her lungs burned.

"The woman was pregnant. Nathan was desperate, aware that his death would destroy her reputation, her name, her life and the life of his unborn child. Before he died, he begged me to marry Susan and give his child the Stone name. I promised Nathan that Susan and her child would never lack for anything, that I would care for them as my own."

"Oh, God."

Rosie's knees collapsed and she dropped to the ground in a puddle of skirts and petticoats, staring up at him.

"I have a wife and a son." Knots rose along his jawline. "After the court-martial I wrote Susan and told her there would be no more long separations. I suggested that we start over. Then the incident with Luther Radison happened, and . . . you know the rest." He pulled a hand down his face. "Nate is my brother's son, Rosie. The boy is old enough now that he needs a father. I swore to Nathan that I would be his son's father."

"Susan," Rosie whispered. The word blackened her tongue. She wished to God that he hadn't revealed the woman's name. Knowing her name made Susan seem as real and fatal as a gunshot.

"It was never a real marriage. In the beginning, Susan was wild with grief over Nathan's death; we were strangers. I accepted a post out west to give us time to adjust before we actually began a life as man and wife. When that assignment ended, I posted for another. A military fort is no place for a family. Consequently, I haven't done well by Nate. That has to change. I owe Nathan and I owe the boy."

"You son of a bitch!" If Rosie'd had her guns at her waist, she would have shot him through the heart. "You already had a wife when you married me!"

He ran a hand over his face, then looked down where she continued to crouch on the ground. "I've thought about that day a thousand times. When I stepped up on the scaffold I honestly believed I had made peace with dying. Then you and Sheriff Gaine threw out a lifeline and, God help me, I grabbed it. I was standing there with the noose around my neck, thinking I was minutes away from death, and suddenly I saw a chance to live. I didn't think about consequences, didn't ask if I had the right to marry or save myself. By the time my mind cleared enough to think, you and I were married."

"You should have told me!"

"At the time, my circumstances didn't matter. You needed help to get a harvest, and I owed you. I considered my time here as an interlude before moving on. In the beginning, it didn't seem possible that you and I would ever mean more to each other than employer and roustabout. I'd clear my debt by helping you bring in a profitable harvest; then I'd return east, and neither of us would be the worse for the experience."

Rosie stared up at him without seeing. Heat bubbled inside her, followed by waves of cold so frigid she thought her blood had frozen. She couldn't stop shaking.

She wasn't married. She never had been. All of it was a lie. That night in the barn, all the compliments she had lived for and drawn strength from, the long nights of tenderness, passion, and love . . . all of it was based on a lie.

She sprang from the ground snarling like a cougar and flung herself on him, hitting, spitting, clawing her nails down his cheeks. She kicked and hammered her fists on his chest, his shoulders, on the sides of his face.

"I loved you!" she screamed. "I quit drinking for you, cleaned myself up for you, quit swearing and smoking for you! I changed myself inside out for you, and all the time you knew you would leave me and go back to *her*!"

Bowie hadn't defended himself against her attack, but now he moved, catching her wrists. "The changes you made, you made for *you*! You can't change for someone else. You have to do it for yourself, and you did! I've done wrong by you, Rosie, and I'll regret that for the rest of my life. But *you* did right by yourself!"

Swearing, screaming every ugly name at him that she could think of, she fought against the hands holding her, finally breaking free. "You're just like Blevins," she shouted, choking on a sob and flinging her hand toward the headstone in the yard. "Except that he used force and you used lies and sweet talk! There's not a dime's worth of difference between you! You both used me and threw me away!"

Whirling, wishing to God that she had let him hang, she lifted her skirts and bolted for the house.

Bowie waited until full darkness before he followed her.

Passion's Crossing was a small, tightly knit community; before the morning train had traveled a third of the distance to Denver, everyone would know that Rosie's husband had cut and run, had never been her husband at all. He was banking heavily that The Day of the Longhorns remained fresh in the minds of the townsfolk and that they would rally to Rosie's support.

Pride would carry her past the worst of the scandal. Unless she started drinking again, she wouldn't place her personal pain on public view. Moreover, she was a spirited, beautiful woman. Eventually there would be another man. He couldn't stand to think about that. The thought of Rosie bedding another man curled his hands into fists and formed a knot of jealous, murderous rage behind his rib cage.

When he entered the kitchen, Lodisha and John Hawkins

fell silent and stared at him with a mixture of accusation and betrayal. Lodisha did not offer to doctor the deep scratch marks raking his cheeks. John Hawkins folded his arms across his chest and turned his face to the wall.

Silently, Bowie passed them, realizing he would miss them almost as much as he would miss Rosie. Clenching his teeth, he knocked on the door of the small bedroom she had not slept in for weeks.

"Unlock the door, Rosie, or I'll break it down."

"Go to hell!"

Like everything else on the farm, the door was flimsy and ready to collapse on its own. It broke open the first time he hit it with his shoulder.

Rosie sat on the bed, propped against the headboard. Light from an oil lamp fell across the revolver in her hand. She'd had time to strip out of her shimmy and petticoats and now wore a pair of dun-colored long johns.

"There's more to say." Guilt burned in his gut when he looked at her. The comment about his being like Blevins had seared him. He had no justification to offer in his defense.

"Choke on it, Stone. And don't come any closer." Raising the revolver, she closed one eye, then sent a bullet whistling past his ear. From deeper in the house he heard the kitchen door slam and understood Lodisha and John Hawkins had removed themselves from the line of fire.

"By next week my attorney should have my legal affairs untangled. I've instructed him to transfer a large sum of money to your account at the bank in Passion's Creek. A week from now, you'll be the biggest depositor in Western Kansas."

She leaned forward and screamed. "Do you think you can ease your conscience by paying me off? Like a whore? I don't want your damned money!" She sighted the gun barrel on his belt buckle and fired, jerking her hand to one side at the last possible second.

"I hate your guts, Stone! I hope your train out of here crashes and you die! I hope you rot in hell!" Raising the hand with the gun, she wiped at the tears streaming from her eyes, then leveled the barrel at his chest. "Do you love her?"

"I told you. Susan and I are practically strangers."

"Did you think about her every time you poked me?"

"For the love of God, Rosie. This is no easier for me than it is for you. Do you think this is the way I wanted it? If it weren't for Nate, nothing could make me leave you. I love you!"

She shot the hat off his head. The bullet shaved so close to his scalp that he felt his hair part.

"You slept with her, didn't you?"

"We never lived as man and wife." He stared at her. "Don't do this," he said finally. The wild anguish in her eyes was like a bayonet in his guts.

"Don't you *dare* tell me what to do!" she snarled. Three bullets whizzed past his face, chunking into the wall behind him. The room stank of smoke and gunpowder.

Firing wildly, she shot all around him until the revolver's hammer came down on empty. Then she threw the revolver at his chest and buried her face in her hands. "I want to kill you! But I can't, and I hate myself for that." She threw out her hands. "You used me! You deceived me and betrayed me. I was a goddamned fool to trust a man again!"

He kicked the revolver under the bed frame, then walked further into the room and sat on the end of the mattress, watching as she jerked her knees up to move away from him.

"I know you won't believe this, but I didn't use you, I love you. And I never intended to hurt you."

"But you did! And, oh God, it hurts so much!"

He placed his hand on her leg. "I love you, Rosie, like I've never loved any woman before. The only thing that could make me walk out that door is the promise I made to Nathan on his deathbed. There's a child out there who believes I'm his father. I owe that boy. I gave my word."

She stared at him, hot tears flooding her cheeks; then she threw herself across the bed and into his arms. Bowie held her while she wept, deep racking sobs of pain and anger. If he let himself believe this would be the last time he would ever hold her, he feared he would explode inside. His chest burned as though one of her wild shots had found its mark, and for one scalding instant he hated Susan, wished to God that he had never married her, despised Nathan for asking it of him.

"I'm sorry," he said, hearing how lame and inadequate it sounded. He stroked her hair, her heaving shoulders, and finally tilted her wet face up to him. "I wish things could have been different."

"I love you, Bowie. Please don't leave me!"

"I love you too, Rosie. But I don't have a choice." He kissed her, tasting salt, tasting her pain and echoes of his own. Then he gently disengaged her arms from around his neck.

"Oh, God!"

"I'll never forget you, Rosie Mulvehey. For the rest of my life I'll see you in every tawny-haired woman."

Her sobs followed him past the shattered door and through the front parlor, then down the porch steps into the yard.

Revolving slowly, he inspected the farm one last time in the moonlight. The barn, the outbuildings, the pasture, the house, the fields, Frank Blevins' headstone, the cottonwoods by the creek. It was a damned dismal place for a man to leave his heart.

When he felt Lodisha and John Hawkins silently watching, he pointed his boots toward the road to town and began walking.

His train for Denver departed at sunup.

Chapter Nineteen

Owl's Butte, Wyoming

"Would you like more coffee?"

"Thank you, no. The stage should arrive any minute." Susan was already jittery. One more cup of Mrs. Alder's strong coffee would jolt her out of her skin.

Knowing it upset Gresham but unable to stop herself, she again peered out of Mrs. Alder's dining room window, nervously squeezing the beaded purse hanging from her wrist. Inside were the telegrams from Alexander Dubage and Bowie.

Scowling, Gresham thrust aside his untouched breakfast and shoved a hand through his hair, leaving it in tousled disarray. Smudges overlay his spectacles. For the first time in Susan's memory, his tie sat askew and his shirt appeared limp and crumpled as if he had slept in it.

"So what happens next? The son of a bitch returns from

the grave, snatches you up, and takes you back to Washington, D.C.? Where the hell has he been all these months?"

"In Passion's Crossing, Kansas. You know that."

This morning's conversation was a rehash of the sketchy details known to them, a discussion repeated a dozen times throughout the last traumatic and devastating week. They had spent hours poring over the telegrams, dissecting them word by word, frantic with shock and speculation, trying to read between the lines, and endlessly debating everything except that which reverberated uppermost in their minds. Their future. In the span of one feverish day their lives had been reduced to a pile of stunning telegrams that destroyed assumptions each had secretly cherished.

"Don't they have paper and ink in Kansas? If for some reason Stone couldn't write to you, surely he could have hired someone else to inform you that he was alive! This is unconscionable, Susan, an unforgivable breach of decency. He let you and Nate believe he was dead. He let his father turn you into the streets all but penniless! Because of his callous disregard you suffered unthinkable mental anguish. And all the while the bastard was alive!"

Reaching across the table, Susan touched his sleeve. "We haven't heard the full story. There must be a reason why Bowie let everyone believe he was dead."

"You're defending him?" An accusing stare shot across the table.

"I'm merely saying there must be a reason. Gresham, please. I beg you not to make this more difficult than it is already."

"How much worse could it be?" he asked, throwing up his hands. "Or did you always suspect he was alive? Is that why you wouldn't marry me? Because you believed he'd come back for you?"

Susan lowered her head. "I think we both wondered if Bowie could be alive. We both knew something was peculiar when Gulliver County wouldn't produce a death certificate." Her eyes contained an endless depth of misery. "If you're asking if I care for Bowie, the answer is yes. The night you told me about Stone Toes Gulch, I confided the circumstances of my marriage. Bowie saved my reputation and he gave Nate a name. Of course I care for him."

"Oh, God," Gresham murmured, thrusting his fingers through his hair.

"But it was never like—"

"Stop. I can't bear to hear any more of this." After removing his spectacles, he tossed them on the table and covered his eyes with his hand. "Stone can give you so many things that I can't. Servants, a big house, trunks full of fashionable clothing. No more money worries. He can give you the life you deserve and want."

"Gresham, please." She was so nervous at the thought of seeing Bowie that she could hardly think. And every time she gazed at Gresham's beloved face a wave of despair washed over her.

The thought of never seeing him again, never holding him again, tore her heart to shreds. Gresham was lover, friend, confidant, and the one person who believed in her. His faith provided her the strength and willingness to reach beyond herself. She could not imagine life without him.

But she was Bowie Stone's wife. If Bowie was coming to take her away from Owl's Butte, the law was on his side.

"Oh, Gresham, I need you so much," she whispered, pressing her handkerchief to her eyes. "Part of me is still that same terrified woman who stepped off the stage in a snowstorm, the same woman who needed a man to tell her what to do. I didn't want to marry you until I knew I could manage on my own and be the kind of wife you want and need. My hesitation had nothing to do with Bowie. When I'm independent enough not to need you, that's the day I'll—" she bit off the rest of the sentence and lowered her head, trying to swallow the lump that choked her.

She would never marry Gresham Harte, not now, not ever. She already had a husband. Closing her eyes, Susan gripped her hands in her lap and fought the whirling sensation that spun her thoughts like bits of confetti.

Bowie was alive. She had to accept that. He would arrive in Owl's Butte within the half hour. The news continued to stun her; the shock had not dissipated. The telegrams in her purse had flipped her world upside down. She had no idea what she and Bowie would say to each other or what he expected from her.

"The damned stage is early," Gresham announced between clenched teeth. "There it is."

Wordlessly, Susan gripped her hands and watched a coil of dust grow larger at the far end of town. The knight of the reins whipped the horses down Main in a showy display, drawing up smartly in front of Mrs. Alder's hotel.

Her husband had arrived.

The bottom dropped out of Susan's stomach. Her knees shook so badly that she didn't know if she could rise from her chair. This was going to be the third most difficult day of her life. Nathan's death, Nate's death, and now Bowie's resurrection.

Instinctively, she swung toward Gresham, wanting to throw herself in his arms and beg him to somehow make everything right. But there was nothing he could do. Nothing any of them could do.

"You promised not to interfere," she whispered, unsure if the statement was intended as a reminder or an accusation.

His dark eyes burned at her across the table. "I love you, Susan. I can't sit by and let him take you away! I agree that you have to talk to him, but—"

They gazed out the window, mesmerized as the stage door

popped open and spit out the first passenger, a large red-faced woman who looked the worse for having spent the night being tossed about like dice in a cup. A white-haired man followed, stepping to the ground behind her.

"I have to go." Susan's corset squeezed down around her spine. She couldn't breathe. Her skin felt clammy. Because Gresham eyed her so intently, she resisted a nervous urge to straighten her bonnet and tug down the lapels of her short summer jacket.

Gresham helped her out of her chair and his fingers brushed the nape of her neck, intending reassurance. "We'll meet at my office first thing in the morning," he reminded her. The tension deepening his voice wound Susan's nerves a little tighter.

"I remember," she said, her eyes on the window and the emerging stage passengers.

"If he allows you."

Turning abruptly, she looked straight into Gresham's angry dark eyes. "I'm not the coward I used to be. I said I'll be at your office tomorrow morning, and I will be."

"I suppose he'll spend the night at your cabin."

Susan stared at him, her cheeks on fire. This was something they had both fretted about but neither had mentioned.

"Damn it!" Gresham raked a hand through his hair, then picked up his glasses and glared down at his fists. "Forgive me. It's just . . . I want to hit something or kill somebody. Stone has no right to do this, but of course he has every right. You're his goddamned wife!"

Susan bit her lip hard enough to taste blood. Ordinarily Gresham Harte recalled his manners in her presence and did not engage in profanity. "You know I love you," she said softly, aware they were attracting the attention of other diners and not caring.

"That's what makes this such a Greek tragedy!"

Throwing etiquette to the wind, she touched her gloved fingertips to his lips. "Even if . . ." But she couldn't talk about leaving him. "I'll see you tomorrow, I promise."

Forcing herself to turn away from him, she placed one tasseled boot in front of the other and passed through Mrs. Alder's lobby and outside onto the covered veranda. Her pulse pounded at her throat and temples, the sound banging like a drum in her head.

She spotted Bowie the instant he stepped out of the stage door. Halting so abruptly that her skirts swung about her ankles, Susan gasped and sucked in a hard breath. For one stunning instant she believed she was looking at Nathan. He wore dark pants and a broadcloth jacket, the fit over the shoulders pulling a little as it always had. She hadn't seen him wear a Stetson before but saw at once that it suited him. Sun had darkened his face to bronzed mahogany, but the piercing blue eyes were Nathan's.

No, not Nathan, not Nate grown to manhood. The man brushing the dust off his shoulders was Bowie.

Staring at him, Susan understood how she had persuaded herself that their marriage might eventually be successful. He so closely resembled the man she had loved. Moreover, she hadn't had a choice, not really. Her options had been utter ruin or accepting Bowie as her husband and savior. She had married him in a state of hysterical gratitude, blessing the ground he trod that he had agreed not to reveal her pregnancy even to his father.

Standing frozen on the veranda, she watched Bowie's gaze travel over her and then beyond and was startled to realize he didn't recognize her. Perhaps Mrs. Winters was correct, perhaps she had changed to the extent that she did indeed stand more erect and carry herself differently. Certainly she no longer hunched her shoulders or scanned each face with fluttery eagerness.

It also occurred to her that Bowie had never observed her wearing high mourning, nor had he known her to choose a sensible hat or dress her hair as simply as she did now. Finally, they had not seen each other in well over a year. Although Susan had been his wife for almost five years, she could count on her fingers the number of weeks she and Bowie had actually spent in each other's company.

Clasping her hands against her waist, trying to conceal her trembling fingers, and nervously aware that Gresham watched through the oval window on the hotel's front door, she stumbled down the veranda steps and stepped in front of him. She had forgotten how tall he was.

"Bowie?" At close quarters she noticed deep scratches running down his cheeks. Various bruises and healing scabs suggested an accident or a fairly recent fight.

"Susan?" He removed his hat and smiled stiffly. "I'm sorry I didn't . . . you look different."

Awkward and ill at ease, they regarded each other in silence, inspecting for changes and finding them. Bowie looked older than Susan remembered. The experiences of the past year had enhanced maturity, had dissolved brash edges of arrogance into something more solidly self-assured. He seemed more muscular, leaner, more a soldier than an officer. A quiet vibrancy glowed deep in his eyes, much as she would have expected from a man who had come within minutes of hanging. Oddly, the changes felt right to her. He impressed her as a man who had walked through fire to emerge stronger, finer, more settled in his own skin.

Observing the speculation in his gaze, Susan wondered what changes he identified in her. Did it surprise him to find her clad in plain serviceable clothing instead of flaunting the newest mode? Was it appealing or off-putting that she met his eyes straight on with no uneasy dropping of eyelids? Would he hear the new self-assurance in her voice, observe it in her step?

Could he sense her budding independence and her growing confidence in her own opinions? All things considered, it wasn't surprising that he had failed to recognize her.

Bowie cleared his throat and touched the bow tie at his collar. He glanced behind her. "Did you bring Nate or will I see him later?"

"Nate is dead," she said softly, lowering her eyes. Each time she said the words aloud, fresh shock brought tears to her eyes. It seemed impossible.

When she was enough in control to look up, Bowie was staring at the peaks of the Tetons, his jaw working.

"I didn't know," he said finally. "Dubage didn't tell me. I'm sorry, Susan."

Until this minute, she hadn't thought of informing Alexander Dubage about Nate's death. Eventually she supposed she would have. It was only in the last ten days that her paralysis had broken and she had begun to function again.

Gathering herself together, she drew a deep breath and gestured toward a buggy and horse. "I rented a trap for the day. I thought you might want to drive out to the cemetery. I always visit Nate on Saturday mornings."

"How did it happen?" Gingerly taking her arm, he led her to the buggy and assisted her inside.

Susan resisted looking over her shoulder at the hotel. Her heart despaired when she thought about Gresham.

After taking up the reins, Bowie asked directions, then turned the trap toward the outskirts of town. Speaking in a halting voice, hardly able to form the words, Susan told him about the Fourth of July social at the lake.

"It's been very hard," she finished, tears strangling her. "Nate was the center of my life."

They traveled a quarter of a mile before either of them spoke again. "I have a hundred questions," Bowie said at length. "I imagine you do too."

"Yes." She twisted her handkerchief between her fingers, unable to halt the nervous gesture. "This is very difficult . . . perhaps it would be easier if we begin with the past."

He nodded and thumbed back the Stetson. "You know about Stone Toes, but how much do you know about what happened with Luther Radison?"

"I can't believe you would shoot an unarmed man. A friend of mine read the newspaper accounts. We're convinced Radison's friends lied on the stand." She slid a look toward him. "What I don't understand is why you weren't hanged. The newspapers reported that your sentence was satisfied. I also don't understand why you didn't notify anyone that you were alive."

A line of knots rose like pebbles along his jawline. "I'll explain that. But first . . . the senator gave his word that he would care for you and Nate while I was gone. Yet Dubage's telegrams indicate that my father disinherited you both." He turned his head to examine her face. "Is it true that you were turned out of the house with only forty dollars?"

Susan fixed her gaze on the open range. She had tossed and turned most of last night anticipating this question and others, trying to decide how she would answer. With truth, or kindness.

She pressed her hands together and spoke carefully. "Your father understood that Nate and I were the primary beneficiaries named in your will. At the time of the senator's death, no one guessed there would be any difficulty obtaining your death certificate or probating your estate." She inhaled deeply. "Your father undoubtedly believed there was no need to provide for Nate and me, as he understood we would be well cared for under the terms of your will. In that context, his decision is blameless and understandable."

Relief loosened the rock-like tightness in Bowie's shoulders. He nodded slowly. "When I first learned what happened, I thought . . . but your explanation makes sense."

After guiding the horse through the ornate iron gates of the cemetery, Bowie braked the trap in the shadow of a pine, the only tree within the cemetery fence. Frowning, he swept a glance across the sun-baked headstones.

"Does the wind blow all the time?"

"Usually." Susan accepted his hand down from the buggy. "Wyoming takes some getting used to. But once you have the eyes to see, it's a beautiful land." She lifted her eyes toward the purple and mauve peaks in the distance. "In spring, wildflowers carpet the range. Even the sage has a silvery beauty. I'm told the sumac is brilliant in autumn." Lifting her skirts, she walked to a small stone and knelt to place a bouquet at its base. "Nate loved Wyoming. There was room for running and playing, fishing and roping, so many new things to enthrall a small boy."

Bowie followed her, bending to read the inscription and examine an etching of a cocker spaniel carved below Nate's name. "He liked animals?"

"Oh yes." Turning aside, she dipped the brim of her bonnet to conceal a spasm of pain. "A friend designed the carving."

"I didn't know him," Bowie said after a moment. "I thought there would be time later. I failed Nathan and I failed his son."

"Nate looked like both of you," Susan said when she could speak. "Dark-haired, blue-eyed, that stubborn Stone chin. He was curious and adventurous, afraid of nothing. Just like you and Nathan. He wanted to go to West Point and be an officer when he grew up." Kneeling, she removed a weed from between the rocks outlining his grave. The pain was not as intense now, but it would be with her always, only a memory away.

Bowie rocked back on his boot heels, his fists opening and closing at his sides. An August breeze meandered across the range, gave the pine a rattle, then moved on. "How did my father die? It was the scandal that killed him, wasn't it?"

Susan glanced up. "No. Your father was proud of what you did at Stone Toes Gulch. He planned to protest your court-martial. He demanded an inquiry." Bowie stared down at her, wanting to believe. "And your father understood about Luther Radison. Not for an instant did he accept that his son could be guilty of murder. You had nothing to do with your father's death. He died loving you and believing in you."

He turned away from her and folded his arms across his chest, looking toward the distant Tetons. "I thought the senator would despise me for disgracing the family name. I thought appearances were more important to him than conscience. I believed I'd carry his disappointment to my grave."

"The senator defended you to anyone who would listen," Susan whispered. Surely God would forgive her for shaping the senator into the father he should have been.

"I mean no offense, Susan, but are you telling the truth?"

"Yes." Ducking her head, she led the way back to the trap. "I'll direct you to my cabin," she said, settling herself beside him, careful not to brush against his thigh.

"A cabin?"

"Log, one room, and very small," she explained, glancing back toward Nate's headstone. "I like it."

"I've always pictured you in a grand house attended by servants." He returned her even gaze. "I apologize for staring. But you're very different from what I remember."

"Yes," she said quietly. "Indeed I am."

"Why on earth did you decide to come to Wyoming?"

During the drive to the cabin, she explained about answering Gresham's ad and his subsequent rejection when he discovered she was a military widow with a small child. She didn't spare Bowie's feelings or her own but related how she had pleaded with Gresham to marry her. "I was desperate. I had no money, no skills, and a child to feed. I didn't know how or if I would survive."

Bowie's hands clenched and whitened around the reins. "I can't express how deeply I regret that you and Nate came that close to starvation. It never entered my mind that such a situation could occur."

"Mr. Harte supplied the eventual solution." She told him about her first visit to Henrietta Winters in County Creek and progressed to anecdotes from her classroom. As she spoke her voice firmed and assumed an unconscious authority.

"You're a teacher," Bowie repeated.

"I love teaching," she said, smiling at his surprise. "I never dreamed that I could make a difference in people's lives or that I could earn a position of respect and trust." The wonder of it shortened her breath even now. "Before you—died—I used to spend my time focused on meaningless frivolities: the next ball, the latest fashion. I doubt I had an original idea or an opinion of my own the entire time I lived in Washington, D.C.. I was wasting my life without knowing it. Now I'm making a useful contribution. It's not always easy; sometimes it's hard. But creating a worthwhile niche for myself feels good. My life is simple now, pared down to the essentials. I like it that way."

They rolled through the outer edge of Owl's Butte and turned up the road toward Susan's cabin. In the distance, she spotted the steeple housing the school bell, white against a cobalt sky.

She never saw the bell steeple without thinking about growth and hard work, about dreams and possibilities. Or without remembering Nate, who hadn't been tall enough to pull the bell rope. She had laughed and counseled patience; he would grow up soon enough.

"I'm glad you didn't hang," she said slowly. "But why didn't you?"

Bowie kept his eyes on the horse's ears. "There's an ordinance in Gulliver County, Kansas, that states a woman can save a condemned man if she agrees to marry him. Rose Mary Mulvehey exercised that ordinance and saved my life. I married her."

Susan blinked and her mouth dropped open. She and Gresham had speculated endlessly over this point. The possibility that Bowie had saved himself by marrying had not entered their minds.

"How could you marry Miss Mulvehey when you already had a wife?"

"At that moment I wasn't thinking about you or Nate." The gaze he turned on her offered no excuse or justification. "Marriage was deemed to satisfy my sentence. I didn't consider the consequences, Susan, I just did it."

Looking into the distance, Susan thought about his situation. "I imagine anyone would have done the same in the same circumstance." She didn't blame him for saving his own life.

"Afterward I couldn't walk away. A sheriff's posse would have come after me. Equally as important, I owed Rosie for saving my life. To pay that debt I stayed with her long enough to plant her wheat crop and see it through to harvest."

Curious, Susan studied his face. "That's why Miss Mulvehey agreed to marry a condemned man? She wanted a hired hand to plant a crop?"

Bowie glanced at her. "If I'd written to tell you and the senator that I was alive, I would also have had to tell you that I'd committed bigamy. I'd have burdened you and the senator with another scandal, and Rosie would not have gotten her harvest. At the time I believed you and Nate were well cared for. I believed I could repay Rosie with minimal harm to anyone."

As Susan watched the cabin draw nearer, her mind cast backward, remembering how hard it had been coping with the senator's death alone, believing herself an abandoned widow, remembering her horror and despair when she and Nate were turned out of the senator's house without enough money to pay a month's expenses. And all the time, Bowie had been alive, married to another woman.

"Tell me about your other wife," she said finally.

Bowie didn't answer until he had guided the trap into her yard. "I can't describe Rosie," he said, following a lengthy silence. "I can feel her, I can see her in my mind. But I can't describe her in a way that would do her justice or help you understand who and what she is. I can tell you this. Until two weeks ago, Rosie didn't know about you and Nate. I'm solely to blame for wronging you; Rosie had nothing to do with it."

"Can she cook and drive a nail?" It was a stupid question, but Susan found herself consumed by curiosity about Rosie.

An explosive laugh emerged from deep in Bowie's chest. "I've never known Rosie to cook anything more complicated than a pot of coffee. But can she drive a nail? Lord, yes! Rosie Mulvehey can string a line of fence faster and better than any man I've ever known. She shoes her own horse, chops her wood, drives a plow. She is arguably the best shot in Gulliver County."

The truth dawned on her as she studied his face. As Bowie spoke of Rose Mary Mulvehey, a variety of emotions transformed his expression. Love, admiration, exasperation, a flash of irritation. Susan had observed the same mixture in Gresham's eyes.

"You love her," she said softly.

Bowie twisted on the seat and his face sobered. "Under law my marriage to Rosie is not legal. My first obligation is to you, Susan." He inhaled deeply. "I gave Nathan my word."

Susan tilted her head and met his eyes squarely. "I have

to know this, Bowie. If you had known beforehand that Nate . . . that Nate was gone . . . would you be here now?"

A struggle erupted in his eyes, a battle between honesty and honor. She watched as a decent man fought to fulfill a long-ago vow.

"No," he said finally, looking at the cabin. At this moment it looked extraordinarily small and primitive even to Susan. "I'm not proud of myself for saying this, but if I'd known about Nate, I probably would have let you continue thinking I was dead." He turned to face her. "But I am here, and I'm prepared to accept my obligations."

Susan folded her gloved hands in her lap. She kept remembering the way his eyes had softened when he spoke of Rose Mary Mulvehey. "Bowie . . . what did you expect when you came to Owl's Butte?"

He hesitated. "When I was in Denver I commissioned a land-man to purchase a hundred acres of horse property in Oregon. I still have contacts in Washington, D.C. and within the military. The cavalry is always going to need and buy horses. I believe raising and selling horses will be a satisfying life."

"You expected to take Nate and me to Oregon?" About as far from Passion's Crossing, Kansas, as he could get. "Is that what you're proposing now? That you and I go to Oregon?"

His jaw clenched. "I made a vow to Nathan and to you. I promised I would take care of you."

"I have some lemonade inside," Susan said before climbing down from the trap unassisted. Suddenly she smiled, the first genuine smile in more than a week. Bowie believed he was obligated to rescue her from a bleak and dismal existence. He thought she needed him. He still didn't realize how much she had changed. "Afterward I'd like to show you my classroom."

"I'd be pleased to see it," he said politely.

Pausing on the cabin's small porch, Susan looked up into his eyes and her heart lifted. From the moment he had mentioned Rosie Mulvehey, she had sensed that everything would work out. "And I want to tell you about Gresham Harte."

"Isn't Harte the man you came to Wyoming to marry?"

"If it hadn't been for Gresham Harte, I would have lost my mind after Nate died. It was Gresham who designed Nate's stone." And so much more. In a very real way, Gresham had helped design her too. More accurately, he had gently prompted her to refashion herself into a person she could admire and respect.

As Bowie's story was incomplete without Rose Mary Mulvehey, so her story was incomplete without Gresham Harte.

The sun peaked in the sky, then slipped toward the mountains. They walked on the scrub range behind Susan's cabin, talking for hours about people and events, filling in details, growing more comfortable with each other and beginning to enjoy each other's company in a manner they had never experienced before.

Smiling with shy pride, Susan related the meeting with the town council. She described her students and what she hoped to accomplish with each. She remembered everything about Nate and spoke of that final day at the lake. And she told him about Gresham Harte, her voice soft and possessive. Blushing furiously, she admitted that she might have committed bigamy herself except she feared marrying out of need. That statement required further explanation, and she spoke for another hour while Bowie listened as a friend might have done, without judgment or comment.

Bowie spoke of the heart-aching trials of a farmer and recalled The Day of the Longhorns, and he told her about the attempted hanging under the cottonwoods. He made her laugh and tugged her heart with his tales about Rosie and Lodisha and John Hawkins. By the end of the afternoon, Susan felt as if she knew them.

"I like Lodisha and John Hawkins. And I admire your Rosie very much," she said, stopping beside the boulder her students played on. "She's very special."

"So are you, Susan," Bowie said, looking at her with those blue, blue eyes, Nathan's eyes, Nate's eyes. "You've become a remarkable woman. I was wrong about everything I thought I knew about you."

She smiled. "Whatever you thought was probably correct. But that person died when you were sentenced to hang. In an odd way, your 'dying' was the best thing that ever happened to me. Because I didn't have you, I had to grow up. I had to learn to stand on my own feet, think for myself, and build a life for myself and Nate." She gazed across the range toward Owl's Butte. "This is my home, Bowie. I've made friends here, good friends. I belong here. Nate is here . . . and Gresham. I could never leave."

He looked down at her. "Will you accept a word of advice from a new friend?"

Her eyes dropped to his mouth and just for one moment, Susan wondered what might have happened if there had been no Rosie Mulvehey and no Gresham Harte and they were meeting now for the first time. Something flickered in Bowie's expression and she suddenly sensed that he was wondering the same thing.

"With the proviso that I'm not obligated to act on that advice," she said with a smile. "I do my own thinking now."

"Needing someone is as much a part of life as breathing. When we no longer need someone, we're alone, the worst kind of alone there is. You are long past needing a man to survive. Don't mistake that kind of need with needing a man— a certain man—to be fulfilled and happy. It isn't the same thing. Time is shorter than we think it is. Don't delay doing something you know in your heart is right."

The dying sun cast their faces in tones of pink and gold. "I'm glad you came," Susan said softly. "I always regretted that I didn't know you well. And I was sorry that I didn't have a last chance to thank you for saving me from ruin and for protecting my secret. I'll always be grateful to you for that. And in a way I'm grateful that you let me think you were dead." For an instant they looked into each other's eyes. "I'm not much of a cook," Susan said, taking his arm. "But I have some supper inside."

Gresham galloped into the yard and reined hard to a skidding halt, peering through the dust kicked up by his bay's hooves.

Son of a bitch! They were strolling arm in arm, and Stone was gazing down at her as if Susan were a bonbon about to be devoured. The bastard was easing into it, holding her arm close to his chest, sliding toward further intimacies. Gresham swore. He had known this would happen. Every cavalry officer he had ever met possessed a slick manner and an overweening arrogance. They believed every settler in the west owed them whatever they wanted when they wanted it. Every swaying skirt was theirs for the taking.

Well, by God, Bowie Stone was not going to return from the dead and lay claim to Gresham Harte's woman. Stone had abrogated that right when he put his wife through a funeral service and left her to starve on the streets. He did not deserve a fine woman like Susan.

Leaping to the ground, Gresham jerked his rifle from the saddle scabbard, then strode toward the boulder beside the schoolhouse. When Stone saw him coming, Gresham raised the rifle to his shoulder, moving forward until he was close enough to make certain he had a kill shot.

"Gresham!"

"Step aside, Susan. I'm going to kill the bastard. He is not going to take you away. I've decided I like you best as a widow."

Stone scowled and his hand dropped to his side arm. "Who the hell are you?"

"I'm the man who fed and cared for your wife when you were playing dead in Kansas. I'm the man who buried Nate and wept while I did it. You abandoned them, Stone. You aren't worth the price of the bullet that's going to kill you. You should have died when you were supposed to. For Christ's sake, Susan, get out of the way."

To his amazement, she burst into laughter. Raising his head from the rifle sight, he stared at her.

"Gresham, you wonderful idiot. Put down that rifle. I want you to meet my husband, Bowie Stone. Bowie, this is Gresham Harte, the man I'm going to marry."

Stone hesitated, then raised his hand away from his sidearm. "Susan tells me you're an attorney. We'd like to hire you to obtain a divorce. Divorces are legal in Wyoming, aren't they?"

"A divorce," Gresham repeated uncertainly. "Yes, I can obtain a divorce for you." He stared hard at Stone. He'd come here in hot white fury, prepared to shoot a man for the first time in his life. Now his victim wanted to hire his services? His mind couldn't easily make the transition. Susan walked toward him, rose on tiptoe and kissed his cheek. Extending a finger, she pushed down the barrel of the rifle.

"Bowie offered a substantial settlement," she said, smiling. "We'll have money to finish the house at the homestead and enough to provide a comfortable income for the rest of our lives."

"I don't want the son of a bitch's money!"

Stone narrowed his eyes. "The money is Susan's. She's entitled to Nathan's estate and I'm assigning it to her. It's what she would have inherited if she and Nathan had married. What she does with it is her decision, not yours."

"Gentlemen," Susan said, stepping between them. She gave them each an admonishing glance, feeling the heat in her cheeks. "I think we can agree this is an awkward circumstance. If I ever knew the etiquette for a situation like this, I've forgotten it." She made a little gesture with her hands. "I have a stew on the back lid and a pie on the sill. If you gentlemen will wash up, I'll have supper on the table in ten minutes. I believe we're civilized enough to share a meal together."

Gresham watched her walk toward the cabin, trying to absorb what had happened. The bizarre nature of the situation had robbed him of speech. He was about to sit down to supper with the husband of the woman he wanted to marry. What in the name of God would the three of them talk about? He swore beneath his breath.

"Do you still think you need that rifle?" Stone asked.

He wasn't so sure that he didn't. He still wanted to shoot Bowie Stone.

Stone tipped back his hat, then started toward the house. "It was never a real marriage, Harte."

Throughout a supper that none of them tasted, Susan and Bowie chatted comfortably, talking about people they knew in common, recalling incidents from the past. Susan had removed the plates and poured coffee before Gresham calmed enough to realize he was listening to a get-acquainted conversation, a conversation between friends, not lovers. Nevertheless, they were husband and wife; hot black jealousy cramped his stomach. He knew what Stone had been trying to tell him out in the yard, but he couldn't decide if he believed it or not.

"Susan? Will you join me for a turn in the night air?" Bowie inquired when he had finished his coffee. He glanced at Gresham. "Excuse us."

There was nothing Gresham could do but seethe and watch Stone lead her outside. If Stone tried to steal her, he'd hunt the bastard to the ends of the earth. Brooding, he stared into his coffee cup.

Susan wrapped her arm through Bowie's and lifted her skirt to step over a rock. "It's hot tonight." She looked up at the stars spangling the black sky. "I'm sorry supper was so awkward. Ordinarily Gresham isn't rude. He's usually a stimulating and charming companion."

Actually the evening had thrilled her. She had never seen Gresham behave this way. Perhaps it was a throwback to her earlier self, but Susan had rather enjoyed watching him compete for her attention, regarding Bowie with glances of dislike and suspicion. The small drama had fascinated her and proved enormously flattering.

"I love him, Bowie. We'll build a wonderful and satisfying future together."

"You've made a good life here," he said, looking toward the lights of the town. "I'm glad for you."

She hugged his arm close to her side, speaking in a whisper. "You're saying goodbye, aren't you?"

Oddly, she felt reluctant to let him go. There was still so much to say, so many questions left unanswered, so many paths they had not explored and now never would. "I'm glad you have Rosie. I'm sorry I'll never know her. I wish you both long life and happiness."

A humorless smile curved his lips as he covered her hand with his. "It's by no means certain that Rosie will have me back." Moonlight shadowed the scratches on his cheeks. "She's just as apt to shoot me."

Susan smiled. "She'll have you back. You'll build a wonderful new life in Oregon."

They walked toward the trap in the moonlight. From the

corner of her eye Susan spotted Gresham, standing in the cabin doorway, watching them carefully.

Bowie turned to face her, taking her hands in his. "I'm sorry for the disappointments and pain that I may have caused you. And I'm more sorry than you'll ever know that I wasn't there for Nate and that I didn't know him."

"I'm sorry too," she whispered. "He was so like you and Nathan. You would have loved each other."

It seemed the most natural thing in the world to step into his embrace. She slipped her arms around his waist, pressing her forehead against his chest. They stood together for a full minute before she moved back and watched him climb into the trap.

"I'll never see you again, will I?" Susan whispered.

For a long moment they looked at each other, then Bowie made a sound under his tongue and turned the horse toward Owl's Butte.

She followed as far as the road, then stood in the moonlight and watched her history recede.

When Gresham slipped his arms around her waist, she leaned back against him. "We never knew each other. It seems so sad."

"If you want to go with him, it's not too late. There's my horse."

Spinning, she turned in his arms and scowled at him. "Gresham Harte, sometimes you are so exasperating!" She dashed a suggestion of moisture from her eyes. "I love you, you idiot. I've never loved any man as much as I love you. Although right now I can't imagine why. You were positively rude at supper. You hardly said two words and you bolted your pie. Now you're sulking."

"What?" He blinked. "I never sulk! And what the hell was I supposed to say? Stop talking to your wife? She's the woman

I'm going to marry? Speaking of that, how could you tell him that you'd finally decided to marry me, when you hadn't told me yet?"

"Are you withdrawing your proposal?"

"Of course not. But I'd like to know what the Sam Hill he said that made you change your mind."

She wrapped her arms around his neck and kissed his chin. "I was looking at things wrong. Needing someone isn't necessarily a weakness. And I do need you, Gresham. I need your encouragement and your patience. I need to love you and know you love me. I need your strength and goodness, and your belief in the future. I need to begin each day knowing you're part of it, part of me, part of us. And I need you to teach me how to hammer a nail."

"Susan, I love you like life itself, but sometimes you make me crazy." She gave him one of those smiles that dissolved his insides and made him think about unhooking her corset and rolling down her garters. When she looked at him like this, nothing else in the world mattered except taking her in his arms and thanking God that she had come into his life.

They stood in the road, arms wrapped around each other's waists, and watched until Bowie Stone's horse and buggy were swallowed by the night. Then Gresham carried her into the cabin, placed her on the bed, and did his damnedest to make her forget she had ever known any man but him.

Chapter Twenty

Gulliver County, Kansas

Rosie sagged against the porch post, clutching a short stack of telegrams. Tears brimmed in her eyes as she reread the last message. A crack sounded as the hard shell broke away from her heart and elation burst through her body.

"Oh, thank you, God!" she yelled at the hot August sky. The anguish of mere minutes ago exploded into wild joy. "Thank you!"

Clamping the telegrams between her teeth, she fumbled in her pants pocket, then pushed some loose coins into the hand of the boy who had ridden out to deliver the telegrams. "And thank you, Johnny Kravatz!"

His freckles spread in a grin. "Good news, Miz Stone?"

"The best! Captain Stone is coming home!"

Bowie was coming back, coming to get her. Unashamed

tears rolled down Rosie's cheeks. Suddenly she felt as weak as a newborn colt, her legs wouldn't support her weight. Gasping, she clung to the porch post to hold herself upright.

"Will there be a reply, Miz Stone?"

"Yes! You tell Mrs. Paltz to send Captain Stone a telegram the minute you get back to town. Tell Stone that I forgive him and I still want him. And tell him to get his behind back here on the next train!"

Forgetting the boy on the porch, not thinking to offer him a glass of water to wash the dust from his throat, Rosie tested her legs, then bolted inside and ran into the kitchen.

"Lodisha! Bowie's coming to get us! We're all going to Oregon. Where's John Hawkins? I have to tell him to start packing. We have a hundred things to do!"

Lodisha looked up from her scrub brush and her dark face broke into a wreath of smiles. "Din't I say the Cap'n he'd be back? Yes sir, I never doubted it, not for a Sunday minute. Guess you can pour out that bottle of blazer you been hiding in yor room, honey girl. You ain't never gonna be needin' the likes of that!"

Rosie had forgotten about the whiskey bottle in the joy and excitement of knowing that Bowie was not lost to her. Countless times she had approached to within a heartbeat of easing her pain by jumping inside of the bottle she'd purchased the day after he left her. But she hadn't done it.

Lord knew she wanted to. The night Bowie walked away from her, jealousy, betrayal and lost love had cleaved her in bloody pieces. The pain of losing the one thing she loved most in this world made her crave a drink like most folks craved air and water.

Since that night she had kept the bottle under her bed, near at hand in case the pain of Bowie's betrayal overwhelmed her and she had to have relief or go screaming crazy.

But she didn't do it. Maybe somewhere deep inside she

understood that her battle with whiskey had nothing to do with Bowie Stone and everything to do with herself.

Maybe the demeaning memories of drunken riots and banging hangovers and the stink of jail time were too strong, too humiliating. Maybe she liked respecting herself. Whatever stayed her hand, Rosie thanked heaven that it had.

When she had John Hawkins and Lodisha seated at the kitchen table, glasses of lemonade in front of them, she read Bowie's telegrams out loud, her face glowing as hot and radiant as the Kansas sun.

Lodisha frowned. "Me and John Hawkins are 'sposed to take Ivanhoe on the train to Orrigon? Where is Orrigon?"

After Rosie explained, John Hawkins nodded. "Raising horses is good. That will be a satisfying life for Captain Bowie Stone and for us. I have heard of this Oregon and this ocean."

"Bowie says he and I will follow as soon as he arrives here to get me."

"What the Cap'n done do wif his other wife?"

"I don't know," Rosie said, jutting out her chin. "He's coming home to us and that's all that matters!"

Maybe Susan had died, or maybe she didn't want Bowie any more. Maybe Bowie had changed his mind about her. Although Rosie was dying to know the story, she would have to wait a week to hear it.

"We have so much to do!" she said, spreading the telegrams on the table to study the instructions and schedules. Lodisha and John Hawkins examined the train tickets.

"Ain't never rode no train a'fore." Excitement sparkled in Lodisha's black eyes. "Reckon I'll need me a new hat. What's the house in Orrigon look like? Do it have a good stove?"

Rosie laughed. "I don't know. All he says is there's a house on the property and he wants you and John Hawkins to get it ready for us. He says we'll live there until we get our own house built."

"I will ride in the freight car with Ivanhoe," John Hawkins decided. "When do we leave?"

Rosie compared the telegram instructions with the date on the train tickets. Her hands flew to her mouth. "You leave tomorrow! There isn't time to buy a new bonnet, Lodisha. You can wear one of Mama's old hats." A frantic look came into her eyes. "We have to pack!"

"What we goin' take?"

They gazed around the kitchen and parlor.

"Not a damned thing," Rosie said after a minute. They looked at each other, then burst out laughing. "Take whatever personal items you feel you can't replace. We'll leave the rest for the mice and the wind."

After a hurried supper, John Hawkins rushed to the barn to pack Ivanhoe's tack and his own few items. Lodisha tied her favorite cooking utensils in a canvas bundle, then ironed the dress and jacket she would wear on the train.

When Rosie was given to understand that she was only in the way, she stepped outside and wandered toward the fields of moonlit stubble.

Sleep would be impossible tonight. Bowie was coming home. Her heart was so full, spilling love, relief, and eagerness, that she had difficulty concentrating on all she needed to do before Bowie arrived to take her to Oregon.

She would give away the cows, pigs and chickens. Miss Raven would be pleased to receive Rosie's books for the new lending library. Reverend Paulson would see that her plow and farm implements went to whoever needed them most.

She walked a short distance into the stubble, as brown and dry as the prairie, then turned to look back. Moonlight didn't make the house and outbuildings look any less shabby. It would be a relief never again to worry about the henhouse collapsing or think about giving the barn another slap of paint.

The house was starting to lean, and the roof didn't look sturdy enough to withstand another Kansas winter.

If memory served, nothing had changed. The farm still looked as bleak as it had the day Rosie and her mother had arrived here in Frank Blevins' buckboard. For fifteen years the place had been nothing more than a bump on the prairie, a patch of dry dirt and tough grass better suited to rabbits and prairie dogs than farming.

Her eyes settled on the distant curve of Frank Blevins' headstone, gray in the moonlight.

Rosie had not beaten him; she hadn't enjoyed a minute of revenge.

Blevins must be laughing in his grave.

Ivanhoe balked at entering the freight car. After a lot of rearing, pawing, and snorting, John Hawkins eventually shouted Ivanhoe up the ramp and inside the boxcar, where he stood rolling his eyes and trembling.

"He will settle down. I will be with him," John Hawkins promised.

Neither nervousness nor excitement disturbed the old Indian's expression. Whatever he thought about uprooting his life, he said nothing. He accepted what life brought. Perhaps he would approve of Oregon and find ways to make himself useful.

Rosie gripped John Hawkins' hand and shook it as if they would never meet again, then she embarrassed him by embracing him in public. He gave her his eagle's talon for luck, then entered the freight car and waited in the shadows for departure.

Rosie hurried down the line of railroad cars and jumped inside the passenger car. Rows of wooden seats lined the narrow interior, which was already crowded. She found Lodisha sharing her food basket with a young mother and two skinny toddlers.

"How long is that food going to last if you're giving it away before you've even left the station?" Rosie demanded, smiling in fond exasperation. Reaching, she straightened the cloth flowers on Lodisha's straw bonnet.

The train whistle blasted in their ears, and somewhere ahead of them cars crashed against couplings.

Bending, Rosie kissed Lodisha's cheek. "An attorney named Milbourne will meet you and drive you and John Hawkins out to the property. We'll be about a week behind you."

Lodisha gripped the edge of the wooden seat. Nervousness vied with the excitement in her eyes. She glanced at Rosie and arched an eyebrow. "They's somethin' we din't talk about, honey girl, but I knows yor secret. Cain't keep no secrets from yor Lodisha."

Rosie frowned as the train lurched under her feet. "What are you talking about? I don't have a secret."

Lodisha's gloved hand rose from the wooden seat to press the front of Rosie's skirt. "I's talkin' 'bout how we gots ourselfs a baby!" She beamed at the young mother seated across from her. "We bin waitin' a long time fer this."

Rosie's mouth dropped. She stared at Lodisha while her mind spun backward, counting.

"Hell's fire," she breathed. "I'm not barren after all." She threw out her hands and gave out a yell that brought the conductor running down the aisle. "I'm going to have a baby!"

The conductor looked her up and down with an expression of disapproval. "Are you riding or staying behind, Mrs.?"

Bending, Rosie looked out the window. The depot was moving. Whirling, she ran down the aisle, blew Lodisha a kiss, then jumped off the slow-moving train.

Grinning like an idiot, she watched until the smoke was only a black smear against the horizon, then she asked Reverend Paulson to drive her back to the farm and pick up anything he thought his needy parishioners could use.

A baby.

After Reverend Paulson had loaded his buckboard and driven away, Rosie sat on the front porch step, cradling her stomach and dreaming how she would tell Bowie about their baby.

After two weeks of pain and uncertainty, life had performed another spin, working out in a glorious way she could never have expected.

There was only one thing missing.

The night wind sighed through the cottonwoods and whispered across the prairie grass. With Lodisha and John Hawkins gone and the livestock given away, silence, broken only by the dry wind and an occasional creak of the floorboards, descended on the farm. A hot stillness weighed heavy with unfinished business, a sense of things left undone, promises unfulfilled.

Fighting up from the depths of a dream turbulent with frustration, her mind pricked by a nameless anxiety, Rosie threw back the thin sheet that covered her and padded into the dark kitchen. She dipped a ladle of water from the bucket on the broadshelf and closed her eyes against wisps of the nightmare that had awakened her.

Wetting her face and throat, Rosie finally opened her eyes to the first streaks of dawn lying faint against the window-panes. She watched the shadows draping Frank Blevins' head-stone slowly change from tones of gray toward pink and blue.

Something powerful and irresistible tugged her forward. Moving like a sleepwalker, she pushed open the kitchen door and stepped into the dark yard, her gaze fixed on the rectangle of whitewashed stones that outlined Blevins' grave.

The hot dawn stillness was so absolute that she heard her

heartbeat accelerating against her ribcage, could hear her breath quickening in her throat.

Slowly, her steps reluctant, she approached the grave and stood frowning down at it, shivering lightly despite the warm air, listening to the silence of being alone.

"It's just you and me now," she whispered, staring hard at the blank headstone. "And the wind and the prairie and the fields."

A breeze teased the ruffle on her nightdress, stirred loose hair around her shoulders. Beneath the rustle of leaves and dry grass, Rosie imagined a harsh chuckle of ghostly laughter.

Closing her eyes, she wrapped her arms around her waist, pressing against the pain of acknowledging that Frank Blevins had won. She would depart this farm in defeat. The agony within that thought clawed across her mind. To leave without besting him was the same as condoning every evil act that Frank Blevins had ever done. It was the same as telling him that beating her mother to death and raping her was acceptable.

Doubling over, Rosie clutched her stomach, feeling sick. She turned anguished eyes toward the stubble in the fields.

She had almost won. Did Blevins know that? If it hadn't been for the stampeding longhorns, she would have taken her revenge. She had come so close this time.

If only she had one more chance . . . all she needed was one more harvest. In her heart, Rosie felt certain that next year she could bring in the most profitable harvest this stinking farm had ever seen. She could do it.

But she wouldn't be here. Panic shot through her body, curling her into a hunched ball. How could she leave before it was finished with Blevins? How could she condone all he had done?

She couldn't.

Revenge had been the fire in her belly for so many years;

revenge the goal that fueled body and soul. She couldn't walk away now, not after all she had sacrificed, all the pieces of herself that Blevins had taken from her. She could not walk away and let Frank Blevins rest unpunished, could not let him win.

Bowie would understand. Bowie loved her, he would agree to give her one more harvest. Next year they would beat Frank Blevins. Bowie would understand that they couldn't go to Oregon until Frank Blevins was punished.

A groan welled up from her chest and Rosie turned tear-wet eyes toward the pink line growing on the eastern horizon.

Next year could bring drought or an infestation of insects or dust storms or tornados. Next year never came. She and Bowie would spend the rest of their lives pouring their sweat and blood into a patch of Kansas dirt.

"I hate your rotten stinking soul!" she screamed at Frank Blevins' grave. "If it wasn't for you, I could leave this hellish place!" Tears ran down her cheeks, catching the first rays of the rising sun. She was shaking all over. "If it takes the rest of my life, I swear I'm going to beat you! I'm going to win!" Tears glazed her eyes and she covered her face in her hands.

Bowie would never understand. He would never stay here for another year, another harvest. When he learned that she couldn't go with him to Oregon, that she couldn't leave Frank Blevins until she had bested him, Bowie would ride away. He would hate leaving her; it would hurt him inside, but he would do it.

Staggering, she fell forward and beat her fists against the top of the headstone. Sobbing, she lifted her head toward the fields and her future. She saw herself growing old on a diet of liquor, labor, and despair. Without Bowie, with only the wind and the prairie and Frank Blevins, Rosie knew she would start drinking again. What would it matter? She saw herself, dirty and ragged, battling the dust and heat and hopelessness year after year after year. Living on promises of next year, fighting to win a victory over a dead man.

"Oh, my God!"

Horror widened her eyes and she stumbled backward from the headstone, staring at it through a mist of tears. Blevins still had the power to destroy her. His hold on her reached from the grave and poisoned her mind, drawing her to him and away from all she held dear.

"No," she whispered, shuddering violently, backing away another step. "You've already stolen so much from me. You can't have my future! No! I won't let you take that too!"

Spinning on the balls of her feet, Rosie gazed wildly about her. She needed to strike him down, needed to break his hold on her now and forever. But how?

It sickened her inside that even for one brief instant she had considered letting Bowie ride out of her life again. Bowie Stone was the only good thing that had ever happened to her. He was her life, her love, her future. And Frank Blevins was not going to take that from her.

Shaking violently, tears streaming down her face, Rosie bolted for the house—the house with all its ugly memories and squeaking hinges and oppressive symbols.

She ran inside and returned with a flaming cone of rolled newspaper. Hands shaking, she circled the hated house, touching the fire to the blistering paint, here, there, beneath the window, beside the door. And she wished with all her soul that she could burn Frank Blevins as well.

The house exploded into flame with a soft whooshing sound. Curls of black smoke shot high into the air. For a moment Rosie stared at it, her heart burning as fiercely as the dry wood.

Then she heard her name, faint and distant. Whirling, she shaded her eyes against the dawn.

Far out on the prairie she spotted a lone rider leaning low on the neck of his horse, flying toward her across the hard dry earth.

"Bowie!" Her throat constricted. "Yes! Oh God, yes!"

Lifting her nightdress above her knees, she ran away from the burning house, away from the past. She ran across the scorched prairie, toward the future and the man she loved more than life itself. Sharp-edged stones tore at her bare feet and the tough dry grass sawed at her ankles. Tears blinded her.

"Bowie! Bowie!"

He jumped to the ground before the horse reached her and ran to catch her as she fell forward. Rock-hard arms closed around her and crushed her against his chest so tightly that she felt his heartbeat pounding as if it were her own.

"I love you, I love you!" Laughing and weeping, she caught his face between her hands and pulled his mouth down to hers, kissing him again and again, not letting him speak, wanting to dissolve into him so they could never part again.

"Rosie." His embrace was so tight and fierce that she thought her bones would crack and she didn't care. All she cared about were his strong arms around her and the kisses raining over her forehead, her eyelids and cheeks. Bowie buried his face in her tangled hair. "I missed you. God, I missed you!"

She slipped her arms around his waist and rested her head against his chest. Standing within the circle of her husband's sheltering arms, listening to his strong steady heartbeat, Rosie felt his love wrap around her and hold her safe.

They stood on the dawn prairie and held each other, watching the house burn. Smoke and sparks swirled in the air, bits of ash, bits of the past. Fiery shadows flickered against Frank Blevins' headstone.

And finally Rosie understood that she had been wrong. It

wasn't a profitable harvest that she had needed to beat Frank Blevins and avenge his abuse. What she had needed was love, something Frank Blevins had never known or experienced. Loving and being loved, that was the most powerful revenge of all.

She turned her back to the burning house, letting it go, releasing the past, and she lifted her mouth to Bowie's kiss, her eyes shining with tears of joy. She took his hand and gently placed it over her stomach. Her smile was radiant.

"I have something wonderful to tell you."

Next year had finally arrived. She had won.